THE DREYFUS AFFAIR

ALSO BY PETER LEFCOURT

The Deal: A Novel

THE
DREYFUS
AFFAIR

A Love Story

Peter Lefcourt

HarperPerennial
A Division of HarperCollins*Publishers*

Grateful acknowledgement is made to Warner/Chappell Music, Inc., for permission to reprint excerpts from "Old Devil Moon" by E. Y. Harburg and Burton Lane. Copyright 1946 Chappell & Co. (ASCAP) (renewed). All rights reserved. Reprinted by permission.

A hardcover edition of this book was published in 1992 by Random House, Inc. It is here reprinted by arrangement with Random House, Inc.

HarperCollins books may be purchased for educational, business, or sales promotional use. For information please write: Special Markets Department, HarperCollins Publishers, Inc., 10 East 53rd Street, New York, NY 10022.

First HarperPerennial edition published 1993.

Designed by Carole Lowenstein

LIBRARY OF CONGRESS CATALOGING-IN-PUBLICATION DATA

Lefcourt, Peter.
    The Dreyfus affair : a love story / Peter Lefcourt. — 1st HarperPerennial ed.
    p.   cm.
ISBN 0-06-097559-8 (paper)

    I. Title.
[PS3562.E3737D7   1993]
813'.54—dc20   92-54926

97 98 ❖/RRD H 10 9

"My burning protest is only the cry of my soul.
Let there be an inquest in the full light of day.
I am waiting."

—EMILE ZOLA, *J'Accuse*

"You win a few. You lose a few. Some are rained out.
But you got to dress for all of them."

—SATCHEL PAIGE

Acknowledgments

I'd like to thank my editor, David Rosenthal, who bought this book on a one-sentence pitch and never looked back, and also my copy editor, Amy Edelman, who cleaned up my act.

THE DREYFUS AFFAIR

I

It was bad enough going 0-for-5 and committing a dumb-ass error that led to two unearned runs in the bottom of the ninth that beat you. Not to mention the postgame buffet of overspiced anchovy pizza and lukewarm lite beer. In Cleveland, no less, on a sticky night with a room in the Embassy Suites that had the loudest air-conditioning unit this side of a 747. This was just your average, everyday run-of-the-mill shit.

What was really upsetting was what just almost happened in the shower. Jesus. He didn't even want to think about *that*. *That* fell into the category of unthinkable things. *That* was banished to the Siberia of his conscious thoughts, where, he hoped, it would freeze to death and never be heard from again.

Often of late, following a road loss, Randolph MacArthur Dreyfus, Jr., a.k.a. The Shovel, found himself having peculiar thoughts. It had nothing to do with the game itself. It was something deeper and more troubling that stuck in his throat with the anchovy pizza and wouldn't go away. He felt like he was about to start crying. Like his insides weren't zipped down securely. He was hitting .335 and was a leading candidate for MVP, for chrissakes. And he was sitting in front of his locker fighting back tears. What the hell was going on?

The error was already history. The official scorer could have gone either way on it. The ball was in the hole, and even if he hadn't kicked it he probably wouldn't have nailed the Cuban. The guy had led the Pacific Coast League in stolen bases last winter.

Bernie Lazarre, the catcher, had gone over to him before the shower and told him that the scoring was fucked and besides he got Axel Most off the hook on the unearned runs, keeping his E.R.A. below three, so Axel actually owed him a favor. Randy Dreyfus wasn't interested in any favors from Axel Most or Bernie Lazarre, or anybody else, at the moment. He wanted to take a walk and think things out.

But you didn't take a walk in the neighborhood around the ballpark in Cleveland. You took the team bus back to the hotel, or you took a cab. Rennie Pannizardi was trying to organize a trip to Omar's, a downtown strip joint, where for five bucks you could have a nude girl sit down on your lap and gyrate for one minute. It was the cheapest hard-on in the American League.

There was one whirlpool free in the trainer's room, next to the one where Willie St. James was soaking his bad hamstring. Randy climbed in and felt his heart turn over as the rush of adrenaline kicked in to accommodate the heat. Maybe he could just sit in the stew pot and bake the peculiar feeling out. He closed his eyes and tried to drift, but Willie St. James's cracked soprano pulled him out of it.

"You know anything about tax-deferred municipal bonds, man?"

"What?"

"My tax guy wants to put me into low-yield bonds and some other shit."

"Oh yeah?"

"Yeah. He says my portfolio is too high-yield."

"That so?"

"What are you in?"

"Bunch of things."

"You know what Ephard's in?"

Randy shook his head.

"Windmills. Those things up north near San Francisco. Ephard's guy put him into a couple of dozen. Ephard says they're going to look good in twenty, twenty-five years. . . ."

One of the trainers came in to tell Randy that Charlie Gonse wanted to see him.

"If he gives you shit about the error, tell him no one in the whole fucking American League could've nailed Morales. The guy runs faster than a Mexican with a chili pepper up his ass."

Charlie Gonse's office was on the far side of the trainer's room, separated by a glass partition through which he could watch what was going on in the whirlpools while he ate his postgame Greek salad. Ever since he got the bad news on his cholesterol count it was all he ever ate. He was up over 220 and convinced that he would keel over dead if he so much as looked at a pat of butter.

The manager beckoned Randy to a chair across from him. Still dripping from the whirlpool, Randy sat down, and a small puddle of chlorinated water began to collect underneath the chair. Gonse polished off the Greek salad with a plastic fork and meticulously wiped an olive stain from his mouth. Then he took out a fresh toothpick and began to work over his upper teeth.

"Can I tell you what I think the problem is here?" Gonse said finally.

"Problem?"

"Lack of focus. That's the problem. E6 in the bottom of the ninth. The bottom of the ninth is no time for E6."

"Charlie, I'm hitting .335. I've got seventy-eight RBI's. So I blew a ground ball. It happens to everyone."

"You're not in the ball game . . ."

Randy closed his eyes for a moment, took a deep breath, and flexed his back. He felt a slight stab in his right rotator-cuff muscle, which had been bothering him since April, when he tried to nail a guy at the plate on a cold night in Boston.

". . . you're spread too thin, you're all over the place. You're Mr. Baseball. Mr. This, Mr. That. You're going to have a goddamn shopping center named after you, for chrissakes. You can't nail a guy in the bottom of the ninth if you're thinking about what you're going to say when you cut the ribbon of a shopping center in Van Nuys. Can you?"

"Charlie, Morales is one of the fastest guys in the whole league."

"Marty Marion would've gotten him. Marty Marion would've nailed him by three steps. Marty Marion didn't have a shopping center named after him."

At this point Randy wished he had gone to Omar's. The chlorine puddle was getting larger. The anchovies were digging in for a firefight. The team had lost a game in the standings to both Oakland and the Angels. His head hurt. The air conditioner in his hotel room sounded like the "Anvil Chorus." And a very weird thing had just happened in the shower.

"You're twenty-eight years old. You got the best swing since Ted Williams. You're the fastest white guy in the league. You've got a nice wife, a family, you're pulling down two point three a year not to mention the TV and merchandising money. You've got a shot at the Hall of Fame if you don't get hurt or start putting powder up your nose. All you've got to do is keep your eye on the ball. You understand what I'm saying?"

"Right."

"And you don't answer your fan mail."

"Huh?"

"My sister Francine's got a kid in Glendale who wrote you a letter a while back. You never answered it. You know what *noblesse oblige* means, Dreyfus?"

"I've got a service that takes care of that."

"Give your service a call. Tell them to take a look for a letter by Ernest Turnack, 3890 El Rosarito Drive, in Glendale. The kid thinks you walk on water. That's it. Over and out."

When he got back to the trainer's room, it was empty except for Willie St. James. Randy didn't feel like discussing municipal bonds with the left fielder so he ignored him and went straight to his locker. Lying in front of it was a bagful of baseballs to autograph and a copy of a *Sports Illustrated* cover story with a note from his publicist clipped to it:

What about the 24th for Arsenio Hall? You'll be on with Bobby Vinton and Princess Caroline of Monaco. Need to know by Wednesday. Please call.

It was going to be a hell of a home stand. First the dedication of the shopping center in Van Nuys and then the Arsenio Hall show. His literary agent told him that if he wanted the hardcover sales of his book to move at all he would have to do the talk shows. Otherwise it would be on the remainder counters in two months selling for $1.98.

He had written *Free Swinger: My Life in Baseball* during the off-season with a wiseass sportswriter from New York, who sat in his den with a tape recorder asking him embarrassing questions. Randy hadn't liked the experience at all, but his literary agent told him it was done that way and that the sportswriter had put Canseco on the best-seller list.

Randy decided to leave the baseballs for tomorrow. He was too tired to sit there and sign them right now. In his locker was a pair of Bill Blass slacks and a Lacoste knit sport shirt. He had twenty-five Lacoste knit sport shirts that his wife, Susie, had bought for him at Bullock's in Sherman Oaks. Five of each color. They wore well and didn't shrink up on you, and he liked the little alligator on the front.

Had he promised to call Susie tonight? There was a problem with one of the twins' orthodontia, or was it a problem with the brakes on the 560 SEL? He couldn't remember. He'd call from the hotel, after he dropped a couple of Nuprin for the headache. Maybe they could do something about the air conditioner.

Maybe he could take a sleeping pill and wake up in the batting cage before tomorrow's game and go 4-for-4 and be out of Cleveland without anything ever almost happening. Things used to be a lot simpler. There was just the matter of getting the fat end of the bat around on the ball, a split-second reflex that he had been born with and lived in fear of losing. Nobody was able to explain why ballplayers lost it. They woke up one morning and couldn't get the job done anymore. It was as if whatever gene or chromosome that handled that operation had been removed overnight. The competition was so fierce these days that if you lost a millisecond on your bat speed you were history.

Fortunately the reporters were all gone by now. What the hell do you say about a ground ball anyway? You picked it up and you threw it to first base, and either it got there on time or it didn't. In this case it didn't. The ball wasn't hit hard and was three steps to his right. Charlie Gonse didn't know what he was talking about. Marty Marion wouldn't have gotten the Cuban. You couldn't have gotten the Cuban with a howitzer.

The team bus was gone, and he had to ask the security guard at the door to call a cab for him. He wasn't going to stand outside the players' entrance at Municipal Stadium in Cleveland trying to hail a cab. The driver had an earring and listened to loud rap music on a portable tape deck, which didn't help the headache that was throbbing behind his sinuses. Randy looked out the dirty windows of the cab as they drove through the war zone around the stadium and headed for the west side. You didn't want to get traded to Cleveland. Not even for a guaranteed $5 million a year and a full package of perks.

When Arizona didn't wind up with a team during the expansion in '95 there had been some talk of moving the Cleveland franchise to Phoenix. But nothing ever happened. They had given L.A. a third franchise instead, which pissed a lot of people off. The networks were calling the shots, and Phoenix didn't have the demographics that the San Fernando Valley did.

Randy Dreyfus had come up in the Angel organization, a first-round draft pick out of USC. He played only half a season in Double A before being traded to the Dodgers and sent to Albuquerque. Even though he had led the Pacific Coast League in hitting, the Dodgers left him unprotected in the expansion draft, and he was snapped up by the Los Angeles Valley Vikings. The Dodgers had been trying to get him back ever since, but there was no way the Vikings' owner, John D. F. White, Sr., or his son, John D. F. White, Jr.—or John/John, as the players called him—would trade him. Not even for Chavez Ravine and Vin Scully, they told Peter O'Malley whenever the Dodgers' owner inquired what it would take to get Randy Dreyfus.

As far as Randy was concerned, the Vikings were probably a better deal than the Dodgers or the Angels. The new 125,000-seat stadium that they'd built on the old Sepulveda Reservoir site between the San Diego and Ventura freeways was far and above the best facility in baseball and a lot closer to his house in Valley View Estates. In the course of a few years, the Whites had put together a team that was a legitimate contender in the American League West.

They had been six games back before Randy failed to throw the Cuban out. Now they were seven out, but it was only July.

The hotel lobby was deserted. The guys who hadn't gone to Omar's were either in the bar or watching soft-core porno movies on the closed-circuit cable hookup in their rooms. At the desk Randy was given two phone messages along with his room key. One was from Susie and the other from Barry Fuchsia, his agent. He was in the final year of a three-year deal and at the end of the year he would become a free agent. The Vikings were trying to extend his contract before Randy tested the free-agent market. The price kept going up in increments of $500,000. Barry said that if they kept saying no he'd get the White boys up over $7 million, maybe even $7.5 million.

As soon as he was in his room, Randy dialed Barry Fuchsia's home number in Encino. The phone rang half a dozen times before a nasal voice answered.

"Yeah."

"Barry, it's me."

"Who?"

"Randy. Randy Dreyfus. You called. Left a message."

"Where are you?"

"Cleveland."

There was a long silence. Randy could hear a TV going in the background.

"Right. Uh . . . I got a call from John/John this morning."

"What did he say?"

"The usual shit. The inmates are taking over the asylum. He's going bankrupt. How good they've been to you. Et cetera."

"How much?"

"Four point seven-five in the first year, five two in the second, a base of six in the third with incentives up to six point seven-five."

"Jesus. What do you think?"

"The elevator's still going up."

"It's a lot of money."

"It's not even August yet."

"Yeah, but what happens if I go into a slump?"

"You planning on it?"

"No, but it happens to everyone. Now and then."

"Listen, you manage not to get killed or maimed between now and October one and I'll get you seven going in with escalators in years two and three and a pension package that'll keep you off the streets in your old age."

"You really think so?"

"No, I'm bullshitting you. I'm not interested in putting a five-hundred-thousand-dollar commission in my pocket. I want to make life difficult for myself."

"Jesus . . ."

"You're not becoming one of those newborn Christians, for chrissakes, are you?"

"No. Barry, listen, maybe we ought to think about this before we say no. You know, sleep on it."

"It'll be hard in the morning, believe me."

"Huh?"

"It was a joke. Sleep on it. Hard in the morning . . ."

Randy got a flash from Siberia. The ugly thought somehow managed to disinter itself from the frozen tundra where he had buried it and fly over the pole to Cleveland. Not now. This was no time for those thoughts. He was in the middle of a contract renegotiation. He fielded it on one hop and flung it back.

"Anyway," Barry Fuchsia was saying, "I turned it down. It's gone. The train left the station."

"Well . . . uh . . . okay, I guess you're right."

"I'm right. Besides, all I have to do is call John/John back tomorrow morning and we'll be at five for year one before I say good morning. You want me to do that?"

"I guess not."

"You're beginning to understand how this works. Get some sleep."

Barry Fuchsia hung up so fast that Randy didn't realize for a moment that he was off the phone. He sat on the bed holding the receiver in one hand, rubbing his temple with the other, before getting up and getting the Nuprin. He washed down two with a glass of tap water that tasted like Lake Erie and went back to the phone to call his wife.

It rang four times before the machine picked up: "Hi. This is Randy, Susie, Molly, and Dolly. We're not home right now, but we left Calvin on guard so if you want to visit bring a porterhouse steak and a suit of armor. Just kidding. If you leave your name and number after the beep we'll call back. Honest. Bye . . ."

Randy hung up. He refused to talk to his own answering machine. He went over to examine the noisy air conditioner. Maybe it was just a dirty filter. A hundred and fifty-five bucks a night, in Cleveland, and they can't keep the goddamn air-conditioning filters clean.

The phone rang.

"Hello?"

"Was that you just now?"

Susie's tone of voice was accusatory, as if she were speaking to a six-year-old who had just stuck his hand in her crotch.

"I don't like talking to machines."

"Randy, you know I never pick up when you're not here. It could be some nut. You never know."

"What's going on?"

"I spoke to the vet."

"The vet?"

"About Calvin. Don't you remember?"

Their dog, a hyperactive two-year-old Dalmatian, had been showing signs of mental unbalance lately. He was drinking chlorinated water from the pool and systematically chewing his way through the leather upholstery in the house. Randy wanted to have him put to sleep, but his eight-year-old twin daughters told him that if he did, they'd never speak to him again.

"What'd he say?"

"Well, he thought that maybe we should see somebody."

"See somebody? What are you talking about?"

"He said that Calvin is probably under some sort of stress. He said there are people who treat these kinds of problems. They see the family and the pet together . . ."

Randy put his free hand on the bridge of his nose and squeezed until his sinuses hurt. Sometimes this technique relieved the pressure that built up. At least until the Nuprin kicked in.

"Do we have to talk about this now?"

"Did you have a bad night?"

"Oh-for-five."

"Who was pitching?"

"La Bella. Look, I got a problem with the air conditioner here. I got to get it fixed and get some sleep. Okay?"

"Okay, but think about what the vet said. There's a three-week waiting list for an appointment to see this guy."

"Right. See you Sunday night."

"Good night. Love you."

He clicked the interrupter and dialed the front desk. They told him that Maintenance had gone home for the night but that if he wanted they'd switch him to another suite. Randy wasn't interested in moving at a quarter to one in the morning. He hung up and went and sat on the acrylic long-wear carpet in front of the TV.

As he assumed a yoga position, he turned on the set. Arsenio Hall was talking to Tina Turner or Whoopi Goldberg, he wasn't sure which. He turned the sound down and tried to get the tension to drift away from his center. Last year the Vikings had brought a yoga instructor to spring training to teach the players relaxation techniques.

Randy tried to fine-tune his center so that it would vibrate sympathetically with the air conditioner. Jesus. Things were really weird. He had just turned down nearly $5 million to play baseball for a year. His manager told him he lacked focus. His dog had a severe personality disorder. And he had nearly lost it in the shower.

All right. Maybe he was making too much of the shower thing. It was an involuntary reflex, completely out of his control. It was probably just a crossed wire anyway. Things were probably getting a little screwed up inside because of the pennant race and the renegotiation. There could be a number of explanations for it.

Anyway, it wasn't what had almost happened in the shower that really disturbed him. First of all it didn't actually happen. There was a difference between something *almost* happening and something happening. There was something worse. And it had been going on for a while now.

Randy finally felt the Nuprin kick in, and the first wave of relaxation spread from his center into his extremities. He watched Tina or Whoopi get up and kiss Arsenio. He started to feel a little better. Maybe it wasn't that important. Maybe he could work around it. Maybe it was just a deep-seated admiration. He was one hell of a ballplayer. Did all the little things right. Nobody in baseball made the pivot better on a double play.

Whatever the case, there seemed to be only one explanation for what was going on. Randy was falling in love. And it wasn't with his wife or with some bimbo he'd picked up on the road. It was with his second baseman.

II

Digger Johnson Pickett, known as D.J., had been the starting second baseman for the Valley Vikings since the first year after the '95 expansion. The Whites had gotten him out of the Kansas City organization, where he had played parts of two seasons with respectable, if unspectacular, numbers. He was a career .285 hitter, knocked in fifty to sixty runs and stole roughly twenty-five bases a year, and, in the words of John D. F. White, Sr., was a credit to his race.

According to the eighty-year-old owner of the Vikings, there was no finer black man in the American League. Willie St. James, on the other hand, called D.J. a house nigger. The left fielder said Pickett took too much shit from the Whites and didn't stand up for black solidarity in the clubhouse. But nobody debated the fact that D.J. was a stabilizing influence in the middle of the infield whom you could count on to move the runner along, bunt, and, in general, make the kind of plays that didn't show up in the box score.

D.J. lived alone in a condo in Thousand Oaks and kept to himself on the road. He never went to Omar's in Cleveland or out drinking. Mostly he went to the movies or just stayed in the room and watched TV. Sometimes he shot a round of golf, but that was about it. In three seasons with the Vikings he hadn't missed a game. He held club records for games played, consecutive errorless chances, bases on balls, and being hit by a pitch. In three years he had been hit by fifty-four pitched balls. Bernie Lazarre said he had steel bones.

He was exactly six feet and weighed 170 on the nose, never gaining or losing a pound. The one peculiarity about him was that before each game he would lie down in the corner of the clubhouse and fall asleep for exactly twenty minutes. No matter how noisy the clubhouse got, no matter how important the game or what was going on, he would close his eyes and nod out. It drove people crazy. There was speculation on the team that he was taking some sort of new drug that didn't show up in the mandatory urine tests.

Late Sunday night, as the team returned from the thirteen-game road trip, during which they had gone 6-7 and lost ground to the two teams ahead of them in the standings, D. J. Pickett sat at a window seat reading *Time* magazine cover to cover. A half-full glass of tomato juice rested in the beverage rack as they cruised thirty-seven thousand feet over Kansas. Most of the team was asleep, trying to beat the jet lag and cumulative effect of all the travel.

Two rows back, on the aisle in the center section, Randy Dreyfus was not asleep. He was trying to concentrate on the speech he was writing for the shopping-center opening on his Toshiba laptop. His publicist said that he should be brief and witty. Tell a couple of anecdotes, the publicist had said, a few inside stories about the team. Randy didn't know any inside stories. All he knew, at the moment, was that he was in trouble.

He found himself looking over at his second baseman and then quickly averting his eyes. He had to pull himself together. This aberration was starting to interfere seriously with his play. Counting the last game in Cleveland through the Baltimore series over the weekend, he was 2-for-18 and had left seven runners in scoring position. He had blown a double play on a perfect feed from D.J. that would have gotten them out of a bad inning.

He had finally decided that he would go see someone during the home stand. There were doctors who dealt with this type of thing. He had read somewhere that these feelings were not uncommon among athletes. In fact, the article had said, it was to be expected.

Like soldiers in combat, they spent a lot of time together in intense situations and became emotionally vulnerable.

Jack Viscotti, the team doctor, had given him the address of a guy to see in Westwood. Randy had told him a friend of his was having marital difficulties. Viscotti said that this guy was terrific. He had treated Jaime Descanzo for a severe manic-depressive disorder, and Descanzo had wound up hitting .341.

Randy would settle for being able to sleep at night without having the troubling thoughts that kept him tossing until 4 A.M. He wanted to get back on track. He didn't need this shit. Like Charlie Gonse had said, he had it all going for him. If he didn't fuck up he'd be in the Hall of Fame with a tax-deferred annuity well into seven figures. No, he certainly didn't need this shit.

Harry Glugg wandered down the aisle with a vodka tonic in his hand. Glugg was looking for someone to talk to, and Randy made the mistake of making eye contact. The big first baseman leaned down over him, spewing vodka fumes, and said, "Whad'ya think of the little black one?"

"What?"

"The little black stew with the maraschino-cherry tits. She looks like a spinner, whad'ya think? Got a place by the airport with a couple of other stews. Whad'ya say we go over there and have 'em sit on our face? Shit, you're married, aren't you? Your wife picking you up?"

Randy nodded to the whole sequence of questions and tried to keep his eyes on the Toshiba screen, hoping that Harry Glugg would go away. But he continued to stand there, swaying slightly as the DC-10 hit an air pocket.

"Your wife's a looker, Shovel."

"Yeah."

"She fuck around?"

"Harry, I got work to do, okay?"

"No hard feelings, all right?"

Glugg lurched toward the rear of the plane in search of another victim. The Toshiba screen was blank except for the words GOOD MORNING. IT'S GOOD TO BE HERE.

Randy hit the SAVE key and leaned back in the seat. His wife *was* a looker. Susie Kent Dreyfus stopped traffic, even in L.A. Five-eight,

118 pounds, blond, blue-eyed, she had been the Rose Bowl Queen the year Randy ran for 165 yards and two touchdowns and took her up to Mulholland Drive, where he proposed to her at the moment of penetration. She said yes just as he shot his load. They were married four months later.

The thing that bothered Randy the most about this whole thing was how he could be married to a looker like Susie, who had almost no sag on her tits even after two kids, and still be interested in a black second baseman. It made no sense at all. He had always liked girls. Before the twins were born he and Susie used to do it almost every night. Now they did it less, but that was supposed to be normal. They were right about at the national average of 2.3 times a week. Except, of course, when he was on the road or in a slump.

He closed his eyes and tried to locate his center, as the yoga instructor had taught him. If he could only doze off for the remaining two hours of this interminable plane ride. Wake up as the wheels hit the runway. He'd make the phone call to the guy in Westwood first thing tomorrow.

But instead of falling asleep he found himself wondering whether he could call D.J. up and invite him out to dinner. There was a little Chinese place in Ventura with terrific wonton soup where nobody ever went. He'd tell Susie he was having dinner with Barry Fuchsia to talk about the contract.

As the plane hummed westward into the night, Randy was beginning to get that giddy feeling again. He dug his fingers into the armrests to try to steady his nerves. It wasn't working. He kept peeking through half-closed lids, noticing how the light from the reading lamp played off the protuberant veins of D. J. Pickett's strong neck.

Susie Dreyfus was wearing a pair of leather slacks with a peach cashmere sweater and an avocado-green Nina Ricci scarf. Standing in the cluster of wives waiting in the United Airlines terminal for the plane from Baltimore to land, she was talking to Karen Most about premenstrual water gain when she saw Randy come through the door. Right away she could tell it had been a shitty road trip. He was dragging his ass and scowling.

He had on a tangerine-colored Lacoste with a pair of Eddie Bauer casual slacks and Reeboks. No matter how hard she tried, she couldn't get him into decent shoes. When they kissed, she could taste the diet Coke on his breath.

She waved good-bye to Karen Most as they headed for the parking lot. The team would deliver his suitcase tomorrow. It was one of the nice little things about the Vikings. That and the wives' parking lot at Viking Stadium, which she had been instrumental in getting the owners to provide.

Susie was chairperson of the Viking Girls, an ad-hoc committee of players' wives who met to suggest ways of improving conditions for the families of ballplayers. They were working on a proposal to provide a day-care center at the ballpark, which Mr. White had promised to give serious consideration.

Randy was sullen as they moved through the terminal and out to the lot, answering her in monosyllables. It wasn't until they were in the 560 SEL and heading north on the 405 that he said anything at all.

"I'm down to .321," he pronounced. "I went one-for-thirteen in Baltimore."

"You never hit well in Baltimore."

"I was lucky to get the hit. I'm uppercutting everything."

"Don't worry. You'll probably go four-for-four tomorrow night."

"Michaelson's starting. I never hit off Michaelson."

They rode in silence the rest of the way, Randy dozing until the headlights picked up the pink-and-gray-trimmed stucco of the hacienda-style house at the end of a cul de sac in Delores Canyon. Valley View Estates was the hottest area in the West Valley. They had gotten in when the market was sluggish, at one point two, and had been told by a broker that they could sell in the high twos right now, all cash, thirty-day escrow.

Susie had decorated the sprawling sixty-eight-hundred-square-foot house in Post–Santa Fe Modern, which her decorator told her was very in at the moment. Even the inside of the garage was done in earth tones. Randy got out and headed for the connecting door to the kitchen as Susie entered the anti-theft ignition code and snapped in the steering-wheel bar.

Even before he'd fully gotten in the door, Randy saw Calvin bearing down upon him. Instinctively, Randy made the pivot, lowering his shoulder, making contact under the front paws and sending the dog flying across the pantry and into the freezer compartment of the Sub-Zero. The Dalmatian landed hard on the Enseñada ceramic tiles. Not bad for a guy who had just spent six hours on an airplane. The next time he came into second hard, Randy'd finish him off.

Opening the fridge, he grabbed a couple of carrot sticks and a diet Coke. He could hear the TV going from the maid's room off the kitchen, where Mikva, the Lithuanian housekeeper, was watching the shopping channel. They had the only Eastern European housekeeper in Valley View Estates. Susie had found her working illegally in Toys "Я" Us and made a deal to send her to computer-programming school after three years.

Upstairs he peeked in the half-opened door to the twins' room. Each of them slept on her back, mouth open, moonlight reflecting off her retainer. Randy estimated he was in for over fifty grand in orthodontia between the two of them. Their eyeglasses rested on the matching night tables. On the wall was a large poster of Joan Lunden, the twins' role model.

It never failed to amaze people how two such perfect specimens as Randy and Susie Dreyfus could have produced a pair of nearsighted, knock-kneed little girls. It was clearly recessive genes going back a few generations. Still, Randy felt a clumsy paternal love for them, even though neither was the slightest bit interested in baseball. His own daughters didn't even know what an Earned Run Average was.

The bathroom off the master suite was done largely in mirrors. From any spot in the room you could see any other spot, and you could see through the exercise nook, where the stationary bikes and rowing machines coexisted with the bonsai plants and potted palms, directly into the bedroom. As Randy stood working the Interplak over his gum line, he could see Susie in the bedroom slipping into a satin negligee from the Victoria's Secret mail-order catalog.

Shit. Not tonight. He was exhausted. His sinuses were killing him. He needed some sleep if he was going to face Michaelson tomorrow night. Not to mention all the other stuff that had happened. That had *almost* happened. He clung to the thought that nothing had actually happened yet. Nothing was going to happen. He'd see the guy in Westwood. They'd straighten things out.

Meanwhile, he checked out the medicine cabinet, hesitated between a Valium and a Xanax, then dropped the Xanax and gargled with Listerine for the scratchy throat he had developed in Baltimore. On the way into the bedroom, he hopped the bike to do a few miles to calm himself down until the Xanax kicked in. Maybe, in the meantime, Susie would fall asleep.

He set the road gradient to twelve degrees and watched as his heart rate climbed above a hundred. Susie turned a page of the paperback she had taken to bed with her. He hoped it wasn't one of those torrid sex novels about Hollywood. Whenever she read those she was insatiable.

The race to exhaustion began. One of them would eventually outlast the other. As Randy moved past three miles and jacked up the gradient to fifteen degrees, he had another unsettling thought about D. J. Pickett: For as long as Randy had known him, he had never seen the second baseman with a woman. He had never heard him talk about a woman. In Cleveland the guy had never had a naked girl from Omar's gyrate in his lap.

Jesus! Maybe this was more serious than he thought. He started to pedal harder.

III

The Randy Dreyfus Shopping Center was in a largely Hispanic neighborhood in Van Nuys off the northbound 405. The day that Randy was scheduled to cut the ribbon was so hot and smoggy you could barely make out the outline of the mountains to the north. In spite of the weather, however, the opening was well attended. The local city councilman, Alfonso Mendoza, was there, along with Ken Teffner, the Vikings PR man, a reporter from *The Valley Tribune,* and Randy's publicist, Teresa Melon.

Susie had dressed the twins in matching red-checkered sundresses, with Mary Jane shoes and sunbonnets. She herself was in a white two-piece Côte d'Azur summer suit and a straw Garbo hat she had found in a boutique on Melrose. Randy had wanted to wear one of his Lacoste shirts and slacks, but she had convinced him that you had to wear a suit when they named a shopping center after you.

They stood out in the sun while Alfonso Mendoza gave a long speech in Spanish. The only words Randy understood were *shortstop* and *pennant race.* Susie was perspiring right through her deodorant pad and the twins were beginning to whine audibly by the time Randy stepped up to the microphone. There was a smattering of applause from the small group of curious people who had stopped to watch the ceremony on their way into or out of the Alpha Beta.

"Hey, how're you doing?" Randy said too close to the microphone. His words reverberated across the mostly empty parking lot. He moved back a step and referred to the speech he had written hastily that morning. "It's a pleasure to be here. It's really an honor for me to be chosen to have this shopping center named after me. I want to thank Councilman Mendoza and the city and Mr. John D. F. White, the owner of the Vikings, for making all this possible. . . . And my wife, Susie, and my daughters, Molly and Dolly, right here beside me."

Another ripple of applause. A drunk loitering around the garbage Dumpster shouted, "Eat pussy!" A security guard was quickly dispatched to deal with him.

"Well, baseball's a great game. You have to play them one at a time. It's a long season, but if you give it your best day in and day out, that's all you can do. . . ."

His publicist had brought a carton of books for Randy to sign, but apparently nobody in the neighborhood read much English. Fifteen minutes after he cut the ribbon, Randy was with Susie and the girls in a booth at Hamburger Hamlet eating a tostada salad.

"Well, I think it's an honor that your father has a shopping center named after him," Susie said.

The twins said nothing, deep into their guacamole burgers. Randy nodded absently. He wasn't thinking about the shopping center. He was thinking about making a phone call. He couldn't remember if the phone booths in the Hamburger Hamlet were private. He wanted to call the doctor in Westwood. In spite of his resolution, he hadn't made an appointment yet.

"Excuse me," he said and headed off toward the restrooms.

The phone was on the wall, in full view of anybody who happened to walk by. How could he stand there and call a doctor who dealt in personality disorders when anybody could walk by at any moment and hear what he was saying? On the other hand, he didn't want to make the phone call from home in case Susie wandered into the room. He had been carrying the number around in his wallet since Jack Viscotti had given it to him. There was another number he had been carrying around with him, a number he had memorized off the players' roster, the number of D. J. Pickett's condo in Thousand Oaks.

The idea of calling him up and suggesting they have dinner on their off night, Thursday, wouldn't go away. Of course, he wasn't going to do it. Not until he talked to the doctor at least. He'd sort this thing out and get back on track.

As he was struggling with these thoughts, standing in the middle of the narrow corridor near the phone, Molly or Dolly—he couldn't actually tell the difference most of the time—entered the hallway on her way to the ladies' room.

"Hi, Daddy. What are you doing?"

"I'm making a phone call."

"Who're you calling?"

"Mr. Gonse. The manager. I . . . want to find out who's playing . . . right field tonight."

"Oh. I'm going to the bathroom."

"That's nice, sweetheart."

He watched as the eight-year-old disappeared into the ladies' room. Susie had decided it was time the girls used the bathroom by themselves in public places. It drove Randy crazy to think about all the potential child molesters who congregated in public bathrooms.

Jesus. Why had he said that to her? What if she repeated it to Susie? Susie would know that he wouldn't call Charlie Gonse from a public phone in a restaurant to find out who was playing right field that night. Randy picked up the phone and pretended to put money inside, waiting for his daughter to come back out of the ladies' room. When she did, he said into the phone, "Well, thank you very much. I'm glad you can accommodate me."

He hung up and said to Molly or Dolly, "Actually, I wasn't calling Mr. Gonse. I was making an appointment to have the brakes looked at on the Mercedes."

"Oh," the twin said. Then: "They have this bathroom in there with long bars on the wall."

"It's for handicapped people, to help them go to the bathroom."

"I don't need any help to go to the bathroom."

"I know. I'm very proud of you."

"Do we have to go shopping in that shopping center?"

"No."

"I'm glad. There weren't any Americans there."

He finally got through to Dr. Fuad from the car phone in the 850i after he dropped Susie and the girls at the house and said he was going to go look for some shirts at Bullock's. The doctor said he was booked solid, but when Randy mentioned that Jack Viscotti had referred him, he squeezed him in for the next morning. Then he had to go to Bullock's and pick out half a dozen new Lacoste shirts.

What kind of doctor was named Fuad?

That evening Randy was standing at shortstop in the top of the fifth, thinking about the doctor's name, when a ground ball was hit up the middle. Normally with a left-handed batter it was the shortstop's ball, but Randy had been thinking about the doctor and got a bad jump. D.J. raced over from the hole between first and second and dove, catching the ball in the webbing of his glove. Then, on his knees, he whirled and fired to first, getting the runner by half a step.

The crowd exploded. Randy stood there watching the second baseman dust his uniform off and trot modestly back into position. It was gorgeous. A play like that you didn't see every night. But Randy knew that D.J. had been covering for him. If Randy had reacted to the crack of the bat, he could have made a routine out.

Charlie Gonse knew it too. When Randy got back into the dugout at the end of the inning, the manager gave him a look. Randy averted his eyes. He didn't want to be summoned for another Greek-salad talk. He was 0-for-2, taking a called third strike in the first and popping to short in the third, and his average was already down another three points to .318.

They were down 4–0 to Milwaukee. They had lost the opening game of the series. They couldn't afford to be swept at home by Milwaukee. Already the sportswriters were predicting that the Vikings were through for the season. They were nine games out and fading.

Randy peered out at the crowd. On nights like this he hated all of them. None of them knew how hard it was to hit a round ball with a round bat. They thought all you had to do was close your eyes and swing. He kept repeating Dr. Fuad's telephone number to himself. The guy must be an Egyptian or something. An Egyptian shrink. How could you talk to an Egyptian about sexual deviation?

Glen Ephard drew a walk. Randy moved on deck as the third-base coach flashed the bunt sign to D.J. Which would put a runner in scoring position for Randy. He didn't need that type of pressure right now. He found himself hoping that D.J. would blow the bunt so that he wouldn't have to bat with Ephard on second.

Unfortunately, D.J. laid down a perfect bunt. The crowd cheered as Randy took the doughnut off the bat and headed toward the plate. Thousands of voices chanted in unison, "Ran-DEE, Ran-DEE . . ."

At the very least, he needed to get Ephard to third, to hit the ball to the right side. The Brewers had one of those young split-fingered-fastball guys on the mound who threw sinking aspirin tablets at you. The first two times up Randy had barely seen the ball.

The guy started him with a slider that nipped the outside corner. The call could have gone either way, but the umpire rang him up. Randy stepped out, knocked some artificial-carpet lint from his cleats, and stared out at the skinny right-hander. Maybe he and D.J. should have lunch instead of dinner. Lunch was less of a thing. You could have lunch with anybody.

"You going to step back in, Dreyfus, or should I change my plane reservations?"

The umpire, Dave Corliss, a fat slob who had never given Randy a call, glared at him. Randy stepped back in. The right-hander threw the next one high and tight, moving Randy off the plate. The ball had to be going at least 95 miles an hour. Randy felt an involuntary buckling of the knees. The protective helmet didn't cover the whole body. There were a number of vulnerable spots exposed to a pathological right-hander with homicidal tendencies.

He stepped out again. He wondered whether Dr. Fuad validated parking. Very few people did anymore. You'd think that for $175 an hour they'd pick up the parking. And it wasn't even a full hour, apparently. Thirty-five minutes. Randy was trying to calculate the price per minute when the Milwaukee catcher said, "Anytime you're ready . . ."

Randy stepped in once more. The right-hander went into his windup and Randy swung before the ball was halfway to the plate. He should have been watching for the change-up. The guy was making him look bad. He stepped out again and looked down at the third-base coach, who was running signs. What kind of sign was he going to give with two strikes and two outs anyway? Hit? Hit a home run? Step back in and stop fucking around?

This time Randy stepped right back in. He wanted to get it over with. The right-hander reared back and threw a rising fastball that Randy barely even saw. By the time he swung the catcher was tossing the ball back to the mound and the Brewers were heading for the dugout.

The organist quickly started playing "The Habanera" from *Carmen*. On the message board there was a Viking Stadium welcome for the San Gabriel Valley Ferdinand Magellan Explorers Club. D.J. emerged from the dugout with Randy's glove. He tossed it to Randy and headed out to second.

Randy thought he saw an empathetic look on the part of his teammate, a look that seemed to say, "Hey, man, it's okay." And a wink. A wink? Did anyone else see the wink?

He'd have to tell Dr. Fuad about the wink. If he was starting to hallucinate, they might have to prescribe drugs. The league permitted drug taking on a doctor's orders. He'd check it out with the team's player rep before the next urine test.

When he left the house at nine the next morning Randy told Susie he was going to take the Mercedes in to have the brakes looked at. It was rare that he was up and out so early following a night game. They had lost 7–0 and were now ten games back, eleven in the loss column.

The traffic crawled slowly through the Sepulveda Pass, inching toward the basin, as the early-morning low clouds hung over the freeways waiting to be burned off by the July sun. Randy yawned and sipped a large container of coffee he had got at the Jack in the Box. He had barely slept, even after a Xanax and 12.7 miles on the stationary bike.

It had been close to 3 A.M. before he drifted into a troubled sleep, tormented by jarring half-dreams of split-fingered fastballs and terrorists surrounding his shopping center and holding the twins hostage. And to make matters worse, he woke to a new twinge of pain in his right shoulder, below the rotator cuff.

He got off at Wilshire and had to push the 560 SEL to get there by nine-thirty. Dr. Fuad's office was on the fourteenth floor of a medical building on Glendon. All the way up on the elevator he considered turning around and going back down to the garage, getting in the car with the bad brakes, getting it up to 140 on the Coast Highway, and seeing what happened when he hit the light at Sunset.

Suite 1410 was marked simply, MENDES FUAD, M.D., A MEDICAL CORPORATION. Randy opened the door and found himself in a small waiting room, with two chairs and a table and another door with two lights over it, one red, the other green. The red one was lit at the moment.

He sat down and grabbed a copy of *People* magazine. Every few minutes he glanced up at the red light as he tried to immerse himself in a story about Pia Zadora. She sure had a nice rack. It was comforting to realize that he could still appreciate a nice rack. He wasn't that far gone yet.

The door opened, and a man of about fifty appeared, wearing a lamb's-wool sweater and baggy trousers and carrying a set of beads in his hand. His hair was thick and sprinkled with gray, his shoulders sagging, his lidded eyes half closed, his entire demeanor like that of a large lazy sheepdog.

"Mr. Dreyfus?" he said in a soft liquid voice.

"Yeah."

"Please come in."

Randy followed the doctor into an inner office, which was small and cozy, with rugs and throw pillows scattered around. There was no desk. Fuad sat down in an armchair and gestured for Randy to take a seat opposite him.

They sat there for a long moment as Randy scratched behind his ear, a nervous gesture that he had little control over. It was dead quiet in the room, except for the sound of an aquarium air pump in the corner and the clicking of the worry beads.

"So, Mr. Dreyfus, why are you here?"

Jesus. The guy didn't fuck around. He cut right to the chase. Randy didn't know where to begin. He found the quiet of the office and the sleepy gaze of the man sitting opposite him disconcerting.

"I'm not sure," he finally mumbled.

"Why don't you just plunge right in."

Randy looked around him. The door was thirty feet away. He wondered if Fuad kept it locked to prevent people from escaping. If push came to shove he could always overpower the guy and get the keys. He looked like he couldn't take a hit.

"You see, the thing is, I've never been to a shrink before."

Fuad nodded slowly, saying nothing.

"It's kind of hard to talk about this."

"I understand. But unless you talk about it, we can't get anything done, can we?"

Now Randy was nodding. But he still wasn't talking.

"All right," the doctor said. "Let's pretend that you're not here about you, that you're here about someone else, a friend. Your friend's got a problem. You're concerned. You want to help. So what's your friend's problem?"

"He almost got a rod in the shower in Cleveland."

"Excuse me?"

"Doc, do you think it's possible for a guy who thinks Pia Zadora's a fox to be queer?"

D. J. Pickett was applying Armor All to the vinyl patio furniture on the terrace overlooking the pool of his condo in Thousand Oaks when the phone rang. He moved inside and across the deep pile rug to the phone, grabbing it just before the fifth ring, when the answering machine would have picked up. He accomplished this with the same superb timing that he demonstrated in making a force play at second, getting to the base a split second before the runner.

"Hello?"

There was silence on the other end.

"Hello?" he repeated and was just about to hang up when he heard a voice on the other end say, "D.J.?"

It took him a moment to identify the voice, though it was familiar to him. It was the context that was confusing. Why would Randy Dreyfus be calling him at home in the middle of the afternoon?

"Hey, Randy, how're you doing?"

"Pretty good. How are you?"

"Okay . . ."

There was another long silence on the other end. D.J. thought they might have been disconnected.

"Randy? You there?"

"Yeah."

"So . . . What's up?"

"Just checking in."

"Huh?"

"Saying hello."

"Oh."

"Well, see you tonight."

"Sure."

"Bye."

And he hung up. D.J. stood there holding the receiver as the line went dead. He hit the interrupter to make sure that Randy had actually hung up, then crossed to his kitchenette and poured himself a glass of iced tea.

He had just had a very peculiar conversation with Randy Dreyfus. He had seen him last night, and he was about to see him again tonight. In fact, between April and October, he saw Randy Dreyfus almost every night of the week. Nevertheless, Randy had called in the middle of the afternoon, approximately three hours before batting practice began, just to say hello.

The guy was in a bad slump. Slumps tended to make you act peculiarly. When D.J. was with the Pirates there was a center fielder who would eat nothing but raw vegetables when he was in a slump. So D.J. decided to chalk it up to slump behavior and went back to Armor-Alling his furniture. It wasn't until that night in the top of the fourth inning, as they were waiting for Bernie Lazarre to throw the ball down to second after the pitcher's warm-ups, that he thought about it again.

Randy Dreyfus said to him, "You want to have dinner tomorrow night?"

D.J. took the peg and threw it to Rennie Pannizardi at third, who tossed it to the pitcher. Meanwhile, before D.J. could react to the invitation, Randy moved back to his position and the batter stepped in. The inning turned out to be interminable. The Brewers scored two unearned runs when Randy overthrew a ball into the first-base-dugout with the bases loaded.

In the bottom half of the inning, Charlie Gonse called Randy over and chewed him out. D.J. sat in the corner of the dugout and wondered how to respond to this very strange dinner invitation from his teammate. Why would a guy with a wife and two kids invite his second baseman to dinner on the one free night of a home stand?

Maybe he had misunderstood. There was a lot of noise out there. During infield warm-ups in the top of the fifth, D.J. said to him, "What was that you said to me last inning?"

Randy looked away, then muttered under his breath the same proposition he had made in the top of the fourth. This time it was pretty clear that Randy was indeed inviting him to dinner the following night.

"Don't you want to spend your off night with your wife?"

"She can't eat for a while. She has a spastic colon."

"Oh. Sorry."

"There's this Chinese place in Ventura's got good wonton soup."

Harry Glugg tossed the ball back toward the Vikings' dugout as the catcher got ready to throw the ball down.

"You want to take it?" D.J. said, meaning the peg from the catcher.

"Huh?" Randy said.

Bernie Lazarre stood there waiting for someone to cover second. D.J. moved into position finally, took the throw, and tossed it to third.

"Isn't Ventura a little far for dinner?"

"You take the freeway, it's less than an hour."

The organist went into an up-tempo rendition of "The Ride of the Valkyries," and the first batter of the inning stepped in. D.J. moved into the hole between first and second for the pull-hitting left-handed batter.

The guy was probably having problems with his wife and wanted to talk to someone. D.J. had to be the last person on the team in a position to give Randy Dreyfus advice on his marital problems, but Randy Dreyfus didn't know that. D.J. sure as hell hoped he didn't. D. J. Pickett had gone to great lengths to keep his private life private. And he was reasonably sure he had never been indiscreet in public.

Of course, there was another possibility. But this possibility seemed highly unlikely. Randy Dreyfus was about as straight as you got. He had a blond, blue-eyed wife, two kids, and a shopping center named after him. D.J. looked over and saw him take his cap off and wipe a strand of blond hair off his forehead. He looked like Jack Armstrong, all-American boy.

It couldn't be. No way. Not America's favorite shortstop. Out of the question.

Wouldn't that be a kick in the head . . .

Randy carefully inserted the cuticle scissors into his nostril to go after a recalcitrant nose hair. It was delicate work, and he kept the shaving mirror angled from below to guide his hand accurately. He was not having much success. He kept sticking the point into the delicate flesh inside his nostril and wincing.

It was 1:07 A.M. as he stood in his mirrored bathroom after yet another loss at home and reviewed the events of the day. It was not your average day, that was for sure. He began by spending thirty-five excruciatingly uncomfortable minutes with the Egyptian shrink trying to understand what was happening to him. Dr. Fuad told him that he would inevitably have to come to terms with his feelings, whatever they were. There was no getting around that. Actually, he told Randy to tell this to his hypothetical friend. Randy had not been able to drop the pretense that he was not the one with the problem, even though the doctor knew and he knew the doctor knew and the doctor knew that he knew the doctor knew.

"Your friend has to accept the validity of his own feelings, doesn't he?"

"Yeah, but he's not sure about this. Maybe it's just a crossed wire."

"Well, you told me he said it went deeper than the incident in the shower."

"Nothing happened in the shower!"

Randy actually shouted these words. Then he lowered his voice, afraid that he could be heard throughout the building.

"What I meant—what *he* meant—was that there's something special about the way they play together. They have this, like, *thing* going, like one of them knows when the other's going to make the double play by stepping on the bag or by throwing to the base. You'd be surprised how important this is. Otherwise you can bump into each other."

"I don't see that as a problem."

"Well, neither does he, but that's not all. He wants to have dinner with him in a Chinese restaurant in Ventura."

"So?"

"All alone. On the one off night of the home stand."

"I still don't see the problem."

"You don't?"

"What's going to happen at dinner?"

"He doesn't know. That's the problem. You see, doc, this is all very new to this guy. He was just sitting in your waiting room thinking about sticking it to Pia Zadora—"

"I beg your pardon?"

"Pia Zadora. She's got a terrific rack."

"I see."

"The thing is he's got a shot at the Hall of Fame."

"Why should his sexual preference preclude his being voted into the Hall of Fame?"

"You don't know much about baseball, do you, doc?"

"I know enough."

"Do they play ball in Egypt?"

"I think we're getting sidetracked here."

"If it's off the pyramid it's a ground-rule double, right?"

It had gone downhill from there. Randy had gotten abusive. Before leaving he had accused the doctor of being a pervert himself and a possible terrorist.

Later that day he had called from the car phone and apologized. They'd made another appointment for Friday.

Randy flinched again as the scissor pinched him. The nose hair was still there. He found the half-gallon bottle of Listerine in the medicine cabinet and began to gargle.

He wasn't sure whether D.J. had actually accepted the dinner invitation. They didn't discuss it after the fifth inning. He'd just go and see what happened. If the second baseman didn't show up, then Randy'd just forget about it and try to go about his life as normally as possible. In fact, after leaving the doctor's office he had gone and bought a copy of the *People* with Pia Zadora in it and taken it with him to the men's room of Bullock's, where he carefully locked himself in a toilet stall and proved to himself that, at the very least, he still swung from both sides of the plate.

An action that may have been profligate, he realized now, seeing Susie emerge behind him in the mirror wearing a black lace bra and panties, a pair of leather boots that went halfway up her calves, and a pair of three-inch spiked heels.

It was too late to get to the stationary bike. She had him cornered in the bathroom.

"Nice outfit," he muttered, turning around slowly with a nervous little laugh.

The next thing he knew she had him pinned against the sink. She made short work of his baby-blue jockey shorts.

Randy closed his eyes, dug in, and swung away.

IV

The principal feature of the breakfast nook of the Dreyfus home was an authentic Navajo table that Susie had laminated to protect against spilled milk. The walls were done off-peach with moldings in burnt sienna. The floor was hand-painted Mexican ceramic tile, at fifty-four dollars a square foot, laid by a Native American craftsman from Santa Fe. When *Home Stand*, the cable-TV program that featured the family life of prominent ballplayers, had sent a camera crew to do a show on the Dreyfuses, Susie had given a guided tour of the house on camera, starting with the breakfast nook. A good breakfast, she said, her lovely and sincere features at three-quarter profile to the camera, was the foundation of a successful day.

On this particular morning, Randy sat with the sports page of *The Valley Tribune*, eating a bowl of spoon-size shredded wheat. The twins were parked in front of the TV watching the last half hour of *Good Morning America*. Susie was fixing herself her morning bowl of figs and oat bran.

She poured in the acidophilus milk and sat down opposite him at the Navajo table

"We have to make an appointment to see the therapist."

"Huh?" he mumbled, momentarily confused. How did she know about Dr. Fuad? He had given the doctor only his car-phone number.

"I told you, he's very busy. If we don't make an appointment now, we won't be able to get in to see him for the next home stand."

"Who?"

"Dr. Levine, the family pet counselor. About Calvin. Remember?"

It would be so much easier simply to arrange for Calvin to have an unfortunate accident. He could slip the Dalmatian some poisoned biscuits. No one would ever know. They didn't do autopsies on dogs.

"You really want to do this?"

"Randy, we talked about this. We're not getting through to Calvin."

It would be better to get someone else to do the dog. This way he could pass a lie-detector test, if it came to that.

"Yeah, okay, sure . . ." he said and went back to the box scores.

"What days are you free?"

"Free?"

"Next home stand. What day should I make the appointment for?"

"Any day is okay."

If he played it right, he would never have to keep the appointment. How expensive could a contract on a Dalmatian be? If you could get a person taken care of, you should be able to get a dog out of the way. He could probably find a guy in Pacoima who'd do it for a hundred bucks.

"Let's go to Nicky Blair's tonight, okay?"

Shit. He hadn't mentioned anything to her yet, hoping to come up with some last-minute thing to cover for him while he was at dinner with D.J. in Ventura. Now he had to get into it over breakfast.

"Uh . . . listen, I may have to have dinner with Barry tonight."

"Barry, your agent?"

"Yeah."

"Why?"

"About the contract renegotiation. We're right in the middle of it."

"Why can't you have lunch with him?"

"Barry doesn't eat lunch."

"Randy, it's the only free night this entire month. I was counting on going out."

"Barry thinks we can get to seven."

"Can't you go to his office this afternoon? Who makes deals at night, anyway?"

"They could call at any time. We have to be prepared for a response. I mean, they could start dicking around with year three . . ."

The phone rang. Randy reached for the wall unit behind him.

"Yeah?"

"It's me, Randy. D.J."

Randy's heart skipped a beat. "How're you doing?"

"Look, you sure you want to have dinner tonight? I mean, we could meet for lunch or a beer tomorrow, before the game. It seems like a long way to drive to have dinner."

"I think it's a good idea."

"You do?"

"Uh-huh."

There was a moment of silence on the other end. Then: "Okay. What time?"

"Eight."

"What's the name of the place?"

"Ching Ming's Fine Cantonese Cuisine."

"Where is it."

"Off the freeway."

"What freeway?"

"The 101. It's right in town. You can't miss it."

"Well . . . I guess I'll see you then."

"Right."

Randy hung up and said, "That was Barry's girl. Felicia. Confirming dinner. I'm going to go take a Jacuzzi."

And he was gone before Susie could respond. She sat there stewing over her oat bran. It was extremely insensitive of him to have made plans on the one free night of a home stand. They always went out on off nights.

This could be another indication that their marriage was in trouble. She was beginning to be concerned. His sex drive was certainly diminishing. She had to make all the moves lately. And last night was very mediocre. A real hit-and-run job.

She hoped it was just a slump. She hoped it would get better once he started hitting again. Dr. Linda Jacobs said on talk radio that lack of sex drive was a serious problem in a marriage. A woman had called in from Palos Verdes and said her husband hadn't slept with her for fourteen months, and when she finally made him go into therapy with her she found out that he had been masturbating three times a day with lingerie catalogs from the Broadway.

Ching Ming's Fine Cantonese Cuisine was on East Second Street between the Drip 'n' Dry Launderette and Bob's Gun Shop. It was cavernous, with pink lacquered latticework and brass wall sconces in the shape of tortured reptiles. The large booths were soft and womblike, smelling of years of saddle soap and soy sauce.

D.J. sat in one of the booths toward the rear, sunk into the spongy leather, absently stirring the sugar in his teacup. He had gotten there at exactly eight o'clock. He was always punctual.

He would try to have Randy Dreyfus get right to the point and be out of there by nine. The menu was not very promising. There were lots of combination plates and the kind of heavy rice dishes that made him constipated. He didn't want to get blocked up during a pennant drive.

By eight-thirty D.J. had gone through an entire bowl of hard noodles and was thinking of leaving when Randy walked in the door. The tall blond shortstop peered into the darkness and, sighting D.J., loped over with that loose, athletic gait of his.

"Jeez, I'm sorry," he said, sliding in opposite D.J. "I hit some bad traffic. You order?"

"Not yet."

Randy picked up the menu. "The wonton soup's real good. So are the spare ribs. You want to order fried rice for two?"

"Sure."

"Nice place, huh?"

"Yeah."

"Harry Glugg told me about it. His brother-in-law lives in town, eats here all the time."

"Uh-huh . . ."

Randy continued to scrutinize the menu. "The pork chop suey's pretty good and so is the moo goo gai pan. Maybe we ought to go with the steamed rice instead—what do you say?"

"Okay."

"Fried rice has a lot of cholesterol. How's your cholesterol?"

"Good."

"So's mine. One-fifty. Doctor says you could run a power plant through my arteries. I don't know—how much cholesterol could be in fried rice?"

"Why don't you just order what you want?"

"Yeah. You're right. I'm going to go with the barbecued spare ribs to start. Want to split an order of egg roll?"

"Fine."

Randy called the waiter, an old man in an ill-fitting gray suit, who trudged over and wrote down their order on the back of a newspaper. Then he trudged into the kitchen, leaving Randy and D.J. completely alone in the empty restaurant.

"How're the brakes on your car?" Randy asked.

"Fine."

"I got this slow leak in the brake-fluid reservoir. I've taken it in three times already. It's a real drag."

"Must be."

"So what's your mother's name?"

"Beg your pardon?"

"I was wondering what your mother's name was."

"Shirley."

"Nice name. Mine's Estelle. Estelle McNamara was her maiden name. How about yours?"

"My what?"

"Your mother's maiden name."

"Beggs. Shirley Beggs."

Randy scratched the back of his neck, flexing his shoulder muscles. The rotator-cuff nerve was still hurting.

"So what do you watch on TV?"

"I don't watch much TV."

"I like to watch *Jeopardy.* I have it taped when I'm on the road, and when I get back I have ten, twelve to watch all in a row. I can fast-forward through the commercials—"

"Randy, why'd you ask me to dinner?"

The question took Randy completely off guard. He looked away, unable to meet D.J.'s eyes. He had no idea what to say. Where the hell was the waiter with the food?

The silence continued for what seemed like hours, Randy scratching his neck, flexing, and D.J. sitting there, hands folded in front of him.

Randy had never noticed before how beautiful the second baseman's hands were. His fingers were long and tapered, his knuckles prominent, his skin smooth in spite of all the ground balls he had fielded. D.J.'s fielding percentage was in the high .980's. He was heading for another Gold Glove season.

Finally, Randy cleared his throat and said, "Well, I thought it would be nice to get to know each other, you know what I mean?"

D.J. nodded but not necessarily as a reply to Randy's question. There was a trace of irony in the nod, a side of the second baseman that Randy had novor eeen before.

"Randy, we've been teammates for three years. We've spent a lot of time on the road together, on planes, in hotels, in clubhouses. During all this time we never had much to say to each other outside of who was going to cover second on a stolen base. So now you drag me up to a Chinese restaurant sixty miles out of town to ask me what my mother's maiden name is."

He looked right at Randy and shrugged. Randy shrugged back. Then D.J. smiled. So did Randy. It was a completely involuntary reaction. The smile just came out of him from somewhere inside. He sat there smiling like a kid, without knowing why.

In the middle of this smiling, the old man trudged over with the wonton soup and spare ribs. Randy sprinkled noodles on the top and dove in. They ate their wonton soup in silence. When they were finished Randy offered D.J. a couple of the barbecued spare ribs. D.J. helped himself to one, dipped it into the plum sauce, and washed it down with a sip of tea.

"Randy, I'm going to tell you something about me that nobody else on the team knows. In fact, very few people in the entire world know. If this got out it would probably be the end of my career. I've gone to great lengths to keep this under wraps but I'm going to tell you. I'm going to tell you because I think you need to know. Randy, I'm gay."

"Right."

D.J. looked at him carefully, searching for signs of sarcasm in his voice. He found none.

"Did you hear what I said?" D.J. asked.

"Yeah."

"Does that make you uncomfortable?"

"Nah."

"You sure?"

"Uh-huh."

There was another long moment of silence before D.J. said, "So what are we doing here having dinner on a Thursday night when you got a wife at home?"

"I don't know."

"Have you ever . . . ?"

Randy shook his head quickly.

"Never?"

"Never."

"Not even when you were a kid?"

"Nope. Nothing happened until the shower in Cleveland."

"What're you talking about?"

"Nothing happened in the shower either, but something almost happened. I'm seeing a shrink. He's an Egyptian. Maybe it'll go away. Maybe it's a crossed wire. I still feel like banging Pia Zadora so it can't be that bad, you know what I mean?"

D.J. looked at his shortstop with newfound compassion. "Jesus, Randy, I don't know what to tell you."

Randy nodded and shrugged. "I mean, I just want to know. One way or another. Is there some sort of test you can take?"

"No. You can't take a test. It's something you just figure out eventually. . . . What about your wife?"

"I don't know. We still, you know, do it. Now and then. She's a good-looking woman. The thing is, D.J., I don't even know what you guys do exactly."

"It's not that hard to figure out."

Randy averted his eyes, embarrassed by the images that were going through his mind. D.J. was quiet for a moment, then:

"Look, can I tell you something? If you're not sure about this, you should probably try and ignore it, see if it goes away. Sometimes it does. Because, I got to tell you, it's not an easy life. Especially these days."

Randy nodded.

"And you might as well kiss the Hall of Fame good-bye if it gets out. This isn't Pete Rose laying down a couple of bets. They'll crucify you for this."

Randy sat there listening with a growing sense of helplessness. He was in deep shit. He suspected that he wasn't really interested in swinging from the right side of the plate anymore. And he was scared shitless of hitting left-handed. Overnight everything had changed. Nothing made sense anymore.

He sat there staring off into space, uninterested in the pork chop suey in front of him.

"Listen, Randy, I'll tell you what. We'll pretend this conversation never happened. Who knows? Maybe it's a crossed wire after all."

Randy nodded absently. Then D.J. muttered, "Pia *Zadora*?"

D.J.'s smile was so broad that Randy found himself smiling back in spite of himself. They both started laughing. What else was there to do?

V

On August 1, when they left on a ten-game road trip to Toronto, Boston, and New York, the Vikings were nine and a half games out of first. While they were on the road, both Oakland and the Angels were at home, playing weak opposition. The writers covering the team were predicting that this road trip was the beginning of the end. No one expected them even to tread water. By the time they returned to the West Coast they'd be thirteen or more games out and down for the count. Wait till next year.

People were calling the sports talk radio programs, sounding off, accusing the players of being overpaid fuckups. There were cries to bring up the minor leaguers and start rebuilding for next year. Realtors began making unsolicited phone calls to the players' homes inquiring about their interest in selling. Charlie Gonse's TV show, *The Manager's Corner*, was sinking in the ratings, losing its time slot to reruns of *Baywatch*. Arsenio Hall canceled Randy Dreyfus's appearance when Catfish Hunter suddenly became available.

But a baseball has a tendency to bounce unpredictably, Isaac

Newton notwithstanding. External forces get screwed up. Entropy kicks in. Collective biorhythms wreak havoc with the laws of thermodynamics. Men with twenty-twenty vision take called third strikes, lose pop flies in the sun. Hamstring muscles get stretched, groins get pulled. Odd things happen. A squibber under the glove, a ball with eyes, a checked-swing looper dropping in with the bases loaded, a strategic wild pitch, a couple of games one way or another, and things could look very different in a short amount of time.

Which is what happened to the Vikings in early August. They defied the bleak prognostications of the doomsayers by going into Toronto and sweeping the Blue Jays while both Oakland and California were faltering at home. They scored thirty-two runs in the three-game series, made only one error, and their pitching staff threw strikes. Balls dropped in. The slump-ridden hitters started to make contact. Randy Dreyfus was 7-for-12 with two doubles and a home run. To everyone's surprise, when they arrived in Boston the Vikings were only six and a half out. Go figure.

Just before batting practice for Thursday night's opener of the four-game series with Boston, Charlie Gonse decided to call a clubhouse meeting. The manager was not known for inspirational pep talks, preferring one-on-one Greek-salad chats in the privacy of his office.

"Okay, so we're on a roll. So we won three straight. So we're only six and a half out. How is it that this team is suddenly playing like a winner? Beats the shit out of me. I see a lot of crap going down, a lot of half-assed strictly minor league comportment that isn't worthy of a contending ball club. I see a lot of stuff out there I go home at night and don't even want to think about, 'less I upchuck my dinner. I haven't seen anybody hit the cut-off man in weeks. I haven't seen a bunt laid down that I couldn't pick up myself and throw the guy out. By three steps. I've seen a lot of horseshit on the bench that I won't even comment on. So just because you swept Toronto doesn't mean shit. You keep going like this and you might as well forget the season. Have I made myself clear?"

Randy Dreyfus sat in front of his locker staring at a box of baseballs he was supposed to autograph. He had been largely oblivious to Charlie Gonse's pep talk because he had other things on his mind. His dinner with D. J. Pickett at Ching Ming's had cleared nothing up. On the contrary, it had made things even more difficult. He now knew something he really didn't want to know.

At his last session with Dr. Fuad, he had related what had gone down in Ventura. The doctor nodded sagely, fondling his worry beads, and said, "Well, now you know what you wanted to know."

"But I didn't want to know *that*."

"Knowledge is power."

Easy for him to say. He wasn't having weird thoughts about *his* second baseman. All weekend Randy had walked around in a stupor. Gonse benched him Saturday night against Texas. On Sunday he took him out in the sixth for defensive purposes.

When he had said good-bye to Susie and the twins on Sunday night he'd had tears in his eyes. He couldn't control himself. It was embarrassing welling up right there in the departure lounge before getting on the charter to Toronto.

During the flight he sat by himself in the back of the plane and tried not to start crying again. And when he got to the hotel in Toronto, he took a couple of Seconal and a hot bath and slept fourteen hours.

He had developed a sort of mental jamming system, a way of blocking thoughts before they entered the danger zone. On the field D.J. and he communicated as they always did, using glove signals to set up pickoff plays and double-play coverage. After the game Randy spent a long time in the whirlpool so as to avoid being around when D.J. was still there.

Then, in spite of all this emotional turmoil, a strange thing had happened. He started hitting again in Toronto. Which made things even more confusing. It was difficult to have a nervous breakdown while you were on a hot streak. His stroke came back just as curiously as it had disappeared. He began to see the ball again. No matter how hard the pitcher threw, he saw the ball like an enormous piñata floating in front of him. All he had to do was swing and goodies came pouring out. Go figure.

Every night the high lasted until he got in the whirlpool. Then he began to fight the depression. He dressed hurriedly, took a cab to the hotel, dropped the Seconal, and passed out. He slept till noon, ordered room-service breakfast, and spent the day watching quiz shows on TV.

After Charlie Gonse's pregame talk in Boston, D.J. came up to Randy at the batting cage.

"How's it going?" he said.

"Fine."

"You're certainly hitting the hell out of the ball."

"Yeah. I made an adjustment in my stance."

D.J. smiled and nodded. The two of them stood there for a moment in silence, watching Bernie Lazarre hit. Then D.J. said, "Look, if you ever want to talk, just let me know."

"Right."

"Just talk. Like friends. Seriously."

"I appreciate that."

And Randy grabbed the bat and stepped in to face Leo Gump, the pitching coach. The first pitch was low and inside, right in his wheelhouse. Randy hit it so far over the left-field wall that Charlie Gonse moved him from second to third in the batting order.

Randy went 3-for-4 that night, including a bases-clearing double, which won the game in the eighth. His average climbed back up over .330. Barry Fuchsia called to tell him that they were up to seven in year two and seven five in year three and that the sweeteners were up a hundred across the board.

In spite of these developments, he was miserable. He lay on the bed and watched TV with lidded eyes. The weather was gorgeous, ideal for playing golf, but Randy never left the room. He couldn't go on like this, even if his average went above .400. It wasn't worth it.

On Friday morning, Randy picked up the phone and called Dr. Fuad in L.A. He left a message on the doctor's machine and had nearly dozed off again when the phone rang.

"Mr. Dreyfus?"

The doctor's voice sounded distant and weary, as always. Randy wondered if he was going to get billed for the phone call. He had had to talk to Arthur Maltz, his business manager, and tell him to pay the Egyptian out of his petty-cash account so as not to leave a paper trail. Susie sometimes read the monthly statements from Maltz, Dilecki and Froemann, an accountancy corporation in Reseda that, for a mere 7 percent of Randy's gross earnings, handled their finances.

"Hi."

"Something wrong?"

Right to the point, as usual. The guy had no bedside manner.

"I'm not happy," Randy blurted out.

"About what?"

"About my life."

"I see."

Silence. Randy could picture him in his office, feeding his fish, clicking his beads, the phone cradled between his neck and shoulder. The guy never seemed to react to anything. Randy could have said that he had just taken out the entire coffee shop in the Ramada with an AK-47 and the guy would've said the same thing: "I see."

"I'm pretty bummed out here."

"About what?"

"You know."

"Well, Mr. Dreyfus, we have discussed that matter a great deal. You can't make feelings disappear just like that. You have to pay attention to them. . . ."

"What the fuck do you want me to do? *Go out* with him?"

Randy had yelled into the phone again. He was doing that more and more lately. He could almost see the doctor moving the receiver away from his ear.

"If that's what you want to do, that's what you must do. It's like eating or breathing. You can't stop doing those things, can you?"

"Doc, what if I told you I wanted to take my weenie out and wave it around in the middle of a schoolyard? Would you tell me that I should do it if I feel like it?"

There was an audible sigh over the wire. Then the doctor said, his voice dropping yet another octave, "This is not criminal behavior. This is behavior between consenting adults. . . ."

"Let me ask you something, doc. And give me a straight answer for once. Are you a lefty or what?"

"I beg your pardon?"

"A faggot."

"No, I am not, Mr. Dreyfus, since you asked, but even if I were, it would be irrelevant to the therapeutic process."

"Some process. I'm worse off than I was when I first came to see you."

"That's quite normal. Self-awareness is a very painful process."

"Yeah, well, I'm not so sure about this whole deal anyway. I went three-for-four last night, and let me tell you something—if Pia Zadora walked into this room right now, I'd stick it right between those big tits of hers. You know, so who needs your opinion anyway."

"I believe *you* called *me*, Mr. Dreyfus."

Unable to come up with a retort, Randy hung up. Fuck him. He was finished with Dr. Mendes Fuad. Who needed to listen to that shit?

Randy got out of bed and wandered over to the window. It was nineteen floors down to the street. It would be a pretty decent splat. There'd be pieces of him scattered around on both sides of the street.

Looking for the window latch, he realized that the windows did not open. It was a No Suicide room, like a No Smoking room. They must have noticed he was depressed when he checked in. They probably trained the desk clerks to recognize the signs.

He stood there at the window for a long time staring down at Boston. Maybe the Egyptian faggot was right after all. Maybe it *was* like eating and breathing. Maybe you just had to go with it.

Squinting at the TV, he read the LED readout: 12:47 P.M. They didn't have to be at the ballpark till five. He picked up the phone and dialed D. J. Pickett's room.

They went to see *Desert Tornado*, a martial-arts picture starring Bobby Mason, in a mall in Cambridge. There were only about a dozen people in the small theater watching the black karate star dismember Iraqi Special Forces soldiers in the deserts of Saudi Arabia.

Randy and D.J. sat there, each with a tub of popcorn, listening to the clean thump of Bobby Mason's hands as he slammed a nonstop stream of Arabs into the sand dunes. The guy never missed, never got under one and popped it up. Every hit was a clean, sharp single up the middle. By the time he was finished, bodies were littered across the sand all the way to Baghdad.

They walked out together into the neon reality of the mall, silently digesting the carnage, feeling drained but satisfied that terrorism had gotten its ass kicked. It was a little after three, two hours before they had to be at Fenway Park.

D.J. stopped to admire a pair of slacks in the window of a men's clothing store.

"You want to do some shopping?" D.J. asked.

"Okay."

It was one of those classy boutique-type places full of expensive European-looking clothes. A guy with a Frog accent came over and asked if they needed help. D.J. asked to see the pants that were in the window.

As the Frog went over to the window to get the pants, Randy realized that he was surrounded by left-handed hitters. The guy definitely didn't walk straight. You could tell a mile away that this guy wasn't interested in Pia Zadora.

For a moment, Randy had an impulse to bolt. To get the hell out of there. To run as fast as he could away from this nest of lefties. He could still get out clean. He could quit baseball and never have to take another shower with twenty-five well-built guys. He had enough in the bank to open a small miniature-golf course or a Toyota dealership. . . .

"What do you think of the color?" D.J. asked.

"Huh?"

"The beige. What do you think?"

"Sure. Looks good to me."

"It won't go with a couple of cashmere sweaters I have. The colors aren't complementary."

"Yeah. That could be a problem."

The Frog handed D.J. the trousers. "Would you like to try them on?" he said. Randy could swear the guy was making eyes at D.J.

"Why not?"

"The changing rooms are in the rear." The salesman pointed to a door marked EXIT just past the men's underwear. "If you like any assistance, tell me."

D.J. walked off with the trousers on the hanger, leaving Randy alone with the Frog. Flexing his fists, Randy was ready to do serious damage. If the guy made a move, he'd be able to slice him in the neck, then finish him with a knee in the solar plexus. This way he would avoid breaking any bones or leaving visible scars. In case there was a lawsuit. Arthur Maltz had put him into a $5 million wraparound liability policy for just this sort of thing.

"Is there anything *you* would like?" The Frog said with a look similar to the one he had given D.J.

"Nah," Randy said quickly.

"We have a special on underwear. Imported. From Italy."

"No thanks."

Maybe he'd just break a shin or a clavicle, nothing life-threatening. It would give him a certain amount of pleasure to drop-kick this guy right through the plate-glass window.

When D.J. emerged from the changing room he looked terrific. The beige pants really brought out how gracefully he was built. There wasn't an extraneous ounce of flesh on his body. It all worked together harmoniously, like a crisp double play. No wasted motion. No unnecessary steps.

"What do you think?" D.J. asked Randy, as he turned and checked out the various angles in the three-way mirror.

"Good. Nice."

"You don't think they're a little too pleated in the front?"

"Nah."

D.J. turned to the Frog and said, "Can you have these altered for me by Monday morning?" The Frog raised his eyebrows and tilted his head, clearly unhappy.

"I do not know. It's not much time."

"I'm going to New York Monday."

"You will not be back?"

"Not this season."

The Frog lost interest rapidly. Randy intervened. "Can't you just do it, man? You know what I mean? It's no big thing. Just put it on the top of the pile, okay?"

The guy stared at Randy with his bored, superior look, probably trying to figure out if this big, tall blond dish was going to get rough and whether or not the idea appealed to him. Randy considered the uppercut knee into the scrotum, a blow that every shortstop in the league knew how to administer to runners coming into second too high and hard.

"Well, all right," the Frog relented after a long moment. "But I am going to have to keep the tailor late."

Fuck him. Randy sent the guy flying over first and into the stands for a ground-rule double anyway. Then he calmly brushed pieces of his private parts off his uniform leg and trotted back to his position.

Later, in the cab on the way to the ballpark, D.J. said to him, "You really got very assertive in there."

"Yeah, well, the guy pissed me off."

"I like assertiveness."

Randy turned away abruptly, afraid that he was blushing. *Blushing.* Jesus. What next?

Then something even weirder happened. The cab hit a bump, and Randy started to cry. Just like that, tears pouring out of him uncontrollably. D.J. looked at him, concerned.

"You okay?"

Randy nodded. But he wasn't okay. He was fucked up. Royally. D.J. took a neatly folded monogrammed handkerchief out of his pocket and handed it to him. Randy blew his nose loudly, muttering, "Fucking allergies."

Milton Sheen, a Boston cab driver for forty-two years, looked back through the rearview mirror at the big blond ballplayer sobbing away in his cab. He shook his head. What a disgusting display. You wouldn't have seen Johnny Pesky bawling in the back of a cab, for chrissakes. These guys were all overpaid drug-addict pussies. He put his foot down harder on the gas pedal, heading for the Charles, and hoped the guy didn't puke all over the backseat.

VI

John D. F. White., Sr., the owner of the Los Angeles Valley Vikings, had accumulated his considerable fortune in the fast-food business. Seoul Food, the chain of Korean restaurants that he had started from scratch in the eighties and built up to be the largest Asian junk-food empire on the West Coast, had been responsible for the lion's share of the $217 million cost of acquiring the expansion franchise in 1995.

When he turned eighty, he named his late-in-life son, John junior, president and chief executive officer of the team and devoted most of his time to playing golf and eating lunch in downtown restaurants with influential old friends from Hancock Park and Pasadena. He smoked cigars, fat panatelas from the Canary Islands, and wrote rambling letters to the editors of local and national periodicals denouncing things like sperm banks and the fluoridation of public water supplies.

John/John was thirty-one and still quaked when the old man entered a room with his virile, energetic walk. The old man was a hard act to follow. It was common knowledge that he was still the power behind the throne.

John/John was short and pudgy with blue-tinted contact lenses that made him look a little spacey. Axel Most called him the Prime Minister of Neptune. He suffered from psychosomatic asthma and kept an inhaler in his desk drawer for blitzkrieg attacks. Now and then in the middle of a meeting he would have to take the device out and start breathing through it, while beckoning for the people in the meeting to continue talking as if nothing out of the ordinary were taking place.

From the time he was five he had been a baseball nut, devising teams and playing make-believe games on the floor of his room with baseball cards. He had played out entire 162-game seasons every year, calling the play-by-play for each one in an imitation of Vin Scully. In his bedroom at home in Holmby Hills he had Nintendo baseball hooked up to a Mitsubishi forty-nine-inch set, and he often lulled himself to sleep hitting 102-mile-per-hour fastballs into oblivion.

On this early-August morning John/John was meeting in his office at the stadium with the Viking Girls, the players' wives' association headed by Susie Dreyfus. They were discussing Susie's proposal to set up a day-care center at the stadium so that the wives could bring their kids and stay for batting practice and the game.

Though the team certainly had the resources to devote a room for the day-care center, John/John was opposed to the idea. When a ballplayer arrives at the ballpark he wants to forget about his wife and kids. He's there to do a job, a tough job, and he doesn't need any more distractions than he already has.

At the moment the team was on a roll, having gone 8-2 on the road trip. They were only five and a half out of first and being taken seriously again as a pennant contender. He didn't need them thinking about report cards and orthodontia right now. Not with Oakland coming in for three starting tomorrow night.

But he wasn't going to dismiss the idea out of hand. Not to Susie Kent Dreyfus. She was a force to be reckoned with. Susie Dreyfus was hot. *Los Angeles* magazine had featured her in a piece they did about women who "had it all." Besides being married to the Vikings' star shortstop and being the mother of two children, she had a weekly call-in radio program, where she fielded questions about baseball, home redecorating, and personal hygiene.

You just didn't say no to Susie Dreyfus. You didn't want it getting out on the air waves that the Vikings were insensitive to women's needs. It was bad public relations. John/John actually considered himself a progressive in this area. He had supported a move to increase the number of toilet stalls in the ladies' rooms at Viking Stadium, in response to the bottleneck problems that arose in the late innings. He sent a hundred dollars every year to Planned Parenthood. He supported the right of women sportswriters to be in the clubhouse before and after the game even if this meant they'd see naked men. It was one of the few issues that he dared to differ with his father on. When John senior heard that women sportswriters wanted equal access to the players after the game, he said, "As far as I'm concerned, a woman has no right being around where exposed genitals are unless she's prepared to do something about it."

Susie Dreyfus was wearing a smart pair of khaki culottes and a cleavage-revealing tank top. John/John began to fear an asthma attack.

"We could convert one of the weight rooms real easy," Susie was saying. "Randy says there are too many of them as it is."

"Sure."

"I mean, half the guys have their own weight rooms in their houses."

"I think it's a great suggestion."

"So when do you think we could get going on it?"

"Pretty soon. I'd like to run it by the Stadium Administration Committee, get some of their input."

John/John eyed the phone buttons lighting up on his console. Calls were being fielded by his secretaries in the outer office. One of them was no doubt from Barry Fuchsia. He was anxious to close the Randy Dreyfus deal. They had gone over $7.5 million in year three now, and they still weren't closed. Maybe he could figure a way to throw the day-care center in as a deal point, just to get it closed. The last thing he wanted was Randy Dreyfus out there on the free-agent market. He might have to have a day-care center in his ballpark to prevent that.

"Well," he said with a smile as he got up. "I appreciate you ladies coming in and visiting . . ."

Susie Dreyfus stayed seated. The others followed her lead. "Do you have a rough timetable on this, John?" she said quietly.

"Well, as soon as the committee has a look at the numbers—"

"When would that be?"

John/John could see that she wasn't going to move until he named a firm date. He was standing there behind his desk confronting a group of seated women, their legs held tightly together in a gesture of defiance, if not sexual withholding. He could feel his bronchial tubes begin to constrict. The inhaler was in the top right-hand drawer, behind the cough drops and the extra-strength Excedrin.

"A month or so . . ."

"The season would be practically over by then," said Karen Most, the wife of his Cy Young Award–candidate pitcher.

They were ganging up on him. He had to get them out of the office before he started gasping for air.

"I'll call a special meeting of the committee. How's that?"

"When?" Susie Dreyfus persisted.

"Tomorrow. I'll call it for tomorrow. We'll get rolling on this right away."

"Great."

"I'll call you as soon as I know."

"Terrific. Thanks, John."

She sat there for one more long moment. John/John had moved around to the front of the desk, farther away from the inhaler.

"Listen, thank *you*. Anytime. My door's always open. See you around." He made a little waving gesture, hoping that this would do the trick.

Now she finally got up. He eagerly shook her hand and those of the other five women. As soon as they'd trooped out, John/John made a run for his desk, reached into the drawer, and groped for the inhaler. A secretary appeared at the door with the phone list just as he got it in his mouth and started sucking in air. Gasping, he waved her in.

She put the list in front of him as he wheezed loudly. He pointed to Barry Fuchsia's number.

By the time the secretary got Barry Fuchsia on the phone, John/John's lungs were nearly clear. He took a deep breath, put down the inhaler, and said, "Barry, I think I have a notion you're going to like. . . ."

They took the Jeep Wagoneer to Dr. Levine's Family Pet Counseling Center on Magnolia Boulevard in Burbank. It was the only vehicle in the family that had nonleather upholstery. Calvin lay in the rear compartment, behind the twins' seat, chewing on a Naugahyde puppy bone. Susie sat in the passenger seat, her hands folded primly in her lap, looking out the window. Molly and Dolly were each reading a back issue of *Ladies' Home Journal*, to which they had their own subscription. Randy drove slowly, spitefully, missing every light he could on Ventura Boulevard.

In spite of his best efforts, they were only three minutes late for their appointment with Dr. Bob, as he liked to be called. Though he assured them he was a qualified Ph.D., licensed by the State of California to dispense psychotherapy, he felt that titles created barriers and that his method was all about breaking down barriers.

"Walls. We put up walls without even being conscious of them."

They were sitting in Dr. Bob's consultation room, a room with a tile floor, drain, and hose to deal with accidents from traumatized pets. He was a tall, athletic-looking man of about forty, in a tight-fitting T-shirt that showed off his pectorals. The Dreyfuses sat on straight-backed vinyl chairs, Calvin at their feet in the "stay" position he had been taught at obedience school.

"The pet often feels that he's not a part of the family. That's the root of the problem. You need to make the pet feel he belongs, include him in family activities, relate to him in a meaningful way. Let me ask you a question, Randy. Do you spend time with Calvin?"

"Yeah. When I'm in town."

"What do you do with him?"

"What do you mean, what do I do? I walk him, give him his dinner, that type of thing."

"What I'm talking about, Randy, is quality time. Do you spend time with your dog doing things that don't have to do with maintenance?"

"Beg your pardon?"

"Do you pet him? Do you talk to him? Do you play with him? Do you relate to him in a manner that communicates love and re-spect?''

Randy looked at the guy, trying to get a read on him. In spite of the pecs, he looked like a wimp. Did Randy *relate* to his dog? Was he kidding or what? Jesus. At five hundred bucks a pop this clown had some deal going. Randy had only agreed to go to placate Susie. Now he was sorry he'd shown up. It was his second therapy session of the day, no less. The morning had begun at nine thirty-five in Dr. Fuad's office in Westwood.

He had told Susie that he was going to take the 850i in for a lube job this time. He was running out of vehicles to get serviced early in the morning. The doctor had promised to give him the first after-noon session that opened up.

Randy had told the doctor about his date with D. J. Pickett in Boston and the subsequent shopping trip and crying fit in the cab.

"I mean, I called the guy *up*. I asked him *out*. It was a goddamn *date*, for chrissakes.''

"So," Mendes Fuad had said, "you telephoned him, you suggested you go to see a film. After the film you accompanied him to a cloth-ing store, where he bought some trousers. And then you started crying in a taxicab and he loaned you his handkerchief. Is that more or less what happened?''

"Yeah.''

The doctor rocked slowly in the bentwood rocker, working the worry beads, his eyes half-closed, while Randy wriggled uncomfort-ably in his seat.

"Perhaps," Fuad said, "it is the beginning of a courtship ritual.''

"What?''

"Courtship. The mating dance. It occurs in all species.''

"What the fuck are you talking about, doc?''

"You are flirting with each other, preparatory to mating. That's what it appears like to me.''

Randy did his best to keep from losing it. If he slugged the guy, he'd have to find another doctor. The thought of going through the introduction and confession with a total stranger again was not appealing. This guy, with all his faults, was at least convenient to the San Diego Freeway.

"Am I getting through to you?" Dr. Bob's wimpish voice penetrated Randy's daydream. For a moment he wasn't sure where he was. Were they talking about mating rituals with his second baseman or relating to his dog?

Randy looked over at the twins, who were staring at him expectantly, waiting for him to give the right answer to this asshole. They would disown him if he didn't try to relate to the dog. It was pretty clear where their priorities lay.

"Yeah, I get the point," he managed finally. "Got to relate, treat him like a member of the family."

"Precisely. I think, Randy, that as the leader of the family your relationship with Calvin is the critical one. He looks to you for sustenance, for guidance, as well as love. He needs you to take charge. . . ."

"Right."

"Now I want you to approach Calvin and show him some affection with this new attitude in mind. I don't want you just to pet him perfunctorily. I want you really to relate to him. To make this a quality interaction."

"Now? You want me to do this now?"

"I think it would be therapeutic. I think it would mean something not only to you but to Calvin. He's very aware of your reactions, and I think he senses what we're doing here together this afternoon."

The twins nodded their heads in unison. There was no getting out of it. He was cornered. He was going to have to perform.

Randy got up and slowly approached the dog, who regarded him with the same expressionless look he always gave him, the look he had on his face when he tried to come into second hard and Randy had to send him across the room on the fly.

"Hey, Calvin, how're you doing?" he said, forcing a smile.

Calvin got up, breaking the "stay" position, and gave a sort of half-yawning little cry. Randy kneeled down in front of him and extended his hand. He rubbed the dog's back and said, "Good dog, nice dog . . ."

"Don't you have a particular pet name for him that you use when just the two of you are alone?"

"Nope."

"Well, now's the time to come up with one. He's ready to hear it."

Randy ransacked his brain for something appropriate to say. Finally, in a barely audible voice, he murmured, "Nice . . . doggie . . ."

Calvin lifted a leg and peed on the floor, right in front of him. The twins giggled. Dr. Bob smiled.

"That's a sign of affection, Randy. That means he loves you and wants to protect you. You've established a bridge that'll take you across the gap that's been separating you. Good work, Randy."

D. J. Pickett and Randy Dreyfus had their second date on the first Saturday of the home stand. Friday night, as they were warming up between innings, Randy asked him if he wanted to shoot eighteen holes in the morning. They agreed to meet at a course near D.J.'s place in Thousand Oaks at 10 A.M.

Randy had made a great effort to avoid wearing noncomplementary colors. He agonized in front of his open closet for a long time before settling on a light tan Lacoste, a pair of beige slacks, and his white Reeboks with brown trim. Then he stood in front of the mirror and admired how it all worked together perfectly.

Though Randy wasn't much of a golfer, certainly not in the same league with D.J., who shot in the low seventies, a round of golf was an opportunity to be alone with the second baseman. Just a couple of ballplayers shooting eighteen holes on a Saturday morning. It was a good chance to get to know each other better. D.J. was a good listener, and Randy found himself talking freely about a number of things he rarely talked about with anybody else.

He told D.J. about his ham-radio hobby. Nobody on the team knew that Randy had built his own transmitter from a kit and spent entire evenings talking to people all over the world. Once he talked with a guy who turned out to be the Prince of Liechtenstein.

"No shit," D.J. said, selecting an iron from the cart.

"Yeah," said Randy. "We're having this conversation about the weather and about food we like, that kind of shit, when he suddenly says that his cook at the palace is Italian and makes great lasagna. So I say, 'What palace?' And he says, 'My palace.' Funny, huh?"

"Yeah."

Randy watched as D.J. chipped perfectly to the green, the ball winding up six feet from the cup. One hell of a shot. The guy was gorgeous to watch on a golf course.

Even with a minus-ten handicap, Randy was behind by the ninth hole, but he didn't care. He was having a good time. He couldn't remember the last time he felt so relaxed around another guy. D.J. made no mention of the crying incident in Boston. As far as Randy was concerned, it was a freak accident, another crossed wire. Mating ritual. Jesus. The fucking Egyptian was out of his mind.

They were done by noon and went to grab a bite at a small Mexican place that D.J. knew. It was dark and nearly empty and they ordered margaritas with their combination enchilada–taco–chile relleno plates. Randy was talking about his favorite Mexican restaurants around the league when D.J. interrupted him.

"Listen, Randy, we got to talk."

"We *are* talking."

"That's not what I mean."

D.J. fingered the stem of his margarita glass for a moment, then continued. "The way I see it, we're going to have a problem, we keep this up."

"What're you talking about?"

"Remember what I told you up in Ventura?"

"Yeah."

"Well, the way I see it, you're heading for problems. Big problems. You're exposing yourself to a dangerous situation."

"You're not . . . uh . . . ?"

"No. That's not what I mean. I've been tested."

The waiter chose this moment to ask if they wanted coffee. They shook their heads in unison and waited for the guy to go away. Then D.J. wiped his mouth carefully with his napkin and said, "Look, I'm just trying to save you a lot of trouble. Actually, both of us a lot of trouble. I mean, we're on the same team. We're a double-play combination. You realize what would happen if it got out? Not to mention the fact we're in the middle of a pennant race here. We're talking about a major distraction here. We're talking about conduct detrimental to the best interests of baseball here. . . ."

Randy sat there nodding without really understanding why he was nodding. He had heard what D.J. said and knew that nodding was not an appropriate response.

And then it happened again. Without any warning, like one of those summer thunderstorms that come out of nowhere. He started to cry again. Loud, hiccuppy sobs that sounded like a choking fit. The waiter turned around and stared. The Mexican truck drivers looked over from the bar. The bartender stopped wiping glasses.

D.J. whipped out another handkerchief and gave it to Randy. When Randy was able to talk again, he glared at the truck drivers at the bar and muttered, "What the fuck you staring at? You never seen a guy get a chili pepper stuck in his throat before?"

Mikva was folding laundry in the avocado-and-rose laundry nook of the Dreyfuses' home in Valley View Estates when she came upon something that puzzled her. It was a monogrammed handkerchief with the initials DJP sewn into a corner. She may have been from Lithuania, but she wasn't dumb. She knew about monogrammed handkerchiefs. And she knew that this one didn't belong to anybody in the household. No, this one belonged to someone else. This handkerchief spelled trouble.

Mikva considered her options. The easiest thing to do would simply be to throw the handkerchief out. She had only fifteen more months before she would start computer school. But if the handkerchief was discovered and caused the type of problems that she imagined it would cause, then there would be a period of instability, followed no doubt by a divorce. She would have to stay with the woman under reduced circumstances, eventually being moved into a smaller house with a less spacious maid's room and possibly without a satellite dish. She didn't like that option at all.

The problem was that Mikva couldn't bring herself to destroy property. It would look bad in the event that there was an immigration hearing. No, that was not in her interest either. So she settled upon a course of action that was neither self-incriminating nor self-destructive. She would put it in Mrs. Dreyfus's drawer, where she kept her delicate things and where Mr. Dreyfus would never look. Then the tramp could dispose of it herself when she found it, and

Mikva wouldn't become an accessory to the criminal act, as she had seen someone become the other night on *Perry Mason.*

If she, Mikva, were married to a handsome baseball player who made lots of money and had a big house with a satellite dish, she wouldn't leave *her* boyfriend's handkerchief around. She muttered *kurva,* which meant "harlot" in Lithuanian, and stuck the handkerchief in Mrs. Dreyfus's drawer, on top of a pile of underwear that only a slut would wear. The woman was not only a whore, she was a dumb whore.

Susie had just gotten home from her aerobics class and went upstairs to change before running to the studio to tape her radio show. She had very little time to slip out of her leotard and into her spandex pants, and she wouldn't even have bothered changing her underwear if it weren't for the fact that she was expecting her period and was concerned about her personal hygiene in case she began to flow that afternoon. She always counseled her listeners to wear clean underwear when they were menstruating.

Her first reaction upon seeing the handkerchief was that Mikva had somehow mixed one of her own handkerchiefs in with the laundry. But by the time she was out the door and into the 560 SEL she had realized that not only were her housekeeper's initials not D.J.P., but that the woman didn't use handkerchiefs, preferring to walk around with wads of Kleenex in her pocket, a habit that had always disgusted Susie.

Susie got the Mercedes quickly up to eighty-five on the freeway. She thought more clearly at high speeds. What was a handkerchief with the initials DJP doing in her drawer? If it wasn't Mikva's and it wasn't hers, then there was only one other person's it could be. And his initials weren't D.J.P.

All the way into the studio, Susie tried, unsuccessfully, to forget about the monogrammed handkerchief. There was no particularly good explanation for it and a number of bad ones. The bad ones could go a long way in explaining the strange behavior her husband had been demonstrating lately.

He kept sneaking off early in the morning to get work done on one of the cars, or to buy more shirts at Bullock's. He now had close to fifty Lacoste polo shirts. She couldn't remember the last time he had approached her to make love. Instead he preferred to Exercycle himself to exhaustion every night. Susie simply couldn't write off his erratic conduct as slump behavior anymore. He was hitting .425 over his last ten games.

But mainly she was struck by the way he walked around with this silly grin on his face half the time, a look that she hadn't seen since he had first fallen in love with her years ago. No matter how hard she tried, she couldn't help thinking that Randy was in love with someone else. Someone whose initials were D.J.P.

The only name with those initials that came to mind was Doris Pannizardi, the wife of the Vikings' third baseman. She was a tall, gangling woman with a bad overbite. The thought of losing her man to Doris Pannizardi was ridiculous. Give me a break. Doris Pannizardi. She'd bite it off.

The thought was so silly that Susie started to laugh. She didn't laugh very long. She was too furious. What was he doing screwing around on her? They had been married barely ten years. She'd never as much as flirted with another guy. When she'd said, "Till death do us part" she'd meant it.

She hoped it *was* Doris Pannizardi. It would serve him right if he got it bitten off.

Since leaving D. J. Pickett in the Mexican restaurant in Thousand Oaks, Randy had been driving the freeways, aimlessly weaving across the grid of the northwest San Fernando Valley. He had no idea where he was, and it didn't matter. Driving calmed his nerves. He was in bad shape. How much longer could he go on like this, breaking out crying in restaurants and taxicabs?

He tried to reach Fuad on the car phone, but got the machine. Where the hell was he, anyway? Was it some sort of Egyptian holiday? The guy didn't look like he had a family or even a wife. In spite of the doctor's denial, Randy suspected he was a lefty. For one thing, the guy wore this pansy aftershave and padded around his office in bedroom slippers. And then there were the fucking fish. Randy had never met a straight guy who played with tropical fish.

But the crying was not the worst of it. That was just weirdness. He could probably learn to live with it, like some sort of permanent handicap. He had seen this piece on *60 Minutes* about guys who uncontrollably shouted out dirty words. In the middle of telling you to shove a hot poker up your ass they handed you a card that said that they had this disease and they couldn't help what they were saying. Randy could get a bunch of cards printed up for the crying.

He kept asking himself how he could be one. He didn't like tropical fish or interior decorating or eau de cologne. He was married to a looker and had produced two children, even if they were girls with bad eyesight. He had spent eight years in organized baseball without getting a rod in the shower. Until very recently.

The fact was he didn't even know exactly what they did when they did it. And what you said afterward. And if you kissed and held hands and that type of shit. He wasn't entirely clear on the mechanical stuff. Maybe it was like a batting stance: You just got up at the plate and did what was natural.

He was so lost in these thoughts that he nearly rear-ended a VW going too slow in the fast lane. Jesus. He was out of control here. He had no idea where he was. It was the middle of a Saturday afternoon, and he was doing ninety on some out-of-the-way freeway somewhere thinking about how you have sex with another man.

He turned on the radio and punched the preset button to the all-talk station. A woman's voice was saying, ". . . I was thinking about converting the room over the garage to an exercise room and getting into shape. I figure if I lose a few pounds my husband won't cheat on me. . . ."

"Don't count on it," another woman's voice said, a very familiar voice.

"You don't think so?"

"Redecorating your house won't necessarily save your marriage, Joanne. The only way of doing that is being vigilant."

"Vigilant?"

"Don't assume you can trust a man just because you've been married to him for ten years. . . ."

Susie Dreyfus's voice sounded uncharacteristically cold and cynical. A chill went through Randy, and as he shifted his bulky frame in the leather luxury of the big Beemer, he felt his scrotum tighten.

VII

As soon as the blonde in the tight leather skirt and the silk blouse with the real pearl stick pin and the Gucci scarf walked into the office, Pete Zabriskie knew she wasn't from Santa Ana. You didn't see that type of threads on the local talent. This one had money and looks and had pulled into the lot in a midnight-blue 560 SEL. This one was from up north. This one was undoubtedly a Yellow Pages job.

ZABRISKIE INVESTIGATIONS—DISCREET, REASONABLE, AND THOROUGH occupied a quarter-page in the West Los Angeles/Beverly Hills Yellow Pages. The 714 area code and the Orange County address attracted business from people who didn't want to hire a detective with an office anywhere near where they lived. It was the don't-shit-where-you-eat category of human behavior. They preferred driving the fifty miles to Santa Ana and paying the mileage charges for Zabriskie to come up to L.A. and work.

It was fine with Pete Zabriskie. Billable hours was the name of the game in any service business. And Zabriskie Investigations, Inc., was billing a lot of hours. If things continued at this pace, he'd clear a hundred and twenty-five by the end of the year. Which wasn't bad for a guy out of Cal State Fullerton and the Downey Police Department.

The blonde told him her name was Smith. Joan Smith. He wrote it down in pencil so that he could erase it when she eventually told him what her real name was. She said that this was the first time she had been to a private detective. They always said that. Like guys with hookers.

Then she took a handkerchief out of her pocketbook and put it on the table in front of him. It was a white linen handkerchief with the initials DJP monogrammed in script on the edge.

"I found this in my husband's laundry. I want to know who it belongs to."

Pete Zabriskie saw a lot of monogrammed handkerchiefs in his line of work. Monogrammed handkerchiefs were a great source of business for him. They were left around, like matchbooks or cigarette butts with lipstick, to create work for private detectives. You didn't have to take a criminology course to know that every man or woman who ever fucked around left clues so that they would be caught. It helped assuage their guilty conscience. It was all about guilt, this extramarital business. Guilt produced billable hours.

"Is that all you want to know?"

This question disconcerted her. She looked like she was working hard to control herself. They all did. The anger was there, right below the surface. If he wanted to expand his business, he could start an assault-and-battery service on the side. One-stop shopping. Find out who it is and then beat the shit out of them.

"I suppose you'll file some sort of report. Is that how it works?"

"That depends upon you, Mrs. Smith. We can be as thorough as you like. It's your call."

"What do you mean?"

"Well, some clients are merely interested in the identity of the owner of the handkerchief. Others would like to know a little more about the circumstances under which the owner of the handkerchief and the investigatee have commingled."

He took some papers out of his desk drawer and handed them across to her.

"We have a basic service and a number of options available. They're all listed there. As you can see, basic surveillance is at an hourly rate and terminates upon the discovery of the person whose identity you are interested in knowing. There is, however, a minimum number of hours required as a forfeiture. Expanded surveillance entails a written report sent to you Federal Express or faxed, as you choose, on a daily basis. It contains not just the name or names but the venues, times, conditions, and relevant circumstances of all meetings between the investigatee and the target person. Finally, there is the comprehensive plan, which combines all the expanded-surveillance features with affidavits from witnesses and photographs—"

"Photographs?"

"Yes. They're useful in court should you choose to go the next step."

She stared vacantly at the papers in her hand. Things were moving very quickly. This guy already had her in divorce court with his photographs and itemized accounts of the whereabouts of the "investigatee."

"Listen, I think you're making some assumptions here—"

"Let's hope so. My philosophy, Mrs. Smith, is expect the worst. Then you can only be pleasantly surprised if it turns out to be better than you think."

She took the expanded-surveillance package and signed a contract. She asked him to FedEx the reports to her office at the radio station. He assured her they would be sent in a plain brown wrapper.

"Will a package addressed to 'Mrs. Smith' reach you at this address, Mrs. Smith?"

"I beg your pardon?"

"If 'Mrs. Smith' is what we call in this business a *nom de guerre*, then you won't be receiving my reports, nor, I have to point out, would the signature on the contract you just signed be valid."

"I see . . ."

He took out a new contract for her to sign. She signed "Suzanne Dreyfus" and wrote out a retainer check for five hundred dollars from her petty-cash account, her teeth tightly clenched.

In the car driving back up to L.A. Susie played heavy-metal rock loud on the Blaupunkt. She felt queasy. She hadn't liked Pete

Zabriskie or his over-air-conditioned, cinder-block office with the secondhand Danish Modern furniture and the secretary who looked like a Delta stewardess who lifted weights. Zabriskie wore tinted glasses and a bad hairpiece and must have bought his suit at K mart. *Commingled?* What kind of a word was that? They were talking about her husband having an affair, not about some sociological phenomenon. This guy couldn't intimidate her with college-board words. Susie had majored in sociology at USC with a phys-ed minor. She knew what *commingled* meant. She even knew how to spell it.

Her thoughts drifted in the smoggy air of southeastern Los Angeles as the Mercedes headed north on the Santa Ana Freeway. Expect the worst. Go the distance. Call Bernie Solov, lay things out. On the come. Just as a precaution. Alimony, child support, and half the pension plan. For openers.

The thing was that she still loved Randy. She had no desire to hurt him. Even if it turned out to be *the worst.* Maybe he was just having some sort of weird early midlife crisis at twenty-eight. Maybe he'd get it out of his system, and it would be smooth sailing from here on in.

By the time she had reached the downtown interchange, she had decided that whatever the investigation turned up she would be understanding and supportive. She would do her best to accept and forgive. And if they wound up in court, she wouldn't take him to the cleaner's. She'd agree to the house, reasonable child support, and a lump sum settlement.

"I want to kill my dog."

Dr. Fuad did not react visibly to the plaintive note in Randy Dreyfus's voice as the shortstop walked fitfully back and forth across the doctor's deep-pile carpet.

"I hate him. He gives me this shit-eating look, drives me up a wall. And my wife and daughters drag me to see this goofball dog shrink, who wants me to spend quality time with him. Quality time! With a goddamn Dalmatian! Can you believe that? So I'm actually thinking up schemes to put out a contract on him. I mean, is that crazy or what? I'll tell you what I think—I'm thinking about offing the dog because it keeps me from thinking about my other problem. The Big One.''

"What's that?''

"Let's not beat around the fucking bush here, doc. You know what I'm talking about. The rod in the shower, remember?''

"Yes, of course.''

"I'm fouling them off here. I'm just standing there protecting the plate with a two-strike count on me, you know what I mean?''

Without a word or gesture Dr. Fuad acknowledged that he knew what Randy meant. He sat in his chair, his slippered feet tucked beneath him, watching Randy pace across his office.

"I'm hitting defensively. That's no good. You got to go up there telling yourself that you can hit the guy.''

"Whom do you want to hit?''

"It's just an example. A figure of speech. I'm trying to hang in there, that's all. I got to hit or get out of the box. That's what he said.''

"That's what who said?''

"D.J.''

"The man for whom you are having these uncomfortable thoughts?''

"That's right, doc. Where have you been all this time? Who do you think I'm talking about? King Kong?''

The doctor did not say anything for a moment. He sat nodding his head almost imperceptibly. The guy never tipped his hand. He just sat there like some fucking cigar-store Egyptian playing with his beads.

"Do you want to know what I think, Mr. Dreyfus?''

"Isn't that what I'm paying you a hundred and seventy-five an hour to find out?''

"No. You are paying me a hundred and seventy-five an hour to find out what *you* think. What I think isn't worth the money.''

"Okay, doc, I'll bite. What do *you* think?''

"I think that you are asking for my permission to sleep with this man.''

"What're you, fucking out of your mind? Why would I do that?''

"Because you are very ambivalent about it, and if you can get me to make the decision for you, then you won't have to be responsible for it."

"Is that so?"

"That is so."

"You know everything, doc?"

"Hardly."

"Because that's not what's going down here. What's going down here is that I have some sort of crossed wire that's fucking around with my head. You're supposed to find that wire and disconnect it."

"I'm not a brain surgeon . . ."

"And I'll tell you something else," Randy went on, not listening. "I got more consecutive errorless games than any other active short-stop in the American League, and I'm only twenty-eight. I don't get hurt, I'm looking at eight to ten more years in the majors, a couple of MVP's, batting titles, maybe a World Series ring. I'm headed for the Hall of Fame, doc. If this shit doesn't get in the way."

"What you refer to, Mr. Dreyfus, as 'this shit' may in fact be an essential part of you. You can't simply have it removed like a bad tooth."

"Why not?"

"Because it doesn't work that way."

Randy stopped pacing and turned toward the doctor, overcome with a sudden surge of sadness. It was all turning bad, and he had no control over it.

"Jesus, doc, I don't get it. Why me? I have this good life going. I'm hitting .331. We got a shot at the division. I'm in negotiations on a three-year deal for close to twenty million. Then this happens, throws a monkey wrench in everything. The whole goddamn ball game. It's like suddenly finding out you have leukemia."

Dr. Fuad got up and walked across to the fish tank. For a moment he peered at the impassive features of a Nepalese gunjafish, the rarest specimen in the tank. "Do you see this fish?" he said. "The striped one?"

"Yeah."

"This fish is a cannibal when put in a tank with his own species. Here, with other species, it shows no aggressive behavior. Why is that?"

"Fuck do I know."

"Nobody knows. And if we don't know why a simple organism like this does something, how can we begin to understand behavior in a psyche as complex as that of a human being?"

He turned to Randy, shrugged, then gave one of his pained smiles. Randy shrugged back. They stood there for a moment, looking at each other, not knowing what to say. Then Dr. Fuad looked at his watch.

"I'm afraid your time is up for today. I'll see you on Friday."

"Right."

"What, by the way, is an MVP?"

"Most Valuable Player."

"I see."

"It's a big thing. Like the Medal of Honor."

"Why won't you get it?"

"They don't give it to lefties, doc."

Fuad stared at Randy inquisitively, but the shortstop decided not to attempt explaining it to him. There was only so much you could expect an Egyptian to understand about baseball.

Parked across the street from Dr. Fuad's building was a nondescript gray Chevy Caprice with 134,000 miles on the odometer. Behind the wheel, chewing on a chicken fajita sandwich, was Pete Zabriskie, who had picked up Randy Dreyfus's trail at 8:42 that morning outside his Valley View Estates home. Zabriskie's billable hours had begun at 7:00 A.M., when he swung the Caprice north on the Santa Ana.

He had tailed the Beemer all the way into Westwood and watched it disappear into a subterranean garage on Glendon. He photographed the board in the lobby that listed all the offices in the building, then waited for Randy Dreyfus to emerge, which he finally did at 10:16 A.M., having been inside the building for thirty-nine minutes. Zabriskie got out of the car and followed his target on foot.

The report that he FedExed to Susie Dreyfus that evening contained the following information:

Subject walked around Westwood for an hour and three minutes, then stopped at a newsstand and bought a copy of *Penthouse* magazine, which he took into Bullock's. In Bullock's he rode the escalator to the top floor, went to the men's room. Subject spent four minutes and thirty-five seconds in the men's room and then emerged, without the *Penthouse* magazine.

At Bullock's the subject purchased a bottle of Pierre Cardin cologne, at $29.99, and a Perry Ellis leather jacket, at $699. He left Bullock's, got on the San Diego north, and headed back out to Valley View Estates. He drove around residential streets, stopping only once, to talk to a man standing beside a truck marked MANUEL RODRIGUEZ—FINE GARDENING with a Pacoima phone number written on the side. The subject spent seven minutes talking to the gardener and was observed handing money to him, amount unknown.

At 1:07 P.M. the subject drove into the In and Out Burger on Macadamia Boulevard for lunch, ate what appeared to be a Double Bonus Burger, got back on the freeway, and put in 176 miles of apparently aimless driving before heading for Viking Stadium. Surveillance terminated at 4:42 P.M. as subject went in the players' entrance at the stadium.

The one thing about Randy Dreyfus's activities that day which had Pete Zabriskie puzzled was the gardener. Everything else checked out, more or less. The forty minutes in the building on Glendon might have been a quickie, though, judging from the lobby board, the building was primarily doctors and lawyers. The cologne was S.O.P. for a guy screwing someone on the side, as were the clothes. The 176 miles of purposeless freeway driving was not unusual for a guy with a problem. People did it all the time in Southern California.

Pete Zabriskie could even buy the *Penthouse* in the can at Bullock's. But he couldn't buy the gardener. That one didn't compute. A guy drives around his own neighborhood for half an hour to find a gardener and give him money. You mailed a check once a month to your gardener and didn't waste your time trying to find him and pay him in cash.

As he drove back to Santa Ana through the early-evening rush-hour traffic, he kept asking himself what possible connection there could be between a gardener named Manuel Rodriguez from Pacoima and a monogrammed handkerchief with the initials DJP.

Pete Zabriskie had found that the seemingly random often turned out not to be random at all but directly connected to the moral turpitude he was hired to ferret out. The random, however, had to be clearly distinguished from the *hinky*, as they used to refer to certain behavior on the Downey Police Department. The *Penthouse* in the crapper at Bullock's, for example, was strictly hinky. A guy with a good-looking wife and a girlfriend somewhere goes into a public bathroom in the middle of the day and whacks off. That was your basic hinky behavior. But spending seven minutes talking to your gardener in front of somebody else's house was an act that could not be explained by mere human perversity. If he could figure out where that was at, he might be on the track that would lead him to the identity of the girl who Randy Dreyfus was schtupping.

Pete Zabriskie decided to check out Manuel Rodriguez Fine Gardening. After he checked out the August *Penthouse*, just to be on the safe side. For all he knew, Randy Dreyfus could be a weenie waver, and he took the skin mag into the crapper as a cover. In this town you had to be prepared to look at all the angles.

VIII

On August 19 the Valley Vikings headed north for a short six-game road trip that would take them through Seattle and Oakland. They had moved into a second-place tie with California, three games behind the A's. A sweep in Oakland would put them in first. A feeling of queasy exhilaration settled over the Viking clubhouse, a feeling that crunch time was approaching, that with six weeks left in the season it was time to make their move.

Randy's renegotiation was stuck in the third year at $7.25 million. Barry Fuchsia said that the elevator was stalled between floors. It was now all up to Randy. He had to perform from here to the end of the season. Otherwise, they were going to have to get off the elevator with $7.25 million and a day-care center.

The final night of the home stand, Randy had gone 2-for-4 with a walk against K.C. He was hitting .338, three points ahead of Cal Corvene of the White Sox. The smart money had him with both the batting title and the MVP, unless he went completely south during the last six weeks. Charlie Gonse told him to stop thinking about anything. "Just hit the goddamn ball," he said. "Don't read the papers, don't watch TV, don't do anything to distract yourself. Just swing the fucking bat."

Charlie Gonse didn't have a clue. In view of what was going on in Randy's life these days it was amazing that he was able to put his uniform on straight. Fuad had written him new scripts for Valium and Xanax after telling him that tranquilizers only retarded the therapeutic process. "Anesthetizing yourself from the pain isn't going to help you," he said. "You have to confront it. You have to assume the responsibility for it. You have to embrace your pain, Mr. Dreyfus. Revel in it. It's *your* pain."

In the meantime, he swung the bat and dropped fifteen milligrams of Valium a day with an occasional Xanax between meals. Before game time he chugged two diet Cokes with caffeine to counteract the tranks and get his reactions sharpened back up. At any given moment, therefore, he was either revving up or tranking down. He didn't spend a lot of time in the same station these days.

D.J., for his part, kept his distance. They had their usual communication between innings about covering the bag, but that was pretty much the extent of it. Ever since the crying fit over the margaritas, D.J. seemed to be withdrawing.

In the bottom of the third in Oakland, with A's runners on first and second, however, D.J. did something that indicated to Randy that he was not entirely indifferent. Buzz Grough had gotten into a jam and loaded the bases with nobody out. Bernie Lazarre called a meeting at the mound to decide where they were going to try to make the play. Randy, Harry Glugg, Rennie Pannizardi, and D.J. trotted in to join Grough and Lazarre.

Randy had been to a shitload of these mound meetings in his career. They always were the same. "What do you want to do?" "I don't know." "Let's go for two, make the play at home if you have a shot. . . ." Randy wasn't listening. He was acutely conscious of D. J. Pickett's hip right next to his. It was jutting out, maybe three inches away from Randy's left hand.

The sound of the catcher's voice pierced Randy's fantasy, pulling him out of the reverie. He nodded quickly and trotted back to his position. When he got there he realized he had no idea what Bernie Lazarre had said.

The caffeine was out of gas, and he couldn't do a Xanax in the third inning. He was on his own. If the ball was hit to him now he was in trouble. He was standing there, panicked, completely lost, when he heard D.J. call his name. Randy looked over, saw the second baseman put his glove between his mouth and the batter, hold up three fingers. Which meant that it was a rotation play and Randy was supposed to cover third on a bunt. D.J. must have picked up on his distraction during the meeting on the mound. Somehow he knew that Randy hadn't heard a word that Bernie Lazarre had said and was covering for him.

As it turned out, the batter hit a gapper into right center that cleared the bases, and Randy didn't have to make a play at any base. But for that brief moment that Randy had crouched down waiting for the ball, lost and vulnerable, he had felt protected. He had felt safe. At that moment, in the bottom of the third at Oakland, Randy had been convinced that there was definitely something special going on between him and D. J. Pickett.

In any event, Randy stayed out of the shower for a good half hour after the game. He'd had to put up with a certain amount of attention from his teammates and reporters because he had gotten a hold of a low inside slider in the eleventh and golfed it down the line for the winning home run. Actually, he had been fooled on the pitch and was bailing out. It was a cheap shot since it was only 310 down the line in Oakland. The ball hit the foul pole a couple of inches above the left fielder's glove.

"Were you looking to hit one out?"

"What'd he throw you?"

"You think you can catch Oakland?"

Et cetera. Randy knew all the answers. It made no difference what the questions were. He could have phoned them in. By the time he had showered and gotten dressed, the clubhouse was empty except for the maintenance guys and the center fielder, Angel Mendoza. Angel "Spic" Mendoza was a wiry little guy from the Dominican, about five-eight in heels, who hit a soft .240 but covered the outfield like a Doberman pinscher. He had been in the bigs for five years and still barely spoke a word of nonobscene English.

Mendoza came up to Randy and said, "Fucking shit, man."

Randy nodded, which was the only appropriate response to give Spic Mendoza when he started running off at the mouth.

"Cocksucking son of a bitch, man," Mendoza said in way of explanation of his first sentence. "You hit fucking shit out of that fucking ball, man."

"Yeah."

"You wanna go get shitfaced?"

"No thanks, Angel."

"*Chinga tu madre,* man," and he walked away, heading for the clubhouse door, leaving Randy alone with the maintenance men. They looked at him impatiently, anxious for him to leave so they could close the place up.

He had one of them get him a cab and was in his room at the Ramada in time for Arsenio Hall. He dropped a V, got under the covers, and drifted off before the first commercial.

Unfortunately, Randy's subconscious decided to put on a floor show for him, and by twelve-thirty he was up again, reeling from some of the weirdest song-and-dance numbers he had ever dreamed. The V usually took care of the strange stuff, flattening it out and enabling him to sleep dreamlessly. But somehow this shit must have slipped by the V. This shit was borderline loony tunes. Jesus.

The fucking Fruitcake Follies had really gotten out of hand. There was stuff there that he was embarrassed to have even in the most private recesses of his imagination. He had dreamed about committing felonious acts in the whirlpool with D. J. Pickett. This baby had gone pretty far before he woke up. This baby had definitely gone beyond the limits.

He was sweating profusely. Throwing off the covers, he got out of bed and went over to the window. Bolted. Another No Suicide room. The word must be out on him. They probably faxed the info around the league. Keep this guy bolted in.

Randy turned the air conditioner up to high, letting the cold air blow across his naked body, drying the perspiration. He stood there for a long time, cooling down, his arms against the wall in front of the air-conditioning vent.

He looked down. He was hard as a rock. He could hit one five hundred feet with it. Jesus. He started to run in place. As long as he kept running, he'd be okay.

Randy was on his third mile when the phone rang. He answered it, still running, out of breath. "Yeah?"

"Excuse me, sir, but the person in the room right under you has called to complain about the noise."

"Right." Randy hung up. He was dripping sweat once again. He went into the bathroom, ran the shower, keeping the water cold. He stepped in and forced himself to endure it as long as he could. Then he toweled himself off and went back to bed.

Between the air conditioner on high and the cold shower, Randy was shivering. He grabbed his knees and balled himself up in the fetal position, trying to keep warm. It was no use. He couldn't get warm, and he couldn't sleep. He got back out of bed, fumbled around in his suitcase, and found a pair of sweats. He put them on and started to pace back and forth.

What the hell was he going to do? Going out for a walk in this city at this hour was out of the question. He'd come back with holes in his body from crack dealers taking target practice with automatic weapons. Suddenly he remembered the weight room. On the road, the team rented an extra suite and put some weight machines in there for the players who wanted to work out in the hotel. He'd go in there and bench-press a few hundred pounds. That ought to do the trick.

Randy grabbed a towel from the bathroom and his room key and exited. He walked down the hallway, past the closed doors of his sleeping teammates, to the end of the corridor.

When he opened the door to Suite 612 he found himself facing the last person in the world he expected to see working out at one o'clock in the morning in the weight room at the Ramada Inn.

D. J. Pickett was doing leg presses, lying on his back pushing the weights up with his feet. From where he stood, Randy could see the straining biceps femoris on the inside of the second baseman's thighs where they protruded from the tight-fitting, blue satin Sharper Image workout shorts.

Randy knew he was in big trouble if he didn't turn around and walk right out of that room. He tried to, but his legs wouldn't move. Instead he just stood there staring dumbly at D.J. and holding the door open behind him like a life raft.

If Randy Dreyfus ever felt any confusion about the basic choreography of the sex act with another man, it dissolved instantly. As he stood watching his friend, he could see clearly how one would proceed if one wanted to.

Randy let the door slip from his fingers, and it slowly closed behind him. D.J. stopped the leg presses and looked up at the big blond shortstop in the sweatpants with the telltale bulge.

They held each other's look for a very long moment. Nobody moved. Nobody ran. Like the Egyptian said, it was basically breathing at this point.

"So what do we do now?" Randy said finally.

"It's your call."

"How do you begin?"

"The same way you would with Pia Zadora."

"You mean you like . . . kiss?"

"We could do that."

"What the fuck . . ."

And as Randy put his arms around his second baseman, he felt a great sense of relief. It was finally over. For the first time in his career, Randy Dreyfus stepped up to the left side of the plate. He dug in, choked up on the bat, and went with the pitch.

IX

Manuel Rodriguez finished pruning the bougainvillea that demarcated the swimming-pool area from the tennis-court area of the Nouveau French Normand château on Delacroix Drive and headed back to his truck just as the sun was sinking behind the rim of Delores Canyon. It was his last job for the day, except for a little extra that he had contracted to do for the baseball player over on Caravaggio Place. The baseball player had slipped him two hundred dollars and asked him to go to his house after dark one night and open the gate to the yard. That was all. Two hundred bucks. No questions asked.

Manuel Rodriguez said okay. A fast two hundred under the table. He didn't have to ask questions. It was none of his business why the guy wanted his gate left open. ¿Quien sabe? The guy was a good baseball player, hitting over .300. His wife was a fox. A nice pair of melons. Why not? A hundred for each melon.

The gardener loaded the power mower and pruning shears in the rear of the '78 Ford wide-body with the retread tires and rebuilt transmission. He ought to spend the two hundred on a couple of new tires, but he didn't like the idea of driving into BFGoodrich and handing over a couple of crisp hundred-dollar bills for tires. This money came out of the sky. This money belonged at the $100 window at Hollywood Park.

Rodriquez put the key in the ignition and waited as the battery turned over with a tired groan and the engine started. He fished a Kool out of the glove compartment and lit it. When he made the turn onto Delores Canyon Road, he didn't notice that there was a gray Chevy Caprice on his ass.

Pete Zabriskie had been on Manuel Rodriquez's tail since morning. While Randy Dreyfus was out of town, he was following up his hunch about the gardener. All day long, as he sat in the Caprice down the street from the enormous houses whose gardens Manuel Rodriquez tended, Zabriskie wondered whether he was way out of line on this one. Maybe the gardener was supplying the shortstop with drugs, or running bets for him, or whatever, and none of this shit had anything to do with the handkerchief with the initials DJP.

But the hours were piling up. As of five o'clock he was into gold time and could bill Susie Dreyfus time and a half. She looked like she could afford it. The 560 SEL had a sticker price in the mid-eighties. And their house in Valley View Estates would go for two easy.

Pete Zabriskie felt a rush of adrenaline when he saw the wide-body turn off the canyon road and onto the cul de sac where the Dreyfuses lived. Son of a bitch. It was about time. He was about to hit a number.

He kept the Caprice about fifty yards behind the pickup, then pulled over and killed the headlights. Reaching into the glove compartment, he found the Nikon binoculars with the nightscope attached. He opened the window and trained them on the house.

The gardener parked the truck right in front, got out, and walked around to the side of the house, out of view. Zabriskie was trying to decide whether to get out of the car when he saw the gardener returning to his truck. He couldn't have been on the side of the house for more than half a minute. Rodriquez pulled the truck into the driveway of the Dreyfuses' house, backed out, and turned around. The private detective ducked down in his seat as the Ford passed him on its way back out to Delores Canyon Road.

Zabriskie waited for the truck's taillights to disappear from the rearview mirror before sitting up again. He was about to get out of the car when he saw a dog run out from the side of the house where Manuel Rodriquez had just been. It was a white dog with black spots, a Dalmatian, and it was running like crazy toward the main road. The dog passed the Caprice without stopping, and in a few seconds, it, too, disappeared down Delores Canyon Road.

Did he follow the dog? Fuck that. He wasn't going to tail a god-damn Dalmatian. He grabbed a flashlight and walked over to the house.

Moving carefully, in case there was another dog around, Zabriskie walked around to the side where Manuel Rodriquez had gone. What he discovered there was a wide-open gate to a fenced yard. He stood for a while studying the terrain, soaking up the details that he could play back later if he chose, before returning to his car.

As Zabriskie drove down the canyon he attempted to analyze the raw data he had accumulated in the last few minutes. It wasn't too much of a stretch to infer from the sequence of events he had observed that Manuel Rodriquez had opened the gate. And that this action caused the dog to escape. So far, so good. The next part was not self-evident, however. Establishing a motive. The gardener did not steal the dog, or anything else for that matter. The gardener came to do this after dark, which meant that he did not want to be observed or connected with the act of opening the gate.

You only had to put the pieces together to see that they all added up to trouble. This set of circumstances smelled like San Pedro with the wind blowing in. Now the job at hand was to connect the gardener and the dog to the identity of the babe who Randy Dreyfus was schtupping.

Cherchez the gardener. Or *cherchez* the dog. This was wild stuff. Shit, this was better than *The Maltese Falcon*. This was beyond weird or hinky. This was fucking bizarre.

Randy Dreyfus was awakened from a dreamless sleep at 8 A.M. The phone rang nine times before the shortstop reached over and picked up, still half-asleep.

"Yeah?"

"Calvin's gone."

Randy could hear his wife's voice clearly on the phone, but it was a moment before he could put it in context. He wasn't exactly sure where he was. He turned over on his back, holding the receiver, trying to adjust to the fact that he was no longer asleep. The realization that he was in a hotel room in Oakland talking to his wife in Los Angeles struck him at approximately the same time that he remembered the weight room.

The weight room. Holy shit . . .

"Randy? Did you hear me? Calvin ran away. Somebody left the gate open."

"Huh?"

The dog. There was the dog as well as the weight room. He had to be very careful. She had him groggy, with his defenses down. He couldn't afford to trip up. Between putting a contract out on his dog and screwing his second baseman, they could probably send him up for a long time.

He tried to force himself awake by slapping himself lightly in the face. Susie continued to talk into the phone in a high-pitched, almost hysterical voice.

"I don't know what happened. The twins swore they didn't leave the gate open. And yesterday wasn't Manuel's day to come . . ."

The gardener. He had paid the guy in cash. There was no way they could trace the money. If the guy tried to blackmail him, he'd slap a lawsuit on him, run him the fuck out of the neighborhood.

"I called the police and reported it. They asked me if I wanted to file a breaking-and-entering report because of the gate . . ."

Giving the gardener the money would make him an accessory to the breaking and entering . . .

"What do you think?"

"About what?"

"About the breaking-and-entering report?"

"Did someone break in?"

"For godsakes, Randy, aren't you listening to me?"

"I got to bed late last night."

"Where were you, anyway? I tried calling you late, after one."

"Huh?"

"Last night. Where were you at one-thirty?"

"I was in the weight room working out."

"At one-thirty in the morning?"

"I couldn't sleep. . . . The dog's gone?"

"That's what I've been trying to tell you. The police won't look for him unless we report the open gate as breaking and entering."

"Well, listen, he'll turn up. Someone's probably found him by now."

"People keep Dalmatians. They're very much in demand, especially one that's trained, with all his shots. And Calvin is so friendly . . ."

Why hadn't he thought of having the gardener take the collar off the dog so he'd be untraceable? They'd take him to the pound and gas him.

"So what do you want to do?" Susie insisted.

Randy didn't want the cops anywhere near him at the moment. Besides the accessory before the fact on the dog rap, he had probably committed a number of felonies in the weight room. The cops were smart. Sometimes they brought you in on one rap and got you to sing on another.

"Uh, listen, forget the breaking and entering."

"They won't look for him."

"They're not going to look for him anyway. Don't worry. He'll turn up. Listen, I got to go work out."

"At this hour?"

"Yeah. I'm on a new weight program."

Susie didn't hang up right away. There was a long silence on the line. Randy could hear her breathing. Then: "Randy, do you love me?"

Jesus. He didn't need this now. With all the other stuff going down, the last thing he needed was a wife who wanted him to whisper shit in her ear.

"Sure," he mumbled, hoping that would do the trick.

"You've been so distant lately."

"Yeah, well, you know, we're two games out."

He heard her sigh on the other end. Another stretch of silence.

"Talk to you later," he said hurriedly and hung up. He lay back on the bed and was swept by a sudden and overpowering surge of memory. His entire body tingled as he played back in his mind the stolen hours with D.J. among the weight machines. He couldn't remember anything in his life as intense, not even the first time with Susie up on Mulholland after the Rose Bowl.

All he could think of, as he lay there, was D. J. Pickett and what they had done last night while the rest of the team slept. He began to blush like a schoolgirl. Holy shit. At the same time, blood began to rush downhill, rising like a mountain stream in spring. In a matter of seconds he was harder than a Louisville Slugger.

At 10:30 A.M. Milt Zola, the head baseball writer for *The Valley Tribune*, was sitting in the coffee shop in the Oakland Ramada Inn polishing off a plate of eggs over easy when he noticed a strange conversation going on in a corner booth. Randy Dreyfus and D. J. Pickett, the middle of the Viking infield, were sitting and whispering to each other.

The morning rush was gone. The place was empty. Full plates of food sat in front of them getting cold. Each time Milt Zola looked up from his edition of *USA Today* he saw that the French toast on their plates was still untouched.

Maybe they were going over a new set of signs. Who the fuck knew. Ballplayers. They all had a couple of screws loose. It was Zola's opinion that the Vikings' pennant chances pretty much rested on the ability of Dreyfus and Pickett to finish strong. They were the heart and soul of the team, the middle of the infield. Pickett was the consummate pro, the ballplayer's ballplayer, making it all look easy. But Dreyfus was the guy with the breakthrough talent. Randy Dreyfus could be the superstar of the decade if he played up to his potential.

Milt Zola finished his coffee, got up, and casually wandered over to the booth in the rear to see if he could drum up a story. He was only a couple of feet away when Randy Dreyfus suddenly stopped saying whatever he was saying to D. J. Pickett, straightened up, and stared at the sportswriter.

"You guys don't eat your breakfast, you're not going to grow up big and strong and beat Oakland."

Pickett turned around and saw him for the first time. "How're you doing, Milt," he said.

"Going over some signs?"

"Right."

"Can I get a quote or two for the early edition?"

Randy Dreyfus shrugged, then nodded without enthusiasm. Milt Zola eased his large frame into the booth next to Pickett and signaled for the waitress to bring him another cup of coffee.

"You guys thinking sweep?"

"There're still two more games up here," D. J. Pickett said.

"Most's going Sunday against De Luca. That ought to be a lock. Tonight's the one you got to win."

"Yeah." They both nodded simultaneously.

"You think this team has the character to go all the way?"

"Sure," D. J. Pickett said.

"Randy, you think they're going to throw at you tonight after the dinger in the eleventh last night?"

Randy Dreyfus shrugged. "Fuck do I know." He started to cut up his French toast meticulously into little pieces.

Milt Zola looked from one to the other. These guys didn't have much to say this morning. He decided to try another angle.

"Tell me something, you guys have been playing together on the same team, right next to each other in the infield, for three straight years. I imagine you get to kind of know each other pretty well, huh?"

Randy Dreyfus stopped cutting up his French toast. D. J. Pickett wiped his mouth with his napkin, even though he hadn't eaten anything. Neither said anything.

"What I mean," Zola elaborated, "was I would imagine you get sort of in tune. You begin to anticipate the other one's moves and reactions on the field, you know what I mean?"

"No." Randy Dreyfus shook his head emphatically.

"You get real comfortable with each other. Sort of like a marriage . . ."

"Huh?"

"You know, like you were married or something . . ."

"What're you talking about, man?" Randy Dreyfus seemed almost incensed.

"It's just an analogy, Randy."

Randy Dreyfus put down his fork and said, " 'Scuse me, will you?

I got to go take a dump." And the big shortstop got out of the booth and exited the coffee shop.

Milt Zola turned to D. J. Pickett beside him. "Something wrong with him?"

The second baseman shook his head. "It's the pennant race. Fucks up your digestive system."

The Vikings won again Saturday night, 5–4. In the eighth D. J. Pickett punched a low outside forkball down the line between the first baseman and the bag, bringing in two runs and putting the Vikings ahead before Hube Henry came out of the bullpen to nail it down. It was a beautiful piece of hitting, a textbook example of going with the pitch.

The clubhouse was rowdy after the game. You'd think they'd won the pennant the way the players were cracking jokes and snapping their towels at one another's asses. It was like a fraternity-house party.

Randy sat quietly in front of his locker with a diet Coke. Glen Ephard came over. "Charlie wants to see you in his office."

"Right."

"You miss a sign tonight or something?"

Randy shrugged. He didn't know why Charlie Gonse wanted to see him. He wasn't in the mood for a Greek-salad chat right now. All he wanted to do was get out of there and be with D.J. They were planning to meet across the Bay in Chinatown for a late dinner. He got up, still in his uniform bottoms and sweatshirt, and walked over to the manager's office.

Charlie Gonse looked up from his cottage cheese and fruit plate and motioned for Randy to enter.

"Have a seat," he said, pushing the paper plate away disdainfully. "This shit'll kill you faster than cholesterol. I swear the cottage cheese tastes like it was scraped off an asbestos ceiling."

"You wanted to see me, Charlie?"

"No. I just called you in here to talk about cottage cheese." The manager was wearing a terry-cloth bathrobe, his head wrapped in a towel. He plucked a toothpick from a dispenser on his desk and started to go at his upper incisors.

"I'm going to lay it right on the line, Shovel. All right?"

"Yeah."

"You got your head up your ass."

"What?"

"You're not in the ball game. I don't know where the fuck you are but you're not between the foul lines."

"What're you talking about? We've won ten of the last twelve games. I've been hitting .432 over that period. I haven't made an error since Cleveland—"

"Numbers. That's all that shit is. Numbers. I'm talking about being in the game. I'm talking about standing out there and having a clue where the hell you are. I got to tell you, Shovel, I look at you out there sometimes and I get the distinct impression you're on another planet."

Randy stared back at his manager, trying to control his anger. The fact that the guy was right had nothing to do with the fact that he didn't deserve this shit. What difference did it make to Charlie Gonse what planet Randy was on as long as he did his job?

"Tell me something. What was the count on D.J. before he hit the double down the line in the eighth?"

Randy look at him incredulously. What kind of a dumb question was that? Who the fuck knew? D.J. probably didn't even know.

"See what I mean?"

"I don't keep track of counts."

"You lose track of the count, you lose track of the game. You remember the count on D.J., you remember what the guy threw him with that count, so next time you're up against him with bases loaded and you got the same count, you know what to expect. You understand what I'm saying?"

Randy nodded. There was no point in contradicting Charlie Gonse about this, or about anything else, for that matter. The guy had to be right all the time. When he went to the bullpen in the ninth and the batter hit one out on his relief pitcher, he was still right. It was always someone else's fault.

"My nephew still didn't get that picture you were supposed to send him."

"I'll take care of it."

"Get your head out of your ass."

"Right."

"That's it. Over and out."

Later that night, at the restaurant in Chinatown, Randy asked D.J. what the count had been on him when he hit the double.

"Three-and-one."

"You remember that shit?"

"I remember that one because I said to myself that Grigan always comes in three-and-one with a slider outside, and I'm going to go to right."

A water chestnut slid off Randy's chopstick and fell on his aqua Lacoste shirt. He was all nerves. It was a miracle he could still play baseball. And play well, no less. He had gone 2-for-4 with a double that night. His average was up to .345.

Randy watched D.J. skillfully scoop up pork, mushrooms, and rice with his chopstick and manage to get it all in his mouth without spilling anything. He had terrific hands. When he scooped up a ground ball he did it in one continuous, graceful movement. Randy could watch him field ground balls all night long. He could watch him eat pork lo mein all night. There was no doubt about it: He was crazy about the guy.

He had never felt like this before, not even with Susie. With Susie, he wanted to fuck her and then wake up at the ball game. It wasn't at all like that with D.J. He wanted to talk to him, to eat in Chinese restaurants, to go to the movies, to feed him perfectly on the double play, laying the ball in chest high so that he could pivot and avoid the spikes of the sliding runner. Most of all, he wanted to go back to the weight room.

It was already after midnight, and they had a day game tomorrow. A crucial game with Oakland. They should be in bed, lights out. But he wasn't at all tired. He felt a wild exhilaration, an excitement he hadn't felt since he was eighteen.

They paid the bill, splitting it down the middle, and wandered around until they found a martial-arts double feature in a large, empty movie house. They sat alone all the way up in the rear balcony. Downstairs were a few other male couples.

After a while Randy and D.J. started to neck. It was wild. He hadn't made out in a movie theater since he felt up Janice Vaccario in the balcony of the Crest Theater in Glendale. They eventually stopped watching the movie altogether. When it got to heavy petting, they grabbed a cab back to the hotel.

They took separate elevators up to the tenth floor. Randy went to the ice machine and got a bucket of ice while D.J. closed the curtains and turned the rheostat down to dim the lights.

Randy let himself in with an extra key. D.J. put out the DO NOT DISTURB sign and deadbolted the door. Then he put a Sinatra cassette into his portable tape deck and disappeared into the bathroom. When he reappeared he had slipped into something he had bought at a North Beach leather shop during the team's last trip to the Bay Area.

"Jesus," Randy muttered, his breath taken away.

"You like it?"

"Yeah." Randy was nodding so furiously that it looked as if he had some sort of spasmodic tic. He stood there for a long moment admiring D.J. Pickett's outfit as the ice cubes melted in the bucket and the room began to spin gently in front of him.

The Man began to sing "Our Love Is Here to Stay." The ice bucket slipped out of Randy's hand and fell to the floor with a wet, whooshing sound. The Rockies began to crumble. Gibraltar began to tumble. They were only made of clay. . . .

X

Pete Zabriskie omitted any mention of the open-gate business in the report he FedExed to Susie Dreyfus. It was his experience that it was counterproductive to provide clients with raw data for which he himself had no clear explanation. All it did was confuse them, leading to panicked phone calls. The whole *cherchez*-the-gardener-and-dog angle was a flyer anyway, and Zabriskie himself was beginning to think he might be barking up the wrong tree, so to speak.

As it was, his reports already contained a sufficient number of interesting items. There was the forty-minute blitzkrieg in Westwood, the jerk-off incident at Bullock's, and the cologne. She could chew on that stuff for a while.

Zabriskie had logged some additional hours checking into the occupants of the fourteenth floor of the building in Westwood. There were two cardiologists, a urologist, an ear, nose, and throat guy, and a shrink. None of them had the initials D.J.P. Nor did the lawyer, who specialized in accident litigation. The escrow company and the investment firm were clean. As far as the Human Resources and Potential Group was concerned, it turned out to be some biofeedback operation run by a New Age dentist whose initials were not D.J.P., nor were those of any of the whacked-out-looking assistants he had working for him.

On Sunday Pete Zabriskie rested. While her detective took the day off, Susie Dreyfus sat on her Mazatlán leather loveseat in the recreation nook off the bedroom, and read and reread his reports. She didn't know whether she was pleased or disappointed that he hadn't turned up anything concrete yet. Though she wanted to know, she also didn't want to know.

The business in Westwood was upsetting enough. Why would her husband make up a story about getting the car serviced, drive to Westwood, go see a doctor or lawyer or investment person, then wander around town and go into Bullock's and buy cologne? As far as the girlie magazine in the men's room was concerned, she chose to ignore that information altogether. That incident was completely off her radar screen. She wouldn't be surprised if Zabriskie had made it up just to fill out the report.

The twins were in their bedroom down the hall, indisposed. When they'd learned that Calvin was gone they had taken to their beds and were refusing food. Susie had driven around the neighborhood tacking up signs with their phone number, and every time the phone rang, she ran to answer it, hoping it would be someone who had found the dog. But still no one had called.

Putting down the latest report, Susie grabbed the remote and zapped the big-screen Sony, which came instantly to life with a close-up of male buttocks rising and falling rhythmically. For godsakes. How many times had she told Randy that if he was going to watch the Porno Channel he should switch to something else before he turned it off so that the twins wouldn't accidentally turn it on?

She ran rapidly through 40 or 50 of the 177 choices that the dish provided. She watched Aerobics for a few minutes, then Home Improvement, where someone explained how to do the plumbing on a Jacuzzi, then a few minutes of *An Affair to Remember*, which made her want to throw up, and was about to turn the set off altogether when a familiar face flashed on the screen. The cameraman came in tight for a shot of her husband as he stepped into the batter's box.

Randy took a ball low, then a strike over the outside corner. He was unshaven, haggard-looking. And his eyes had this peculiar, almost dreamy look. It was as if he weren't entirely there, as if he weren't thinking about what the pitcher was going to throw him next but about something that had nothing to do with the game.

He was thinking about the woman with the initials D.J.P., no doubt. She had considered the possibility that the woman traveled with him, a road groupie, but that didn't explain his clandestine morning trips to Westwood or that Thursday-night dinner with Barry Fuchsia.

Randy stepped out to knock the dirt out of his cleats with the head of the bat. The camera came in close again. Susie continued to study her husband's face. It was not familiar to her. He looked slightly demented. Who was this man?

During the bottom half of the inning, the camera picked him up again as he completed a 4–6–3 double play. Jumping over the sliding runner, he made the throw beautifully to first, nipping the batter by half a step. The announcer went on about how Dreyfus and Pickett were the slickest double-play combination in baseball.

In the middle of this the doorbell rang. Susie flipped on the security-system intercom. She heard a woman's voice begin to say something, only to be drowned out by barking. The twins must have heard the barking too, because they were out of their beds and at the door before her.

Calvin had come home, retrieved by a neighbor who found him chewing the leather off her patio furniture. The reunion with the twins was emotional. They all spent a great deal of time letting Calvin know how much he had been missed. She and the twins caressed him, talked to him lovingly, gave him strokes. As Dr. Bob had explained, it was important to reinforce a dog's self-image. A dog with weak ego strength was an unhappy dog.

"Where have you been, you naughty dog?" Molly scolded. Susie explained to her daughter that it was counterproductive to bawl Calvin out. He would misinterpret it as displeasure that he had come back. No, they had to be supportive and loving.

She couldn't help wondering, however, as she went to the kitchen to get his bowl and fill it with a large helping of fiber-rich Balanced Diet dog food, recommended by Dr. Bob for firm stool contour, not only where her dog had been the night before last, but where her husband had been. Lifting weights at one-thirty in the morning?

Forget it. He was in bed with D.J.P. Maybe she ought to upgrade to the comprehensive plan.

John D. F. White, Jr., was having his usual Sunday lunch with his father on the poolside patio of the old man's mansion in Hancock Park. On Friday he had spent the morning escorting the steering committee of the Viking Girls through the stadium to choose a spot for the new day-care center, and now he was reporting the results to his father.

"There's the third weight room, over near the visiting club's equipment room. I figure we can give them that."

Barely acknowledging what his son was saying, the old man served himself another helping of shrimp salad and belched loudly.

John/John went on. "The point is, they're very determined. Susie Dreyfus is the leader. I can't get her to budge on this. . . ."

"Where's it going to stop?"

"What?"

"We pay them millions of dollars, give them the best accommodations, trainers, equipment, now they want us to take care of their goddamn kids too. Why not wipe their asses while we're at it?"

"It's actually not a bad public relations move. It shows us as a progressive-minded organization—"

"You know what it shows us as? A bunch of assholes. A bunch of pussy assholes."

John/John felt his bronchial tubes begin to constrict. The old man had that florid look on his face which meant he could explode at any minute.

"It'll help us close the Randy Dreyfus deal."

"We're still not closed on him?"

John/John shook his head. A little more color rose in his father's face as he pushed the shrimp salad away and reached for a Davidoff from a leather case in the pocket of his Hawaiian sports shirt.

"If I can get the day-care center, then I think his wife will get him to sign at seven two five for year three."

John senior lit the Davidoff, carefully rotating the end to get an even ash. When he was finished, he exhaled deeply, blowing the smoke right over his son's head, and said, "They're putting a goddamn gun to our heads. That's what they're doing."

"He's eligible to become a free agent at the end of the season."

"You take care of them, you develop them, you make them a star, you give them a goddamn nursery school for their goddamn kids, and what do you get in return? The right to guarantee them over seven million dollars three years from now."

"It's the going rate."

"Why the hell don't we just give them the whole deal, the stadium, the hot-dog concessions, the TV money? We're just goddamn ticket sellers. We stand there and sell the tickets, then hand the money over to them . . . after taking care of them and their goddamn kids. I don't know why I didn't stay in the fast-food business. All I needed were some Mexicans at minimum wage and a clean crapper. . . ."

John/John waited for the tirade to subside. He had heard it before, many times, knew it practically by heart. When his father finally ran out of gas and sat there sucking petulantly on his Davidoff, he said, "I think there's a deal at seven seven five, seven and a half, and seven two five, with sweeteners of two fifty on on-base percentage and errorless games, with maybe an interest-free loan of two point five and an option year at five. If we throw in the day-care center."

"Why don't we throw in my left nut while we're at it?"

"Dad, it's just a converted weight room with a couple of checker games and a UCLA student to take care of the kids."

"Can you imagine putting in a day-care center for Eddie Stanky? You know what he would have told you to do with your fucking day-care center?"

The door to the house opened, and a Filipino servant emerged with a portable telephone. "Phone call for you, Mr. John."

John/John took the phone and heard the flat voice of Barry Fuchsia on the other end.

"Sorry to bother you on a Sunday, but I figure neither of us can afford to take the Sabbath off these days, seeing as we still have this open deal, am I right?"

"Right, Barry. How are you?"

"That depends on you, John. Randy wants me to talk to the Dodgers, but I told him we had the makings of a deal here."

"I was just talking to Dad about it, as a matter of fact. He's fine with the day-care center."

"What about year three?"

"Year three'll fly."

"We're going to want a little bump on the sweeteners, say three fifty and four on on-base percentage."

"I thought we agreed on two fifty."

"We did. But that was on Tuesday. Today's no longer Tuesday."

John/John took the phone away from his ear for a moment and wheezed. He took the inhaler out of his pocket, took a large suck off it, and waited.

"You there?" Barry Fuchsia inquired.

"Um-um," John/John mumbled, buying time for the medicine to dilate the bronchial tubes sufficiently. Finally, he took a deep breath and said, "I'm going to have to get back to you on that, Barry."

"The train's not going to be in the station too much longer, John."

"Right."

"Oh, yeah. I almost forgot. We're going to want a Ph.D. in child development running that day-care center. Is that going to be a problem?"

John/John looked at his father, who was trying to dislodge a piece of shrimp from his teeth with the edge of his tongue, and muttered that he didn't think it would be.

As Susie watched the players get off the plane at LAX that night she wondered if the bitch was on the same plane. Did he see her openly on the road? Did the other players know? Was this just another example of the universal male conspiracy to fuck around on their wives? Nobody talked. Everybody covered for one another. There was undoubtedly an entire parallel set of women to be used only away from home. They kept them, all together, in an apartment in Manhattan Beach, and chartered a plane for them when they went on the road.

She could swear she saw them winking to each other just before they gave their wives the perfunctory kiss. All except Harry Glugg, who was dead drunk and kept trying to put his arm around one of the stewardesses. The Vikings were in a buoyant mood, having just swept Oakland to climb into a first place tie with the A's. But Randy looked anything but buoyant. He walked with the slouch he adopted when he was in a slump, and when he gave her her perfunctory kiss, she could smell booze on his breath. Randy almost never drank anything but an occasional lite beer.

In the car on the way home he was more sullen than usual. You would have thought he had gone 0-for-12 instead of being the star of the series. And as soon as he got home he went right to bed, skipping the stationary bike, not to mention her.

Which was fine with Susie. She wasn't about to make love to a man who was cheating on her. The cold war would go on until she had the proof she needed, and then she would confront him and make her demands, and they would go from there, depending on the sincerity of his contrition.

He better fucking beg her forgiveness. She wanted him on his knees, humble, no attitude. Then she'd consider taking him back. Maybe . . .

Shit. It would be a lot easier to handle this if she didn't still love him. She could go to the lawyer, stick it to Randy, and get on with her life. If she played it right, she could have a piece of him for some time. He was in negotiation for a long-term deal at over $7 million a year. Having a piece of Randy Dreyfus would be a going concern.

She went into the bedroom and sat down on the edge of the bed. He slept with his hands around the pillow like a child with a doll. There was an innocence to his blond features, a sweetness to his face. His breathing was even, untroubled. He looked as if he were dreaming of low inside fastballs. Sitting there watching him sleep, she couldn't imagine him engaged in adultery with the woman whose initials were D.J.P.

Where had it all gone? Not too long ago they were on top of the world. *Southern California Lifestyles* had named them one of the ten most dynamic couples in town. Randy was leading the league in batting. The Vikings were making a run at the pennant. Her call-in radio show was the highest-rated program in its time slot. Their master bathroom had been featured in *Creative Plumbing*. The twins were on the waiting list at Buckley. Their dog was mastering his personality disorder.

And now they were just another sordid statistic, another Southern California marriage washed up on the shoals of adultery. It was enough to make you want to cry. Which is exactly what she did. Susie Dreyfus sat there sobbing as her unfaithful husband slept the exhausted sleep of the overextended.

XI

According to the notebook that Pete Zabriskie kept for Wednesday, September 3, Randy Dreyfus made three additional stops after his forty-minute quickie in the building on Glendon. First he went to the Ralphs on Pico, where he bought a package of extra-lean chopped meat. Then he drove to Builders Emporium, where he bought a container of Liquid-Plumr. Finally, he got on the Ventura heading west to Valley View Estates, where, instead of going home, he wandered around, as he had done before, until he located the wide-body Ford with the bald tires that belonged to his gardener, Manuel Rodriguez.

Pete Zabriskie was unable to overhear the conversation that took place between the two men. It lasted five minutes, with Randy Dreyfus doing all the talking. The Mexican nodded from time to time and then accepted the chopped meat, the Liquid-Plumr, and what appeared to be a nice chunk of money from the ballplayer.

As Zabriskie followed the Beemer back toward Los Angeles, he tried to make some sense out of the transaction he had just observed. Supplementing your gardener's pay with hamburger meat and drain unclogger seemed to be the type of behavior that would have to be relegated to the category of hinky. It could no longer be

considered merely random, and its weirdness was outside the purview of any perversion that Pete Zabriskie was familiar with. In his
line of work he had developed a very catholic view of perversion,
but this number was strictly *sui generis*. This baby was as hinky as it
got.

In order to keep up with the 850i, the private detective had to
keep the Chevy's accelerator pressed against the floor. They by-
passed the San Diego and headed through the Cahuenga Pass to
Hollywood, got off at Gower, and headed south to Sunset. The subject drove the car into the Sunset Gower Studios, stopped at the
gate, and said something to the guard, who pointed in the direction
of a soundstage.

It wasn't worth the trouble to bullshit the guard and keep the
surveillance up at close range. The guy was undoubtedly shooting
some commercial or TV promotion. All the ballplayers did that
these days. As if they weren't paid enough just to go out and play
catch every night.

Instead, Zabriskie drove over to the drive-in window of the Jack
in the Box and got a Breakfast Jack and a cup of coffee. Then he
found a shady spot on Gower across from the lot, parked, and let
himself shift into the semiconscious state he adopted when doing
surveillance. He was able to induce a partial trance in which he
could catch some Z's while remaining alert to any possible reap-
pearance of the subject.

Closing his eyes only partially, which allowed enough light to
come through to alert him to any significant change in his field of
vision, Zabriskie drifted off on the fumes of the midmorning traffic.
He sipped his coffee, nibbled on his Breakfast Jack, and thought
about chopped meat and Liquid-Plumr.

Inside Stage Three, meanwhile, Randy Dreyfus was being made
up by an anorectic girl named Desirée in preparation for the filming of an athlete's-foot commercial. He was the official spokesman
for Meditex anti-fungal foot powder, as well as for Aunt Dot's Extra-
Strength bran muffins, Carlyle chain saws, and Stu's, a chain of
cellular-car-phone stores with fifty outlets from San Luis Obispo to
the Mexican border.

They had dressed a set to look like a locker room, and Randy,
along with a dozen extras in and out of baseball uniforms, was

going to demonstrate the effectiveness of Meditex. It was the last thing that Randy felt like doing at the moment. These things always dragged on for hours. Instead of being able to sneak up to Thousand Oaks before batting practice, he'd be stuck here sprinkling powder on his feet until it was time to go to the stadium.

To make matters worse, he had to do the spot dressed only in a towel. That's why, his agent explained, they paid the big bucks for this one. A quarter of a million a pop. The bran muffins were only a hundred grand.

"Please keep your eyes closed," Desirée said.

Randy yawned and kept his eyelids tightly clasped together as the girl worked on his face. He was exhausted. He had woken up at 4 A.M. and had had to fight the impulse to get in the car and go see D.J. And then he hadn't been able to get back to sleep and lay in bed, tossing and trying to figure out how he was going to get through the rest of his life, not to mention the next day.

"Hey, Randy, how're you doing?"

It was the voice of Marv Schuster, the director of the commercial, and Randy opened his eyes prematurely and got an eyeful of pancake makeup.

"I told you not to open your eyes," Desirée scolded.

"Right . . ."

"You look over the script?"

"Uh-huh," Randy lied. He had glanced at it while waiting for traffic lights this morning. Then he had gotten seriously distracted by other things. First there was the session with Fuad, which had gotten extremely uncomfortable, with the Egyptian actually suggesting that he had been a closet lefty his *entire life*. Then his decision to take another shot at offing the dog and his arranging for the hit with Manuel.

"We've made a couple of dialogue changes." Schuster thrust a new script into Randy's lap and walked off.

"Please. Don't open your eyes," Desirée sighed. "We're almost done."

Randy didn't get a look at the new script until he was in Wardrobe, which consisted of a rather small towel, held up by gaffer's tape and kept closed by a strategically located safety pin. They were getting a lot of beefcake for their 250 grand. The wardrober was a skinny little lefty with spiked hair. He looked like he'd fall over if you breathed on him too hard.

The wimp lefty finally released him into the hands of the assistant director, who led him to the set, where the other ballplayers were waiting around amid the athlete's-foot fungi, in various states of undress. There were balls and bats scattered about, open lockers with designer clothes.

Someone came over and shoved a light meter in his face, then shouted something to a guy up on a camera crane. A few of the guys nodded at him, and Randy returned the nods with his practiced reciprocal nod, which amounted to a barely discernible movement of his head, a kind of subliminal nod.

"We're going to pick you up coming out of the shower, Randy, and dolly with you along the row of lockers to the locker over there, where the product is . . ." Marv Schuster was explaining the shot, an arm around Randy's shoulders, his breath reeking of Tic Tacs.

"Now there's some business going on as you cross the room. The background is going to be ad-libbing conversation. When you pass Jeff over there, he's going to say, 'Way to go, Shovel. You really nailed that guy,' and you're going to nod, a kind of half smile, half nod, like you're acknowledging the remark but you're also modest. You follow me?"

"Yeah," Randy mumbled.

"Then when you get to the locker, you reach in, pretend you're looking for the product, then turn back, three-quarter profile to camera left, and say, 'Hey, who swiped my Meditex?' Then we'll cut. Got it?"

Randy nodded. He'd figure it out. They never got serious until the nineteenth take anyway, and by that time he'd have it down cold.

"Okay, everyone, positions," the assistant director called. As Randy walked back to the shower room door, the guy called Jeff smiled at him.

Jesus. Was it starting to show? Did everyone know, or was it only the lefties? He remembered hearing that a lefty always could smell out another lefty. They could walk into a room and spot a guy right off . . .

Randy was so disturbed by this thought that on the first take he turned the wrong profile to camera and said, "Hey, who wiped by Fedimex?"

Milt Zola sat in the press box at Viking Stadium and filled out his score sheet. Axel Most was going against a young left-hander who was 15–3 for Kansas City and Most's chief rival for the Cy Young Award. The San Juan Capistrano Swallows, an a capella choir, had entertained the pregame crowd with a medley of Neil Sedaka songs. At the moment a group of car salesmen from a Honda dealership in the Valley, all wearing baseball caps and buttons that said I GOT MINE IN RESEDA, were trying, unsuccessfully, to organize a wave out in the left-field pavilion.

Zola took a bite of his overcooked chili burger, felt his stomach cringe, drank some coffee, and waited for the game to begin. His eyes idly scanned the field, where the managers were meeting with the umpires at home plate to exchange lineup cards. In the dugout the players sat around and fidgeted, played with gloves, bats, balls, talked quietly among themselves. Out in the bullpens, the starting pitchers loosened up.

It was all part of the desultory pregame ritual—the same formalities that had been going on forever. And Milt Zola barely took notice of it. He had covered so many baseball games that he was able to take in a great deal at one time without focusing on any particular activity to the exclusion of the whole picture.

Which is why, no doubt, he was struck that evening by a certain anomaly in his field of vision. D. J. Pickett was at the water cooler taking a drink of water. Standing beside him and engaged in what appeared to be intense conversation with him was Randy Dreyfus. What struck Zola wasn't what was going on, which was simply a conversation at a water cooler, but the body language of the two ballplayers. There was something in the picture that didn't compute when he played it against the catalog of the millions of images he retained from all the baseball games he had covered as a sportswriter. He didn't know exactly what was wrong with the picture, but his instinct told him that something was out of kilter. There was an unidentified blip on his radar screen.

Zola didn't think any more of it until the fourth inning, when Kansas City had a runner on second with one out in a scoreless game. Dreyfus kept looking over at the bag, ducking in behind the runner to keep him close. But when the runner moved to third on a grounder to the right side and Dreyfus continued to look over toward second base, Zola started getting that same strange feeling he had gotten before the game—the sense that there was something wrong with the picture. Why was the shortstop looking at second base when there was no runner there? Was there some sort of sign that Pickett was supposed to give to Dreyfus? With a runner on third and two out?

It didn't add up to anything that Milt Zola could fathom. During the rest of the game he found himself watching Randy Dreyfus and D. J. Pickett. After a while he made himself stop, convinced he was imagining things. Maybe he had just seen too many goddamn baseball games. Maybe he was burned out at fifty-five, hallucinating things from the press box.

Milt Zola was not hallucinating. Down on the field, Randy spent a great deal of time stealing looks at his lover. In the dugout between innings he sat as far away as possible from D.J. to avoid the temptation of reaching out and touching him. They had a few stolen moments around the second-base bag while the pitcher warmed up. Then the catcher threw the ball down to second, and they were separated once more.

Just before the top of the eighth, as Axel Most threw his warm-up pitches, Randy stood a few feet to the left of second base and whispered loudly, "I got to see you."

D.J. fielded the grounder from Harry Glugg and threw it back side-arm. Then he turned toward Randy and shook his head, as if to say, This is no place to have this conversation.

"Why not?" Randy whispered plaintively, just as Glugg lobbed a two-hopper in his direction.

"Later," D.J. whispered back. Randy fielded the warm-up grounder and threw the ball into the box seats behind first base. Harry Glugg watched the ball sail over his head, eliciting roars of laughter from the crowd, then turned back and looked at Randy incredulously. By that time, fortunately, Most had taken his eight warm-up pitches, and Bernie Lazarre threw the ball down to second. D.J. cut in front of Randy, took the peg, threw it to Rennie Pannizardi at third, and returned to his position.

The Vikings' seven-game winning streak ended that night when Randy dropped a pop-up in shallow left-center, allowing two runs to score. Though the scorer gave the guy a hit, it was charitable scoring. Charlie Gonse told a reporter that his brother-in-law could have caught that ball in his wheelchair. So could his grandmother. And she'd been dead thirty years.

Randy showered, dressed, and was out of the clubhouse in record time. He sat in the 850i in the players' parking lot, three cars away from D.J.'s emerald-green Jaguar, and waited. The Jag was just like D.J.—sleek, graceful, responsive. He stared at it longingly. Whenever another player came out of the door, Randy ducked down to make himself invisible.

By the time the second baseman emerged, there was only one other car left in the lot, Charlie Gonse's Honda. Randy got out of his car, walked around to the passenger door of the Jag, and knocked on the window. D.J. looked up, sighed, then smiled and unlocked the passenger door. Randy quickly slid in, feeling the delicious cool smoothness of the rich leather under his ass.

D.J. looked around nervously, then felt Randy put his arms around him, smelling the Brut cologne and the Revlon extra-strength conditioner.

They began to neck furiously in the front seat of D. J. Pickett's Jaguar.

Meanwhile, Milt Zola was sitting in Charlie Gonse's office trying to get some copy before deadline. Gonse was still in his uniform, sitting at his desk, the remains of a Greek salad in front of him. "I don't know what the hell's wrong with Dreyfus," the manager lamented. "Between you and me, he's got his head up his ass."

Though the manager's hyperbole was not entirely accurate with regard to the activity Randy Dreyfus was engaged in at the moment, it was not that far off either.

At four o'clock that morning Pete Zabriskie woke up abruptly in his two-bedroom, one-and-a-half-bath condo in Anaheim Hills. He bolted straight up in bed and sat there, rigid, incredulous, as the circuits in his febrile brain finally connected, and the solution to the puzzle presented itself.

Holy shit. Infuckingcredible.

He turned on the lights, deactivated the carpet sensors of his state-of-the-art security system, and went into the kitchen. Pouring himself a tall glass of cranberry cocktail, he sat down on one of the bar stools and considered the human condition.

The perversity of man never failed to amaze him. Just when he thought he had seen it all, the entire spectrum of human greed and ambition, passion and folly, he stumbled upon something new to add to his catalog of aberrant behavior.

Zabriskie sat there, sipping his cranberry cocktail, and reflected upon the sad fact that men were driven to acts of madness in a largely random and existential manner. You never knew what was coming at you. It was the job of people like Pete Zabriskie, free-lance knights, to tilt against the windmills of disorder and deca-dence.

Frankly, he had backed into this one. He had tripped over it while he was looking elsewhere for a much more conventional example of moral turpitude. The data had been stored in his head, waiting to be accessed by the right sequence of signals. The sequence had finally arranged itself in a significant pattern: the gardener, the money, the open gate, the runaway dog, the chopped meat, and the Liquid-Plumr.

Jesus Christ! What else did that all add up to? He must have been blind not to have seen it before.

The fucking guy was trying to whack his dog.

XII

Molly and Dolly, sporting their matching Esprit jumpers, sat in the family nook and waited for the school bus to honk. On the large-screen Mitsubishi, set into the Santa Fe limestone wall, Joan Lunden was talking to a nutritionist about calcium deficiency. Calvin was chewing quietly on the leather footstool of the Marco Mitrani recliner, so quietly that neither girl noticed until Susie came in from the kitchen and caught him *in flagrante delicto.*

"Calvin, stop that. Right now."

The Dalmatian slinked away guiltily as Susie stood there, hands on hips, frowning.

"Mommy," said Dolly, "you're not supposed to yell at Calvin. That's what Dr. Bob said. Remember?"

"I know. But unless he gets the point soon, there's not going to be any furniture left in this house."

They had another appointment with the dog counselor that week. Susie wondered whether they shouldn't be going to a marriage counselor instead. Randy had gotten home late again last night and gone right to bed. The game had been over by ten, and it was close to two before she heard him come in.

She had thought about simply confronting him with the evidence, handing him the handkerchief and Zabriskie's reports and seeing how he reacted. But the reports were all circumstantial, as was, for that matter, the handkerchief. He could deny everything. And then he would be more circumspect, which would make it more difficult for Zabriskie to get the goods on him.

The school bus honked. She hurried the twins out the door, and as she stood there watching them march primly up the steps and take their seats, she wondered whether she really wanted to deprive them of a father. And what if Randy wound up marrying this D.J.P. woman? Then the twins would have some bimbo as a stepmother.

Tears began to well in her eyes. Again. This was ridiculous. This had to stop. She couldn't allow herself to become completely unglued. She had too much to do.

It was clear to her that she needed someone to talk to. Unfortunately, she couldn't confide in any of the Viking wives. That was too close to home. Karen Most had mentioned a shrink in Westwood who was apparently very good with family relationship problems.

Back in the breakfast nook, she found Karen Most's number and dialed it.

"Hi, Karen, it's Susie Dreyfus . . ."

Karen Most sounded groggy, and then Susie remembered that the Mosts didn't have any kids and had no reason to be up at seven forty-five in the morning.

"Did I wake you?"

"No . . . not at all," Karen Most lied.

"Listen, remember you told me about that therapist in Westwood who specializes in family problems?"

"Uh-huh."

"Well, my sister-in-law Toby's mother is having some marital problems and asked me if I knew anybody and I thought of that guy you told me about. What's his name?"

"Fuad."

"What?"

"Fuad. F . . . U . . . A . . . D."

"That's a . . . peculiar name."

"He's Egyptian."

"Really? Do you happen to have his number?"

"How many shrinks named Fuad can there be in the book?"

"Thanks."

She hung up, got out the West Los Angeles phone book, and found a listing for a Mendes Fuad, M.D., in Westwood. She copied the number down, then went into the exercise nook to do ten miles of cross-country skiing.

Mendes Fuad's answering machine took a phone call from Suzanne Kent—Susie Dreyfus's maiden name, which she thought preferable to use in a situation like this—while the doctor was in session with her husband. Fuad sat on the overstuffed armchair, playing with his beads and listening to the big blond baseball player talk about what had happened the previous evening after the ball game.

"I couldn't believe it, doc. I mean, right there in the Jaguar. In the parking lot of Viking Stadium."

Dr. Fuad merely raised an eyebrow and waited for his patient to go on.

"I'm out of control. I don't know what the fuck I'm doing anymore. All I can think about is being with him, every day, every moment. Even in the middle of the game. I spend half the time staring at him. I can't afford this shit. We're only a game out of first place. . . ."

The doctor nodded slowly, scratched his chin with his long, chiseled, hairy fingers.

"I don't know how much longer I can handle this," Randy went on. "The distraction's killing me. I dropped a pop fly in the top of the ninth last night that cost us the game. It's September. It's nitty-gritty time. We got a shot at the whole thing this year. The pennant, the Series . . ."

After a long, charged moment, Fuad said, "I suppose it's a question of priorities."

"What do you mean *priorities*?"

"What's more important? Your feelings for this man or winning the World Series?"

"Doc, it's not like I have a lot of choices here. I'm out of control."

"You're in love."

"How the fuck can I be in love with a *man*?!"

Randy was shouting again, and Fuad let him cool down for a moment before saying, "The same way you can be in love with a woman. Why not? Millions of men are in love with other men. Why don't you just accept it? And we can go from there."

Randy looked at him plaintively and said, in a quiet, aspirated voice, "Do you have any idea what would happen if this got out?"

The doctor shook his head.

"They'd never let me into the Hall of Fame."

"So?"

"So!"

"What's so important about being in the Hall of Fame?"

"You don't understand, do you?"

"Explain it to me."

"It means you're one of the best who ever played the game. You have to be voted in. By sportswriters. They give you this plaque made of copper, with all your records engraved on it, and it hangs in this museum in Cooperstown."

"Cooperstown?"

"It's in upstate New York."

"I see. . . . So you have a plaque made of copper hanging in a museum in upstate New York. Is that it?"

Jesus. The guy really didn't get it. Randy looked at him, totally exasperated.

"Doc, can I tell you something?"

"Of course."

"Maybe you should go back to Egypt and practice there."

When Fuad looked at him with an injured expression, Randy added, "Nothing personal, okay?"

As Pete Zabriskie swung the Chevy out into the fast lane of the San Diego northbound, three cars in back of the Beemer, he wondered where the day's odyssey was going to take him. From the looks of it, they were headed back to Valley View Estates.

Even before he went back to sleep early that morning, he had decided that he wasn't going to report the dog contract to the blonde. In the first place, he hadn't been hired to find out if her husband had homicidal feelings for the dog. It was outside the terms of their agreement, which stipulated that he ascertain the identity of the party whom Randy Dreyfus was schtupping. The ballplayer wasn't schtupping the Dalmatian. In the second place, failure to report a dog contract amounted to failure to report a conspiracy to commit a felony, which, he remembered from his stint on the Downey police force, was itself a felony. He didn't want to mess with that shit. It could cost him his license.

Still, as he drove north through the Sepulveda Pass, he couldn't help wondering what drove a man to get his gardener to feed Liquid-Plumr to his dog. What the hell happened anyway? Did the dog's intestines dissolve like rust off bathroom pipes?

The extent of human depravity in the world never failed to fascinate Pete Zabriskie. In his line of work he wound up seeing it all, the full spectrum of hinkyness. In addition to the squalor that he was hired to uncover, there were the accidental detours in dark alleys, like this one, where he was looking for one thing and stumbled on something else. There were Maltese Falcons all over the goddamn place.

But this particular day turned out to be uneventful. He followed the Beemer to a golf course in Thousand Oaks, where the subject met one of his teammates for a round of golf. It was the black guy, the second baseman. Zabriskie didn't follow baseball too closely but recognized this guy from TV. The detective hung in until the back nine, and then decided to wrap up the tail for the day. By the time Randy Dreyfus finished eighteen holes he wouldn't have enough time to go meet the schtuppee and slip it to her before he had to be at the ballpark.

The day was a write-off. Eighteen holes of golf with a teammate. If anything, he seemed to be getting farther and farther away from discovering who owned the handkerchief that Susie Dreyfus had found in her underwear drawer.

Later that afternoon Randy Dreyfus lay naked on satin sheets in the darkened bedroom of D. J. Pickett's condo listening to the quiet hum of the air-conditioning system and deciding that the beer commercials had it all wrong. It didn't get any better than this. He couldn't remember the last time he had felt so good, not even when he went 5-for-5 with seven runs batted in against Chicago.

The second baseman was in the kitchen, getting them something to drink. Randy let his eyes wander around the room, taking in the furnishings. It was a strange feeling to be in another man's bedroom. Ballplayers saw one another's hotel rooms, but they almost never saw their bedrooms.

Everything was tasteful and understated, in soft, harmonious colors. The furniture was antique, rich dark wood, perfectly finished. The walls had restful paintings on them. There was a large armoire facing the bed that contained a collection of close to a hundred sweaters.

D.J. returned from the kitchen in a short terry-cloth bathrobe, carrying a pitcher of iced tea and two glasses. He poured them each a glass, then sat down on the bed beside Randy.

"Cheers," D.J. said, clinking Randy's glass.

"Up yours," Randy replied with a big grin. And then they both giggled.

"You okay?" D.J. asked.

Randy nodded. *Okay* was not exactly the term he would use to describe all the conflicting emotions inside him at the moment. He took a sip of the iced tea and said, "It's just kind of weird, you know what I mean?"

"Yeah."

"I mean . . . when did you realize that you, like . . . wanted to do it with another guy?"

"A long time ago. As long as I can remember."

"Did you ever used to do it with girls?"

D.J. shook his head. "I'm a virgin." He laughed out loud. "I tried once when I was in college. Blond cheerleader type, cute as a button. Couldn't have done any better than this one. She came up to my room after the Penn State game . . ."

"What happened?"

"Nothing. Equipment failure."

"You couldn't get one?"

D.J. shook his head. "Spaghetti . . . By the time I was thirteen, I had it pretty much figured out. I used to hang around the gym watching the guys work out."

"How old were you when you first did it?"

"Fifteen. A sailor picked me up in the Greyhound station."

"Jesus."

"It's a way of life. You just kind of go with it."

"Are you sorry?"

"What do you mean—am I sorry?"

"I mean, if you had the choice, would you rather be straight?"

D.J. shook his head.

"Why not?"

"Then I'd have to fuck women."

They both laughed, then sat there as the laugh petered out, replaced by a gradual sense of sadness as they realized that the afternoon was dissolving. Soon they'd have to get up, get dressed, and drive to Viking Stadium to rejoin the real world. They sat there in silence as the thinning afternoon light filtered through the Levolors. There were a hundred questions in Randy's mind. He didn't know where to begin.

"D.J.?" he said quietly.

"Yeah?"

"What's going to happen?"

D.J. smiled at him and shrugged. "I don't know."

The second baseman reached out and gently caressed the side of Randy's face. It was a gesture full of tenderness. Randy felt himself start to choke up. He took a large gulp of iced tea to keep a lid on things and lay there listening to his heart beat.

Manuel Rodriguez had kept the chopped meat overnight in his sister's refrigerator in Pacoima. When he had taken it out that morning, it was a little brown around the edges. It still looked, however, like it would do the trick.

The ballplayer had given him five hundred bucks cash to mix it with Liquid-Plumr and leave it in his yard near the azalea bushes that afternoon. He had said something about a coyote that was threatening his children. Manuel Rodriguez wasn't dumb. The last time the guy had given him two hundred bucks to leave the garden gate open. You didn't have to be a rocket scientist to figure out this one.

So the ballplayer wanted to kill his dog. So he didn't want to do it himself. So he gets his gardener to do it for him, pays him a lot of money. ¿Quien sabe?

It wasn't Manuel Rodriguez's problem to figure out why the ballplayer didn't like his dog. Five hundred off the books was a nice payday. He thought again about new tires as he swung the Ford off Delores Canyon into Caravaggio Place. He was driving around on rubber as thin as tortillas. Sooner or later he was going to have a big bang. But five nice crisp hundred-dollar bills . . . He could put one each on the nose in five straight races or put the whole enchilada on a long shot and buy himself a new Mazda RX7 with racing stripes.

He parked the truck in front of the big house at the end of the cul de sac and turned off the motor. He grabbed the bag with the Liquid-Plumr and chopped meat, got out of the truck, and went around to the rear to get a hedge trimmer, just in case he ran into the blonde with the nice tits. Once last year he had caught her sunbathing without her shirt on. Jesus María.

In the back of the house there was a patio, a swimming pool, an expanse of grass leading to a gently sloping hillside covered with ice plants, and a fence, where Manuel had planted azaleas on the instructions of the blonde.

Never having poisoned a dog before, Manuel Rodriguez wasn't sure just how much Liquid-Plumr to put in the chopped meat. The guy hadn't given instructions, figuring probably that anybody who lived in Pacoima knew how to do this type of thing. They didn't kill dogs in Pacoima. Mexicans were very fond of animals.

The dog was in the house, barking at him through the sliding-glass patio door. It was a firehouse dog without a lot of brains. Manuel never liked this dog very much, even though he was fond of dogs in general and would never have poisoned one without being paid good money. But as far as he was concerned, a Mazda RX7 was worth this particular dog's life.

He took the chopped meat out of the bag and opened up the plastic wrapper. It was getting browner every minute and starting to smell rancid. But this dog looked like he would eat three-day-old bird shit. He pounded the meat, trying to soften it, then took out the bottle of drain unclogger. The skull and crossbones were displayed prominently. Working carefully, he removed the safety seal, then the cap, and poured a healthy amount onto the flattened lump of meat. Then he put on his work gloves and kneaded the meat like he was making meat loaf. When he was satisfied that the Liquid-Plumr had saturated the meat, he divided it into four separate patties and deposited one beside each of four separate azalea bushes across the expanse of the backyard.

When he was finished with this, he spent a few minutes trimming the oleander with the hedge trimmer before calling it a day. As he drove down Delores Canyon, he thought about stopping for a six-pack in the 7-Eleven just before the freeway entrance. He deserved it. It had been a good day's work. Five hundred bananas.

Adios, dog.

"I feel like I'm losing my grip on things, like I have no control over my life anymore . . ."

The man sat there, hands folded in front of him, and nodded slowly. He didn't say anything. He had said very little since she had been in the small, dark, womblike room. She found the place vaguely depressing. If it were up to her, she would have given it some color and light, cheered it up a bit.

"I don't know . . . what to . . . do."

He nodded again. She sat there waiting for him to say something, to help her out, but he continued to look at her with lidded eyes. Here she was pouring out her soul, and the man looked like he was asleep.

Where in God's name did he get those drapes? They looked like they were designed for a mortuary. And the carpet was a cheap acrylic. There were a couple of knockoff Currier and Ives reproductions on the wall that you could pick up at a garage sale for a few bucks. How did he expect anybody to feel better about their life in a room like this?

"So," he said finally, "you are angry."

"Yes I am."

"You feel betrayed."

"Yes I do."

"What do you want to do about these feelings?"

"I don't know. I'm confused. That's why I'm here. I mean, I still love him. I really do. But every time I think about it, it makes me crazy."

He nodded some more, then drifted off into another one of his prolonged silences. She found herself staring at the fish tank in the corner. It made a bubbly sound that she found very distracting. Between the fish tank and the worry beads, it was a wonder you could hear yourself think.

He finally stopped nodding his head and said, "You know, life is a very strange business. We discover things about ourselves all the time, our capacity for love and for anger and our level of tolerance for pain. Anger and love are just two faces of the same coin. They feed on each other."

She took all this in without blinking. It sounded to her like the kind of stuff you found on inspirational greeting cards.

"You see," he went on, "this is what we have to look at. What is really inside you. Is the anger an appropriate response to your husband's infidelity or, rather, is the infidelity a pretext for you to vent the anger you feel on other accounts? Is the infidelity actually *convenient*?"

She looked at him to see if there was a trace of irony in his eyes, but she couldn't tell. They still looked half-closed to her. What in God's name was he talking about? This thing was anything but *convenient*. It was putting a monkey wrench in their entire life. It was threatening to blow apart the whole package.

She shook her head to indicate that he didn't understand at all. "No," she said emphatically.

"I beg your pardon?"

"That's not the problem at all. Believe me, there is nothing *convenient* about this."

He gave her an indulgent smile, as if she were a child, and shrugged. "You never know," he said. "I have a patient who discovered after many years of being an adult and being married that he actually preferred men to women. All his life he had twisted his insides up to deny what his real nature was. He had been living in the wrong body. Maybe you are living in the wrong life?"

"Look," she said, "it's the only life I have, so even if I am living in the wrong life, I don't see what I can do about it. The point here is that my husband is screwing around with another woman. And it makes me furious."

"Is there a lock on the front door of your house?"

"A lock? Of course."

"Does it open from the inside?"

"What do you mean?"

"Can you be locked inside your house?"

"No. Of course not."

"So?"

He smiled a big, broad, smug smile, as if he had just revealed the secret of the universe to her. Then he sat there sagely nodding to himself and clicking his worry beads furiously.

Whomp. The ball came out of the pitching machine, big and juicy as a grapefruit, and Randy drove it deep into the alley in left center. He couldn't miss. Anything it threw at him he hit. He stood in the batting cage and sprayed vicious line drives all over the park, while his teammates and the few hundred early birds in the stands watched in awe.

From his private box behind home plate, John D. F. White, Jr., was watching too. They still hadn't closed Randy Dreyfus. The old man had decided that the last offer was the final offer. He wouldn't give a penny more. Out of principle. "All he's going to get is my left nut. That's it. I'm keeping the right one." John/John had tried to convince him that the couple of hundred thou increments on the sweeteners were not worth arguing about at this point, but the old man had dug himself into a trench and refused to budge.

As John/John watched his shortstop take batting practice, he knew that the Vikings had to keep him at any cost. You didn't find a superstar like this every day. Randy Dreyfus could not only do it all —hit, run, field—but he was the type of ballplayer you wanted on your team. Blond, blue-eyed, good-looking wife, two kids. And he was the right color. Though he didn't consider himself prejudiced, John/John had to admit that they were taking over the game. It wasn't as bad as the NBA yet, but in a couple of years you would have trouble fielding a team with more than one or two white faces on it. It was becoming a marketing problem. Your average working Joe was beginning to wonder whether it was worth twenty bucks to come out to the park and watch a bunch of overpaid black and Spanish guys with attitudes play baseball.

The phone in his box rang. John/John looked at his watch. Too late for Barry Fuchsia to call. Besides, the ball was in their court. Barry Fuchsia wouldn't be calling with a lower number. Barry Fuchsia didn't know how to subtract. He picked up and said, "John White."

A little girl's voice was on the line. "I need to talk to my daddy. Please."

"Who is this?"

"Molly Dreyfus. They told me you were the only one who had the authority to let me talk to my daddy while he was taking batting practice."

"Isn't your mom there?"

"No, she's in Westwood."

"Are you all alone?"

"No. Mikva's here but she's Lithuanian."

"Well, your dad's down on the field right now."

"Please. I have to talk to him. Right away."

"Are you okay?"

"No."

"What's wrong?"

"Please. Let me talk to my daddy."

"Okay. Hang on."

John/John put the cellular phone in its case and sent an usher down to give it to Randy Dreyfus, who had just stepped out of the batting cage.

Randy picked up. "Hello?"

"Daddy?"

"Yes, honey, something wrong?"

"Calvin . . ."

The Liquid-Plumr. Finally. He started to prepare a condolence speech to give to his daughters.

"What about Calvin?"

"He found something in the yard."

"What did he find?"

"A dead coyote."

In the background he heard the sound of a Dalmatian barking, the high-pitched neurotic sound that he so hated. He rubbed his eyes, sighed, then muttered, "What are we going to do with that dog . . . ?"

XIII

On September 19, with two weeks left to go in the regular season, the Vikings were back in first, clinging to a slender lead in the Western Division of the American League, a half-game over Oakland, two and a half over California. They had wrapped up a mediocre 7–6 home stand—the entire team in a hitting slump except for Randy Dreyfus, who went 22-for-48, a sizzling .458 pace, bringing his league-leading batting average up to .353—and were leaving for a short six-game swing through Texas and Kansas City.

The writers were questioning how long Randy Dreyfus could carry the team. His hitting, along with the steady play in the field of his double-play partner, D. J. Pickett, seemed to be keeping the Vikings afloat. The rest of the team was floundering.

Randy's contractual difficulties with the Vikings management were well publicized. The mail was heavily in favor of re-signing him at any cost. In a memo to the Whites, Ken Teffner, the Vikings' vice president of public relations, stressed the "political considerations vis-à-vis the demographic breakdown of the target marketing population."

"What the hell does that mean?" John D. F. White, Sr., growled at his son when the memo crossed his desk.

"That means he's white," John/John replied.

"Since when is being white worth twenty million dollars for three years?"

"He's only asking for nineteen. . . ."

Barry Fuchsia assured Randy that the deal would be closed before the end of the season. All he had to do was continue hitting. In fact, if he kept up the pace of the last few weeks, the elevator might even rise a few more floors before they had to get off.

Before the opening game against Texas, Charlie Gonse gave another one of his pregame talks to the assembled players. He gathered them in the clubhouse after batting practice and said, among other things, "As far as I'm concerned, it's all up to you. You can shit or you can get off the pot. There are lots of little things that don't show up in the box score. And I'm not seeing a lot of those things being done. I can't remember, frankly, the last time I saw someone hit behind the runner except when he couldn't get around on a fastball. It all adds up. You reap what you sow. In spite of what anybody tells you . . ."

Randy sat in front of his locker, signing baseballs and glancing now and again across the room, where D.J. was sitting on a stool, eyes closed, apparently in deep concentration. Randy knew he was asleep. The second baseman refused to give up his pregame nap, not even for one of the manager's pep talks.

Things would be a lot easier for them on the road. At night, Randy could sneak into D.J.'s room and stay there until dawn, slipping out before risking being discovered by a maid or a teammate in the hall. During the day, they could go to movies together or play golf without arousing suspicion. They had to avoid any public displays of affection, but this made it all the more exciting when they finally got together behind closed doors.

Randy felt as if he were on a sailboat being blown slowly and surely toward the horizon, with no idea what was on the other side. And he didn't care. He was riding an incredible high, loose and full of mad energy, swinging the bat with power and accuracy, running the bases like a deer in winter, waiting for night to celebrate with his lover. It was all crazy and wonderful. Maybe the Egyptian was right. Maybe he just had to go with it.

They won 7–2 that night, with Randy going 3-for-4 with a walk, and D.J. hitting one of his rare home runs. After the game, they went to a Mexican restaurant in Dallas and drank margaritas and ate themselves silly. Then they took a cab back to the hotel, holding hands just out of the view of the cab driver, and, following the usual security precautions, met in Randy's room.

They put out the DO NOT DISTURB sign, turned up the sound of the TV to muffle any cries of enthusiasm that might pass through the thin walls, and retired for the night.

The morning after her husband left for Dallas, Susie Dreyfus telephoned Pete Zabriskie in his Santa Ana office. It had been some time now that the private detective had been investigating Randy, and there was still no indication who the other woman was. All he had submitted in his FedExed reports were mileage charges for a series of seemingly aimless wanderings around town. She had pretty much stopped reading them.

"Pete Zabriskie," he announced after the bimbo secretary had put her through.

"This is Suzanne Dreyfus."

"How're you doing?"

"Mr. Zabriskie, let me get right to the point. I'm beginning to wonder if you are going to find out what I asked you to find out. It's been well over a month already."

There was a pause on the other end, then he said, "Let me explain something to you, Mrs. Dreyfus. Private investigation is a painstaking process. We operate in a scientific and systematic manner. We can't perform miracles."

"I'm not asking for a miracle. I just want to know who my husband's sleeping with."

"You are assuming that all we have to do is proceed in a straight line and we will eventually reach our objective. You are assuming that this is a linear activity."

"I beg your pardon?"

"We don't simply move from A to Z, Mrs. Dreyfus. We have to explore avenues of opportunity, detours that sometimes take us many miles from the main road. Every single one of them needs to be checked out before we can proceed. No stone can be left unturned."

"You mean to tell me, then, that you have absolutely no idea who this woman is?"

"Did I say that?"

"Well, you haven't given me any indication that you're on to something."

"I have been exploring some potentially promising leads."

"Like what?"

"I believe that it's counterproductive to discuss a lead unless it develops into something substantive."

"So, that's it—you have nothing to tell me?"

Zabriskie let the phone slip down slightly below his chin and exhaled slowly. He had an earful to tell her, but it was nothing she wanted to know. What was the point of telling her that her husband was trying to whack the family dog? How would that comfort a woman in her condition?

"Let me put it to you this way, Mrs. Dreyfus. What I have to tell you is not directly relevant to the question of your husband's infidelity."

"What?"

"It's merely fragments of the mosaic. As soon as I have the whole picture, you'll be the first to know."

Susie sighed. She was getting nowhere. Then she asked him a question that had occurred to her more than once. "What if he only sees her on the road?"

"The road is out of my jurisdiction."

"Do you think he could, like, fly her around with him to different cities and sneak her into his hotel room?"

"That's feasible."

"Then I'd never find out, would I?"

"It's been my experience that men always leave fingerprints. And sooner or later your husband will too. You can count on it."

•   •   •

After D.J. slipped out of his room at five-thirty that morning, Randy went back for a luxurious second sleep, waking after ten. He got up and went down to the weight room for fifty bench presses before having room service send up a large bowl of spoon-size shredded wheat with fresh strawberries on the side and a copy of *USA Today*.

Over breakfast he scanned the scores of the other games. Oakland had lost in Seattle, which meant the Vikings were a game and a half up. The morning line had them 6–7 favorites against Texas tonight. Things were looking good. There was a whole day in front of him before he had to go to work. D.J. and he were going to check out Neiman-Marcus for sweaters.

He showered, shaved, put on a peach-colored Lacoste shirt and a pair of bleached jeans, and was about to ring D.J.'s room when his phone rang.

"Hey, how're you doing, Randy?" It was Milt Zola.

"Okay."

"Listen, I want to get your reaction to a quote. Okay?"

"From who?"

"The old man."

"What'd he say?"

" 'The way things are going, pretty soon I'm going to be working for Randy Dreyfus.' "

"He said that?"

"Direct quote."

"Holy shit."

"I can't print that, Randy."

"You want a reply?"

"Yes, I do."

" 'It's a free country.' "

"Is that it?"

"That's it."

"What exactly does that mean?"

"It means that Mr. White is free to work for anybody he wants."

Randy told D.J. about Zola's call in the cab on the way to Neiman-Marcus. "What the hell are you going to do with all that money anyway?" D.J. said.

"I don't know. Buy six thousand sweaters, travel around the world, buy myself a ball club and hire only lefties . . ."

D.J. smiled and resisted the temptation to reach over and muss his hair, an affectionate gesture that he often did when they were alone. It was getting increasingly difficult to keep his hands off him in public.

In the Neiman-Marcus men's shop, an immense cornucopia of designer clothing, D.J. picked out three new cashmere sweaters—off-beige, gray, and olive—and Randy bought an expensive lavender cardigan and two long-sleeved silk shirts. Then D.J. convinced Randy that he needed to buy some pants to go with his shirts and sweater.

They selected a pair of Armani trousers for $375. Randy had never spent so much on a pair of pants. He asked D.J. to accompany him into the changing room to check out the fit. They went back through a narrow corridor to a bunch of small cubicles, empty at the moment. Each one had a door, a mirror, and a hook for hanging clothes.

The sudden appearance of the cubicle and the mirror and the oasis of privacy in the middle of the large, air-conditioned desert of Neiman-Marcus's men's shop had a strange effect on them. They were both overtaken by the same impulse at the same time. It was reckless and foolhardy. They were in a public place. The cubicle doors were flimsy. Someone could walk in at any moment.

It may have been that, after spending a morning watching each other try on sweaters, they were so predisposed. It may have been the fact that Neiman-Marcus had a high enough regard for its clientele that the management didn't think it necessary to put a notice in the cubicles that they were under hidden-camera surveillance. Or it may have been that they merely lost control simultaneously, giving way to their affection in the wrong place at the wrong time.

Whatever the case, the shortstop and second baseman of the Los Angeles Valley Vikings engaged in what could be construed in the State of Texas as an indecent act in a public place. And the act was recorded on videotape by a hidden surveillance camera designed to incriminate shoplifters, not photograph embraces between members of the same sex, albeit different races.

• • •

The head of security for Neiman-Marcus, H.A.L. "Hal" Porter, had an extremely broad view of just what constituted an indecent act in Dallas County, Texas. He had been sitting at the console, nibbling on a take-out burrito, waiting for something interesting to take place in one of the women's changing rooms, when the image of Randy Dreyfus and D. J. Pickett flashed across the screen. It took him several seconds to make sense of the strange activity in Dressing Room Number One. He had never seen two men kissing before, and he kept staring, convinced that one of the two figures would eventually turn out to be a woman.

The fact that they were not only both men but that they were of different colors had a visceral effect on Hal Porter. He gagged on his burrito. Jesus H. Christ. Faggotry *and* miscegenation! In broad daylight! In *Neiman-Marcus*!

As soon as he managed to dislodge the errant shred of chili pepper from his esophagus, he strapped on the Magnum with the shoulder holster, grabbed a pair of handcuffs, put on his tailored Neiman-Marcus jacket and his Stetson, and rushed out of the security office. By the time he had taken the escalator down two floors to the men's shop and arrived at the dressing area, Randy was standing in front of the mirror in the open dressing cubicle checking the fit of the trousers. D.J. was sitting on the bench inside and saying that he thought he could go at least one size smaller. If not two. There was no longer any indecent miscegenation going on.

Hal Porter already had the goods on them, however. He said, without any preamble, "I'm placing you under arrest for indecent behavior in a public place. You have the right to remain silent. You have the right to an attorney. If you can't afford an attorney, one will be provided at no cost. Come on out of there, lean up against the wall, and spread 'em."

Randy looked at the heavyset guy in the cowboy hat and spiffy boots and merely blinked. The speech had barely registered. All he could manage was, "Huh?"

"Listen, mister, I suggest you comply if you don't want to add resisting arrest to the other charges."

"What charges?" said D.J.

"Indecent behavior in a public place, creating a disturbance, and sodomy."

"What?"

"You heard me."

"Who are you?"

"Halbert Alvin Leroy Porter, head of security for this store and a sworn deputy for the Dallas County Sheriff's Department, and I got you on videotape."

Randy still didn't budge. He was thinking about taking the fat guy out, but he had only one free hand at the time. The other one was holding up the Armani trousers.

"Look, there's been some misunderstanding here. We haven't done any of the things you're talking about," D.J. said.

"I'll be the judge of that, mister. Now I want both of you against the wall with your legs spread right now."

Randy looked at D.J. the way he looked at him just before he tossed him the ball on a double play. Are you ready? Here it comes . . .

D.J. shook his head quickly, trying to stop Randy from doing anything rash.

"Can we just talk this out for a minute?" D.J. said to Porter in his most ingratiating voice. "I really think if we just discuss this nice and calmly, we can straighten everything out."

Ignoring him, Porter took the walkie-talkie out of his back pocket and said, "Bill, you there?"

After a moment, a crackling noise came back: "Yeah, Hal?"

"Go get Jim and Felix and get on up to the men's changing rooms ASAP. We got ourselves a situation here."

More crackling, then, "Ten-four, Hal."

"You're making a big mistake," D.J. persisted.

"Really?"

"A wrongful-arrest suit against this store is going to run into a lot of money."

"That so?"

"Do you know who we are?"

"No, sir."

"You're obviously not a baseball fan."

"No, sir."

Randy was still standing in front of the mirror holding up the pants that were too large for him. He couldn't believe they were really going to have to take shit from the little fat guy in the big hat.

"Why don't we just get the hell out of here, D.J.?" he said, starting to step out of the Armani trousers so he could put his jeans back on. At that point H.A.L. Porter took the Magnum out of the shoulder holster and drew a bead on Randy.

"Keep your pants on, mister."

Bailing ballplayers out of jail was one of the duties implicit in the responsibilities of being vice president of public relations for the Los Angeles Valley Vikings. It went with the amorphous territory of keeping the ball club's image as favorable as possible. On the road, the vice president of public relations was also the ranking officer, unless the general manager or one of the Whites had made the trip, which was not the case in Dallas.

So when Ken Teffner got paged in the hotel coffee shop over lunch and told by Charlie Gonse that he had just gotten a call from D. J. Pickett saying that he and Randy Dreyfus were being held in a downtown Dallas jail, he was prepared to get the petty cash out of the hotel safe and go get them.

When he asked the manager what the charges were, Gonse replied, "Fuck do I know."

"How much bail money do I need?"

"Fuck do I know."

Teffner took two thousand dollars in cash, which would be plenty to cover a drunk-and-disorderly charge, and hailed a cab downtown. His first indication that they had a problem on their hands was the presence of half a dozen TV minivans in front of the police station. A couple of drunk ballplayers usually didn't draw such attention. Certainly not in Dallas, where they routinely mowed down presidents.

Inside the police station Teffner found a madhouse of reporters, minicam units, cables, microphones. He fought his way to the desk and identified himself as a representative of the Los Angeles Valley Vikings with bail money for Randy Dreyfus and D. J. Pickett.

A reporter near the desk, overhearing this, signaled to his crew, and the next thing Ken Teffner knew he was standing before a firing squad of TV lights, microphones shoved in his face. The reporters were all screaming at once, and he couldn't understand much of anything except for one word that seemed to stick out by its very incongruity. *Sodomy.*

Since the word had no frame of reference for Ken Teffner in this situation, he merely turned away from the camera and back to the desk sergeant and asked for the bail forms. The desk sergeant informed him that bail would be set at the arraignment that afternoon.

Teffner looked at him blankly. "Arraignment?"

"That's correct. There are felony charges against them."

"What the hell did they do?"

"Committed an indecent act in a public place so as to cause an outrage against public morality and decency, to wit, engaging in sodomy . . . Article One-eight-six-A, State of Texas criminal statutes."

Ken Teffner was a fairly unflappable man, but what he had just heard from the desk sergeant was enough to make him begin to drench the armpits of his gray tropical Dacron suit. It was completely unthinkable. Two ballplayers on the Vikings arrested for *sodomy*! In *Dallas*!

This couldn't be true. Randy Dreyfus was married, for chrissakes. And D. J. Pickett was black. They'd been playing in the same infield together for three years. They were superstars. Randy Dreyfus had a shopping center named after him. He was leading the league in hitting.

It took Ken Teffner a long moment to pull himself together. The cacophony behind him mounted. He tried his best to ignore it.

"Look," he said, "there must be some misunderstanding here. You're talking about two very well-known baseball players. This has to be a question of mistaken identity."

"We have a sworn statement from a Dallas County deputy sheriff. And we've got videotape."

"Videotape?"

"Yes, sir. They were apprehended in one of the changing rooms at Neiman-Marcus."

"They were committing *sodomy* in a changing room at Neiman-Marcus?"

"That's what the report says."

Teffner exhaled deeply, felt a tinge of acid begin to make contact with his preulcerous stomach wall. This was a public relations nightmare of the first order, and he, Ken Teffner, was standing right in the middle of it. He realized that whatever had actually happened in the changing room at Neiman-Marcus, he had to make some statement to the press before this went out over the wires completely uncooked. He could not afford to remain silent in the face of what appeared to be the entire media establishment of the city of Dallas.

Turning back toward the cameras, he held up his hand to get some quiet. The roar died down to a mild din. Teffner cleared his throat and winged it.

"Though I haven't had a chance to talk to either Randy or D.J. yet, I am confident that there is no truth whatsoever to the charges filed against them. There has undoubtedly been a grievous mistake here that will be cleared up very quickly. These are two fine young men, ballplayers and good Americans, and the Los Angeles Valley Vikings organization is behind them a hundred percent. Thank you."

Teffner found Randy and D.J. in a holding cell downstairs, being watched by an officer lest they commit another outrage against the public morals. D.J. was lying calmly on a bench, looking as if he were merely taking a pregame snooze. Randy, still wearing the Armani slacks that were a size and a half too large, paced back and forth, holding his pants up.

Teffner was allowed a few minutes to talk to them through the bars. He spoke in a whisper, so that the cop on duty wouldn't hear.

"Look, first of all," he said, "I want you to know that there's no way anybody's going to believe those charges against you. We'll get a lawyer on this right away and have you out of here with an official apology by the store and the City of Dallas."

D.J. nodded, but without much conviction. Randy looked like he wanted to put his fist through someone. Neither of them, however, said anything. There was a long, awkward silence. Then Teffner said, somewhat sheepishly, "What actually *did* happen?"

"Look, Ken," D.J. said, "why don't you just find a lawyer who can get us the hell of here, okay?"

"What do I tell him?"

"Tell him that Randy was trying on a pair of pants when this little fat guy with a gun came in and arrested us."

"That's all?"

Another long silence. D.J. realized there was no point in keeping it from Teffner. They had them on videotape.

"Before that we were kissing."

All the way back to the hotel, Ken Teffner tried to map out a clear-headed and orderly manner of proceeding. He reminded himself that he was not a lawyer and that the legal problems involved were not his concern. His job as vice president of public relations was first and foremost to protect the public image of the Los Angeles Valley Vikings and, collaterally, to protect the image of baseball, which was the product his employers were marketing.

As soon as he contacted the club's legal counsel in Los Angeles, the lawyers would take over. And then he would, as always, be expected to march along picking up the pieces. There would be a hell of a lot of pieces to pick up on this one.

He still couldn't believe it. Randy Dreyfus and D. J. Pickett kissing in a changing room in Neiman-Marcus. How did you play this story? Was there an angle that you could turn around and use to your advantage? Guy gets messed up on drugs, drinks too much, gambles, leaves his wife—you could play up the rehab and contrition angle. But this?

It had to be just an aberration, some sort of gag they were pulling that unfortunately got recorded by the surveillance cameras at Neiman-Marcus. Couple of guys screwing around after a few beers. Boys will be boys.

Nevertheless, there was a hollow feeling inside Ken Teffner when, back in his room, he dialed Burton Meeker, the club's chief counsel, who had to be paged off a racquetball court in Century City. The gray, patrician-looking lawyer stood dripping sweat as Ken Teffner told him that the shortstop and the second baseman of the Vikings were in a Dallas jail waiting to be arraigned on public indecency and sodomy charges stemming from an incident in a changing room in Neiman-Marcus.

"You're not serious," Meeker said in his quiet, authoritative voice.

"I'm afraid so. They say they have them on videotape from a hidden surveillance camera."

"Have you spoken to them?"

"Just for a minute."

"What did they say?"

"They said they weren't committing an indecent act."

"What *were* they doing?"

"Kissing."

"Kissing?"

"Kissing."

There was a moment of astounded silence. Then Meeker murmured, "They were kissing in a changing room at Neiman-Marcus?"

"Apparently."

"Why were they doing that?"

"I don't know, Burt."

After getting off the phone with Meeker, who had to call his office for a referral to an attorney in Dallas to appear at the arraignment, Ken Teffner called Charlie Gonse. When he told the manager what had happened, Gonse said, "You realize how this fucks up my lineup for tonight?"

The next call should have gone to Larry Zwick, the general manager, but the Whites didn't give him a great deal of power. He was an ex-manager they'd kicked upstairs, a figurehead, with the Whites doing most of their own negotiations and letting Zwick take the fall for the bad news. There was no point in calling him. Nobody ever did.

Finally, there was the call that Ken Teffner dreaded most. This situation was beyond the scope of comprehension of John D. F. White., Sr. or Jr. Baseball was practically a religion to them. The game was sacrosanct, a totem of the American way of life.

He couldn't let them hear about it raw on the six o'clock news. It would kill them. Teffner nervously dialed the number of the Vikings office and asked to be put through to John D. F. White, Jr.

When John/John got on the phone, Teffner took a deep breath and said, very quickly, "This may not be as bad as it sounds but Randy Dreyfus and D. J. Pickett were arrested a few hours ago in Dallas for committing an indecent act in a changing room at Neiman-Marcus."

All Ken Teffner could hear on the other end was an excruciatingly plaintive wheeze.

By the time the Dallas district attorney's office saw the videotape and realized that H.A.L. Porter's understanding of what constituted sodomy was excessively broad, Burton Meeker and John D. F. White, Jr., were already on a plane for Dallas; Gene Sandheur, a local criminal attorney retained by Meeker, had gotten a copy of the complaint, seen the defendants, and was trying to track down a judge to dismiss it summarily; and Ken Teffner was engaged in serious damage control, trying to get through to the networks and the press syndicates to put a lid on the story before it went out over the wires like a raging forest fire. Teffner was doing what he could to stamp out the sparks. But calling up UPI to deny that two ballplayers on your team had committed sodomy in a department-store changing room was a difficult phone call at best.

Getting a tip from a friend at a Dallas daily, Milt Zola was down at the police station, working the cops, trying to get a piece of the story. At the moment, he was the only L.A. reporter in town. It wouldn't be long before they sent everybody and his brother down here. He was going to have to file something tonight, and at the moment he had no idea what the hell had actually happened. He couldn't help wondering, though, if the strange vibrations he'd had about Dreyfus and Pickett were premonitions or astute observations. Was he psychic or just very perceptive?

Meanwhile Randy and D.J. were given a meal of egg-salad sandwiches and iced tea, which neither of them touched, and refused to sign autographs for any of the cops in the police station. The lawyer had come and gone, promising to do what he could to get them out of there as soon as possible. It all depended on what was on the videotape, he said. D.J. told him exactly what was on the videotape, and the lawyer assured them that it didn't constitute sodomy in the State of Texas.

By 5 P.M. the district attorney had decided to drop the sodomy charge and was debating with his colleagues whether two men kissing in a department-store changing room constituted an indecent public act. There was no precedent on the books that anybody could find. Homosexual relations between consenting adults had been decriminalized in Texas. That the act was performed in a public place was what was legally ambiguous. Nobody knew what to do.

While they were still debating the issues, Gene Sandheur located a judge and got him to issue a writ of habeas corpus, putting the ball squarely in the district attorney's court. Either charge them or let them go.

Reserving the right to refile charges at a later date, after a more thorough investigation was performed, the district attorney issued the order to release the two ballplayers from jail. Unfortunately, this occurred some time after the deadline for most evening news broadcasts.

At six o'clock, as most Americans were sitting down to dinner and the evening news, they learned that the shortstop and second baseman of the Los Angeles Valley Vikings had been arrested for committing an indecent act in a changing room of a Dallas department store. Later on, during the ten o'clock news, the story was updated: The alleged sodomists had been released from jail pending the filing of new charges.

XIV

Susie Dreyfus was driving north on the San Diego after her radio program when she heard the news out of Dallas. She got off at the next exit, pulled into a Bob's Big Boy, and sat there trembling for nearly an hour. The security guard came over to ask if there was something wrong. She stared at him blankly, restarted the engine, and took off.

At the Dreyfuses' home in Valley View Estates, Mikva had her TV tuned to The Shopping Channel and didn't hear the news. Nor did the twins, who were upstairs planning out their wardrobe for the upcoming week in the daily wardrobe journal that Joan Lunden suggested they keep. The phone began to ring off the hook. After the first five calls, Mikva stopped answering.

Pete Zabriskie was home in his den in Anaheim Hills kicking back when he heard the anchor of the six o'clock news tease the story. Then, after he heard the details, Zabriskie muttered, "Holy shit. *Cherchez* the fucking second baseman."

Manuel Rodriguez was having a beer in the El Chollo lounge on San Fernando Road when the story came over the bar TV. The Spanish-speaking clientele hardly reacted to it. Rodriguez stared at the screen and shook his head. The dog-killing baseball player was a very strange *hombre*.

On the way home to his house in Pacific Palisades, Mendes Fuad, M.D., was listening to National Public Radio news, which did not choose to broadcast the story that evening. And even if they had, Fuad would not have been surprised. He'd seen this coming for some time now.

Perhaps the greatest consternation occurred in the visitors' clubhouse at Arlington Stadium, where a TV was on in the trainer's room. Willie St. James and Glen Ephard were getting rub-downs when the local anchor cupcake announced the news of the arrest in the voice she reserved for earthquakes and plane crashes.

The two ballplayers looked at each other to see if they hadn't hallucinated the news report. The trainers stopped working, staring blankly at the set. Nobody said a word. Nobody even blinked.

In his office Charlie Gonse was laboring over his lineup card when St. James and Ephard, in their towels, knocked on the door.

"Yeah," Gonse said.

The two players entered the small office and stood there for a moment silently until the manager growled, "What?"

"Did you hear about Randy and D.J.?" Ephard ventured.

"Yeah," said Gonse.

Some more silence. Then St. James said, "What're you going to do, Charlie?"

"I'm going to put Jarvis at short and Caliper at second. You got any better ideas?"

When they were finally released from jail, Randy and D.J. took separate cabs back to the hotel. It had been decided by Ken Teffner that, given the circumstances, neither of them should play that night. Randy left first, slipping out the back door of the police station to avoid the press, but when he got to the hotel he found that there was a group of reporters waiting there.

He told the driver to keep going and drop him at a Burger King a few blocks past the hotel. He ordered a double cheeseburger, fries, and a chocolate shake and sat in the corner eating his dinner, hoping that no one would recognize him.

It was only now, as he sat sucking on his straw, that he began to realize just how deep the shit was. At the police station he'd been running on adrenaline. Now he was out of gas, and the ramifications of what had happened began to hit him.

At the moment it all seemed too overwhelming to deal with. All he wanted to do was curl up and go to sleep. But he didn't know how to get back up to his hotel room without facing the TV cameras. How long could he hide out in the Burger King?

He decided to call the Egyptian. In a pay phone in the parking lot, he dialed the shrink's number, got the machine. After the message and the beep, he said, "Listen, doc, I'm in big trouble here if you haven't heard yet. The shit has hit the old fan. Call me at the Embassy Suites in Dallas when you pick this up. I sure hope you pick this up. What're you doing now, anyway? Buying food for your fish or something? Jesus!"

Randy left the booth, turned in the direction away from the hotel, and started walking.

For his part, D. J. Pickett walked straight through the reporters and into the hotel. He said nothing, made eye contact with no one, got his key and a stack of phone messages, and took the elevator up to his room.

The messages were all from the press. He threw them in the trash basket, took the phone off the hook, and went into the bathroom. Running the shower full force, he got under it and stayed there for half an hour, trying not to think about anything at all.

At about this time, Burton Meeker and John D. F. White, Jr., landed at Dallas–Ft. Worth Airport. They grabbed a cab and headed into town, arriving at the Embassy Suites only to find a horde of reporters milling around in front.

Not even bothering to check in, they took the elevator directly to Ken Teffner's suite. The PR man was on the phone with ESPN, pacing the room, explaining, "There are no charges whatsoever against them. It was all a mistake. We're expecting a statement and apology from Neiman-Marcus any minute. . . . What was that?"

Teffner took a hit off his diet Coke, then said, "No, I haven't seen the videotape, but there's nothing compromising on it, believe me. . . ."

John/John sat down on the couch, while Meeker searched the room for a minibar.

"As soon as we've had a chance to see it and to talk to the boys, we'll have a statement. That's it for the moment." Teffner hung up and turned to the two men. "You won't believe what's going on," he sighed.

"Are they still being held?" Meeker asked.

"They're out. As of six-fifteen this evening. No charges filed for the moment."

"Are they at the ballpark?"

Teffner shook his head. "I didn't think, what with all that's going on, that they ought to play tonight."

"Right," John/John said without conviction. Completely at a loss, he began quietly to wheeze.

"So legally, at the moment, there's no problem," Meeker said.

"Not if they don't refile."

"There may be no legal problem but that doesn't mean we don't have a problem. A major problem. We have a public relations Chernobyl on our hands. How the fuck do you get a drink around here?"

"You have to go down to the bar."

"What kind of a hotel is this?" Meeker went over to the refrigerator and opened it. "You don't even have a beer in here?"

Teffner shook his head. The phone rang again. He picked up. "Ken Teffner . . ." He covered up the mouthpiece with his hand and whispered, "It's NBC."

"Tell them to call back," Meeker said.

"We'll have no comment for another hour," he said into the phone and hung up.

"Ken, do me a favor. Take the phone off the hook, will you?"

Teffner took the receiver and laid it on the faux ebony end table, then sat down opposite the two other men.

"Are they in the hotel?"

"I don't know," said Teffner. "Dreyfus isn't answering his phone, and Pickett's is off the hook, according to the hotel people."

"All right, let me see if I have this straight. As far as you know, the two of them were kissing in the changing room at Neiman-Marcus. Is that it?"

"As far as I know."

"Nothing more?"

"That's what they told me."

Meeker put his hand on the bridge of his nose and rubbed his sinuses, shook his head and sighed deeply. "Ken, do you know what's going on between the two of them?"

"No."

"Look, we might as well get down to brass tacks here. Are these guys diddling each other?"

Teffner shrugged. "I don't know."

"Ballplayers don't kiss each other."

"I know. I mean, it's hard to believe, isn't it? Randy and D.J.?"

"All right," said Meeker. "First we've got to talk to them, find out what actually happened, then we have to figure out how to handle it."

"The longer we go without making a statement, the worse it's going to be," said Teffner.

Meeker nodded, wondering if he could go down to the bar and bring up a bottle of I. W. Harpen. It was getting harder and harder to get a drink in this goddamn country. He turned to the team owner and said, "John, I think you ought to call your father."

John/John sat there, terror-stricken. He did not want to make that phone call.

"He's going to hear about it on the news, if he hasn't already."

John/John took the inhaler away from his mouth, caught his breath, and mumbled, "What . . . do I say?"

"I guess you better say that the middle of his infield has sprung a leak," said Burton Meeker with a perfectly straight face.

Francis "Fritz" Esterhazy III, the commissioner of baseball, had just made himself a very dry Beefeater martini in his thirty-ninth-floor apartment on Central Park South when he was called to the phone. Easing his bulk into a leather armchair, he sat and listened to one of his administrative assistants recount what had happened in Dallas.

As he was listening, he grabbed the remote-control device from the end table and flicked on the giant TV across the room. Instantly the enormous screen filled with the image of a crowd of reporters standing outside a hotel. Simultaneously listening to the aide on the telephone and to the television, he pieced together the essential developments of what was to be subsequently referred to around baseball as "the Dallas business."

His very first reaction was annoyance that the placidity of his evening had been ruined. He and his wife were to go out for a quiet evening of good food and relaxed conversation about summer homes and fly fishing at a small Northern Italian place in the East Fifties with another couple, an old Princeton friend and his wife. It did not take him long to realize that the plans for the evening would have to be jettisoned.

Fritz Esterhazy was chosen as commissioner largely because he could navigate skillfully among divergent interests. After a career in investment banking in which he made a great deal more money than he could ever possibly use in this lifetime, he had headed up a number of foundations and commissions, where his abilities as a quiet and effective negotiator were greatly appreciated. Then, in the mid-nineties, after labor unrest and drug problems had plagued the game for more than a decade, the baseball owners approached him to bring his low-key, lubricative management style to the game in the hope of ending the turbulence.

At sixty-two, Fritz Esterhazy was a man at the top of his game. He had everything he wanted in life and was looking forward to smooth sailing from here on in. He anticipated another five years as commissioner, enough time to bring baseball into the full flower of health, and then a sybaritic retirement with a rose garden in Mount Kisco, winter months in Palm Springs, the occasional baseball dinner or Hall of Fame inauguration. What he did not need at the moment was a major scandal. And that apparently was what he had.

Almost immediately he realized that if it turned out to be more than a misunderstanding or a prank, it would constitute a deadly attack on the integrity of the game. What had supposedly happened in the changing room in Dallas violated fundamental notions of morality inextricably connected with the game of baseball. There was no way that the sport could accommodate this behavior. It was quite simply heretical, in the purest sense of the word.

Ballplayers were far from perfect human beings, but they were not sexually deviant with one another. They could cheat on their wives, patronize whores, carry on with women on the road, but they could not succumb to the charms of their fellow players. Not in America. Tennis players could. Even football players. They were just athletes. Baseball players were knights of the royal garter.

Whether he liked it or not, Fritz Esterhazy was the defender of the faith. He walked around with the Holy Grail in his pocket. It went with the territory. Baseball had survived the Black Sox scandal, the war, the reserve-clause challenge, drugs, and the Pete Rose business . . . and now this. A couple of ballplayers, stars on a pennant-contending team, one black, one white, get caught with their pants down in Dallas. The entire country was already aware of it. Something had to be done.

And unfortunately, it was going to be Fritz Esterhazy's call. There was no way to pass the buck on this one. He was going to have to decide if this was "conduct detrimental to the best interests of baseball," as it was written in the boilerplate of every contract signed by a ballplayer. And if it was, excommunication was the prescribed remedy.

As he called downstairs to get his car brought around, he thought of the decision that the Archbishop of Canterbury had had to make with regard to Thomas More. This one was more or less in the same ballpark.

Randy had no idea where he was. He had wandered into a shabby part of the city. There were no cabs anywhere. His feet were killing him. He must have walked five miles.

There was a bar on the corner, the door open, the ball game on. He could hear the low-key hum of the fans in the stands, a sound he always found comforting.

He entered and stood for a moment watching Glen Ephard go down swinging, badly fooled on a low outside slider. Then he got change from the bartender and called a cab. While he waited, he watched the game. The Vikings were getting killed, 10–1. Jarvis had made two errors at short.

The cab driver took him back to the hotel through strange parts of the city. The guy made him through the rearview mirror but must have been too embarrassed to say anything. He had the ball game on the radio. It was now 13–1.

Due to an unsubstantiated rumor going around that Randy and D.J. were on a plane back to L.A., the crowd of reporters in front of the hotel had thinned out somewhat, but there were still enough of them to make entering the hotel unnoticed impossible. Randy paid the driver and hurried toward the door, head down. A guy with a microphone moved to block his way, and Randy lowered his shoulder and took him out cleanly, knocking him into a crowd of other reporters. He hurried through the revolving door, got his key and messages from the front desk, and made the elevator a few feet ahead of the vultures.

Upstairs in the hallway, a couple of enterprising guys were camped outside his room. As Randy approached, one of them started to raise his camera, but Randy got his foot into it and punted it twenty yards on the fly with good hang time.

Once inside his room, he deadbolted the door and stood there for a moment, catching his breath and feeling the adrenaline slowly dissipate. He looked down at the crumpled messages in his hand. Among those from reporters, newspaper editors, and TV personalities, were ones from Mendes Fuad and Ken Teffner.

He went over to the telephone, its message light blinking frantically, and dialed the Egyptian's home number.

"Yes?" The shrink's voice sounded like it was underwater.

"It's me, doc."

"Yes . . ."

Jesus! Is that all he could say, like he hadn't heard anything? Didn't he watch TV or listen to the radio? Didn't he know what the fuck was going on?

"You heard the news, right?"

"Yes. What seems to be the problem?"

"What seems to be the problem?! My whole goddamn life is fucked up. How's that for a problem?"

"I see."

"What am I going to do?"

"What do you want to do?"

"What do I want to do? I want everything to go back to the way it was before. I want to play baseball and . . ."

"And what?"

"And . . . you know . . ."

"No, I don't know."

It took a moment for Randy to actually say it. "I want to be with him."

"I don't see that that's outside the realm of possibility, do you?"

He really didn't get it. Maybe in Egypt it was all right for ballplayers to kiss in changing rooms, but it didn't go over so hot in this country.

"Doc, they're going to rake us over the coals."

"Perhaps. But if you can do what you want to do, that is, play baseball and be with him, what difference does it make?"

"You don't understand. The guys on the other teams, the bench jockeys. They're going to kill us. And the writers are going to write all this shit."

"There's nothing to be done about that."

"And what about my wife and kids?"

"That will be painful. But as I have said to you before, growth is pain."

Taking the phone with him, Randy walked over and opened the window shades. He was six floors above an interior atrium. The windows were sealed. Another No Suicide room.

"You know something, doc, I couldn't even jump out of the window here if I wanted to. They seal them up."

"Do you want to?"

"It'd solve a shitload of problems."

"Perhaps, but it would leave you with one big problem."

"What's that?"

"You'd be dead."

"So, doc, I should just grow and have pain. Is that it?"

"That's it."

"Thanks a lot. I'll be in touch."

He hung up and tried D.J.'s room, but there was a busy signal. Phone off the hook. It was one floor down. Did he dare try to sneak down there with the reporters all over the place? He decided to call Ken Teffner first.

"How're you doing?" he said when the PR guy picked up.

"Randy, is that you?"

"Yeah."

"Where have you been? We've been trying to reach you for hours."

"I took a walk."

"Listen, could you come down here? We'd like to talk things over with you."

"Who's there?"

"John's here and Burt Meeker."

"Anybody else?"

"So is D.J."

"D.J.?"

"Uh-huh. We've been kicking this thing around together, all of us."

"Oh yeah . . . ?"

"Come on down. We'll fill you in. I think we're getting a handle on this."

As soon as Randy walked into Ken Teffner's room and saw D.J. sitting on one of the couches next to John/John, he smelled that something had gone down. There was a look on his lover's face that read capitulation. A deal had been cut in his absence, and he was about to be pressured into signing off on it.

Teffner greeted him with a big smile, pumped his hand, and led him into the room, introducing him to a guy in a suit that had to cost over a grand easy.

"Burt Meeker. Randy Dreyfus."

The guy got up and shook his hand. "How are you, Randy?"

Randy nodded.

"Hell of a season you're having."

"Yeah . . ."

"Sit down, Randy. Want a Coke?"

"No thanks."

Randy sat down on a chair beside D.J., so he wouldn't have to look at him in front of the others. The game was going on the TV, the sound turned down low. Randy could see that they were down to the mop-up guys in the bullpen.

"Let me tell you where we are on this, Randy," Teffner began. "According to D.J., the whole thing's been blown completely out of proportion. You guys were just messing around, having a good time. Nothing really happened over there in that dressing room. It was just horseplay. . . ."

Horseplay? Jesus. They had to be kidding.

"So here's what we're going to do," Teffner continued. "We're going to call a little press conference with both of you and put it out on the wires. No big thing. We'll kid around a bit, laugh, make the whole thing a big nothing that just got blown up by the press. You guys could sort of like kiss and make up. You know, a big buss on the cheek, that kind of thing. It could actually be terrific, you know, kissing to make up for a kiss. . . . So what do you think?"

For a moment, Randy didn't say anything. He turned to look at D.J., but the second baseman avoided his eyes. Then he turned back to Teffner and said, "I want to talk to D.J."

"What?"

"I want to talk to D.J. . . . alone."

Teffner looked at Meeker, who looked at John/John. Nobody said anything for a moment. Then Teffner smiled uneasily and said, "Randy, we're all on the same team here . . ."

"Could you guys go take a walk down the hall or something?"

The three men hesitated for a moment, then got up, not looking very happy about it. As soon as they had exited, Randy went over and turned up the sound on the TV. They could have the room under surveillance. You never knew.

Then he walked back and stood in front of D.J., arms folded.

D.J. shook his head sadly and said, "Randy, it's no use. We got to cop a plea here."

"Yeah, but did you hear what they want us to do?"

D.J. nodded.

"You want to do that shit?"

"Not particularly. But I don't see that we have a whole lot of choice. This thing could get very messy."

"A fucking press conference?"

"Look, all we have to do is say we had a couple of beers, got a little silly, and were . . . wrestling in the changing room."

"Wrestling?"

"Yeah. Screwing around. Like he said, horseplay."

Randy walked over to the window. He stood there for a long moment, his back to D.J.

"Listen," D.J. went on, "there's this clause in the contract that everybody signs about conduct detrimental to the best interests of the game, or some bullshit like that. The commissioner can decide to invoke it. He could throw us out of baseball. For life."

Still not facing him, Randy said very softly, "What about us?"

"Huh?"

"What about us? What about you and me?"

"What do you mean?"

"Is this it? Is it over?"

D.J. didn't respond, and Randy was afraid to turn around and look at him. Finally, D.J. said in a quiet, pained voice, "I don't know, Randy. We're fucking with our entire futures here."

"Yeah . . ."

"It's not just you and me. It's your wife, your kids. There's the rest of the team, the pennant race. . . . There are a lot of things going down here."

Randy peered through the No Suicide windowpanes out into the murky Dallas night. From somewhere across town he could hear a police siren. In the room behind him was the steady patter of the local announcer describing the play-by-play of the bottom of the eighth inning of a game that was, for all intents and purposes, already over. They would lose a half-game in the standings, maybe a full game, depending upon what happened later that night on the Coast. Randy didn't give a shit about any of it.

All he could think about was that he was standing less than ten feet away from the man he loved. He wanted him to come over and hold him, comfort him, assure him that what had happened in the changing room in Neiman-Marcus that day was not just horseplay. Nothing else mattered to Randy Dreyfus at the moment.

Everything else was just a ball game.

XV

Milt Zola had been to his share of press conferences in his career, but the one that was held in the atrium of the Dallas Embassy Suites the day after the Dreyfus-Pickett business was among the more peculiar ones. Besides the press from Dallas, there were network stringers and writers who had taken the first flight out of L.A. that morning. The giant atrium was filled with reporters and cameramen, while businessmen, caught coincidentally in the middle of this sudden media storm, fought their way through the cables to get their complimentary breakfast.

At precisely 10 A.M., Randy Dreyfus, D. J. Pickett, John D. F. White, Jr., and Ken Teffner appeared at a table set up at the far end of the atrium, away from the steaming hot plates of French toast and pancakes. Each man had a microphone in front of him and a glass of water. Randy Dreyfus and D. J. Pickett were wearing sport jackets and ties and were seated at either end of the table, separated like a couple of boxers at a prefight weigh-in ceremony. Everyone looked glum.

Teffner switched on his mike, cleared his voice, and peered out into the assembled photographic equipment. "Good morning. Boy, some turnout. You'd think we'd just clinched the division." Big smile. "Though, after what the Rangers did to us last night, we're pretty anxious to get out of Texas." Another big smile. No laughs. Teffner was playing to a tough house.

"In any event, we'll try to make this quick so that you guys can get on with your work today. I'll start by reading a prepared statement and then open up for a few questions."

He took a piece of paper out of his jacket pocket. "Yesterday at approximately one-thirty P.M., two players on the Los Angeles Valley Vikings, Randy Dreyfus and D. J. Pickett, were arrested in a department store in Dallas as the result of a videotape recorded by a surveillance camera. Upon examining the videotape and determining that the arresting officer had misunderstood the behavior that appeared on it, the Dallas County district attorney's office dropped all charges against Randy Dreyfus and D. J. Pickett and released them from custody. The publicity surrounding the incident, unfortunately, created the impression that certain immoral acts had been committed. Nothing could be farther from the truth. The ballplayers, who are teammates and good friends, were merely engaged in some spirited hijinks as a way of dissipating some of the tension that inevitably occurs during a tight pennant race. In any event, Randy Dreyfus, D. J. Pickett, and the entire Los Angeles Valley Vikings organization sincerely regret any inconvenience or embarrassment to the City of Dallas that this incident may have caused."

Teffner cleared his throat again in the way of peroration and put away the paper as questions were shot at him from all over the room. He pointed his finger in the direction of the NBC correspondent. "Fred?"

"Can you describe a little more precisely what these . . . *hijinks* were?"

"Wrestling, kidding around, jostling each other. You know, ballplayers do this sort of thing all the time. I mean, after a big win, they grab each other, they hug each other—it's perfectly normal. . . ."

As soon as Teffner took a breath, more questions were shouted and hands were raised. Teffner selected a woman who worked for UPI.

"Why were they in the changing room together?" she asked.

"Well, Randy was buying a pair of trousers. And D.J. was telling him how they fit. Right, guys?"

He turned to the two ballplayers, who dutifully nodded. Teffner recognized the baseball writer from the *Los Angeles Times*. "Sid?"

"Were they drunk?"

Teffner had anticipated this one and had a prepared response. "Randy and D.J. had in fact had a few beers. Maybe one too many. As I've said, sometimes during a close pennant race, a ballplayer has a tendency to take a drink. In any case, they have both agreed to confer with our team substance-abuse counselor with the possibility of entering a program should it be determined that there is a problem in this area. . . ."

Before Teffner had a chance to select the next reporter, a question was shouted out loudly and distinctly from the rear. "What about the tape? Can we see the tape?"

It was a question that Teffner wanted to avoid, but everyone in the room had heard it as, presumably, did the TV audience that would see excerpts of the press conference taped for their local news later that evening. He needed to defuse the issue of the tape quickly and efficiently.

"The tape," he said, "is in the hands of the district attorney's office. And since it is not being considered as evidence in a prosecution, it would seem to me that no useful purpose would be served in making it public. One more question and that'll be it."

Teffner quickly pointed at a reporter in the first row, someone he didn't know. Any port in a storm. "Sir?"

The man glanced at his notebook, looked up, and said, "At any point during these so-called hijinks did the lips of Randy Dreyfus and those of D. J. Pickett make contact?"

The question floated through the room like a wave of tear gas. It resurrected the idea of the kiss, the imagery that Teffner had been laboring so assiduously to erase from the public's imagination. He needed to field this one cleanly and get it to first before the runner. His best shot was a joke. So he turned to Randy and D.J. with a big smile and said, "Hey, were you guys necking in there or what?" As he said it, he laughed loudly.

It worked. It got a Pavlovian response. Everybody laughed. Almost everybody. The reporter who'd asked the question didn't laugh. And neither did Milt Zola.

During the photo opportunity that followed, there were a number of shots of Randy planting a big kiss on D.J.'s cheek and vice versa. It ran on the front page of the New York *Daily News* with the headline A KISS IS JUST A KISS.

As a stroke of public relations brinksmanship, Ken Teffner's performance was virtuoso. The press conference was a masterfully deft piece of footwork in the face of a very treacherous situation. The public bought it. The story played the evening news that day and then died a quick death, relegated to the status of an anecdote.

There were a few smoldering embers, cracks made by other ballplayers, bench-jockeying, an ad-hoc reference here and there in a writer's column, the usual bevy of bad jokes. How do you get to second base on the Vikings? Kiss the shortstop. And so forth.

But by and large Teffner had pulled it off. He had sold Chernobyl as a minor nuclear incident, barely worth discussing. The Whites should have given him a promotion and a raise. Fritz Esterhazy should have given him a knighthood. He should have been voted into the Hall of Fame. Ken Teffner had managed to preserve the integrity of the game of baseball.

There were a few people, however, who didn't buy it, who had trouble dismissing the incident as tension-relieving hijinks in the midst of a pennant race. Susie Dreyfus, for one, found herself troubled by the revelations made at the press conference. She sat in her breakfast nook, watching excerpts from it on television, staring at the strange man in the sport jacket and tie who was her husband. They must have given him the tie. He never took one with him on the road.

After her fit of temporary catatonia the previous night in the Bob's Big Boy parking lot, she had driven directly home, given the twins dinner, then retired for the night, telling Mikva to let the machine answer the phone, which had not stopped ringing since she'd walked in the door.

She had taken a Halcion and went to sleep adrift in anger and confusion. When she had awoken this morning, she felt drugged and awful. Having managed to get the girls off to school, she had been sitting haggardly over reheated coffee, trying to figure out whether to call him, when Mikva came in to tell her that her husband was on television.

Susie flipped on the kitchen TV and saw clips from the news conference. She listened as Ken Teffner explained that it had all been a mistake, that nothing had really happened in the changing room in Neiman-Marcus. She should have been relieved. Randy wasn't kissing his teammate, after all.

And yet she didn't feel relieved at all. If anything, she felt worse. What about the handkerchief? The goddamn handkerchief wouldn't go away. Knowing who it belonged to did not necessarily answer the question of what it was doing in her husband's laundry.

There were probably a number of good reasons why her husband wound up with his second baseman's handkerchief. Maybe he borrowed it during a sudden sneezing attack. Maybe they were doing magic tricks and Randy forgot to return it. Maybe it got hot suddenly and he needed to shield his head from the sun. . . . But she wasn't crazy about any of these explanations. And there were still the strange jaunts around town, the aimless driving on the freeways, the 1:30 A.M. workouts in the weight room on the road.

No, Susie Dreyfus was not comforted by the press conference that morning. One way or another, she was convinced that she was losing her husband. And she didn't know what to do about it.

Another person who didn't buy Ken Teffner's dog-and-pony show was Milt Zola. The veteran sportswriter had been around too long to accept certain behavior on the part of ballplayers. Kiss or no kiss, ballplayers didn't accompany each other into the changing rooms of department stores. In the first place, they didn't shop for clothes together. They went with their wives when they were home, or they went alone. Ballplayers bought new golf clubs together, fishing tackle, hunting equipment. They bought porno videos and brought them back to play on the hotel VCR. They hung out together in bars with go-go dancers and loud music. They worked out together in health clubs. But they didn't buy trousers together and help each other with the fit. That one didn't compute.

Milt Zola had the feeling he was sitting on a very big story. This baby could blow sky high. He wondered if he was the only sports-writer in L.A. who had picked up the signs even before the Dallas incident. And if he was, what the hell was he going to do about it?

Pete Zabriskie didn't buy the story either. His bullshit meter was finely calibrated, and this one registered in the red zone. As far as he was concerned, the owner of the handkerchief was D. J. Pickett, and the two guys were pulling each other's chains. End of story.

It pissed him off that he had missed the faggot angle and let himself be sidetracked by the dog-snuffing business. Christ, he had trailed the guy right to his boyfriend and walked away from it. There they were, the two of them, on the golf course in broad daylight. They probably snuck off into the woods and did each other. He could have nailed them with the telephoto he kept in the glove compartment.

He'd have to call the blonde now and ask if she wanted to go for the full package. Eight-by-ten glossies. They always went over well with the lawyers. The guy would settle out of court and fast.

In his office on Park Avenue in New York, Fritz Esterhazy switched off his TV and breathed a deep sigh of relief. He had spent the greater part of the previous evening reviewing various responses that he would have to make to the situation, filling half a legal pad with notes.

Now he could put away the scribbled press statements and go back to eating osso buco with his friends.

Whether or not he believed the story out of Dallas was another question. Fritz Esterhazy had not gotten to be commissioner of baseball because of an overscrupulous dedication to ferreting out the truth. He had reached the stage in life where the truth was more often a bothersome detail to be accommodated than a value to be pursued. What was important was continuity and tradition. The game had to go on. It was bigger than any individual or any problem. There was the endless succession of innings ticking away in their leisurely rhythm, the slow accretion of statistics, the ebb and flow of victory and defeat. It was his job to ensure that this process continued unimpeded.

So, feeling he had dodged a bullet, the commissioner returned to the soft-edged business of his job. On his desk were a number of suggestions from his staff about who should sing the national anthem for the opening game of the World Series, now less than a month away. Among the listed names, which included Luciano Pavarotti and Barbra Streisand, was the Mormon Tabernacle Choir. Given the moral climate in the country these days, that wouldn't be a bad choice.

Charlie Gonse, sitting in the manager's office in the visitors' clubhouse in Arlington Stadium, had a list in front of him as well. His consisted of players available to play that night. Ken Teffner had called him an hour before to say that Dreyfus and Pickett would be back in uniform for the game. And not a moment too soon. They were on the verge of losing a series to the sixth-place Texas Rangers.

Like Fritz Esterhazy, Charlie Gonse was not overly concerned about what had actually happened in Neiman-Marcus. He had been around ballplayers too long to let himself get sidetracked by their problems. As far as he was concerned, most of them had a couple of screws loose. If you examined them too carefully, you'd probably wind up locking up all of them. What Charlie Gonse was concerned about was winning ball games. Oakland had beaten Seattle the night before, and the Vikings were now clinging to a half-game lead.

The players dribbled in for early batting practice. Rennie Pannizardi had a hamstring that needed taping, and he sat in the trainer's room talking to Bernie Lazarre about the press conference that morning.

"You catch Randy and D.J. on TV today?"

"Yeah."

"You got to watch what the fuck you're doing in this town, huh?"

"Yeah."

"You fart the wrong way, they put you in jail."

"Yeah."

Lazarre was getting a bruised thumb worked on. It had been jammed the last night of the home stand and hadn't felt right since.

"Guy like Randy, married to a fox . . . what kind of shit're they trying to lay on him?"

"Yeah."

"I mean, imagine wanting to fuck D.J. when you could stick it to Susie Dreyfus?"

"Yeah."

Both Randy and D.J. arrived late, skipping batting practice. None of the others said much to them besides nodding and mumbling hello. Spic Mendoza came over to Randy and said, "Son-of-a-bitching fuck, huh?"

Randy nodded quickly, hoping he would go away.

"Shit-ass motherfucker, that's what I think, that asshole put you and D.J. in fucking jail, Randy."

"Right, Spic."

That night Randy felt as if he were playing the game underwater. His timing at the plate was badly off. He struck out twice and flied to right the first three times up. Fortunately, nothing hard was hit to him in the field and Axel Most was on the mound, so they were still in the ball game in the eighth inning.

Randy kept glancing left toward the bag, trying to catch D.J.'s eye. Al De Mun, the infield coach, was waving a towel out of the corner of the dugout, frantically trying to get Randy's attention and move him farther toward the hole, but it was too late. The guy hit a two-hopper that skidded between Randy and Rennie Pannizardi into left field.

Randy wasn't in the game. He wasn't even in the goddamn ballpark. He didn't know where he was. They won the game that night in spite of him, Glen Ephard hitting an opposite-field, wind-blown home run in the eleventh. After the game, he skipped the postgame buffet, showered, and grabbed a cab back to the hotel. He sat in his room and waited for D.J. to get in, ringing his room every five minutes.

When D.J. finally picked up, he said, "You want to get together?"

There was a pause on the other end before D.J. replied, "Randy, I think we got to cool it for a while."

"How long is *a while*?"

"Until this blows over."

Randy nodded to himself, twisting the phone cord around his finger, then he said, "D.J., can I ask you a question?"

"Go ahead."

"Am I just another guy in your life?"

"No."

"You mean that?"

"Yes, I do."

"So . . . what are we going to do?"

"I don't know."

There was another long pause. Randy didn't know if he could take the wrong answer to the next question. "D.J.," he said, "what if I came over late, about one . . . ?"

"Tonight?"

"I'll be real careful."

Another long pause, then Randy added, "You know, this Hall of Fame shit. When you think about it, it's just a copper plaque on the wall someplace in upstate New York, right?"

It seemed like forever before D.J. replied. "I'll leave the door unlocked."

XVI

Don Amarillo, the substance-abuse counselor for the Vikings, flew out to Kansas City to see Randy Dreyfus and D. J. Pickett. As Ken Teffner had assured the press, if there was an alcohol problem here, they would nip it in the bud.

Amarillo was a former ballplayer, a pitcher on the Orioles in the eighties who had drunk himself out of a promising career. He had written a book, *Crash Landing*, which recounted his meteoric plunge from stardom. Since then he had become a leading figure in the substance-abuse field, touring the country, lecturing and consulting.

He was a six-foot-four-inch black man with a swift, athletic stride and a homicidal smile, the same smile that used to intimidate batters when he was throwing high inside fastballs at ninety-eight miles an hour dead drunk. It was a miracle that he hadn't killed anyone, given that he could barely see the plate most of the time.

Teffner made sure the team's move was picked up and reported by the media. He wanted it known that the Vikings were a progressive organization that understood the problems of substance abuse among big-league athletes. They were going to deal with this incident and put it behind them.

The morning after the team arrived in Kansas City, Amarillo arranged to meet with each of the two ballplayers in his hotel room. Randy was first. He sat on a straight chair, six feet away from Amarillo, also on a straight chair, and did his best to maintain eye contact with the guy. He looked to Randy like a professional killer.

"Hey, Randy, I want you to know right from the top here that whatever the problem is, we're going to fix it. Together. You and me. We're going to come out of this in A-one condition. You understand what I'm saying?"

Randy nodded.

"I know where you're at. I've been there. I know how tough it is out there in the glare of all that publicity and money. The pressure's on. Every turn at bat. Gotta do it, gotta get a hit, gotta come through. So maybe you think you need a little hand dealing with the shit, right?"

"Right."

"So you take a drink or a snort or an upper or whatever the hell it is to give you the edge or just get you through it. But pretty soon it doesn't give you any edge at all. It becomes *the* thing. You find yourself out there thinking about it all the time. Waiting on it. Figuring, 'As soon as I get through this inning or this game I can get back in there and have a drink.' That's all there is. . . . You with me here?"

"Uh-huh."

"I pitched drunk for nearly two seasons. Let me tell you something. If I didn't do that shit, I could've pitched for twenty years. I had a right arm that was a gift from God, Randy. And you know what I did with it? Fifty-seven games, career record fourteen and thirty-one, E.R.A. four point eight seven. Goddamn waste . . . So let's talk. What's going on?"

Randy looked at him and shrugged, trying to match the sincerity of Amarillo's expression.

"Hey, it's just you and me here. There ain't no one else around. Nothing you tell me leaves this room. So whaddaya say? Want to tell me what's going on?"

Randy felt that if he didn't say anything at all, the guy might get out of line. So he confessed. "I . . . had a beer the other day."

"All right. There's a start. You had a beer. Good. Very good. How many?"

"One."

"One beer?"

"A Miller Lite."

"You're telling me you only had one beer?"

"Uh-huh. I had it with a pizza at lunch. Sometimes when I have pizza I like a beer. I prefer lite beer because it doesn't fill me up."

Amarillo's ironclad features broke out into a frightening smile. For a moment Randy thought he was going to laugh out loud. He got up and went to the window, looked out for a moment, then turned around and looked back at Randy. He wasn't smiling anymore.

"Okay, you want to bullshit me? Fine. You waste your time, my time, nothing gets done. Randy, don't you see that the only way to begin this process is to admit there's a problem? I understand. I've *been* there. I know it's hard to say it. But you gotta say it. You got to start by saying, *'I got a substance-abuse problem.'* "

Randy wasn't entirely sure that the guy was playing with a full deck. He could go off the rails, pull a knife out of his pocket. He used to throw the ball ninety-eight fucking miles an hour drunk. There was no telling what he was capable of doing. So he said, "Okay, so maybe I have a substance-abuse problem."

Amarillo flashed his big, lethal smile. He walked back over to Randy and said, "Good. Very good. Now was that so hard?"

"No . . ."

"I want you to know, Randy, that you just took the first and most difficult step. Get up."

"Huh?"

"Stand up."

Randy got up. He noticed they were about the same height, but the guy had hands the size of meat hooks.

Amarillo opened his arms wide and said, "I'm going to give you a hug. This hug is going to be our contract, yours and mine, to begin the job of taking care of the problem. This is the most important moment in your new life, Randy. Come here."

Randy hesitated, calculating his options. If the guy was a lefty he could be in for a hell of a scene, but he wasn't interested. There was only one man in his life right now.

"Come on," Amarillo urged, "make the commitment. Today's the first day of the rest of your life."

Randy allowed himself to be hugged by Don Amarillo. What the fuck. If he was going to have a substance-abuse problem, he might as well do it right.

Randy Dreyfus's newly revealed substance-abuse problem had immediate repercussions on his commercial career. Barry Fuchsia got a call from the president of Meditex expressing the company's concern about the image their star athlete was projecting. First the business in Dallas, and now a drinking problem. Barry Fuchsia assured him that the Dallas business was over and done with, a misunderstanding with the local police, and that the substance-abuse thing was minor. They were putting him in a program just as a precautionary measure. Not to worry. Randy Dreyfus didn't have a drinking problem.

Randy got a call from his agent in the hotel in Kansas City.

"What the hell's going on with you?" he said, not even saying hello.

"What do you mean?"

"First this bullshit in Dallas and then a substance-abuse program. How do you expect me to close this deal when you keep pulling this shit?"

"Barry, nothing happened in Dallas. Didn't you see the press conference?"

"Yeah, I saw it. It didn't do you a whole lot of good, you know. Spokesmen for athlete's foot powder don't screw around in the changing room at Neiman-Marcus."

"We weren't doing anything."

"Yeah. Well, next time buy your clothes mail-order. What's the story with the booze?"

"Nothing. The team sent this guy out to see me. We talked, that's all. You know, like I have a beer now and then."

"You shitting me?"

"No."

"Listen, we're at a very critical stage here. You fuck up and they're going to let you go free agent. And then it's a whole new ball game. The elevator goes back to the ground floor. You understand what I'm saying?"

"Right."

"Lay off the sauce, okay?"

"Okay."

After he hung up, Randy realized that Fuchsia hadn't said anything about the deal. Were they still stuck on performance incentive clauses? Would they ever close this deal? Did it matter?

Randy wasn't at all sure what was important anymore. There was his career, there was the pennant race, there was Susie and the twins, there was the Hall of Fame, and there was D.J. Why couldn't he have them all? Why couldn't he just play ball, then do an hour in the weight room with D.J., go home occasionally and have dinner with Susie, take the twins out to the park, win the batting title, sign for $7 million in the third year with an option for a fourth, and get elected to the Hall of Fame?

Why not have it all? Hit for the cycle . . .

The phone rang. Randy picked up and heard the gravelly voice of Milt Zola.

"Hey, Randy, how're you doing?"

"All right."

"Can I buy you a drink—I mean, a cup of coffee?"

"Gee, I don't know, Milt, I'm kind of busy at the moment."

"Look, Randy, I think there's something going on with you and the Vikings. I think they're jerking you around."

"You talking about the contract?"

"I'm not talking about the contract."

"What are you talking about?"

"Substance abuse."

"Hey, I talked to a guy. It's being taken care of."

"Listen, I've been a baseball writer for twenty-seven years, and I can spot a boozer a mile away."

"Well, you know, we're working on the problem. We're going to lick it. You know, one day at a time . . ."

"Randy, you don't have a substance-abuse problem."

"You talk to Don Amarillo?"

"Don Amarillo works for the Vikings."

"Who the hell are you to tell me I don't have a fucking substance-abuse problem, Zola?"

"I'm just doing my job. It's a story, and I got to run with it."

"Listen, you print that I don't have a substance-abuse problem, and I'll sue your ass off for libel."

"My husband's cheating on me and I don't know whether it's with a woman or a man, and what's really weird is that I don't know which one is worse."

Mendes Fuad sat impassively in his overstuffed armchair, chin resting on his long hairy fingers, listening to Susie Dreyfus. From time to time he nodded slowly to give some indication that he was actually following the monologue and not merely drifting off in the drowsy midmorning air. The worry beads clicked in desultory rhythm with the sucking-air sound of the fish tank's motor. Susie paused to catch her breath, then resumed.

"Losing him to another woman makes me angry. Losing him to a man makes me sad. It makes me think that maybe it was my fault. Maybe I did something horrible to him to turn him off to women. Maybe I, like, castrated him or something."

"If this is in fact the case," offered Fuad, in one of his rare apostrophes, "it occurred long before you knew him, possibly in the genetic configuration that he received from his parents or even his grandparents. Feeling guilty about it is basically a smoke screen for your anger."

"But how can I be angry at him for something he can't control?"

"Control has nothing to do with it. You are angry at him for putting his penis into somebody else instead of into you. It basically comes down to that. Putting penises in the wrong places."

Susie did not like the image. Almost everything this man said, when he said anything at all, was upsetting to her. What was the point of spending $175 an hour and coming out feeling worse? This was the last session. Definitely. She wasn't coming back again.

She left the office in a state of curdled fury and drove to

Hollywood to do her radio program. She was in no mood to dispense advice to women about menstrual cramps and contact paper in their pantries, but somehow she would have to get through it. She just hoped that no one wanted to talk about cheating husbands.

As she sped down Wilshire, she decided that it couldn't go on like this any longer. She would have it out with Randy once and for all. They were living in a state of suspended animation. Coming and going in the same house, sleeping side by side in the same bed, sharing the paper every morning in the breakfast nook. While on the road all this stuff was happening. He gets caught in the changing room in Neiman-Marcus with his second baseman. He's giving press conferences, talking about joining an alcohol-abuse program. Alcohol abuse! Randy had two beers and he fell asleep.

He was due back from Kansas City Sunday night. It was time to put the cards on the table, clear the air. No more bullshit. She would ask him point blank where he was putting his penis. And then, as far as she was concerned, he could keep it there.

The Vikings won two out of three in Kansas City and managed a split of the road trip, losing only a game in the standings to Oakland and California. Randy was back in a slump, popping everything up. In addition to all the other distractions in his life, he had to spend long afternoon sessions with Don Amarillo getting hugged. He had no time to see D.J., who had to do morning sessions with the substance-abuse counselor.

He and D.J. were afraid to talk on the phone and afraid to meet in the middle of the night in each other's rooms with all the attention focused on them now. Randy was convinced people were watching them. He couldn't get Milt Zola's phone call out of his mind. How much did the writer know? And what was he going to do about it?

As he sat on the plane flying west over the Rockies, he realized that in a few hours he would have to face Susie. He hadn't called her all week, not even during the business in Dallas, and she was probably furious. What was he going to tell *her* about substance abuse and hijinks in the changing room at Neiman-Marcus?

With all this coursing through his beleaguered brain, as well as the memory of having gone 5-for-23 on the trip, he was not prepared to be summoned for a chat with his manager. Charlie Gonse sent Al De Mun to get him.

Randy put down the copy of *USA Today* that he wasn't reading, and followed De Mun up the aisle. He found Gonse slumped down in his seat doodling on a piece of paper.

"Sit down, take a load off," the manager said to Randy, waving De Mun off.

Randy said, "You want to see me, Charlie?"

"No. I sent Al down to get you so you could sit here and keep me company."

"What's wrong?"

"What's wrong? He asks me what's wrong? I got a team that's sinking like the *Titanic*. I got a shortstop who hits everything two miles straight up in the air and who can't throw a paraplegic out from the hole and looks half the time like he doesn't even know what city he's in, let alone what team he's playing. That's what's wrong."

"I had a bad road trip."

"If you didn't spend your time trying on pants in department stores and hitting the sauce maybe you would have had a better road trip."

"I'm in a program for the drinking."

"Yeah. Great. How about a program for playing baseball? How about a program for hitting line drives into the gaps? How about a program for taking a three-one pitch and drawing a walk now and then so that we could win a ball game? Why don't you join one of those programs?"

Randy sensed they were not communicating very effectively. But, at the moment, this might be preferable to discussing some of the actual problems in Randy's life. And so he sat there and nodded and let the manager go on in his usual haphazard manner until he was abruptly dismissed and sent back to the rear of the plane.

On his way he passed D.J., and they locked eyes for a brief moment. There he was, his lover, sitting with his copy of *Time* magazine and his glass of tomato juice. Randy's heart filled with tenderness. He wanted badly to be with him. He wished he were going home to D.J.'s condo in Thousand Oaks tonight, where they could be together on the big bed with the satin sheets.

Back in his seat, he opened *USA Today* again, but the words swam in front of him. He put it down and closed his eyes. He felt like shit. He felt like his life was coming apart at the seams like a badly stitched baseball. Growth is pain. Just like the Egyptian said. Right.

Fuck him. And his fish.

They had dinner in the family nook annex, Randy, Susie, and the twins, with Calvin lying on the Navajo throw rug in front of the sandstone hearth. Molly and Dolly did most of the talking, prattling on about the other girls in their class and how badly they dressed. Randy and Susie sat opposite each other, avoiding eye contact.

After dinner and TV, the twins went off to bed, and Randy and Susie were left alone on either end of the coral-and-beige sectional sofa staring blankly at the screen. After a few minutes Susie picked up the remote and switched the TV off. Suddenly it was dead quiet in the room except for the sound of Calvin chewing on his leather doggie toy.

"Randy, we have to talk."

He nodded, looking away.

"There's something wrong, isn't there?"

He nodded again, then shrugged, as if to qualify the nod.

"I feel like we're miles apart," she went on. "We don't communicate anymore, we don't touch. We don't make love . . ."

He scratched the back of his ear and stretched his neck as if to get the kinks out of it, a gesture he often made when stepping out of the batter's box after a called strike. Then he stepped back in and fouled one off.

"I've been going through some problems," he said.

"What kind of problems?"

"I've been popping the ball up."

She glared at him, anger flashing. "I don't believe this! I'm talking about a crisis in our marriage and you're talking about popping the ball up! Is that the only thing that matters to you?"

Susie looked straight at him for a long moment, then came in with the high, hard one.

"Is there somebody else?"

"What?"

"Are you involved with somebody else?"

"I don't know."

"What do you mean you don't know? You either are or you aren't involved with somebody else."

"It's not that simple."

"Why don't you try to explain? Maybe I can understand."

Where did he begin? The rod in the shower in Cleveland? The Chinese dinner in Ventura? The weight room in Oakland? How could he explain things to her? So he sat there and said nothing at all. Finally, she asked him, "What happened in Dallas, Randy?"

"You mean that crazy thing in Neiman-Marcus?"

"That's what I mean."

"Nothing."

"Nothing? It was all over the news."

"D.J. and me were messing around and some asshole security guard arrested us. The whole thing was ridiculous."

"Randy, maybe you ought to see someone."

"You mean like a shrink?"

"Yes. Maybe a shrink can help you figure out what you're doing messing around in a changing room with another guy."

He held her look without blinking. It was three-and-two. The payoff pitch was on its way.

"And when you figure out the answer to that question, maybe you can figure out if you're still interested in being married to me. I'd sort of like to know."

With that, she got up abruptly and walked out of the room, leaving Randy alone with the dog. He sat there for a long time replaying the conversation in his head, trying to figure out what had actually been said. Not a whole lot. He had merely hung in there fouling off pitches, waiting her out.

What happened in Dallas, Randy?

Calvin came over and put his chin in Randy's lap. It was a gesture of affection, and it took Randy completely off guard. The dog that he had tried to get rid of, not once but twice, was offering his sympathy. Randy found himself absently caressing his head.

He wondered if you could strangle a dog. How difficult would it be for a man with strong hands, like Randy, to cut off the air to his windpipe? He could say that the dog choked on a bone. He had done everything he could to save him, artificial respiration, the Heimlich Maneuver, but it had been too late. The dog died in his arms on the way to the emergency room. . . .

But Randy no longer felt like murdering the dog. Given the state of his life, he needed all the friends he could get. Maybe they were finally starting to bond, like Dr. Bob had said they should. He sat there scratching Calvin gently behind the ears, in the spot that he liked, every now and then letting his thumb slip down to feel the contours of the dog's throat.

The actual videotape of the hijinks in the changing room at Neiman-Marcus had been seen only by H.A.L. Porter, the Dallas County district attorney, and several members of his staff. After the district attorney decided not to file charges against Randy Dreyfus and D. J. Pickett, he imposed a gag order. He called his staff into his office, closed the door, and told them that he didn't want this stuff going around. It was bad for Dallas, bad for baseball, bad for America.

"We don't need this type of publicity in Dallas. As far as I'm concerned, the incident is closed, and I don't want to hear about it again and I don't want you going home and telling your wives and families about what you saw on that tape. You didn't see anything on that tape that's worth telling anybody else about. Whatever inversion of the laws of nature you believe you may have observed on that videotape is not, in my judgment, a violation of the laws of the State of Texas at this time, and therefore not within the purview of this office. Basically, it's none of our business or anybody else's. Have I made myself clear?"

The deputy D.A.'s nodded in unison. And that was that. They filed out of the office, sworn to secrecy. The videotape would remain in the lower right-hand desk drawer of the district attorney's desk until such time as he could get around to disposing of it. He planned to take it with him next time he went fishing and deep-six it in Lake Whiting, chained to a block of cement.

XVII

The John D. F. White, Sr., Day-Care Center, as it was to be called in spite of the old man's opposition to it, was inaugurated on September 28, the opening night of the final home stand of the season. In a ceremony before the first game of the crucial three-game series with Oakland, Susie Dreyfus thanked the Viking organization for providing them with the first day-care center in baseball.

Surrounded by the players and their wives and children, Susie, looking chic but casual in a tan-and-azure cotton frock with a cardigan over her shoulders against the chilly San Fernando Valley night air, stood in the on-deck circle and gave a short prepared speech.

"I'd like to thank the Whites, father and son, and the whole Viking organization for making this day-care center possible. When we approached Mr. White last August with our idea, he was immediately responsive and provided the funds and the space to go ahead with the project, which we are proudly dedicating this evening.

"I think that this marks a historic moment for baseball in demonstrating its commitment to the American family as the backbone of our nation. A family that plays together, stays together. . . . And now let's go out there and beat the A's."

Applause rocked Viking Stadium from the sold-out crowd. They loved it. Randy stood beside his wife, holding Molly or Dolly's hand, as pictures were taken and the stadium organist played "God Bless America" in fight-song tempo.

D. J. Pickett, not having a family to display, sat in the dugout with Spic Mendoza and Charlie Gonse, who had refused to have anything to do with the day-care center, which he considered to be yet another distraction among too many others in ballplayers' lives.

"Fucking bitch son of a shit," Spic Mendoza said to D.J., who nodded absently. He was watching Randy with his wife and children. They looked gorgeous out there, the four of them, the American family. You might as well put them on the flag. He felt like a home wrecker.

Even though he hadn't encouraged Randy, had in fact discouraged him, he could have stopped it. He should have stopped it. D.J. had seen right from the beginning where it was leading.

And now it was too late. The truth was that every day D.J. was becoming more attached to this big beautiful sweet guy. This was not someone he had picked up in a bar. He found himself thinking about him in ways he had never imagined with other men in his life. And these thoughts were unsettling.

D.J. had led a very self-contained life. He lived simply, putting his money in the bank, so that after the legs went he would have enough to slip quietly off into the country somewhere and open a bed-and-breakfast. He hadn't planned on anything complicated or messy getting in the way. And this was certainly complicated and messy. They had dodged a bullet in Dallas. He shuddered every time he thought about how close they'd come to blowing the whole thing wide open.

"Bastard prick shitass mother . . ." Mendoza continued to mutter as the wives and children went back into the stands and the players returned to the dugout. D.J. tried to get his mind on the game. The pennant was on the line. They needed two out of three to win it.

As he trotted out to his position, D.J. avoided looking over at shortstop. Keep focused. Play the game. Hit the ball, catch it, and throw it. That was all there was to it. When he took the throw from

Bernie Lazarre and tossed it to Randy, the shortstop smiled at him.

This was no time for smiling. This was game time. But the smile was so sweet, almost shy, that D.J. couldn't get pissed off at him. And when Randy went into the hole and threw out the Oakland leadoff batter by half a step, D.J. felt a thrill go through his entire body. It was a hell of a play, Randy making the throw practically from the edge of the outfield grass.

Up in the owner's box, John D. F. White, Jr., was thrilled as well, but for somewhat different reasons. He was a few small deal points away from closing Randy Dreyfus. After months of negotiation, he was about to tie up the shortstop for three years with an option on the fourth. And it would cost him only $20 million and a day-care center.

The Dallas thing was behind them, and now he was on the verge of owning the best player in baseball. The Great White Hope of the San Fernando Valley. Watching him and his wife and daughters during the pregame dedication ceremony, John/John realized that he was buying the whole package. Randy Dreyfus would be the jewel in his crown.

The jewel in his crown got a hold of a low inside fastball in the bottom of the first and hit it halfway to Palmdale, officially ending his slump. But as Randy trotted around the bases to a tumultuous ovation, he wasn't thinking about the home run he had just hit. Or about the game, or the Western Division championship. He was thinking how he would slip out early tomorrow morning, call D.J. from the car phone, and arrange to meet him at some out-of-the-way Motel 6 in the desert with an air conditioner and an ice machine.

For some time now Arthur Maltz, the business manager who handled the Dreyfuses' finances, had been growing increasingly puzzled by a series of checks that his clients had been writing against their respective petty-cash accounts. Maltz had been in the business of serving wealthy people long enough to understand the need for slush funds, euphemistically termed petty-cash accounts, to camouflage the spending of money that one spouse did not want the other to know about. There were numerous reasons for such expenditures, and Maltz made it a practice not to delve into these matters. He merely balanced the books.

In this case, there was a rather large amount of money being paid out of Susie Dreyfus's petty-cash account to a company called Zabriskie Investigations, Inc., in Santa Ana. It was clear that she was having her husband followed for the usual reasons that women hire private detectives to follow their husbands. That one was strictly pro forma.

There was another series of checks, however, that was not so easily explained—a series of checks written by both Randy and Susie Dreyfus to the same person, a certain Mendes Fuad, M.D., a Medical Corporation, in Westwood. Whatever business was being transacted with Dr. Fuad was being done by both husband and wife secretly from each other. He wondered why a husband and wife would be seeing the same doctor without telling each other about it. For one thing, the tax angle was unfavorable. Since the petty-cash funds were not used for medical expenses, they were losing a significant amount of money on medical deductions.

But Maltz kept his mouth shut.

And so did Mendes Fuad. The psychiatrist's job was helping people navigate through the land mine–infested terrain of their psyches, not marriage counseling. That Susie Dreyfus was in his office talking about her husband, who had been there a few hours earlier talking about his lover, a fellow baseball player, was merely an accident of scheduling. One event had essentially nothing to do with the other. It was, as he had explained to Susie Dreyfus, about the deployment of penises, pure and simple. Where they were put, why, and how those involved felt about it. Everything else was wallpaper.

Fuad listened to Susie Dreyfus recount her conversation with her husband at three o'clock the following afternoon, after having had a session with her husband at ten o'clock that same morning, during which he hadn't even mentioned the conversation. Which tended to prove the doctor's point that people lived in skewed universes. He had told Susie that, whether she wanted to accept the fact or not, she had gotten her answer from her husband when she asked him if he was involved with someone else. *I don't know* was an answer.

And now it was up to her to decide whether she wanted to digest it or not.

Susie left the office with an upset stomach, vowing once again that this would be her last session with the sleepy Egyptian in the threadbare cardigan and bedroom slippers, and drove south to Santa Ana, where she was supposed to meet with Pete Zabriskie. The private detective had telephoned her at the radio station and told her he had some news for her that he'd prefer to give her in person.

Zabriskie offered her a cup of coffee, which she declined, then ushered her back into his private office with the arctic air-conditioning on high and the smoggy Santa Ana light coming through the sliding-glass windows.

He sat down at his metal desk, took out a file, then looked across at Susie Dreyfus and broke into a smile that showed an extensive amount of bad dental work. "I'm afraid, Mrs. Dreyfus, that I have discovered the identity of the owner of the handkerchief inadvertently left in your husband's laundry some time ago."

He paused for dramatic effect, running his fingers absently through his hairpiece. "Before I tell you I should warn you that it's probably going to be very upsetting."

"I think I can handle it."

He nodded, coughed, looked back down at his file, and said, "I believe it belongs to a man named D. J. Pickett, who happens to play second base for the Los Angeles Valley Vikings."

"No shit."

"Pardon me?"

"I figured that out already myself. Some time ago."

"I see . . ."

"The fact that he had D.J.'s handkerchief doesn't necessarily mean that they are . . ." She couldn't get herself to say it. Even in her sessions with Fuad she had trouble actually saying the words *sleeping together*.

"No, it doesn't. It's merely circumstantial."

"Yes. It's circumstantial," she repeated.

They sat for a moment not saying anything, the faint hum of the traffic from the Santa Ana Freeway audible from outside.

"Well," said Zabriskie, clearing his throat, "if you would care to upgrade to the comprehensive plan, I could provide documentation that would make things less . . . circumstantial.''

She nodded.

''It's up to you.''

''I don't know,'' she murmured. *I don't know* was an answer, wasn't it?

Did she really want to know? She sat there unable to make a decision. Zabriskie realized he would have to give her a gentle shove in the right direction if he wanted to extend his billable hours. With this in mind, he decided that maybe he'd better, after all, inform her of a collateral aspect of his investigation, as a way of letting her know that he had been on the job with diligence.

''There's something else you might as well know,'' Zabriskie said after another very long moment of silence had passed. ''This is circumstantial too. But somewhat less so.''

''What's that?''

''I have reason to believe that your husband harbors hostile feelings toward your dog.''

She walked out of the office without firing him either. She didn't seem able to fire anybody these days, starting with her husband. When Zabriskie began telling her about the gardener and the Liquid-Plumr, she stopped him. There was only a certain amount of weirdness she could handle. She was on overload right now.

She signed the contract for the comprehensive plan and told him to call her when he had the goods.

''Are you out of your fucking mind or what?'' Gus Mercer, the sports editor for *The Valley Tribune,* said when Milt Zola laid out his suspicions about the Randy Dreyfus–D. J. Pickett substance-abuse story. ''Why would they invent a booze problem if there wasn't one?''

''To cover up a bigger story.''

''Like what?''

''Like what really happened in Dallas.''

Mercer sat in his small cluttered office, trying to eat his lunch and get his assignment sheet worked out while his head baseball writer was laying out some cockamamie left-field sidebar. The story was the pennant race and not what had happened in Dallas. That was last week's story, and it had folded on them like a bad horse. Now Zola was trying to beat it to death.

"Look, Milt, what are you trying to say here? That these guys are blowing each other? No one'll believe it in a million years."

"I can't prove that. I don't even want to prove that. But I want to find out how the Vikings covered it up. That's the story."

"How can you do one story without doing the other?"

"I don't know."

"Listen, you fuck with the Whites, you're going to wind up getting eighty-sixed from the clubhouse. Then what're you going to do? How are you going to cover baseball in this town if you can't get into the clubhouse?"

Milt Zola sat there shaking his head. He knew that he was sitting on a very big story, but he couldn't find the handle on it. One of the dangers of being a reporter was winding up knowing something you didn't want to know. He felt like he was walking around with a hand grenade and playing with the pin.

"Gus, it's Watergate. It's corruption in high places . . ."

"Who do you think you are—Bob Woodward? Look, just go out there tonight and write about the goddamn game, will you? They win tonight, they clinch the pennant."

"But what if it's true?"

The editor put down his tostada grande, belched up some stomach gas, and looked at him sourly.

"Okay. Suppose you do the story and suppose you find out that the second baseman and the shortstop of the Los Angeles Valley Vikings are sucking each other's weenies. Nobody in America wants to read that story. That's like the ozone layer. Nobody wants to know about it. Do you really want to write that story?"

"I don't know."

I don't know was an answer.

Randy sat on one end of a row of chairs arranged roughly in a semicircle around Don Amarillo. D.J. sat on the other end. Between them were an assorted bunch of recovering substance abusers telling their stories. Group therapy was an essential part of Don Amarillo's program, and he had insisted that Randy and D.J. attend these sessions as a crucial step toward licking their problem.

It was a very long hour. All Randy could think of was the motel in Palmdale where he had arranged to meet D.J. after the therapy session. If they could get the hell out of here by noon, they'd have two hours together before they'd have to head back to town for batting practice.

"What do you think about that, Randy?" Don Amarillo's booming bass voice interrupted Randy's daydreams.

He blinked, remembered where he was, and said, "What was that?"

"What do you think about what Walt was just saying?"

"Uh . . . what was he saying again?"

"How his drinking was a way of punishing his mother for not loving him enough."

"Yeah . . ." He nodded vigorously to add conviction to his response.

"What about you?"

"Me?"

"Why do you think *you* drink?"

He looked back up at Amarillo and shrugged.

"Come on, man, don't bullshit us. Everybody's real here. Nobody's hiding behind denial. So, come on, talk to us. Why do you drink?"

Randy stole a quick glance across the room at his lover, who was sitting there, looking terrific in a light-weight cotton sweater and faded jeans. If he could just get through this and get out of here . . .

"Gee, I don't know . . ." he mumbled.

I don't know was an answer.

Pete Zabriskie sat outside in the Chevy Caprice, crouched down in his surveillance doze. Beside him on the front seat was the Nikon with the telephoto. With that baby he could nail you through a hotel window from a parachute.

He had seen both of them go into Don Amarillo's office in Marina del Rey an hour before. They had arrived separately.

When they left, they left separately, without even saying good-bye to each other. Dreyfus got into the baby-blue Beemer. Pickett got into a green Jag.

Zabriskie knew he'd hit pay dirt when, tailing the Beemer on the Hollywood heading north toward the Simi Valley, he picked up the green Jag in the rearview, about half a mile back. These guys were getting pretty cagey, but you had to get up earlier than that to put one over on Pete Zabriskie.

The motel was off Route 14 just before Palmdale. Zabriskie was able to roll past and pull into a Chevron station two hundred yards down the road, from where he could see Dreyfus go into the office, emerge with a key, and pull the Beemer over in front of one of the rooms.

Zabriskie leveled the Nikon, focused, and framed the shot to include the room number clearly. Fucking Japs. With this lens you could make the room number at two hundred yards. The rest was fish in a barrel. He sat and waited for the green Jag to pull in the motel. Then he watched D. J. Pickett go into the office, emerge with a key, and enter a different room.

About two minutes later, he saw Pickett leave his room, walk down to the ice machine, and load up with a bucket of ice. Zabriskie panned him with the camera, keeping the trigger finger steady, waiting for Pickett to turn and quickly open the door of the room that Dreyfus had checked into. *Click.* Nice and easy on the shutter.

He got it in one. Like a trained assassin, Pete Zabriskie didn't waste a bullet.

At a little before five-thirty that afternoon, Bob Bob Baker entered the Dallas County courthouse building and, waving at the security guard, walked up the marble staircase to the second floor. He wore a Stetson, a linen suit, and boots with heels high enough to get him up to five feet five inches on a good day.

Baker was a free-lance reporter who hung around the courthouse, hustling stories, looking for angles. And as far as he was concerned, he had found one last night at H.A.L. Porter's seven-card hold'em game in the den of his split-level out in west Dallas. Baker had gotten himself invited to it and had left after writing a marker for more money than he could cover.

But the marker would be small change if he could manage to cash in on the information that the Neiman-Marcus head of security had let drop between hands. Somewhere in the district attorney's office was an item that, if still there, could be worth a great deal on the open market. *If* it was still there. And *if* he could lay his hands on it. Since it was no longer evidence in a criminal action, it would not necessarily be stashed in an evidence locker. It was a long shot, but Bob Bob Baker was not the kind of guy who liked to bet chalk. He figured it was worth a look see.

He walked down the hallway past the deputies' offices. When he got to the D.A.'s office, he saw Mary Ellen Gethers, the secretary, at her desk. He took off his hat and smiled his best good-old-boy smile. "Howdy do, Mary Ellen."

"Hello there, Bob."

"How come you're working so late?"

"Well, you know how it is," she said with the practiced expression of the born martyr.

"Wesley gone home?"

"Sure has."

"Now don't that just set your teeth itching. He's home sipping his Jack Daniel's, while his faithful secretary is still at her post."

"Ain't that the truth."

"You go on home and get some rest, hear?" he said, replacing his Stetson and walking out. Across the corridor was a men's room. Bob Bob Baker entered, chose a stall, sat down, and waited for Mary Ellen Gethers to go home.

Fritz Esterhazy had flown out to L.A. to attend the final three-game series between the Vikings and the A's that would decide the pennant. He wanted to be on hand for the postgame festivities and the presentation of the trophy for the divisional championship.

It was a beautiful late-September evening with a harvest moon hanging out over the Sepulveda Pass behind the center-field stands. He sat in the Commissioner's Box, next to Gene Jaress, the American League president. There was a capacity crowd on hand, a palpable excitement in the air. This was what it was all about. A tight pennant race right down to the wire, two good teams, a beautiful night under the stars. The two teams having split the first two games, the winner of tonight's game would clinch.

The game was exciting right from the start. The A's loaded the bases with one out in the top of the first. Charlie Gonse had Al De Mun wave the infield in at the corners and at double-play depth up the middle. Randy and D.J., still basking in the glow from their afternoon in Palmdale, cheated a few feet closer to each other.

D.J. held up his glove and signaled one finger to his shortstop, which meant that he would take a throw from the pitcher. Randy nodded, then felt his lips pucker and had to stop himself from blowing a kiss.

The ball was hit past the pitcher just to the right of the second-base bag. The two steps D.J. had cheated made the difference. Diving, he backhanded the ball on a short hop, and, while still in the air, shoveled the ball to Randy coming across the bag. The shortstop tickled the base with his toe and threw to first a microsecond before jumping to elude the upturned spikes of the runner coming in hard to break up the double play.

The umpire hesitated for just a second, then threw up his hand. The place exploded. Randy casually brushed off his uniform and trotted in just behind his second baseman, his eyes on the firm contours of D. J. Pickett's buttocks outlined against the tight-fitting polyester uniform pants.

"You won't see a better double play than that," Gene Jaress enthused to Fritz Esterhazy.

The commissioner nodded agreement. "It's as if those two were an extension of each other."

Randy singled sharply to center in the bottom of the first and stole second but died there when Glen Ephard got under one and hit it to the warning track.

The game moved along, inning after inning, crisply played, no errors, no runs. By the seventh inning, with the starters still in there but tiring, the managers began to play around with pinch hitters and defensive switches. The chess game had begun. Charlie Gonse sat in the corner of the dugout, his windbreaker zipped up tightly, dictating moves to his staff of coaches.

The crowd sang "Take Me out to the Ballgame" during the seventh-inning stretch. The TV cameras featured Susie Dreyfus and her twin daughters behind the first-base dugout singing hand in hand, and when they flashed the image on the message board in left field, there was a spontaneous outburst of cheering for their star shortstop's beautiful family.

The A's had a chance to go ahead in the top of the ninth. They had a runner at third with two outs when the next batter hit a checked-swing dribbler out to the right of the pitcher's mound. The ball was trouble right from the beginning. It squibbed out past the pitcher and seemed to die on the grass. The runner on third was nearly across the plate before D.J., charging as soon as he had seen the inside fastball jam the hitter, barehanded it and, in one continuous movement, got the ball to first to nip the batter by an eyelash.

From the press box Milt Zola wrote 4–3 on his scorecard and then circled it. It was a hell of a play. A major league play. And when the Vikings failed to score in the bottom of the ninth, it was clear that it had saved the ball game and the championship.

They went into extra innings, both bullpens going at full throttle. This was crunch time. There was no tomorrow, as Teddy Yackamow, the voice of the Vikings, reminded the radio audience tuned in from San Luis Obispo to Rancho Cucamonga. It would be settled here tonight, under the lights at Viking Stadium, one team to go on to the League Championship Series and the other to go home for a long winter of golf.

As the game went on, inning after inning, Randy began to want it to go on forever. Then he wouldn't have to talk to the Egyptian or to Don Amarillo or to Barry Fuchsia or to Dr. Bob or to Charlie Gonse. He wouldn't have to face his wife and her questions. He could stay out here in the field beside his lover playing baseball forever. They would stay young and in love, feeding each other perfect double-play tosses, cheating toward the bag, flashing their signals secretly behind their gloves.

It was beautiful. Tears began to form in Randy's eyes as he thought about how happy he was at that moment in the top of the fourteenth inning of a scoreless tie for the American League West Championship.

Charlie Gonse saw things a little differently. As far as he was concerned, they were in deep shit. He was down to his last pitcher, and the guy had gotten away with a couple of terrible pitches in the top of the thirteenth. It was only a matter of time before someone took him deep. Gonse cringed when, with two on and two outs, the Oakland batter drilled one up the middle. But Randy Dreyfus gobbled it up and shoveled it to Pickett for the force at second.

The top of the order was up in the bottom of the fourteenth. Mendoza, Pickett, and Dreyfus. Charlie Gonse called Randy over to the corner of the dugout near the tunnel to the clubhouse and said, "Shovel, I'm going to lay it on the line to you, all right?"

"Sure, Charlie."

"We're out of arms. There are no more bullets in the cannons. Next inning, they're over the top of the fort with their tomahawks— you understand what I'm saying?"

Randy nodded.

"It's time to live up to your goddamn shopping center."

Mendoza took a called third strike. Randy walked out to the on-deck circle as D.J. stood in against the ace of the A's bullpen. The guy led the league in saves and had an E.R.A. of 1.24. He threw sinkers that bit off tiny corners of the plate.

Randy slipped the doughnut over the thin end of the bat and hefted it over his head, feeling his shoulder and back muscles stretch. He watched D.J. fight off the sinkers, working the count to three-and-two, then fouling off four straight pitches before lining one inside first and down the line.

All 125,000 people were on their feet. D.J. rounded first and headed for second as the right fielder went deep into the corner to play the carom off the wall. D.J. rounded second and, not even looking at the third-base coach, put his head down and aimed for third. It was a race between man and ball, with D.J. sliding in a split second before the tag.

Randy stood in the on-deck circle, marveling at the beauty of what he had just seen. He waited for a moment, letting D.J. bask in the glow of the adulation pouring out from the stands, before walking slowly up to the plate amid the deafening roar of the crowd.

"Ran-DEE. Ran-DEE."

This was it. A hundred and sixty-one games, thirteen and a half innings had come down to this moment. He was facing the toughest pitcher in the American League with an opportunity to win the division championship and live up to his shopping center.

Randy stood outside the batter's box, staring down at third, where Al De Mun was running signs. He wasn't looking at Al De Mun's signs. He was looking at D.J. and he was getting an inspiration. Not only did they have to win the game right now, but they had to do it in an unforgettable manner.

What he had in mind had nothing to do with the bullshit signs that Al De Mun was running. What he had in mind was the last thing that anybody in the stadium was thinking about.

It would be gorgeous. It would be the type of thing that, years later, would count when the Hall of Fame elections took place. They would remember this moment, bottom of the fourteenth, runner on third, one out. The percentage play was the sac fly or the ground ball to the right side. But Randy wasn't interested in percentages at the moment. He was interested in greatness.

He closed his eyes for a brief moment and sent the message down the third-base line to D.J. He sent it with everything he had, knowing that his lover would pick it up, just as he had picked up all the other silent signals between them over the years.

When Randy finally stepped in, he didn't even bother looking down at third, where D.J. took his lead off the bag, inching down the line in foul territory. The pitcher glared in at him, shook off the first sign, shook off another. Randy didn't give a shit what they threw him. He was ready for anything.

Nobody in the entire ballpark, however, not even Milt Zola, who had covered baseball for twenty-seven years, or Fritz Esterhazy or Charlie Gonse, was prepared to see Randy Dreyfus square around to bunt. Nobody, apparently, except D.J., who was already heading for the plate.

There was a collective sucking in of air, as 125,000 people watched Randy Dreyfus push the change-up gently toward the third baseman, who had been playing so deep that he didn't even reach the ball before D. J. Pickett crossed the plate with the winning run. As Randy jogged merrily to first base, he was the happiest man alive.

The suicide squeeze. It was Russian roulette with five bullets in six chambers. But when it worked, there was nothing in baseball more beautiful to watch: the runner on third going with the pitch, a dead duck unless the batter made contact. It was all on the line in one split second of perfect timing.

Many things were said about the play that won the American League Western Division Championship for the Los Angeles Valley Vikings that year. It was called audacious, brilliant, spectacular, breathtaking. . . . One of the only dissenters was Charlie Gonse, who called it idiotic, but his disclaimer was lost in the joyous pandemonium of the postgame celebration.

The locker room was full of reporters, TV cameras, league officials, Viking executives. There was the presentation of the trophy, accepted by John D. F. White, Sr., from American League president Gene Jaress. The old man gave a rambling speech in which he talked about American manhood and terrorism, among other things. The networks went to commercial in the middle of it, came back for a few remarks by Fritz Esterhazy, then got Charlie Gonse on camera. When asked why he called for the suicide squeeze in that situation, Charlie Gonse replied, "Only an idiot would have done that." The remark was interpreted as ironic and self-deprecating. One of the headlines in the morning's sports pages was IDIOT'S DELIGHT.

But the nation wanted the heroes, D. J. Pickett and Randy Dreyfus. They wanted them in their living rooms, on their TVs. They were pushed forward toward the cameras, microphones thrust in their faces. How did they feel? What was their reaction when they got the squeeze-play sign? Were they surprised? Did they think it would work?

D.J. shrugged and said, "Well, you know, it's part of the game. We were lucky. It worked. Tomorrow's another day. We still got to beat the Yankees . . ."

Randy stood beside him grinning foolishly. All he could do was smile. Susie, watching from a TV in the day-care center, had the unsettling feeling that her husband was losing his grip on reality. Milt Zola thought that Randy Dreyfus was going to start giggling on nationwide TV. Randy stood there, his perfect set of white teeth shining under the TV lights, until the microphone was thrust in front of him and he was asked how he felt.

"Terrific. Just great," he said, still grinning like the idiot Charlie Gonse considered him. "Like a million bucks," he replied.

A reporter in the back of the room shouted, "You mean twenty million bucks, don't you, Randy?"

"Hey, sounds good to me . . ." Randy laughed. And he continued to laugh as the cameras clicked. He and D.J. put their arms around each other and hugged. The emotion of victory. The standard locker-room embrace of the winners, the heroes.

The picture was on every sports page of every paper in the country the following morning. The country reveled in their two young gods. They celebrated this vision of American manhood at its finest until another picture appeared the next day.

This picture was also of Randy Dreyfus and D. J. Pickett embracing. But this time they had their tongues down each other's throats.

XVIII

The videotape that Bob Bob Baker had stolen from the Dallas County district attorney's bottom right-hand desk drawer was brokered upward through a series of middlemen until there was a copy in nearly every television newsroom in America, as well as a brisk business in the home-entertainment market.

Most of this commerce occurred within twenty-four hours of the actual theft. Bob Bob Baker cashed out early, accepting the first offer from a national tabloid, who sent a plane down to Dallas to pick up the videotape. The scandal sheet made still photos of the choice moments, and then the tape was copied and resold, eventually working its way up to the stations and networks.

When the story broke, Ken Teffner was in his office in Viking Stadium talking on the phone to a member of the Los Angeles County Board of Education about the possibility of naming a San Fernando Valley Junior High School after Randy Dreyfus. He put the educator on hold and took the call from a UPI guy. After listening briefly, he asked him to hold and told the educator he'd have to get back to him about the junior high school.

"You want to run that by me again, please?" Teffner said. The UPI guy told him that he had in his possession a videotape that showed beyond a shadow of a doubt that what occurred in the Neiman-Marcus changing room in Dallas a few weeks before was more than merely the exuberant hijinks of two ballplayers who'd had a couple of beers.

"What were they doing?"

"They were kissing," the UPI guy said.

"Well, as you know, during the heat of a pennant race—"

"This has nothing to do with the pennant race, believe me."

"How do you know?"

"They have their mouths open and their hands all over each other."

"I see," replied Ken Teffner.

"Would you care to comment on behalf of the Vikings?"

"Well, I really wouldn't have anything to say until I saw the videotape."

"I'll have a copy at your office in an hour."

When the tape arrived, Teffner locked the door, switched on the VCR, and sat at his desk watching the shortstop and second baseman of the Vikings act like two horny teenagers on a date. When it was finished, he put his head in his hands and sat for a long time trying to figure out where to begin. What could he possibly do in the face of evidence in living color that Randy Dreyfus and D. J. Pickett were seriously necking? Besides their tongues in each other's mouths, Randy Dreyfus's left hand was caressing D. J. Pickett's buttocks.

This was substance abuse of an entirely different nature. This was Pearl Harbor. This time they had sunk the whole fleet. . . .

His phone rang. He picked up and got Burton Meeker on his car phone from Century Park East.

"Did you hear?" the lawyer asked.

"I've already seen the tape."

"Is it the real thing?"

"It's the real thing."

"Kissing on the lips?"

"Lips, tongues, the whole business."

"Is that all?"

"A little bit of light petting."

"Light petting?"

"Randy's got his hand on D.J.'s ass."

"Is it moving?"

"It certainly is."

There was a moment of static as the Silver Shadow negotiated the corner of Santa Monica Boulevard. Then Meeker said, "You realize that it's not just the faggot stuff? It's the whole substance-abuse cover-up story too."

"I realize that."

"I hate to tell you this, Ken, but they're going to make you look like Ron Ziegler."

"Yeah, well, if I'm Ziegler, Burt, you're John Mitchell."

Most of the TV stations that aired the video fogged out Randy's left hand caressing D.J.'s buttocks, at least on the six o'clock news, and before showing it they ran a disclaimer to the effect that the following clip was not suitable for family viewing. Nevertheless, millions of American families watched the necking session together in dumbfounded silence. Many parents, not wanting to discuss it over dinner with their children, merely pretended not to see it; others mumbled explanations in the manner of Ken Teffner's hijinks story; one man in Mobile, Alabama, lifted the TV set up and threw it out the window; another man in Little Rock, Arkansas, went out to his pickup, got the shotgun off the rack, and poured fifty rounds of ammunition into the side of his barn.

In a few places around the country, notably in New York City's West Village, the videotape was greeted with hoots of laughter and a great deal of celebration. In a bar on Christopher Street, an unfogged version of the necking session was taped off the air and then projected continuously on a large-screen monitor. Each time the tape ran out, the bar's patrons shouted, "Play it again, Sam!"

But in Los Angeles, and particularly in the San Fernando Valley, the tape was viewed with consternation, sadness, and feelings of betrayal. Just twenty-four hours before, these two young men had been their knights in shining armor, their heroes and exemplars. And now they were the shame and laughingstock of the nation. Many people merely refused to believe it, convinced it was a hoax, a bad joke perpetrated by doctoring the tape to make it only appear as if the two ballplayers were doing what they were doing. Various experts on tape doctoring were interviewed on TV, explaining how you could completely alter a videotape before airing it.

While all this was going on, the nation waited for a statement from the two ballplayers, the Los Angeles Valley Vikings, or the commissioner of baseball. The two ballplayers were in their motel room in Palmdale, where they were not listening to the radio or watching television. On behalf of the Vikings, Ken Teffner was making no comment pending a discussion with the individuals involved, and Fritz Esterhazy was "out of his office and unreachable."

The wife and family of one of the individuals involved, however, were not unreachable. Fortunately, Karen Most had telephoned Susie to warn her not to let the twins watch TV when they got home from school and then blurted out, "I'm so sorry."

"About what?" Susie asked.

"It must be terrible. If you need anything at all, just call, okay?" And she hung up.

Almost immediately the phone rang again and a reporter from a local all-news station asked her what her reaction was to the tape.

"What tape?" Susie asked.

"The tape of your husband and D. J. Pickett," the reporter said. "Did you have any suspicions—"

Susie hung up on him and switched on CNN. She had to wait through a commercial and the international news segment before the story played. She sat there in her spandex aerobic-exercise outfit and watched her husband kissing D. J. Pickett. And as she watched it she began to cry, not so much because of what all this would mean to her marriage and to her future, but because of the passion she saw in that kiss. It had been a long time since Randy had kissed her like that. Large, gulping sobs began to wrack her whole body as she realized that her marriage was doomed.

She sat there crying herself out as the phone rang off the hook. Then she pulled herself together, threw some makeup on, and hurried to pick up the twins at school before the reporters got to them.

Oblivious to the media circus going on around him, Randy drove blissfully home from Palmdale with Frank Sinatra's *Songs for Swinging Lovers* on the tape deck. Tapping his foot to the rhythm, he had the Beemer on cruise control at seventy-five and his radar fuzz buster set to pick up any lurking cops.

He sped across the San Fernando Valley, feeling like a million bucks, or, as the guy had said, twenty million bucks. Tomorrow they were leaving for New York to play the Yankees for the American League pennant. He was hitting .338 and had a shot at MVP. And he was in love with a wonderful guy. What more could he want?

As he drove up Delores Canyon, he felt like a surfer on the crest of the big one, heading for a beach that was too far in the distance to see distinctly. But as soon as he turned onto Caravaggio Place, he saw the rocks. Surrounding his house was an armada of TV minivans and cameras. The street was lit up like a movie set.

What the hell were all these reporters doing in front of his house? There were no police cars, ambulances, fire engines. It could only mean . . . Holy shit!

He hit the brake with the intention of jamming the car in reverse and getting out of there, but the reporters had already spotted the BMW. They moved toward him en masse, while another minivan, parked at the end of the street, pulled across the entrance to the cul de sac, blocking off his retreat.

His home was under siege. They had his wife and daughters trapped in the house, access and retreat cut off. All he had to protect himself was the Beemer. He threw the electric door locks and turned up the volume on the tape deck. Frank Sinatra bellowed "Old Devil Moon."

He felt like he was in the middle of a street riot in some Third World country as the reporters swarmed around the car, aiming their cameras like assault weapons. Randy kept his foot on the brake to hold back the powerful engine. Grabbing the car phone, he dialed 911. When the operator asked him what the emergency was, he told her his house was surrounded by reporters and he couldn't get in. She told him that those circumstances did not constitute a 911 emergency and to call his local precinct.

Fuck this. It was his goddamn house, and they weren't going to prevent him from entering. He eased his foot off the brake and moved forward slowly, watching reporters scatter in his path. A sound truck blocked off direct access to his driveway, but Randy saw a small opening between two vans. He cut the angle, jumped the curb, and drove over his front lawn, trampling Manuel Rodriguez's azaleas, then, turning the wheel sharply, aimed for the garage.

They ran after him with their cameras, overflowing onto the front lawn, as Randy hit the garage-door remote and accelerated for the home stretch. The big door lumbered open a few seconds before the Beemer got there, and Randy hit the remote as soon as he cleared the door, which shut behind him, sealing up his castle like a closing drawbridge.

He sat there, his hands gripping the wheel tightly, his heart beating wildly, listening to Frank, who was practically screaming by now.

". . . on a magic carpet ride. Full of butterflies inside . . . Gotta cry, gotta croon . . . gotta laugh like a loon. . . . It's that Old Devil Moon in your eyes . . ."

He found Susie and the girls quietly eating supper in the dining nook. Calvin sat obediently in the corner. The TV was not on.

The Dalmatian got up and came over to greet his master. Randy scratched him behind the ears. Nice doggie.

"Hi, Daddy," said Molly or Dolly.

"Hello, honey," Randy replied.

"We're having meat loaf," the other one said.

"That's terrific. I'm starved," said Randy, sitting down in the bosom of his family.

Susie handed him the meat-loaf platter without comment. He helped himself to a large piece.

"All those people outside the house. They want to talk to you about the World Series, but we said you weren't home," said Molly or Dolly.

Randy nodded, close to tears.

In the dark, almost lugubrious dining room of his Hancock Park mansion, John D. F. White, Sr., sat at dinner with his son. Conversation was sparse. Since watching the six o'clock news, the old man had had very little to say about anything. He ate without appetite, rebuffing all attempts that John/John made to discuss the situation.

It wasn't until the cherry cobbler was brought out that he muttered, "We'll trade them."

"Who?"

"Both of them. We'll put them on the block together. Special price. Two fruits for the price of one."

"It's past the trading deadline, Dad."

"Then we'll give them away."

"Without them, we're not going to win the Series, let alone beat the Yankees."

The old man stared down the long table at his son, whom he could barely see in the low light. He often wondered whether this asthmatic pussy was really his. It must have been recessive genes. Surely he deserved better.

"Let me ask you something," he grumbled. "Do you really want these two perverts to represent the Los Angeles Valley Vikings?"

"They're just two players out of twenty-four."

"Hitler was only one German."

"Dad, I really think you have to put this in perspective—"

"It makes me want to puke. They're all over the goddamn place. The movies, the House of Representatives, the fucking Post Office . . . But not in baseball. Not on my team . . . And to think I was about to give that faggot twenty million bucks. . . ."

The Filipino houseman entered with a phone.

"Who is it?" asked John/John.

"Mr. Esterhazy for Mr. White. Senior."

The old man grabbed the phone and said, without any greeting or introduction, "It's a sad day for baseball, Fritz."

"Yes it is, John."

"First the drugs, now this. What's next? Arson? Kidnapping? Armed robbery?

"I'm afraid I'm going to have to hold an investigation."

"Just toss 'em the hell out, Fritz. On their asses. You've got the power to do that."

"John, I've got to look into this whole matter. It's a little more complicated than that."

"Complicated? You saw the tape."

"What they did is not strictly against the law."

"Are you serious? There's no law against that in this country?"

"I'm afraid not."

"Well, I'll tell you something—it's about time we passed one."

"John, I want to see your boys in New York when they get off the plane tomorrow. My office."

"Give 'em hell, Fritz. Tell 'em what they did was a disgrace to everything this country stands for. Tell 'em I didn't go into Sainte-Mère-Eglise with the Eighty-second Airborne just so they could do disgusting things in department-store changing rooms. . . ."

By the time Fritz Esterhazy hung up the private line in his Mount Kisco home, he'd had an earful of John D. F. White, Sr. The old man was over the top on this, which would only make things worse. He needed to subdue the explosive passions that the issue would arouse. He needed to exercise his skills at mediation to navigate between the extremes on both sides. He needed to determine what really was in the best interests of baseball.

There was an image that wouldn't disappear from his mind's eye. As he was hurrying to catch a cab, he caught a glimpse of an extra-late edition of the *Post* that had just hit the stands. On the front page there was a photo of a little kid in his room with Viking pennants and pictures of Randy Dreyfus all over the wall. The headline read SAY IT AIN'T SO, RANDY.

He managed to get rid of the reporters, for the night at least, by calling the Valley View Estates private security police, who drove up to Caravaggio Place and enforced the regulations against nighttime parking. The vans drove off down Delores Canyon like an army breaking camp. It became very quiet on the street.

Randy went in to kiss the twins good-night. It took all his strength not to fall apart right there in the bedroom with its dotted lace curtains, town-and-country wallpaper, and cut-out pictures of Joan Lunden.

They would find out tomorrow at school. How long could the news be kept from them? As Randy kissed each one tenderly on the forehead, he wondered when he would see them again. He was leaving for New York tomorrow. After that, his future was uncertain. Susie would probably demand that he move out. He would have to comply. Then what?

He walked down to the exercise nook, thinking that ten miles on the stationary bike would calm him down and help him think things out. When he entered, he found Susie on her rowing machine.

He hopped on the bike and started to pedal. The two of them pedaled and rowed, side by side, until they were both sweating and exhausted. When they were finished, Susie got towels for both of them.

"Thanks," he said.

"Sure."

He sponged the sweat off his face and neck as Susie sat down on the edge of the fiberglass Jacuzzi. When she spoke it was in a calm, measured voice. She had promised herself that she would be understanding and nonjudgmental.

"So . . . how long has it been going on?"

"It's hard to say. I mean, I kind of first got the . . . idea in Cleveland back in July."

"So that's when it started—in July?"

He shook his head. "No. Nothing happened for a while. I . . . didn't think, I mean, I wasn't sure . . . You see, this really surprised the hell out of me."

"You're not the only one."

"I'm sorry."

"I understand. It's . . . You got to be what you are."

"That's what the shrink says."

"You've been going to a shrink?"

"Yeah. Ever since I got the . . . ever since Cleveland."

"Does the shrink think, like, you're . . . one?"

"It's hard to tell with this guy. He doesn't say a whole lot."

"I'm sorry, but I have to ask you a personal question."

"Go ahead."

"Given what's going on out there, did you and he . . . take precautions?"

"Huh?"

"Did you have safe sex, Randy?"

"Oh, *that.* Yeah. We got it covered."

"I'm glad to hear that."

"No problem."

"Well . . . I hired a private detective to follow you."

"You did?"

"Yes. After I found a handkerchief with the initials DJP in your laundry."

"You mean all this time I was being followed?"

"He wasn't very good. For weeks he didn't find anything out. Then, after the Dallas business, he told me the handkerchief belonged to D.J. Pretty good guess. And he had all these crazy ideas. I mean he was actually trying to convince me that you wanted to kill Calvin. Can you believe that?"

"Really?"

"Uh-huh."

"No shit."

"He said you were trying to poison him."

"*Calvin?* Why would I want to poison Calvin? He's a great dog."

They sat for a while in silence, Randy still straddling the Exercycle, Susie on the rim of the Jacuzzi. Finally she asked the question that had been nagging at her, though she already knew the answer. "Are you in love with him?"

Even after all this time, the question still embarrassed Randy. Especially from his wife, whom he still also sort of loved, but apparently in a different way than he loved D.J.

"I don't know."

I don't know was an answer. But she wasn't going to leave it at that.

"I think you are. And I'm . . . very happy for you."

And with that she burst into tears.

• • •

Milt Zola stared into the green void of his computer screen, upon which only one sentence appeared: BASEBALL IS PLAYED BETWEEN THE FOUL LINES. This sentence had been written over an hour ago and had been sitting there quietly waiting to be followed by other sentences.

The digital clock in the newsroom read 10:55. He was thirty-five minutes away from deadline for the morning edition, and, for the first time in twenty-seven years, he wasn't sure he was going to make it. The Dreyfus-Pickett story was already teased on the front page, in a box below the fold, and was the lead sports-page story, with several sidebars accompanying it. Zola had two columns on the facing page, and he had intended to write something thoughtful to try to put the issue in perspective.

But as the minutes ticked off, he continued to sit there, unable to write more than the one sentence. Mercer had already tried to tout him off the Watergate angle. He was right: It would be professional suicide to cut off access to the biggest baseball story in town by alienating the Whites. And yet he couldn't get the idea out of his mind that Randy Dreyfus and D. J. Pickett were going to become victims of an orthodoxy that, in some ways, was more conservative than the Catholic Church.

Zola knew that baseball would be severely shaken by this event, an event that had nothing to do with the integrity of the game. It was going to be blown completely out of proportion; sides were going to be drawn; a great deal was going to be said and written that did not concern what went on between the foul lines, which, as his forlorn first sentence indicated, was what really mattered.

The Vikings were leaving in the morning for New York to open a seven-game series with the Yankees for the right to play in the World Series. And yet this fact was barely mentioned on the sports page. There were pitching matchups, injury reports, quotes from the managers—the dramatic context of the League Championship Series—and nobody was writing about any of it. Instead they were writing about an event that took place weeks ago in a Dallas department store, an event that, as far as Milt Zola was concerned, was not only not between the foul lines; it wasn't even in the ball park.

The phone rang. It was the composing room wanting to know when his copy was going to be ready—he was holding up the whole page. He told them ten minutes and hung up. Turning back to the screen, he reread the sentence and sighed. He wasn't going to write this particular story tonight. He didn't have it in him right now to find the words to say all that he wanted to say. Certainly not in ten minutes.

He hit the DELETE key, clearing the screen. On his desk was the standard Viking press kit, sent out by Ken Teffner's office that morning before the story broke. It contained the usual inane quotes about playing them one at a time, not being overconfident, and so forth.

Zola waded through the material with his practiced eye, culling out the significant information from the standard PR bullshit. Then he turned to his keyboard and banged out 750 words about the upcoming American League Championship Series without once mentioning the videotape or the incident in Dallas. Given what was being written on nearly all the other sports pages around the country, Milt Zola had pretty much of a scoop.

In order to avoid the press, the Vikings switched departure terminals for their charter flight to New York. But Randy and D.J. still had to get through the patrols surrounding their houses. Having underground parking, D.J. was able to get out unscathed. He waited for someone else in his condo to leave, and then, using the other car as camouflage, drove out on the guy's tail. By the time the reporters realized it was him and were able to get to their vehicles, D.J. was doing eighty-five en route to the Ventura Freeway. They wouldn't catch him. Not in the Jag.

Things were more difficult for Randy. The press had started assembling before dawn, the noise waking up Calvin, who then woke up everyone else in the house. The Dalmatian ran from window to window like a demented Paul Revere, barking madly at the gathering multitudes.

Randy had to call the sheriff's office as well as the Valley View Estates security patrol to clear a path for the Beemer. Just before he left the house, Susie said to him, "I just want you to know that whatever you decide it's okay with me."

He nodded, kissed his daughters good-bye, petted his dog, and headed for the garage. Once in his car, he started the engine, hit the remote, and, as the drawbridge swung down, backed out over the azaleas, past the cameras.

Because his phone was off the hook, Randy arrived at the wrong terminal and had to be rescued by one of Ken Teffner's people and redirected to the secret terminal, which, by the time he got there, was no longer a secret. Reporters were milling around waiting for him as soon as he walked in the door.

Teffner managed to get him past the cameras and into the security area, where the team was waiting to board the plane. The ballplayers tried to appear casual, but there was a palpable tension in the air.

"Hey, Randy, how're you doing?" Axel Most said. A couple of the others waved. John/John, the general manager, Larry Zwick, and Charlie Gonse were huddled together in one corner. The writers who covered the team were in another. D.J. sat all alone near the window. They did not look like a team that had just clinched their division and were about to fly to New York to play for the league pennant.

Spic Mendoza walked by and said, "Fuck shit, huh?"

"Right," Randy replied. He was watching D.J., wondering what he was going through, how he had managed to get home last night, whether there were reporters in front of his house as well.

The second baseman looked like he was in one of his pregame trances, his eyes half-closed, his hands folded in his lap. Randy had barely slept the night before. Even after the stationary bike, the hot tub, and ten milligrams of Valium. He had finally drifted off around 3 A.M., just a few hours before Calvin began to report the arrival of the enemy.

On the plane Randy popped another V, stretched out across an empty row in the back, and dozed fitfully all the way to New York. When they arrived at JFK, there was a limo waiting to take Randy, D.J., Ken Teffner, Larry Zwick, and John/John directly to Fritz Esterhazy's office in Manhattan.

There was some desultory talk about the traffic, but that was pretty much the extent of conversation in the limo as it fought its way into Manhattan and uptown to Fritz Esterhazy's Park Avenue office. Randy looked out the window and wondered what he was going to say to the commissioner of baseball.

There were more reporters waiting in front of Fritz Esterhazy's office, and Teffner again navigated them through the receiving line and up the elevator to the commissioner's fortieth-floor office.

The office was furnished with baseball memorabilia, framed photos of big moments in the history of the game: Aaron's 715th home run, Larsen's perfect World Series game, Bobby Thomson's ninth-inning blast in the Polo Grounds that sunk the Dodgers in '51.

Everyone was very cordial. Five minutes of strained small talk, and then Fritz Esterhazy asked to be left alone with Randy and D.J. When the others had retreated into the outer office, the commissioner beckoned the ballplayers to sit down on the deep leather armchairs facing his large mahogany desk, then eased his large, ex–Princeton quarterback frame into the chair. He sat there for a moment, looking from one of them to the other, and then said, "Well, boys, what are we going to do about this?"

Randy and D.J. glanced at each other and then looked back at the commissioner.

"We have a nasty little problem on our hands here, and we need to put our heads together and see if we can come up with a solution," the commissioner went on. "I'm going to have to ask you to lay it on the line for me. I need to know just how serious this thing is."

"What thing?" D.J. asked.

"Your relationship."

"With all due respect, Mr. Commissioner, I don't see that that's any of your business."

"I wish it wasn't, D.J. Frankly, I'm not particularly interested in delving into other people's sexual proclivities. But unfortunately my office requires me to protect the image of the game, and the sexual proclivities of two prominent stars of the game has a great deal to do with that image."

He leaned back in his chair for a moment, removed his glasses professorially, and gazed beyond them out the window, where the view extended all the way to the East River.

"Let me see if I can put this in perspective for you," he continued.

"Baseball is not just a sport. Baseball is the expression of this country's most cherished values, among which heterosexual relations and monogamy figure prominently. What happened in Dallas is a violation of both of these values and therefore of baseball itself. You must understand that."

Randy felt two beads of sweat drip simultaneously from each armpit. It was one of the surefire signs that he was starting to lose it. He went over to the bat rack and chose a piece of lumber.

"Every kid growing up in this country looks up to baseball players as heroes," the commissioner continued. "You are the role models for an entire nation's youth. That is an awesome responsibility, but one you willingly take on when you go out there between the foul lines. . . ."

Randy wrapped his hands around the narrow end of a thirty-five-ounce bat and aimed at the middle of Fritz Esterhazy's skull.

"Now, if what happened is just a passing thing, a little deviation that, for whatever reasons, you indulged in, then I feel we may be able to live with it. After all, everyone makes mistakes. Nobody bats a thousand, do they?"

Randy stepped in, choking up just a little on the bat.

"So what I am asking for is an assurance that whatever happened is over and done with and that it will not repeat itself. Can you give me that assurance?"

"You want something in writing?" D.J. asked, his usually even temper beginning to flare around the edges.

"I don't think that would be necessary. I'll accept your word as gentlemen and ballplayers."

Randy let go and swung hard at the low inside fastball. "Listen, Mr. Commissioner," he blurted out, "I don't do drugs, I don't gamble, I don't beat up on my wife or fool around with little kids. I play a pretty good shortstop, I hit .338 this year, best in the league, and only made sixteen errors in the field. I don't argue with umpires, never got thrown out of a game, and I have a shopping center named after me. So as far as I'm concerned, I'm a pretty good American."

Smiling indulgently, Fritz Esterhazy got up and came around the desk to stand in front of the two men. "I admire your convictions, Randy," he said, "and I respect them. I didn't mean to imply that you were not a good American. However, here's the long and the short of it. As far as I'm concerned, major league baseball cannot accommodate an open sexual relationship between the shortstop and second baseman of a division championship team that may be on the way to the World Series."

He paused to let the statement sink in, then he said, "So you're going to have to make a choice."

"What's our choice?" D.J. asked.

"Go back in the closet and stay there for as long as you're in the game."

"How do we do that?"

"You make a brief statement, say the affair is over and that you're sorry it happened, and stay the hell away from each other."

"Is that all?"

"I think you should both seek some counseling."

"Sort of like substance abuse, right?" D.J. snapped.

"Right."

Like the various hotel rooms that Randy had been staying in lately, this office had a No Suicide window. But he was convinced that if he got the shoulder down low enough, just below the sternum, he could send the guy through the glass and on his way to Queens. Then they could really boot him out for conduct detrimental to the best interests of baseball. . . .

"What happens if we don't agree to do this?" he found himself saying.

"Well, then I'd have to seriously consider invoking Article Nineteen.

"We could appeal it," said D.J.

"You cannot appeal Article Nineteen. Article Nineteen is unappealable. Its sole criterion is conduct detrimental to the best interests of baseball in the judgment of the commissioner."

There was a long moment of silence, then D.J. said, despair already in his voice, "It's your bat and ball—is that what you're trying to say?"

"Precisely."

XIX

The players' entrance at Yankee Stadium was mobbed by the press, the curious, and the weird. The NYPD had beefed up the security detail to try to avoid incidents. Besides the reporters and their crews, there were people representing various oddball groups, carrying signs that said things like FAGGOTS, GO BACK TO IRAQ and SODOMY IS A MORTAL SIN.

Randy and D.J. rode through this bedlam in the limo and were escorted through the door by the police. Once inside, they found more TV cameras following them through the corridors until they disappeared into the sanctuary of the visitor's clubhouse—from which the press had been banned by Charlie Gonse.

As soon as they entered, the room became dead quiet. The players had been sitting in small groups talking among themselves, wondering what the commissioner was going to do to Randy and D.J.

Opinion about the affair was far from unanimous. Rennie Pannizardi thought that they should be given a separate locker room because frankly he didn't want to take his shower in the same room with them. "They can do what the fuck they want in private but not in the shower room with the rest of us around."

Willie St. James was now even further convinced that D. J. Pickett was a house nigger and said that as far as he was concerned it was not entirely impossible that he wasn't getting it on with John/John too, who, as far as he was concerned, if he wasn't a faggot acted like one.

Axel Most said it was none of anybody's business and Bernie Lazarre sort of agreed, provided that they didn't expose anybody's family to it. And Harry Glugg said that somebody ought to hit on Susie Dreyfus; it was a fucking shame to let that body go to waste.

But when Randy and D.J. walked in, nobody said a word to them. Nobody even looked at them. Suddenly they all were busy oiling their gloves. Even Spic Mendoza had nothing to say for once.

Charlie Gonse walked out of his office, surveyed his double-play combination, and asked, "You suspended?"

"Not yet," D.J. said.

"Glad to hear it."

Gonse looked around at his players and decided this was a good time for a pregame talk.

"All right, listen," he announced, taking a fresh toothpick out of his pocket and unwrapping it. "As far as I'm concerned, this is a game of scoring runs. You got to score more runs than the other team. That's basically it. So all this other shit that's going around, as far as I'm concerned, has nothing to do with scoring runs. You want to get distracted by peripheral activities, you're not going to have your head in the game. The next thing you know you're five runs down and the wind's blowing in from left field. They got people running around this city ought to be locked up. They're going to be screaming all sorts of shit from the stands, trying to get you out of the game. Tune them out. Switch the station. Tune into the game. Think about runs. Hit the ball, run fast, get around the bases. This is not a game has anything to do with peripherals. Okay. There's Chinese for the buffet after the game."

The players nodded and dispersed, some wandering into the trainer's room, others going back to their lockers to finish dressing.

Randy's and D.J.'s lockers were on opposite ends of the clubhouse. Randy sat down on the stool in front of his locker and looked around at his teammates. It was as if he and D.J. weren't there.

What the fuck was wrong with these guys, anyway? Hadn't they ever seen a goddamn lefty before? They were acting like D.J. and he were some sort of contaminated Typhoid Marys.

He and D.J. hadn't had a chance to talk. They had walked out of Fritz Esterhazy's office promising to think things over. From there they went straight to the limo, accompanied by Teffner and John/ John, and the four of them rode in silence all the way up to the Bronx.

And in the midst of all this shit, they had to play baseball. Jesus. Just hit the ball and score runs. Easy for Gonse to say. Randy didn't even know who was pitching for the Yankees. There was one guy on the team he couldn't hit for shit, a tall, skinny left-hander who threw cut sliders and forkballs at him all the time. He hoped to hell it wasn't that guy.

He looked over at D.J., who was the only one on the team who would look at him. He smiled. D.J. smiled back. Randy felt a tingle inside. It was that old devil moon in his eyes. Thank God for that.

New York was a tough town under the best of circumstances. As far as Randy Dreyfus was concerned, the people there all looked like they slept in the subway and carried concealed weapons. And to make matters worse, the tall, skinny left-hander with the cut sliders was on the mound.

A lot of ugly things were shouted down from the stands that night. And Randy could feel the glare of the TV cameras on him every-where—in the field, at the plate, in the dugout.

The first time Randy came up to the plate, there were roars, catcalls and howls. In spite of the beefed-up security precautions, fistfights broke out in several places in the stands. The cops had to eject a dozen people. Randy stood in there and tried to tune out everything but the tall skinny left-hander glaring down at him like an ax murderer.

Even though he couldn't hit this guy for shit he was going to hit him tonight because sitting in the Commissioner's Box behind first base was a guy who was threatening to throw him and D.J. out of baseball. It might be the commissioner's fucking bat and ball, but before Randy gave the bat back, he was going to do what he did best with it.

The left-hander was going to start him out with a fastball in on the hands. He always did. Randy laid off it, fouled the next one off, eventually working the count to three-and-two. Then he waited on the slider low and away. He adjusted his feet, strode into the ball, and rifled it into right field for a solid single.

As he stood on first base, he noticed that Sid Bernouz, the Yankees' first baseman, a guy you usually shot the shit with, didn't say a word to him. With two outs Bernouz was supposed to be holding the runner on, but Randy had the impression the guy was standing as far away from him as he could.

Glen Ephard walked, then Bernie Lazarre put one in the stands in left, and the Vikings were up three zip. Which didn't do anything to make the mood of the crowd less ugly.

Back in the dugout Charlie Gonse chewed harder on his toothpick. He didn't like leads. Leads made you overconfident. Axel Most was on the mound. If he was on his game, three runs would theoretically be enough. That type of overconfidence could really kill you.

Ken Teffner, John/John, and Larry Zwick sat in the row behind the Commissioner's Box, but none of them had his mind on what was happening onto the field. They had met briefly with Esterhazy before the game, and the commissioner had told them he was very concerned about the situation and would be deciding on a course of action soon. In the meantime, a lot would depend upon the attitudes of the individuals involved.

Ken Teffner had a pretty good idea what that meant. He had been sitting in his seat, doing his best to ignore the obscenities shouted from the fans above them and trying to come up with a campaign to deal with the situation. As he had told Burton Meeker, this one wasn't going to be easy.

John/John wasn't much help. Every time Teffner brought the situation up, he just shook his head and started to wheeze. Zwick's solution was to ride the season out and trade them in the winter. The old man had already asked him to float an offer around to see if anyone was interested. It was unusual to offer two star players as trade bait during a playoff series, but Zwick had dutifully called around the league. So far there were no takers at any price. Everyone was waiting to see what Fritz Esterhazy was going to do.

The commissioner sat in his Burberry, doing his best to keep the mustard from the obligatory hot dog from dripping in his lap, and watched Randy Dreyfus and D. J. Pickett play. They were the heart and soul of the Viking team. Without them, the Vikings would never be able to go all the way, which was too bad. It would make his decision all the more difficult. But he would not shirk his responsibilities. As his old friend Dick Nixon used to say, when the going got tough, the tough got going.

Fritz Esterhazy believed that history always put exceptional men in the right position at critical moments. Abraham Lincoln, Winston Churchill, FDR. Baseball was fortunate to have as its commissioner, at this particular moment in its history, a man worthy of the solemn responsibilities of the office.

The Vikings won 4–3 on a sacrifice fly by D. J. Pickett in the ninth. By the end of the game, the police had ejected over a hundred fans for fighting and throwing objects onto the field. Among the objects thrown at Randy and D.J. were a vibrator, a jar of Vaseline, and a variety of ripe fruits.

The clubhouse was quiet in the face of victory. The Chinese buffet didn't go over very big. The sportswriters, finally allowed into the locker room, were told that only questions about the game would be tolerated, that anyone asking personal questions would be asked to leave.

As far as Milt Zola was concerned, that policy was clearly a violation of the working rules of sportswriting, not to mention the First Amendment. But, keeping a low profile, he helped himself to a paper plate of moo goo gai pan, then went over to D. J. Pickett, who was fielding questions about his sacrifice fly from a group of reporters.

"What'd he throw you?"

"Change-up."

"Were you expecting it?"

"Uh-uh."

"You hit it anyway, didn't you?"

"Apparently."

"How'd you feel about it when you hit it?"

"I got under it, hit it lousy. Just happened to be a guy on third with less than two outs. Otherwise it's a routine fly ball."

The writers drifted off to talk to Axel Most about his seven-hitter. Zola sat down on a stool beside D.J. and said, "How's it going?"

"Pretty good."

"Look, I'm not supposed to talk to you about this, but I think you're going to need some friends in the press. And I want you to know that I could be a friend."

D.J. looked at him, searching his face for signs of duplicity. You really had to be careful with writers. They all said they were your friends and then they fucked you over in print.

"That so," he said, not without a tinge of mockery in his voice.

"Uh-huh. I think you guys are about to get a raw deal."

"Yeah?"

"Yeah. And I think there's a fight worth fighting here. So if you want some help, let me know."

And he got up and walked away. D.J. watched him leave the clubhouse, a big, lumbering guy in a wrinkled raincoat. As soon as he walked out, Ken Teffner, Larry Zwick, and John/John entered. They went around slapping everyone on the back.

Then they came over to D.J. Big smiles.

"Hey, hell of a hit."

D.J. nodded.

"Three more and we're in the Series."

"Right."

Teffner knelt down so that he would be at eye level with D.J. It was his sincerity posture. "What do you say we have some breakfast tomorrow morning?"

"Breakfast?"

"Yeah. We'll have it sent up to my room. Sit around, shoot the shit."

"Yeah, well, you know, I'm not very big on breakfast . . ."

"Great. Say about nine?"

As soon as he got back to the hotel, D.J. tried calling Randy in his room, but the phone was off the hook. When he went down the hall to knock on Randy's door and still got no answer, he started to worry. He was considering getting a passkey from the front desk when it occurred to him where Randy probably was.

D.J. pushed open the door to the weight room and found the shortstop doing leg presses on the machine. He stood watching Randy strain to push the weight back up against the spring, grunting from the effort. When he finished the set, D.J. threw him a towel and watched as he sponged the sweat off his face and neck. He looked beautiful, his chest glistening with a light patina of perspiration, his blond hair spilling haphazardly over his forehead.

"How are you doing?" D.J. said.

"I did fifty leg presses. Not bad, huh?"

"That's not what I meant."

Randy threw the towel away, got up, and flexed his shoulder muscles. "Not so hot."

"It's a bitch, isn't it?"

"I guess it's my own fault. You warned me this was going to happen."

"It's not your fault. We just fucked up in Dallas."

"Yeah, but sooner or later they probably would've nailed us. You know, my wife had a private detective following me. She found your handkerchief in the laundry."

"No shit."

"We were being tailed by a private eye just like in the movies."

"How'd she take it?"

Randy shrugged. "She said that anything I want to do is okay with her."

"It must be pretty rough, you know, with the kids."

"Yeah . . ."

Neither of them said anything for a while, then D.J. said, "They want to see me tomorrow morning in Teffner's room for breakfast."

"What do you think they're going to say?"

"They're going to try to turn us against each other, split us up. Divide and conquer."

"Fuck 'em."

"You heard what Esterhazy said."

"I don't like that son of a bitch."

"Like he said, it's his bat and ball."

"Can't we get, like, a lawyer or something? I mean what about the Players Association?"

"It's Article Nineteen. You agreed to it when you signed your contract. There's no appeal."

Randy walked over to the window and looked down over Manhattan, still alive with traffic even at this late hour. For once he didn't give a shit whether it was a No Suicide room. He wouldn't give them the satisfaction. "I mean," he muttered, "you heard that shit he wants us to do. It'll be worse than Don Amarillo. We'll have to go into some electric-shock therapy or something. . . ."

"Teffner'll figure out some bullshit to make it fly."

"You really want to do that shit?"

"It's your call."

"What do you mean, it's my call?"

"Look, Randy, I got enough in the bank to do okay if they throw me out of baseball. I got no family and a small nut. But you're about to sign a multiyear deal worth a lot of money. You could own this town. You got more to lose than I do here. You want to get out now, I understand."

Randy turned around and gave D.J. a desperate look. "Get out?" he said on the verge of tears. "How the fuck do I *get out*?"

D.J. came over and put his arms around him, and the big shortstop started to cry in earnest.

When D. J. Pickett entered Ken Teffner's hotel suite shortly after nine the next morning, there was a palpable sense of collective anxiety floating through the room. He had the feeling that Zwick, Teffner, and John/John had been up for hours, drinking coffee, perspiring in the already-humid New York morning that had managed to infiltrate through the air conditioners.

Larry Zwick was on the phone with the general manager of the Baltimore Orioles and quickly cut the conversation short. John/John was staring blankly at the TV, watching a rerun of *The Andy Griffith Show*. Teffner ushered D.J. to a chair.

"Hey, how you doing, D.J.?"

"Okay."

"What can I get for you? Some French toast and sausage? Couple of eggs over easy?"

"Just a little coffee."

"You sure?"

"Yeah."

John/John shut the TV off and came over, offering his hand in a strangely formal gesture, as if they were meeting for the first time.

"D.J.," he pronounced in his thinly aspirated voice.

Teffner brought over the room-service coffeepot, and set it down on the table next to a basket full of croissants.

"Have one. They're terrific." He gestured to the basket.

"No thanks."

Zwick came and sat on one of the chairs by the couch.

"You sleep okay?" he asked.

"Yeah."

"Hell of a sac fly."

"Thanks."

"Clutch hit . . ."

"Listen," said D.J., "I don't generally do breakfast, so could we deal the cards?"

There was a moment of uncomfortable silence. John/John sucked some air into his congested bronchial tubes. Zwick recrossed his legs.

"We want you to know, D.J., right at the beginning," Teffner said, "that everybody in this organization has the highest regard for you, including Mr. White."

"My father often says," John/John joined in, "that you are as fine an example for black people as there is in this country. And that includes Harry Belafonte."

"Unfortunately," Teffner went on, "this . . . situation with Randy Dreyfus is extremely awkward for the Vikings. . . . You see, D.J., we have to look at this from a marketing perspective. Baseball is no longer just a game—"

"Why isn't Randy down here too?"

Teffner stopped, momentarily derailed by the question. "Beg your pardon?" he muttered.

"Why aren't you talking to us together?"

Teffner fiddled with his May Company men's shop tie for a moment and then said, "Let me level with you, D.J. We don't think Randy is as reasonable as you. He tends to fly off the handle very easily. We thought it would be easier to communicate if it was just the four of us."

"So what's the deal?"

"Well, we've spoken with Fritz Esterhazy, and he's pretty much laid out his position. And we want you to know that if you're willing to work with him on this, we'll do everything in our power to work with you."

"Work with us?"

"D.J., I really think we can ride this out. It's not going to be easy, but if we all pull together on this, we can get through it."

"Frankly, I'm not so clear on just what everyone wants us to do at this point."

"Well, that would depend upon the commissioner, of course. I assume he would stipulate certain actions, and we would work with him and you to facilitate matters . . ."

For a moment D.J. was afraid he was going to start laughing. What the fuck *were* they going to do? Claim the whole thing was an optical illusion? More substance-abuse therapy?

It was roughly at this point that D. J. Pickett decided he was no longer interested in being a credit to his race. He'd let Harry Belafonte carry the banner himself from here on in. He looked from one to another of the three men facing him and then said in a controlled voice, "Ken, I don't think even you can sell this one. They have us on film. Everybody in the country has seen it. So the only thing that's left is to say we're sorry and we won't do it again. I got to tell you the truth. We're not sorry. And whether or not we do it again is none of your fucking business."

Then he got up, smiled, and said, "Thanks for breakfast."

XX

Barry Fuchsia's phone had been ringing off the hook for days. Every major newspaper, magazine, and book publisher was after a piece of the story. And they were all waving around a lot of cash.

Fuchsia had tried to get through to his client in New York, but Randy wasn't taking phone calls. He finally resorted to faxing the traveling secretary and telling him to have Randy call him immediately. Which he finally did, the morning after the first game.

"Hey, kid, how you doing?" Barry Fuchsia said as Randy sat in his barricaded hotel room eating a room-service breakfast.

"Things are pretty crazy, Barry."

"You're telling me. I got half the country wants to talk to you. I can't go to the bathroom without the phone ringing and someone wanting you on TV. I got *Donahue, Geraldo, Oprah,* Barbara Walters . . ."

"That's great, Barry, but what about the Vikings?"

"What about the Vikings? They can take a number."

"This is going to screw the deal up. You said—"

"I know what I said. But that's when we were talking about substance abuse. Substance abuse is a nonstarter. Nobody's interested in drunks and coke freaks anymore. They already did that movie. But this is a draw. This is heat."

"Heat?"

"Listen, I got a call from a guy at CBS wants to make a TV movie about you. Maybe even get Costner to play the lead. . . . The upfront money won't be great but we could roll it into a development deal, set up a production company—"

"Barry, what the fuck are you talking about? I'm a baseball player."

"Let me tell you something, Randy. You never put on a uniform again, you can still be a rich man. The book rights alone'll cover the first year of any baseball deal, and I'm just talking domestic . . ."

When he finally got Barry Fuchsia off the phone, Randy was no longer interested in his breakfast. He pushed away the bowl of soggy spoon-size shredded wheat and lay back down on the bed. Things were swirling around so fast that it was hard to focus. He didn't even know where to begin to sort out his problems. He wondered what they were telling D.J. downstairs in Ken Teffner's suite. Were they cutting a deal without him?

The phone rang. He had forgotten to take it back off the hook.

"Hello?"

"Hey, how'd you like to suck my big fat dick?" said a voice with a Spanish accent. He thought it was Spic Mendoza until the obscene caller went on. "I'll be waiting for you in the bathroom in the Times Square IRT Station, third stall from the door—"

Randy slammed the phone down. Jesus! It was coming at him from all directions now. The phone rang again almost immediately. He let it ring a number of times, then cautiously picked it up.

"Hey, guess what I told them they could do with their ball and bat?" It was D.J.

"What?"

"Choke up on it."

"No kidding?"

"No kidding. Take two and hit to right."

"Jesus."

Neither of them said anything for a moment. Then Randy said in a whisper, "I guess it's just you and me now, huh?"

"That's the way it looks."

Game Two of the American League Championship Series was played before another sellout crowd. Security was even tighter this time. Everyone entering Yankee Stadium had to pass through a metal detector, even the working press, which had swollen beyond the usual number for a playoff game. It was SRO in the press box.

Which pissed Milt Zola off. He was crowded on both sides by reporters with no sports background, who were not there to cover the game. They didn't even keep score. Instead they sat there, barely paying attention to the action on the field, trading rumors about *the situation*.

The big question—the question that was on everyone's mind—was what Fritz Esterhazy was going to do. And when. The commissioner had been very tight-lipped, saying only that he had met with the players involved and was reviewing the situation carefully before making a decision.

Zola was pretty sure that Esterhazy was going to invoke Article 19. There was immense pressure on him from the owners. They had issued a vaguely worded statement to the effect that there was no place in baseball for behavior that deviated from contemporary community standards of morality.

Zola figured that Esterhazy was stalling for time. If the Vikings were beaten in the playoffs, then the decision to throw out their two key players would be much less controversial. But if he had to exclude them from the World Series, he would come under a lot of heat. So for the moment at least, Zola was sure Fritz Esterhazy was rooting for the Yankees.

The Yankees, however, weren't making things any easier for the commissioner. A key error in the third inning led to two unearned runs, and the Vikings were up 5–3 going into the ninth. If they could hang on and go back to Los Angeles with a two-zip lead, they'd be in excellent shape.

When Randy came up in the top of the ninth, the mixed chorus of boos, catcalls, and cheers descended from the stands. Thanks to the metal detector, there were few objects thrown on the field, though someone did manage to smuggle in a gay porno magazine and float pages down like paper airplanes.

As Game Two began to slip away, the Yankees themselves were starting to get ugly. Randy could clearly hear the word *faggot* from the New York dugout, and when he looked over there briefly, he saw two of the players, towels wrapped around their waists like skirts, doing a mock kiss.

As Randy stepped in, Mike Melovsky, the Yankee catcher, said, "Which one of you sticks it in the other?"

Randy ignored him, keeping his eyes straight ahead on the pitcher. Melovsky kept at him. "Coon like that must have a pretty big one. You choke up on it or what?"

When the pitch came it was high and hard, moving in toward his head. Randy managed to get his left biceps in front of it. The umpire waved him to first base. Randy glared out at the pitcher. It was clearly deliberate, but the umpire didn't issue a warning. Randy looked toward the Viking dugout. Nobody moved. Nobody was going to come out and help him if he went after the pitcher. The trainer didn't even come out to see if he was all right.

He trotted down to first base, refusing to rub his shoulder, which hurt like hell. The guy must have thrown the ball ninety-eight miles an hour. In the stands, the crazies were carrying on again. They had invented a new type of wave, which they called the gay wave. Instead of throwing your hands above your head, you waved your left hand in a limp-wristed salute. There had been a ringing editorial about it in *The New York Times* that morning.

As the gay wave rolled through the stands, Sid Bernouz came over to hold Randy on first.

"Nice town you got here, Sid," Randy said.

The tall, lanky first baseman said nothing. He didn't even nod. Randy looked down at third, where Al De Mun was running signs. He was shooting blanks. Maybe Al De Mun didn't think there was a play on, but Randy Dreyfus was going to put one on.

He took his lead, drawing a throw, reading the pitcher's move. After three throws he got the move down, detected its weakness. He went on the first pitch to the plate, coming in spikes high, beating a good throw by Melovsky and managing to get a nice piece of Slick Carrera's knee in the process.

Carrera rolled over in the dust, then got up, glaring at Randy. No contest. The guy was five-eight in high heels. The Yankee shortstop just spat on the ground, muttered, and went back to his position.

Randy wasn't finished with Mike Melovsky yet. There were more bases to be stolen. Charlie Gonse must have sensed what Randy was planning because he flashed a red light to Al De Mun, who hung the sign out loud and clear.

Randy touched the visor of his cap to indicate he caught the sign, then went back to reading the pitcher's move. Carrera tried ducking in behind him, but Randy didn't bite. He moved off far enough to draw a throw, and then a bluff and then another throw. Finally he took a step past the invisible line that every catcher draws in the sand, and when Melovsky signaled for the pickoff, Randy took off. The throw went wide to the right and under Carrera's glove, skipping into center field, and Randy waltzed into third with a shit-eating grin on his face.

He was now close enough to the Yankee dugout to hear the insults. The Yankees went at him mercilessly. Randy didn't give a shit. Turning his back to them, he took a big lead off third.

Milt Zola watched in amazement from the press box as Randy Dreyfus moved down the line. He was taunting the pitcher, dancing like Jackie Robinson used to do to the crackers in the late forties. He was going one-on-one with the Yankees and making them look bad.

In the Viking dugout Charlie Gonse was splintering his toothpick. What the hell was Dreyfus doing? There was no one out. A sac fly, ground ball to the right side would bring him in.

But Charlie Gonse didn't understand his shortstop's priorities. All Randy Dreyfus was thinking about was that he was now ninety feet from Mike Melovsky. He wanted a piece of him. And out or safe, he was going to have him.

Perhaps the only other person in the ballpark who knew what Randy was going to do was Milt Zola. Zola understood myth and retribution. He realized that Randy Dreyfus had an appointment with Mike Melovsky, who had called for the purpose pitch that had started the whole thing off.

Randy looked down the line. Glen Ephard, standing in from the left side, gave him a clear view of the Yankee catcher. There was no point in even being coy about it. The point wasn't to steal home. The point was to get his shoulder into the Yankee catcher and bounce him off the foul-ball screen.

Randy went on the first pitch, a fastball down the pipe. Melovsky was waiting for him with the ball, mask off, blocking the plate. So much the better, thought Randy as he headed right for him.

He lowered his shoulder and accelerated off the back of his powerful calves, which were tuned to perfection by all those leg presses in the weight room. Just before he made contact, he thought of Fritz Esterhazy's smug Princeton smile.

It did the trick. He hit Melovsky so hard that he knocked the 225-pound Yankee catcher clear back across the plate and halfway to the on-deck circle. As the ball rolled out of Melovsky's glove and bounced away, Randy raised his hand in a clenched fist.

Choke up on that, fuck face.

Sitting on the sand-colored leather settee in the entertainment nook of her Valley View Estates home, Susie Dreyfus watched her husband put away Mike Melovsky and the Vikings win Game Two of the American League Championship Series. She had been sitting there since the beginning of the game, five-thirty West Coast time, compulsively munching carrots and avocado dip, her eyes focused on the TV screen but her thoughts a chaotic tangle of contradictions.

Even though the security police had finally cleared the reporters from the front of the house, photographers continued to cruise by hoping to get a shot of her or the girls. She had kept Molly and Dolly out of school and had done her best to keep them away from the TV, but it was impossible to insulate them entirely from what was going on.

She had explained that Randy and she were having marital problems and that because their father was a famous baseball player, everyone was making a big deal out of it. The twins, however, watched enough TV soap operas to get the picture.

"Is Daddy having an affair?" was the first thing out of Molly's mouth.

Susie shrugged, sort of nodded, then shook her head, then nodded again.

"With his secretary?" asked Dolly.

"Daddy doesn't have a secretary," Susie said limply.

"So who's the home wrecker?" Molly asked.

"It's sort of complicated . . ."

"Are you going to get divorced?"

Susie did another combination of vague, contradictory gestures.

"Are you going to take him to the cleaner's?"

Susie's father had asked pretty much the same question, though a
little less crudely, when her parents had called from Phoenix after
the news broke. Her mother babbled a great deal of nonsense and
told her that she and the twins could come live with them, and then
her father, a lawyer, had gotten on the phone and explained that
she was in a position to do quite well in any divorce settlement.

"You have special factors involved here, certainly with respect to
custody, you understand, not to mention financially . . ."

It was not something she wanted to understand right now. Even
when Zabriskie had sent the Palmdale motel pictures to her radio-
station office and she was confronted with the undeniable reality of
the affair, she had been unable to feel the same anger she had felt
upon initially discovering the handkerchief.

Mostly now she felt a vague sadness inside her. Instead of a desire
to hurt and punish Randy, she felt a peculiar sympathy, almost tenderness, toward him. As all this blind confusion and hatred swirled
around him, a sort of maternal instinct kicked in. He seemed so
alone and vulnerable in the middle of this maelstrom of media
attention and public outcry.

In a sense, it was easier for her to accept that the home wrecker
was a man and not another woman. The rejection was more
oblique. Randy had just gone off in another direction; some collection of hormones inside him switched themselves around, and he
felt a completely different set of desires. There was nothing to be
done about it.

She had decided that she would not ask him to move out of the
house. In fact, he could even sleep in the bedroom if he wanted. She
would pick him up at the airport, as she always did, and drive him

back home and talk to him about his batting average or his problems with pitchers or anything else he wanted to talk about.

As far as she was concerned, it wasn't all about where men put their penises, as Fuad claimed. Though she couldn't help wondering where Randy actually *did* put it. The very thought embarrassed her. She quickly put it out of her mind and turned off the TV.

She removed her skirt and sat down on the Navajo throw rug, assuming the Flowering Tree yoga position. Her arms became limbs beginning to bud, her legs and waist the trunk through which the sap rose. Slowly she began to tune out thoughts of penises and custody settlements and center her consciousness on the simple act of putting out leaves.

They had changed the location of the arrival gate of the Vikings' charter from New York in an attempt, once again, to avoid the TV cameras, but once again the word leaked, and by the time Susie arrived, she had to run the gauntlet of minicam units before reaching the lounge.

It was a good thing she had dressed. She often picked Randy up in a pair of jeans and a sweatshirt, but tonight she was wearing authentic Hopi silver earrings, a beige cashmere sweater over a long plaid skirt, and black leather high-heeled boots. Microphones were shoved in her face, and pert little Asian women with cute hairdos asked her if she was going to take Randy back and what it was like knowing her husband was seeing another man behind her back. Susie walked right through without stopping and made her way into the lounge, which was protected by airport security cops.

She was greeted there in much the same way that Randy and D.J. were when they arrived at the visitors' clubhouse at Yankee Stadium a few days before. The clusters of wives and girlfriends immediately grew quiet. The women all gave quick little nervous waves and cracked smiles, then turned away. Nobody said a word.

Finally Karen Most walked over in her Bullock's jogging suit and Reeboks. "Hi," she said, attempting a sympathetic smile.

"Hi."

"How're you doing?"

"All right," Susie lied.

The two women then stood there for a moment, not saying anything. The other women stood in their clusters not saying anything either. Outside the glass partition, TV cameras rolled, spewing out footage of all this silence.

"This must be very difficult for you," Karen Most said finally.

Susie gave her the same kind of half-nod, half-shrug she had given her children.

"Did you . . . have any idea?"

Susie shook her head. She was hoping that Karen Most would shut up because otherwise she was going to break into tears.

"I guess it's kind of the last thing you'd think of . . ."

Susie nodded, clenching her teeth. It was a yoga technique called stemming the tide, which was supposed to control excessive menstrual flow, but Susie had found it effective in stressful situations.

"Is there anything I can do?"

Susie shook her head, concentrating energy in her solar plexus, contracting the muscles to staunch the flow.

"So are you going to do the car pool tomorrow morning?"

Susie shrugged. "I don't know." *I don't know* was an answer. But Karen Most wasn't buying it.

"I sort of need to know because otherwise I have to cancel the workout session with my trainer."

"Okay."

"Okay you're going to drive? Or okay you're not going to drive? I mean, I don't mind driving. It's just that I need to know one way or the other. I mean, I understand, what with all that's going on, if you can't . . . then I'll cancel the trainer . . ."

Fortunately the plane arrived just then. The wives and girlfriends gathered at the door to greet their men while Susie stood back and waited, feeling the silent glare of the TV cameras on her back. As usual, Randy was one of the last off the plane. He was wearing a nice-looking light green sweater and a pair of European-style slacks. He had started dressing better over the past month or so. That should have been her first clue.

Surprised to see her, he gave a little awkward half-smile. She recognized the gesture and felt a twinge inside her. She gave him a quick peck on the cheek for the benefit of the TV cameras, and, taking his hand, walked out with him.

This time they ran the gauntlet of Asian women with microphones together, and this time the reporters backed off a little because Randy had the same look on his face that he had had before he hit Mike Melovksy.

The cameras followed them out to the 560 SEL. Susie got behind the wheel, and they drove off, leaving the reporters running for their minivans. By the time the Mercedes reached the freeway, Susie had lost them.

In the car on the way home Susie talked about the twins, school, the dog, replacing a water heater in the master bathroom. Business as usual. Randy nodded, muttered a few short answers, and that was that. It wasn't really all that different from their usual conversations on the way back from the airport.

The twins, in matching Petit Bateau dresses, greeted Randy at the door. Susie had told them that no one was to talk about marital problems. They had a quiet dinner of lasagna and salad, and then Randy went downstairs to the playroom and shot pool for several hours.

Though Susie told him that he could sleep in the bedroom, he chose the guest house, on the other side of the pool. He dropped a Halcion and was nodding out before ten.

Just before he dropped off, he heard a scratching sound at the screen door. He tried to ignore it, but it persisted, and finally he got off the foldaway bed and went to the door. Calvin was standing there in the moonlight with a soulful look in his eyes.

Randy shook his head as sternly as he could. "No, Calvin. Go away."

The dog didn't budge. More stern looks and verbal discouragement didn't do any good. Randy finally opened the door and let the dog in.

The Dalmatian immediately jumped onto the bed. Randy shoved him off and climbed in, turning off the light. After a moment, he felt the dog jump back on the bed and nuzzle up close to him.

What the fuck.

Randy mumbled, "Nice doggie," and fell asleep.

XXI

The Vikings won Game Three by a score of 8–1. Paddy Clamm, a journeyman left-hander and spot starter, pitched the game of his career, limiting the Yankees to one run and five hits in seven and two thirds innings. Randy went 2-for-5, with a double and a triple, and D.J. hit one of his infrequent home runs.

The sellout crowd at Viking Stadium, though not as ugly or vociferous as the fans in New York, was nonetheless affected by the publicity surrounding the two star players. There was no gay wave, but there were pockets of hostility up in the stands, booing and catcalling when Randy or D.J. came up to the plate. Mostly, though, there was a sense of stunned confusion and betrayal among the Viking faithful.

The city had been polarized by the controversy. Its normally casual, laid-back rhythm had been jarred by the events into a frenzy of reaction. The call-in radio programs discussed nothing else. Twenty-four hours a day people expressed themselves forcefully on the issue, one way or the other. Everyone seemed to have an opinion. There was a great deal of sermonizing and invective floating over the airwaves.

One caller from Tarzana suggested that after the two offenders were thrown out of baseball and criminally prosecuted for public indecency, all other players should be made to sign a heterosexuality oath. An ex–big league ballplayer now living in retirement in Palm Springs said that in his twenty-two years in the game he had never seen "one" and, in his opinion, "they" shouldn't be permitted to play since most of "them" were more interested in interior decorating anyway. A schoolteacher from Mission Viejo thought that baseball should now become an R-rated entertainment, with no kids under seventeen admitted to the ballpark without an adult.

Leaders of various gay and lesbian organizations hailed the situation as evidence that gays were normal, well-adjusted people in all walks of life. The more radical faction of the gay-rights movement threatened a national boycott if any punitive action was taken against the two players.

It began to look like a no-win situation for Fritz Esterhazy. Whatever decision he made was going to be unpopular. The commissioner sat in his den on Central Park South and watched the third game on television. He had decided not to fly out for the West Coast games. He wanted to be out of the spotlight, sheltered from the enormous media attention that was swirling around the situation.

Earlier he had spoken on the phone with Ken Teffner and John D. F. White, Jr., and learned that Dreyfus and Pickett were not going to cooperate. They had refused to play ball with him, as it were. Which left him very little room to maneuver.

Fritz Esterhazy did not like being backed into a corner. It violated his sense of the unwritten rules of negotiation. You had to give the other guy a little room to play his cards. What Fritz Esterhazy did best was navigate between difficult alternatives and come up with an acceptable solution. But in this case he couldn't do that without the cooperation of Randy Dreyfus and D. J. Pickett, and it didn't look like he was going to get it.

As the Yankees went down in Game Three, things began looking worse. He was going to have to throw two star players on a World Series team out of baseball. Or deal with the consequences of letting them play.

The commissioner was sitting in his darkened den, sipping a watered Chivas, absently watching the ninth inning of the game, now hopelessly out of reach, when his phone rang. He saw from the blinking light that it was his private line, a number that very few people had. It was 11 P.M. His wife was already in bed. He had no idea who would be calling him on this line at this hour. He picked up the phone.

"Hello?" he said.

There was a brief moment of silence, and then he heard a disembodied male voice say, "Mr. Esterhazy?"

"Yes. Who is this?"

"Would you hold for a moment for the president?"

Esterhazy quickly drained his Chivas, as if it were somehow wrong to be drinking while talking to the president of the United States. He got up, flexed his back, waited. He had met the man briefly on Opening Day in Philadelphia, where he threw out the first ball. They had sat together and eaten their hot dogs, surrounded by Secret Service agents, before the president made a discreet exit after the third inning.

How the hell did he get this number? And what did he want?

"Fritz?" He heard the younger man's vacuous midwestern voice on the other end of the line.

"Mr. President . . ."

"Sorry to bother you at this hour, but it's beginning to look like the Vikings are going to the World Series, isn't it?"

"That seems to be the case."

"Pitching. And strong defense up the middle. That makes the difference."

"Yes . . ."

"Let me tell you why I called, Fritz. I'm concerned. I'm concerned about our youth. Where are they going? What do they believe in? How are they going to get along in a world of diminishing resources? When these concerns begin to fill me with despair, do you know what I think about?"

"No, sir."

"I think about baseball and I immediately feel better. I say to myself, There will always be baseball. In spite of the problems of our cities, of pollution, crime, drugs, there will always be nine innings, three outs, three strikes. Pitching and a strong defense up the middle will always make a difference."

"Yes it will."

Then, in a quiet, solemn voice, the president said, "Baseball is an island of cleanliness and purity surrounded by a polluted and chaotic sea. It's our last hope. If baseball goes, we might as well kiss all the rest of it good-bye. The whole thing collapses. Like a row of dominoes. Are you following me?"

"I believe so, sir . . ."

"Good. I knew I could count on you, Fritz. I'm pleased that you see things this way. Give my best to Marjorie."

And the line went dead. The commissioner stood there holding the phone for a second, before laying it down softly in its cradle. He walked back over to the liquor cabinet, poured himself another Chivas, threw a couple of ice cubes in it, and took a deep gulp. The president of the United States had just called with a new wrinkle on the domino theory.

Fritz Esterhazy knew more about the national debt than that idiot knew about baseball, yet that didn't stop him from expressing an opinion. Everyone had an opinion on what he should do, from the president of the United States to his wife—whose name was Margaret, not Marjorie—to the owner of the Los Angeles Valley Vikings.

In a letter to the editor published in that morning's *Los Angeles Times*, John D. F. White, Sr., had written: "Baseball has been going on for a long time, and it has no place for this sort of thing just as it has no place for drugs or gambling or any other immoral activity that wants to rear its ugly head, regardless of race, color, or creed."

At 4 A.M. Randy lay wide awake and naked on the foldaway bed in the guest house. Beside him Calvin snored peacefully. It was hot even with all the windows open. The Santa Anas had blown in yesterday morning, bringing the accumulated heat of the desert with them. The temperature had reached 101 in Reseda, 110 in Palm Springs.

He could hear the whirring of the twin six-ton Carrier air conditioners cooling the house where his family slept. Otherwise, it was dead quiet in Valley View Estates. Randy lay there thinking about the shambles that his life was in. The day before he'd had a session with Mendes Fuad. He had paced around the small office in Westwood, trying to get a grip on things.

"Things are getting out of hand here, doc."

"How's that?"

"We have a good shot at the World Series and I could be thrown out of baseball. I got reporters every morning in front of my house, where I'm not even living. I'm living in the guest house, sleeping with my dog, who I tried to kill a couple of months ago. I spend all my time thinking about D.J., but I can't see him because of the reporters. And . . ."

Randy took a couple of turns around the office without saying anything. Finally Fuad said, "And what?"

"This is a biggie."

"Yes?"

"I don't think I can hit from the right side anymore."

"Beg your pardon?"

"Pia Zadora."

"Pia Zadora?"

"Not interested anymore. Pasadena . . ." Randy made the tits sign, then indicated his reaction by showing his index finger collapsing from a rigid position. The doctor got the point.

"Hmmn . . ." Fuad intoned quietly.

"Is that all you can say? I mean, what if you woke up one morning and discovered you were a paraplegic?"

"You're not a paraplegic. You're a homosexual."

Fuad's words kept reverberating through Randy's head. *You're a homosexual.* It sounded to him like a death sentence. He was an outcast. His conduct was detrimental to the best interests of baseball. Esterhazy was going to throw him out on his ass, and he was going to have to make his living going on *Donahue* and telling his story.

How the fuck was it all going to end up?

He had no idea. Which was why he was lying in his guest house at 4 A.M. unable to sleep. There was only one thing that would enable him to sleep now. Did he dare? The guy liked his sleep . . .

Shit, batting practice wasn't until four o'clock in the afternoon. They could sleep in.

Calvin woke up as Randy was zipping up the fly on his L.L. Bean camping shorts. The Dalmatian, dumb as he was, picked up immediately on the situation. He jumped off the bed and parked himself in front of the screen door with a forlorn look. Whither thou goest . . .

Fuck. Randy opened the screen door and told him to go take a leak. He didn't want to have to walk him later.

"Why don't I hate him? I mean, I should be feeling a lot of anger here, shouldn't I? He cheated on me. He snuck around and . . . and slept with a . . . man . . ."

She still had trouble pronouncing the words. She had to stop herself from saying *slept with another man,* which was not at all an accurate description of what had happened. Fuad was wearing that ridiculous cardigan in spite of the Santa Anas. He nodded absently and jiggled his worry beads as she sat across from him in the cheap imitation leather chair and unburdened herself.

"The thing is . . . I feel just the opposite. Suddenly I have all this tenderness for him. I want to protect him and mother him. He looks so lost. . . . Is that weird or what?"

"Tenderness is not a weird emotion."

"Even toward a man who's in love with another . . . with someone else?"

Fuad shook his craggy head slowly, got up, walked over to the fish tank, and sprinkled some fish food in the water. Susie was starting to get pissed off. All this time she had been pouring out her soul, he was thinking about his goddamn fish.

"I mean, I don't know what to do," she went on. "Should I be there for him, talk to him, help him get through this, or just walk away from it? Maybe he doesn't want to talk about it with me . . ."

Fuad stood there observing the fish, saying nothing.

Susie felt like picking up one of his cheap ceramic vases and cracking it over his skull. She could claim he tried to put a move on her and it was self-defense.

"And now, what's even crazier is he's suddenly developed this thing with the dog. I mean, Calvin and he never even related to each other before. In fact, we went to see somebody in Burbank about the problem, a family pet counselor . . . Dr. Levine? Bob Levine? Maybe you know him . . ."

Fuad shook his head. More silence. She wondered whether the vase was heavy enough to do the trick. Maybe he'd just have a concussion or start bleeding on the awful fake Persian rug.

"Are you listening to me?" she finally cried, exasperated.

The Egyptian turned away from his fish and looked across the room at her with a strange self-satisfied smile. "Very good. Excellent," he said softly.

"What do you mean, *very good*? What are you talking about?"

"You're getting angry at me, aren't you?"

"Frankly, yes."

"Why?"

"I get the feeling that you're not listening to me."

"That I don't care? That I've turned away from you?"

She nodded quickly, instinctively drawing her knees together, suddenly feeling on the defensive. She was afraid he was going to start talking about penises again.

"Perhaps you don't understand what my role is in this process. I am a lightning rod. I collect anger, fear, anxiety. You save your tenderness for your husband and your anger for me. It's a good system, isn't it?"

She nodded again, though it made no sense to her. It was just more of his convoluted bullshit at a $175 an hour. There was a guy she'd heard about in Sherman Oaks. He worked with relaxation techniques and diet, and you didn't have to talk about sexual organs and lightning rods.

"So, tell me, Mrs. Dreyfus, what do you really want to do to your husband?"

"I told you. I want to help him, protect him, put my arms around him and hold him . . ."

"Yes, of course, and squeeze him very hard, so hard in fact that his blood circulation is cut off and he starts turning blue. Isn't that what you really want to do?"

It was at that point that she picked up the vase and threw it at him. She missed him. The vase hit the wall and splattered. Fuad

folded his hands in front of his soft belly, smiled, and said, "Beautiful . . ."

They lingered over their breakfast like an old married couple. D.J.
made waffles with an antique waffle iron he had bought in a garage
sale in Mendocino. Calvin lay stretched out contentedly on the floor,
chewing on a baseball.

It had been late, after noon, when they woke up. There were
already reporters out in front of the building. Randy had to take
Calvin for a walk in the underground parking garage, where the dog
meticulously sprayed the tires of the neighbors' cars.

Just before falling asleep, Randy had decided to tell D.J. about a
dark secret from his past. He had been carrying this ugly incident
around for too long and needed to get it out in the open.

"Listen, there's something I got to tell you," he whispered as they
lay in each other's arms in the sweaty afterglow of making love.

"Hmmn," D.J. murmured distractedly.

"It's important."

"Can't it wait till the morning?"

"I don't think so."

D.J. rolled over and looked up at him with a smile. "You're married."

Randy shook his head. "This is serious."

"Oh, shit. You're pregnant . . ."

"C'mon, D.J., let me say this."

"All right."

He had trouble getting it out. He lay there trying to figure out how
to say it to make it sound less awful than it was. Finally, he just
blurted it out.

"I tried to kill my dog."

"Huh?"

"I put a contract out on him. With my gardener. Chopped meat
and Liquid-Plumr."

"*Calvin?* You tried to knock off *Calvin?*"

Randy nodded.

"What happened?"

"A coyote ate it and died."

D.J. looked at Randy for a moment and then burst out laughing. After a moment Randy joined in. They lay there laughing for a long time. When they stopped, it got very quiet in the room. There was nothing but the low hum of the air conditioner and Calvin's snoring.

"So now you know," Randy said softly.

"Now I know."

"Pretty weird, huh?"

"It's not so bad."

"Do you still . . . ?" He couldn't bring himself to say the words.

"Do I still what?"

"You know . . ."

D.J. didn't say anything for a long moment. Then he lay his head against Randy's chest and whispered, "Yeah, I guess I still do."

Randy drifted contentedly into a deep, delicious sleep and woke up feeling wonderful. He lay in bed enjoying the luxury of not having to sneak back to his own room, as he had to do on the road. He watched his lover sleep, listened to the soft, even cadence of his breathing, admired the litheness of his body, uncoiled and relaxed.

It was the first time that he allowed himself the luxury of studying at leisure the body of a naked man. There was so little he knew about men, how they were put together, how they functioned. And now he lay there marveling at the perfection of the male anatomy, the way it all worked together harmoniously and economically—like a perfect double play.

He closed his eyes and tried to imagine Susie lying there, or even Pia Zadora, and was unable to conjure up the image with any pleasure. How could he have gone all those years denying himself? It was amazing to him that he managed to hit at all from the right side of the plate.

When D.J. finally opened his eyes, Randy kissed him gently and said good morning. They fell into a sleepy embrace and were soon going at it again with such energy that Calvin started to bark and climb up on the bed with them, as if he wanted to get in on the act.

Randy kicked him off the bed with a smart jab of the foot. The dog skidded across the polished hardwood floor and came to rest against the chest of drawers.

Jesus. His dog was a lefty too.

• • •

While Randy Dreyfus and D. J. Pickett were eating waffles in Thousand Oaks, a meeting was taking place behind closed doors in Fritz Esterhazy's Park Avenue office in New York. Present were Emmett Zion, owner of the Cincinnati Reds; W. Pointer Smith, owner of the Kansas City Royals; and Vincente Parza, owner of the Texas Rangers.

The men sat in dark leather armchairs sipping Chivas Regal and eating pistachio nuts. ESPN, the volume low, was on the thirty-four-inch TV that occupied much of one side of the office. Zion, whose Reds were up three games to one against the Phillies and were the odds-on favorite to represent the National League in the World Series, had arranged for the meeting. He had recruited Smith and Parza, knowing they shared his sentiments, and all three were now pleading for the ultimate penalty against the two sinning ballplayers.

"I can't begin to tell you, Fritz," said Zion in his low, boozy voice, "how this thing's been going down in Cincinnati. Do you know I've got over a hundred season-ticket holders threatening to cancel their tickets for next year if I permit those two queers to play ball in my stadium? I've had a mess of advertisers pull out from our local TV broadcast. I've had letters from schoolchildren, entire classes' worth, telling me they'll never come see another baseball game as long as there are homos playing on the field. Now, can you believe that? Children turning their backs on baseball . . . Is there anything more perilous to the future of this game than a nation's youth walking away from it?"

"My point exactly," Smith chimed in. "You see, we're not just talking about moral turpitude here. We're talking about flaunting sin. I'm not sure this game can survive the spectacle of two ballplayers openly carrying on with each other. Surely if anything fits the definition of conduct detrimental to the best interests of baseball, this is it. Suppose they start going around together in public and on the TV shows? How can we countenance that?"

"Throw 'em the hell out on their asses," said Zion.

Esterhazy nodded and took a long, thoughtful swallow of his Chivas. "The problem, however, isn't quite that simple, Emmett," he said finally. "The fact remains that what they did, however shocking it may be to people in this country, is not against the law. And, strictly speaking, it really doesn't affect the game per se."

"Now how can you say that, Fritz?" Emmett Zion looked sincerely hurt. "You're asking me to let my ballplayers get on the field with them. For one thing, what about the medical situation?"

"Beg your pardon?"

"AIDS. How do you expect a ballplayer to slide into second base when one of those guys is covering?"

"Emmett, you don't get AIDS from sliding—"

"The hell you don't. What happens if one of them drools on you? Right in your mouth."

"Drools in your mouth?"

"That's right. You ever look at a picture of a guy sliding? Nine times out of ten the mouth is open."

"That's right," said Smith. "First thing you ought to do is have them tested. That ought to settle the whole question."

Esterhazy drained his Chivas, sucking the last drop out from beneath the ice cubes. If he had another one, he would start to lose his grip on the situation, which was already shaky enough. He was getting it from all sides. That morning he'd gotten a call from the ACLU warning him that if Dreyfus and Pickett were suspended, they would bring a lawsuit against him for violations of the Sherman Antitrust Act and the Fourteenth Amendment, among other things.

He had been chosen by the owners to represent their interests. But he also had a responsibility to the game, to its traditions and values, to all the commissioners who had gone before him. Looking over his shoulder was the ghost of Kenesaw Mountain Landis, who had rescued baseball from the morass of the gambling scandals in the twenties. Judge Landis would have handled the situation firmly. He wouldn't have worried about the Sherman Antitrust Act or the Fourteenth Amendment.

Esterhazy looked at Vincente Parza, the multimillionaire construction king and owner of the Texas Rangers, who hadn't said a word yet.

"What do you think, Vince?" he asked the compact, immaculately dressed man who had been sitting there quietly, his hands folded in front of his chin.

"You want to know what I think?" Parza repeated in a hoarse voice.

"Yes. What would you do in my place?"

"Let 'em play."

"Jesus, Parza, I thought you were on our side here," said Smith.

"Who says I'm not on your side? They make me sick, the two of them. But you throw 'em out you make them martyrs. You let them play, you make them victims."

"What do you mean, victims?" Esterhazy asked.

"We don't have metal detectors in our stadium in Texas. We don't believe in them."

Parza said this as if the conclusions to be drawn were obvious. They weren't. "What the hell you talking about?" Emmett Zion demanded.

"First game they play down in our stadium next year someone's bound to take a shot at 'em."

Esterhazy got up and walked across the room. He opened the liquor cabinet, took out the bottle of Chivas, and poured himself another drink.

"Batting third, the shortstop, number twelve, Randy Dreyfus . . ." The P.A. announcer's voice echoed through the packed stadium. Randy trotted out to join his teammates on the third-base foul line amid a reverberating chorus of boos. He gritted his teeth and forced himself to high-five the guys along the line and then stood there riding it out.

The boos continued through the introduction of the other players. Along the first-base foul line, the Yankees joined in the booing, allying themselves with the crowd. John D. F. White, Sr., in his box behind the home dugout, booed as well. The old man turned around to the crowd and raised his arms in a gesture of encouragement.

"That ought to show people how Los Angeles feels about sodomists," he said to his son sitting beside him. John/John nodded weakly, not altogether convinced that having your star player booed in his home ballpark was a good thing.

John/John had a lot on his mind these days. The deal he had been painstakingly working out over many months to secure the services of Randy Dreyfus had been shelved by his father, who refused even to discuss the matter. John/John had had to call Barry Fuchsia and tell him that they were temporarily suspending negotiations. The agent told him that the next time he called, the price would be significantly higher, provided, of course, that Randy Dreyfus was still available, which was highly unlikely. His client, Fuchsia said, was actively exploring other opportunities, both in and out of baseball. Take a number.

The booing didn't stop when the game began. Every time D.J. or Randy got up at bat or made a play in the field, it started up again. Randy tried to tune it out and concentrate on the game, but it was difficult to ignore. This was his hometown; these were supposed to be his fans. If he couldn't get support from them, what could he expect in Cincinnati? Cincinnati was a lynch town.

In the fourth inning, the Yankee pitcher, a hard-throwing right-hander, hit D.J. in the helmet with a high inside fastball. D.J. went down in a heap and lay there without moving. Randy felt his heart stop. The trainers rushed out in the sudden deadly silence of the stadium, interrupted by some scattered cheers from the hard cases in the crowd.

Randy felt faint, unreal, as if he were watching the scene underwater. Staring blankly out at the field, he began to consider the unthinkable. If anything was seriously wrong with D.J. Randy would murder the pitcher.

It felt like forever before D.J. moved. Slowly he got up and dusted himself off, his knees wobbly. The trainers were shining little flashlights in his eyes, talking to him.

Charlie Gonse turned to Bo Caliper, the utility infielder, and told him to go run for D.J. There were more cheers as Caliper went down to first base and the trainers helped D.J. back to the dugout. They took him down the stairs to the tunnel that led to the clubhouse.

Following the trainers into the tunnel, Randy caught up with D.J. and put his hand on his arm.

"Hey, you okay?"

D.J. nodded. "Yeah."

"Don't worry, I'm going to fix that guy."

Randy waved off the trainers and took the second baseman in his arms. As the two men embraced, the trainers looked away discreetly.

"See you later," Randy whispered and ran back up the tunnel to the dugout. He got there just as Harry Glugg made the last out. Grabbing his glove, Randy trotted out to shortstop and tried to accustom himself to the unfamiliar figure of Bo Caliper beside him at second.

Randy thought about what he was going to do to the pitcher when he came up in the bottom of the inning. He was calm, determined, deliberate. He was going to avenge the attempt to kill his lover. He would do it simply and emphatically, concentrating his rage and making it a lethal weapon. All he had to do was focus his fury and aim it with precision.

There was still no score when Randy stepped up to the plate in the bottom of the fifth. The booing resumed. Randy shut it out. He shut out everything but the task at hand. He concentrated his energy in the direction of the pitcher's mound. The crosshairs of his anger converged in the middle of the pitcher's forehead. If he hit the ball hard enough, his fury would guide it to the right spot.

The guy glared down at him from the mound. Randy glared back. The pitcher started Randy off with a change outside. Randy didn't even blink. He wasn't going to waste his time with that shit.

His fingers squeezed the bat handle, his grip firm but not tight. He felt the murder in his wrists and forearms, the cold, calculating murder that he was about to commit. All he needed was the fastball. Sooner or later the guy would have to throw it.

He dicked around with change-ups in and out, working the count to 3-and-0. The next one was going to be the pitch. Randy stood there wondering if they'd give him the gas chamber for this. He deserved it. It was cold-blooded and premeditated. He had never felt so calm in his life. He was going to murder this man with a baseball through his skull.

The pitch came in low and hard. Randy brought his front foot forward, shifted his weight, and got the fat end of the bat around at the perfect moment. It met the ball squarely in the middle of the plate. He knew he had hit the ball perfectly, heard the gorgeous sound of wood vibrating.

Unfortunately he got under it a sixteenth of an inch, and instead of killing the pitcher, the ball headed over the pitcher's head and on a line into the center-field stands, four hundred feet away, stopped only by a concrete girder. It hit the girder so hard that it bounced back onto the field.

"Shit," Randy muttered, dropping the bat and heading for first. As he rounded the bases to the grudging cheers of the crowd, all he could think of was the sixteenth-of-an-inch miscalculation that had saved the pitcher's life. It was the second time in a month he had planned a murder that didn't work out.

Fritz Esterhazy watched Randy Dreyfus's home run from his den in his Central Park South apartment. Beside him was a yellow legal pad upon which he had written the twentieth version of the press release he would issue the next morning if the score held up and the Vikings went on to the World Series.

The nineteenth version of the press release had spoken about contemporary community values, about the timeless traditions of organized baseball, about Kenesaw Mountain Landis and the moral turpitude of the times. It was a labored attempt to clothe what was essentially a pragmatic decision in high-minded rhetoric. But when the commissioner saw the Yankee pitcher throw at D. J. Pickett's head in the bottom of the fourth, he had a sudden inspiration. The beaning had given him the idea for a completely different approach, one he liked much better.

He grabbed his pen and wrote furiously. When he was finished he had filled up five pages in which he maintained that the health and safety of both ballplayers and fans were seriously jeopardized by the present climate surrounding the Vikings. He mentioned the numerous incidents that had occurred since the affair had been brought out into the open. He cited the doctrine of clear and present danger and his duty as commissioner to protect the integrity of the game. He quoted Justice Holmes's dictum about shouting "Fire!" in a crowded theater. He concluded by saying that he was taking this action in order to protect baseball, its players, and its fans from the fires of violence and disorder that were raging all around them.

He put his pen down and felt a deep sense of satisfaction. He had found the solution to the problem. It was clearly in his purview as commissioner to protect the health, welfare, and safety of the players and fans. He was no longer making a moral judgment; he was acting in conformity with the duties of his office.

He went over to the window and looked out into the inky night over Central Park. Down there people were being murdered, raped, and mugged. He could do nothing about those things. But he could make sure that when people went out to the ballpark, they wouldn't be exposed to such dangers. At least not while Fritz Esterhazy was commissioner.

In the morning he would edit the five pages down to a few terse and powerful paragraphs. Then he would call his press secretary and have him put it out in time for the afternoon papers. Perhaps tomorrow he might even put through a call to the president, assure him that the matter had been taken care of, and remind him that they were looking forward to his throwing out the first ball Friday night in Cincinnati.

Randy drove home to Valley View Estates and his guest house and dog. He dropped a Halcion but was unable to sleep. An acute sense of anxiety floated through him, a sense of impending menace. He was overcome with the realization that nothing would be safe or easy from now on. They had people throwing fastballs at their heads, obscene phone calls, an uncertain future.

That morning Randy had received a letter from his mother, who lived in Lakeland, Florida, and hadn't written him in years. He dutifully sent her Christmas cards with photos of Susie and the twins and called her once a year on her birthday. The letter read in its entirety:

Dear Randolph,

I am writing to tell you that as far as I'm concerned you are no longer my son. I am thankful that your poor father did not live long enough to go through this shame because it would have killed him.

Your ex-mother,
Estelle Dreyfus

When your own mother cut you loose, things were pretty bad. Even Sirhan Sirhan's mother didn't disown him. She visited him every day in prison, brought him homemade pastries.

Randy tossed and turned on the uncomfortable foldaway bed in the guest house, not knowing that the next day things would get even worse.

XXII

The suspension of Randy Drey-
fus and D. J. Pickett for conduct detrimental to the best interests of
baseball made the early edition of the next evening's newspapers.
The story ran on the front page, in most cases above the story of the
Vikings winning the American League pennant. The headlines read,
in large type: ESTERHAZY BOOTS BAD BOYS OUT, and, in smaller type,
VIKINGS CLINCH PENNANT.

Fritz Esterhazy's press release was reprinted in its entirety, with
excerpts used as springboards for a host of sidebar stories entitled
"Clear and Present Danger," "Violence in America," "Fire in a
Crowded Theater," and so forth. The evening TV news shows led
with the story, some of them rebroadcasting the Neiman-Marcus
changing-room tape.

The commissioner was interviewed at the airport, before board-
ing a plane for Cincinnati. He said that the decision had been an
agonizing one, that he had been guided by his concern for the
welfare of the game, first and foremost, that all other considerations
were subservient to that principle. He regretted having to take the
action on the eve of the World Series, but he couldn't afford to take
the chance of violence marring the fall classic. The integrity of the
game was bigger than any of the individuals involved.

Sitting in a bar at LAX and waiting for his flight to Cincinnati to be announced, Milt Zola watched Esterhazy's performance on TV with a sickening feeling in his gut. He put down his Dos Equis, afraid that he was about to throw up. In all his years covering baseball he had never seen a more disgusting turn of events.

The integrity of the game! The integrity of the game involved watching the best players compete for nine innings on a field with ninety feet between the bases. How could the World Series be the World Series if the best shortstop and second baseman in the majors were not out there playing?

The team's flight was announced. When Zola reached the departure lounge he found Ken Teffner in animated discussion with Randy Dreyfus and D. J. Pickett while the other players stood around as if they were watching a play.

"Look," Teffner was saying, "I'm sorry. We only heard an hour ago. We tried to reach you. We called your house. We called D.J.'s place. You weren't there. Neither of you."

Randy Dreyfus looked at him as if he wanted to spit on him. "Are you saying we can't get on that plane?"

"I'm afraid so. The travel's not authorized. Mr. White's orders."

"What the fuck . . ."

"Randy, please. Don't make a scene. It's not us. It's the commissioner. He made the ruling. We can't do anything about it."

Rennie Pannizardi stood a few feet away and nodded, as if to indicate that he agreed with the commissioner's decision. Randy turned to him, his eyes blazing.

"You agree with him, Pannizardi?"

The third baseman shrugged.

"Who the fuck won the game last night? It wasn't for me, you wouldn't even be going to Cincinnati."

"That so?"

"Yeah."

"So where were you guys this morning? Sucking each other's Popsicles?"

It took the combined efforts of D.J., Harry Glugg, and Axel Most to keep Randy from killing Rennie Pannizardi. D.J. managed to drag him away as the rest of the Vikings and Teffner went through the gate to board the plane. The team writers, who had all witnessed the scene, were wondering if they had enough time to phone in the story before the flight took off. They all looked at one another suspiciously, waiting to see if somebody made a run for it. If nobody made the phone call, then they could all wait to file from Cincinnati.

Zola watched this scene with amusement. Pack cowardice. Typical. Nobody was going to move until everyone moved. They'd all miss the plane rather than give one of them a scoop. He decided to lead the group onto the plane. He turned and walked through the gate. One by one, the others followed, looking over their shoulders to make sure that no one stayed behind to phone in the story.

The story—that is, Randy Dreyfus and D. J. Pickett—stood there in the middle of the now-empty departure lounge. They had just learned, from the mouth of the Vikings' vice president of public relations, that they had been suspended from baseball for life.

For a long time they didn't move, overcome by a sense of inertia and despair. Where were they supposed to move *to*, anyway? Their lives suddenly had no direction. They had no place to go.

Finally, Randy said, "You want to go get some Chinese?"

They sat in Ching Ming's Fine Cantonese Cuisine eating pork lo mein and egg rolls. Randy had a couple of beers in spite of his promise to Don Amarillo that he would call him before having a drink. They had driven most of the way to Ventura in silence, both of them still in a state of semishock.

"The fucker actually did it," Randy said.

"Uh-huh."

"Suspended for life. That's a pretty long time."

"Yeah."

"I didn't think he was actually going to do it. I mean, actually throw us out."

D.J. picked at the lo mein listlessly with his chopsticks.

"You know what gets me?" Randy went on. "There are guys doing drugs, drinking, beating up on their wives. Nobody's going after them. . . ."

"Yeah . . ."

"It was that goddamn security guy in Neiman-Marcus."

"If it wasn't him, Randy, it would have been someone else. Sooner or later you fuck up. You can't live your whole life in the closet."

Randy ate for a while in silence, then: "Can I ask you a question?"

"Shoot."

"If you knew then what you know now, would you still . . . you know . . . ?"

"I did know then what I know now."

"Really?"

"That's what I've been trying to say. I went into this with my eyes open. And I'd do it again. Okay?"

Randy felt a surge of warmth inside him as he looked across the table at his lover. D.J. didn't say that type of thing very often, and Randy found himself blushing just a bit. Jesus.

They sat there eating their lo mein in the empty restaurant. When they finished, they opened their fortune cookies, read them to each other, laughed.

"What does yours say?" D.J. asked.

"Take two and hit to right."

They laughed some more, then Randy said, "So what do we do now?"

D.J. shrugged and shook his head. "Shit if I know."

"I never thought about what I'd do if I couldn't play ball. I figured I'd worry about it in another ten years."

"It's not something you want to think about."

Randy played absently with the sugar shaker, turning it around and around in his large hands. "You know what I've always wanted to do?"

"What's that?"

"Take a trip when I didn't know where I was going."

"What do you mean?"

"Just get in the car and drive. No plans, no obligations. Just go."

"Sounds great."

Randy shrugged, smiled, then shrugged some more, as if he were talking to himself. Then he said, "What do you say?"

"Huh?"

"What do you say we do it?"

"Us?"

"Yeah."

"Shit, I don't know—"

"You want to stay in this town?"

"Not particularly."

"It's fucking October. You'd never know it around here. Let's go see the leaves change."

"Where?"

"How about Maine? I always wanted to go to Maine. I like the name. Don't you?"

"Yeah."

They sat there for a moment, thinking about Maine. Then Randy smiled sheepishly and said, "You know where it is?"

They were in the conversation nook, Randy on the peach bean-bag couch, Susie on the burgundy La-Z-Boy recliner. Calvin sat at Randy's feet looking up devotedly at him. The conversation was halting and painful, as Randy did his best to explain the trip he was going to take. Susie listened attentively and then said, "You're just going to take off? Just like that?"

"Yeah."

"Where're you going to go?"

"Sort of to Maine."

"*Maine?* Why are you going to Maine?"

"I always wanted to go to Maine."

"What are you going to do in Maine?"

"I don't know."

I don't know was an answer, probably the best one she was going to get. She smiled without conviction. Then: "You're going with . . . him, I suppose?"

"Uh-huh."

"When are you going to be back?"

"I don't know."

Of course. There seemed to be no point in pressing him for answers. But there were things she had to know. They couldn't go on like this, living in this in-between world forever.

"Randy, are we going to get a divorce or what?"

"I don't know. Things are pretty weird right now, you know what I mean?"

She found herself nodding supportively. Things certainly were weird. *Weird* was putting it mildly.

"I just want to know. I want to make some plans, figure out what to do."

"I understand. Look, as soon as I figure out what I'm going to do, I'll tell you."

"What about Molly and Dolly? You've got to tell them something. You can't just go away without saying anything to them."

"I'm going to talk to them."

"What are you going to tell them?"

"I don't know."

They lapsed back into silence. Susie walked over to the window that looked out on the side yard and the racquetball court. She was wearing a blue cotton sweater and spandex pants. She had lost four pounds since she had discovered the identity of her husband's lover, and she looked terrific.

"Can I ask you something else?" she said quietly, not looking at him.

"Sure."

"Is it . . . does it have anything to do with . . . me?"

"Does what have anything to do with you?"

"You know. The . . . thing with D.J. . . . ."

"No."

"I didn't, like, turn you off or anything?"

"No way. You're a fox. It's just like a different ball game. You sort of get interested in vanilla instead of chocolate. That's all."

She began to feel her insides give way. Taking a deep breath, she closed her eyes, coagulated her tear ducts. When she had pulled herself together, she said, still without looking at him, "The girls are upstairs in their room. You better go talk to them."

Randy marched up the stairs, Calvin trailing behind him, to try to explain to his eight-year-old daughters that he was in love with another man, that every time he saw that man the Rockies crumbled and Gibraltar tumbled. There was nothing he could do about it. He was only made of clay.

It's hard enough talking about your sex life to your eight-year-old twin daughters. But doing it with a picture of Joan Lunden staring you in the face is particularly trying. Randy averted his eyes and did his best to ignore her.

The twins sat on their respective beds, in their matching Naf Naf jumpers, watching their father pace around the room, Calvin pacing in his footsteps. Randy had been searching without much success for the right way to get into the conversation, the best angle from which to explain the odd turn his life had taken.

After a couple of false starts, he lapsed into silence. Molly or Dolly finally broke the ice. "Mommy said you're having an affair but it's not with your secretary."

Randy stopped in his tracks, Calvin banging into him. He looked at his daughter and said, "Is that what she said?"

"Well, she didn't want to talk much about it. She kept starting to cry. But we sort of figured things out anyway."

"So who is it with?" asked the other one.

"It's . . . well, you see, it's complicated."

"We understand. We're almost nine."

"Yeah, we even know what joint custody is and menopause."

Randy walked over and sat down on Molly or Dolly's bed, folded his hands in front of him. "Uh . . . you see, I kind of made a new friend. And this friend, who's a very nice person, and I have gotten very close. It has nothing to do with Mommy. It's like chocolate and vanilla ice cream. They're both good, but sometimes you find yourself liking one or the other for no reason at all. You understand what I mean?"

The twins nodded. Randy plunged on, sinking deeper into quicksand with every word. "So if you start to like vanilla, it's not because there's anything wrong with chocolate. It's just that it tastes different and you wind up wanting to eat it all the time. I mean, you still sort of like chocolate . . . and if there wasn't any vanilla around you could still eat chocolate. . . ."

He felt the quicksand start to seep into his mouth. "Well, anyway, this friend and I have decided to spend some time together. We're going to take a trip."

"What about the World Series?"

"I'm going to skip that this year."

"How come?"

"I want to take this trip instead."

"Can't you take this trip after the World Series?"

"By then the leaves will all be gone. You see, we're going to see the leaves change."

"Where?"

"Maine."

"Where's Maine?"

"It's this place on the East Coast. They have lobsters there."

"Are you going to be gone for a long time?"

"I don't know."

"Are you ever going to come live in the house again?"

"I don't know."

"Boy, there's a lot you don't know."

Randy nodded. It was true. He had never in his life known so little.

"What about us? Are you still going to be our daddy?"

He flexed his stomach muscles to keep himself together, managing to nod and say, "Of course, sweetheart. I'll always be your daddy. No matter what happens."

"So what's your new friend's name?"

"D.J."

"Just like the name of the guy on your team."

"Yeah . . . it's the same name. It's the same . . ."

He couldn't bring himself to say it. But it didn't matter. With all the soap operas the twins watched, they were way ahead of him. He might as well not have bothered with the ice cream metaphor.

"Daddy, you're not *gay*, are you?" asked Molly or Dolly.

Randy found himself smiling in a kind of cockeyed way. It was pointless to deny it. What the fuck. Everyone else in the world knew.

"Sort of," he said, the silly grin still on his face.

Molly and Dolly looked at each other, and, as if to confirm their observation, one of them said, "Just like that new intern on *General Hospital*." The other one nodded in affirmation.

"Is it really like vanilla ice cream?"

"Well . . . it's just . . . look, I just want you to understand . . . to understand that I. . . ."

He couldn't go on. He broke down and started to cry again, like the time in the cab in Boston. It came out in torrents. Sitting there on Molly or Dolly's bed, he wept like the Mississippi. Calvin climbed up in his lap and started to lick his tears. Randy pushed him away, but he kept coming.

"Boy, he really loves you, Daddy."

Randy nodded through his tears.

Molly or Dolly went and got one of her embroidered handkerchiefs. Randy dried his eyes and finally managed to stop crying. He sat there, catching his breath, Calvin in his lap.

"You know what I think?" said one of the twins.

"What?"

"I think Calvin likes vanilla ice cream too."

"Yeah," said the other one, "I think you should take him to Maine with you and D.J."

"No . . ." Randy protested.

Both twins nodded simultaneously with an air that indicated the matter was settled. There was no use protesting anymore.

Randy hugged and kissed both of them. He got up and went to the door.

"Don't worry, Daddy," one of them called after him. "Mommy said she wasn't going to take you to the cleaner's."

"I'm glad to hear that," mumbled Randy as he stumbled out the door with his dog.

A great number of people were trying to get in touch with Randy Dreyfus and D. J. Pickett. There were reporters, book publishers, movie producers, TV talk-show bookers, the whole gamut of media people clambering for a piece of the hottest story of the year. Barry Fuchsia was inundated with phone calls, faxes, telegrams, options, advances, firm offers for the rights to the story of the love affair between Randy Dreyfus and D. J. Pickett.

But Barry Fuchsia was unable to get in touch with his client, who wasn't answering phone calls from anybody these days. The phone on Caravaggio Place was interminably busy. No one could get through.

In addition to the media people, there was a host of other people who wanted to get in touch with the two ballplayers—from the American Civil Liberties Union to the Gay Rights Coalition. Not to mention the weirdos of all persuasions, the hate callers, the lovesick men wanting a date or a lock of their hair.

But Randy Dreyfus and D. J. Pickett were not interested in talking to any of them. They were heading east on Interstate 10 in D. J. Pickett's green Jaguar without a car phone. They were speeding through the night on their way to Maine, with only two small suitcases and a Dalmatian.

They had slipped out under the cover of night and, at four in the morning, were heading east on the San Bernardino into a gradually lightening sky. They were going to Maine to see the leaves change color, and they didn't have anything to say to anybody.

They were free men. They didn't have to worry about making contact, hitting behind the runner, shading the pull hitters into the hole. They didn't have to listen to obscenities hurled at them from the dugouts and the stands. They didn't have to worry about incentive clauses and options. All they had to do was keep driving east.

They sped through the early-morning desert, breathing the dry air, the Jaguar doing a cool ninety on the flat stretches. It was the beginning of an adventure. They had no idea where evening would find them, and they didn't care.

They rode in silence, side by side, listening to Sinatra on the tape deck. Through the rearview mirror they could see a number of bridges burning in the distance behind them.

XXIII

Riverfront Stadium in Cincinnati was packed for the opening night of the World Series between the Vikings and the Reds. The national television audience was treated to a pregame show featuring sixth graders dressed in white shirts, red ties, and blue jackets singing a medley of Stephen Foster songs, followed by a group of drum majorettes from area high schools in a synchronized baton-twirling exhibition.

In the stands, banners proudly displayed slogans like: WE'RE PORN FREE AND PROUD OF IT and AMERICA IS ALIVE AND WELL IN CINCINNATI.

From his box along the first baseline, the president posed for pictures and threw out the first ball. It was a floater that barely made it to the catcher's glove, and it took a nice backhanded scoop by Ernie Kecko, the Reds catcher, to save the chief executive from a wild pitch.

"I should have warmed up in the bullpen," the president said to Fritz Esterhazy beside him, who joined the crowd in Pavlovian applause.

"You were just wasting one, Mr. President," Esterhazy replied with his *noblesse oblige* smile.

Esterhazy settled down for the game, uncomfortably wedged among the Secret Service agents. He wasn't particularly thrilled to be sitting next to the president of the United States in an open stadium. Besides the fact that he would have to make conversation with him for at least three innings, being in proximity to the president made one a potential target for an assassin's bullet. All it had to do was go wide a few inches and Fritz Esterhazy would be under six feet of dirt in his family plot in Mount Kisco with an American flag on his coffin.

"Well, Fritz," said the president, as the first inning got under way, "I'm glad we've put this unfortunate incident behind us."

"Yes . . ."

"This country has enough problems facing it as it is. We certainly don't need baseball being polluted by inversion."

"No, we don't," replied Esterhazy, wincing at the mixed metaphor.

"You'll go down in the history of the game with the great commissioners, alongside Mountain Landis and Estes Kefauver."

They sat there with their hot dogs, dabbing the mustard with napkins provided by the Secret Service.

"The franks are a little underdone, don't you think?" the president said, handing his half-eaten hot dog surreptitiously back to the Secret Service agent beside him. "You can't be too careful what you eat these days. Next thing you know you're in Walter Reed with trichinosis, which, I'm told, is no picnic."

"So I hear."

"Been trying to cut down on my yeast intake."

"Is that so?"

"Between you and me, I don't have half an hour to spend in the john every morning."

Esterhazy nodded absently, hoping the president would not pursue the subject.

"I've got to tell you, Fritz, when I first heard about those two in the dressing room in Dallas, I was heartsick. As if this country didn't have enough troubles. You know, we've got them all over Washington. Not much you can do about that. Unlike you, I can't throw them out for conduct detrimental to the best interests of the country. I have the Congress to contend with . . . and there are some people over in the House—I tell you, you wouldn't want to get into a steam bath with them."

Fortunately, the president left with two outs in the home half of the third. He shook Esterhazy's hand and invited him down to the White House for a game of softball on the south lawn after the season was over. The commissioner thanked him and breathed a sigh of relief that the president and his gang of armed thugs were gone.

He settled down to watch the game, a scoreless tie until the Reds came up with five runs in the bottom of the fourth. All unearned. The Viking road-company double-play duo, Bo Caliper and Howie Jarvis, made two errors back to back that opened the floodgates.

Milt Zola sat in the press box, watching this poor excuse for a World Series game. He had been sent to Cincinnati to write an article about it. How could he write about this game and not mention the gaping hole in the middle of the Viking infield and why it was there?

His editor had warned him. Don't bite the hand that fed him.

Milt Zola was fifty-five years old and had next to nothing in the bank. He rented a ramshackle bungalow in Silver Lake and drove an '85 Honda Accord with a bad master cylinder. He was twenty-five pounds overweight and needed a hemorrhoid operation and a new bridge on the right side of his mouth. This was not a time to be taking chances. And yet . . .

Milt Zola loved baseball. It was a point of reference for his entire life. He could no longer remain silent. He would write the truth and, like Martin Luther, tack it up on the church door. Let them excommunicate him. Let them burn him at the stake.

What was the point of living his life if they started screwing with the few absolute truths that were left in this world? How could he genuflect before Howie Jarvis or Bo Caliper?

By the time the final out was made in the Reds' 8–3 victory over the Vikings in Game One of the World Series, Randy Dreyfus and D. J. Pickett were settled into the Farmer's Daughter Motor Inn outside of Papillion, Nebraska. They hadn't even bothered to see the game on TV. Instead they sat propped up on the overstuffed mattress, eating Kentucky Fried Chicken and watching *The Pride of the Yankees.*

Randy's eyes welled up during Gehrig's farewell speech at Yankee Stadium and he had to go into the bathroom to blow his nose.

"Goddamn allergies," he muttered when he returned. He took a long hit from his diet Coke and sat back down on the bed.

They had traveled straight through, stopping only for gas and food and walking Calvin, going through D.J.'s entire collection of Frank Sinatra cassettes. They hadn't talked much in the car, preferring to watch the scenery and listen to The Man.

Now, sitting in their motel room in the middle of America, Randy felt the exhilaration of not knowing exactly where he was. He was flying free, navigating by the seat of his pants, heading east across the darkened continent.

"Boy, this is wild, huh?" he said.

"Yeah."

"I mean, we could be anywhere, you know what I mean?"

D.J. nodded, got up, and did some stretches, limbering his hamstrings as if he were about to come up to bat.

"So what do you think we're going to do in Maine?" Randy went on enthusiastically.

"Anything we want to."

"Yeah. . . . We could do just about anything. We could go fishing. You ever go fishing?"

D.J. shook his head.

"Neither have I. But we could try. What the hell? How hard could it be? You put a rod in the water and wait around, right?"

"Right."

"There's a whole shitload of stuff we can do. We can play miniature golf. I love miniature golf. . . ."

D.J. lay down on the floor and began to do sit-ups. Randy watched him, admiring the perfect form, the flatness of the stomach, the calves flush against the floor.

"How many of those fuckers you do?"

"Two hundred."

"Every night?"

"Uh-huh . . ."

"Jesus. That's something."

Randy watched him do the first hundred, then went off to take a shower. He closed his eyes, letting the water run against his face. For the first time in months he felt relaxed. He was floating free, living from hour to hour. His life was an adventure full of new scenery every day. And he didn't have to get up tomorrow and try to get the fat end of the bat on the ball.

Instead he was going fishing with the man he loved. Jesus. Life was marvelous. He felt a flush of pleasure go through him, and he started to sing, his voice echoing in the shower.

"You make me feel so young . . . you make me feel like Spring has sprung . . ."

It was a gray, sodden morning with late-night and early-morning low clouds along the coast that would burn off by midday. Well before then, a big flatbed truck with two men inside pulled into the Randy Dreyfus Shopping Center in Van Nuys. It carried a crane and equipment to dismantle the large neon letters that shone brightly over the shopping center day and night.

They parked the truck and went into Dunkin' Donuts for some breakfast before starting work. They were in no rush. They figured they could do it in three hours and put in for the entire day. No point breaking their necks.

After half an hour of coffee and doughnuts, they went back out to the truck and pulled it around so that it was in proximity to the column rising high above Van Nuys Boulevard. They had put the sign up to begin with several months ago, and now they were replacing it with another sign.

They had been hired by the landlord of the shopping center, who had responded to a petition, signed by the various tenants, asking that he remove the name of the Los Angeles Valley Vikings' shortstop and former role model from their shopping center. In its place they had decided to put the name of a more upstanding American.

The problem was the new guy's name had a lot of letters in it, and the job was going to be expensive. Still, the tenants voted to foot the bill. They didn't want their businesses associated with a man who had been thrown out of baseball for conduct detrimental to the best interests of the sport.

The men removed the large neon letters, easing them down into the truck with the aid of the crane and replacing them with the new letters. At eleven they knocked off for lunch at the Pizza Hut. Then they went back out and finished the job. They were done by two-thirty and drove out onto Van Nuys Boulevard toward the entrance to the 405.

The former Randy Dreyfus Shopping Center was now named for a man who was born in Austria and demolished hordes of people with high-tech weapons on the movie screens of America. He was unavailable for an inauguration ceremony—he was on location in the Mojave Desert filming his latest movie, *Terminator 9: The Holocaust.*

As they traveled east through Iowa, Illinois, Indiana, Ohio, and into western New York State, the foliage became progressively more colorful. It was breathtakingly beautiful. They drove through small rural towns, stopping to let Calvin out to pee and trample through the leaves like a slap-happy deer.

It was Indian summer, a warming sun low in the sky. The earth smelled rich with harvest. There were fresh vegetable and pumpkin stands everywhere. They stopped and bought apple cider and bread and cheese and picnicked by the side of the road.

Out here in the real world the leaves changed color in October and the air cooled down at night and there were no palm trees or yucca or purple-and-pink shrubbery or brown air. They had forgotten about California and they had forgotten about baseball. Then, driving east from Utica, they were suddenly reminded of it.

They came upon it by surprise, an enormous sign on the side of the road. It was the last thing on their minds. They hadn't planned on visiting the place, except when they were to be inducted. That had been, of course, before they were excommunicated.

They looked at each other.

"What do you say?"

D.J. shrugged. "Why not?"

You couldn't miss the place. There were tour buses everywhere, all headed there. They drove up and found a parking spot for the Jag. Randy took Calvin for a short walk and then put him back in the car with the windows open wide enough for ventilation but not wide enough for him to get out.

"Sorry, guy, no dogs allowed."

Calvin whined unhappily. Randy looked him straight in the eye and said, "Listen, if you do a number on D.J.'s upholstery, I'm getting the Liquid-Plumr. You got that straight?"

They waited on line to buy their tickets with the tourists in straw hats and sensible shoes. Then they entered the large brick building and walked among the exhibits, stopping in front of the display cases, looking at the old bats and gloves. They stared at the black-and-white photographs of the greats of the game, read about DiMaggio's fifty-six-game hitting streak, Vander Meer's consecutive no-hitters, Maris's 61st home run, Larsen's perfect World Series game, Aaron's 715th, Ryan's no-hitters . . . And the old timers: Hornsby, Cobb, Medwick, Dean, Gehrig, and the Babe . . .

It was all there, displayed and annotated—the heroic feats of dead ballplayers. This was supposedly what it was all about. You made it in here, you got life after death. You got a chance to keep throwing the baseball. Old Cy Young was still going at it after 511 wins.

Jesus. You'd think he'd be tired by now. You'd think he'd want to throw in the glove and kick back and forget about having to hit the corners and keep it low. After all, it was only a game. You got up there and took your hacks, and, at best, seven times out of ten you failed.

They wandered into the inner sanctum of the shrine, the Hall of Fame wing, where the plaques were displayed. It was dead quiet with all the bronze faces staring at you from the walls like mummies. It was like being in a goddamn church. Randy walked over to the D's. Dean, Delahanty, Dickey, DiHigo, DiMaggio, Doerr, Drysdale, Duffy . . . He imagined himself on the wall, between Doerr and Drysdale, his features etched in copper, his feats enumerated below.

RANDOLPH MACARTHUR DREYFUS, JR. (1970–   ): BATTED RIGHT, THREW RIGHT. LED THE AMERICAN LEAGUE IN HITTING FIVE TIMES. FOUR

Suddenly the words of Mendes Fuad, M.D., a Medical Corporation, came back to him: *It's just a plaque on the wall someplace in
upstate New York.*

He looked at D.J. standing beside him, lost in thought too.

"So what do you think?" Randy said.

"It's just a piece of copper."

"Yeah. That's exactly what it is. A piece of copper hanging on the
wall. Who needs it?"

Randy reached over and took D.J.'s hand, squeezed it. He no
longer gave a shit what people thought. Let them throw them out
for conduct detrimental to the best interests of the Hall of Fame
while they were fucking at it.

The Vikings won Game Two of the World Series when, with the
bases loaded, Harry Glugg, badly fooled on an inside fastball, bailed
out and hit an opposite-field pop fly that cleared the right-field wall
by half an inch. Four runs scored, and that was it. Axel Most pitched
an eleven-hitter; everything else was hit right at someone.

After the game, Charlie Gonse said that if the game was a fish he
would throw it back. As far as he was concerned they'd lost and
were now down two games to nothing, and he was going to manage
accordingly. The Vikings had their work cut out for them. They had
serious trouble up the middle. Howie Jarvis and Bo Caliper were a
combined 1-for-16 with three errors between them. But Charlie
Gonse didn't speak of the absence of Randy Dreyfus and D. J. Pickett. No one was permitted to refer to them. They were like dead
relatives who had disgraced the family and whose names were
never to be uttered again.

Milt Zola sat in his room at the Riverfront Hilton, with a view of
the Ohio River and the stadium, and stared at the blank screen of
his Toshiba laptop.

He had sat through a pathetic excuse for a World Series game,
wondering what he could possibly write that would convey the exquisite banality of the nine innings he had just witnessed. The

conspiracy of silence was total. Nobody, not even the network-TV commentators, wanted to touch the subject. Like Gus Mercer had said, it was like the ozone layer. Nobody wanted to hear about it.

Zola walked over to the window and looked down at the city beneath him. He had never liked this town, with its tight-assed midwestern morals and small-town boosterism. How could you trust a city with no hookers or X-rated movie houses? What did people do with their baser instincts?

As he stood there by the window, he thought of a play in the fourth inning of the game that night. The Reds had a runner on first with two outs. It was an obvious steal situation. Zola watched to see if Jarvis and Caliper were using glove signals to indicate who would cover. They didn't do a thing, just stood there chewing gum like a couple of cows out to pasture. When the guy went on the first pitch, as the whole goddamn stadium knew he would, Jarvis and Caliper looked at each other to see who was covering. The hesitation made Bernie Lazarre double-pump, and the base was stolen.

How could you call this the World Series? He wasn't going to dignify it with an article, not even a paragraph. Instead, he was going to write what had to be written. He couldn't stop himself any longer. The article had been building inside him since he'd first learned of the suspension. And he would do it tonight, stay up all night if he had to, until he had said what he wanted to.

It would be his swan song. The Whites would take away his press card and his Viking Stadium parking sticker. They'd scrape it ceremoniously off the windshield with a drum dirge in the background. The paper would offer him early retirement on a reduced pension. Fuck it. He'd move to Florida and open a fishing-tackle business in the Keys and wait for his hemorrhoids to finish him off.

He already knew what the title of the article was going to be. He walked quickly back over to the Toshiba, a wild new energy pulsing in his veins. He hit the CAP LOCK key, centered the cursor, and typed the two-word headline:

I ACCUSE

The Devil's Island Cabins (FOR RENT BY THE DAY, WEEK, OR MONTH) were clustered around a cove off Lake Pinoski in northeastern Maine about twenty miles outside of Caribou. It wasn't the easiest place to get to, but Randy Dreyfus and D. J. Pickett got there four and a half days after getting on the San Bernardino Freeway in Los Angeles and heading east.

There wasn't too much farther east they could have gone without a boat. After their visit to Cooperstown they continued through Vermont and New Hampshire and into Maine, watching the leaves thin out on the trees and smelling the beginnings of winter around the corner.

When they passed the sign that said WELCOME TO MAINE: THE PINE TREE STATE, Randy had D.J. stop the car. He got out and walked around confirming the fact that there really was a Maine, that it wasn't someplace they had stuck on the map just to fill in the blank spots.

"So this is it," he said to D.J. as Calvin ran around in circles chasing insects.

"This is it."

"Son of a bitch. We actually got here, huh?"

"Yeah . . ."

Then they got back in the car and drove for a few more hours. It was getting late. They were hungry. There was a sign on the road that said GOOD FOOD. They followed a long, narrow dirt road through the woods to a clearing, where they came upon the office of the Devil's Island Cabins and Conrad, the proprietor.

Conrad was a thin, hairy man in a Red Sox cap and flannel shirt. He didn't talk much, showed them the best cabin he had, which rented for fifty-seven dollars a night. It was right on the lake with its own jetty and rowboat.

"What about the good food?" D.J. asked.

Conrad looked at his watch and said, "About forty-five minutes."

"Where?"

Conrad pointed to a ramshackle building off the office and left them alone.

The cabin was two rooms with a stone fireplace, old furniture, plastic flowers, and pre–World War II plumbing. There were dried cornhusks on the walls and a sampler that said THE LORD HELPS THOSE WHO HELP THEMSELVES.

It wasn't the Ramada Inn, but they had their own dock that gave directly on the lake and as much privacy as they could want. They sat on the jetty and watched the last of the sunset drop into the lake before going over to the building that Conrad had indicated.

There was only one table set, and Randy and D.J. sat down at it. After a few minutes Conrad emerged from the kitchen with two bowls of split-pea soup, which he placed unceremoniously in front of them, and then withdrew without saying a word.

They looked at each other and sampled the soup.

"Pretty good, huh?" said Randy.

"Great."

The next course was pork chops and mashed potatoes, which Conrad brought out, again without comment. Finally, when he brought the apple pie à la mode for dessert, Randy made a stab at conversation.

"You a Red Sox fan?"

Conrad looked at him for a brief moment. When he spoke, he seemed to be on the point of spitting. "Not so as you'd know it."

"I thought maybe you were, seeing as you're wearing that hat."

"Got it at Fenway Park thirty-one years ago."

"You don't follow the game anymore?"

"Too long a drive."

"What about on TV?"

"We don't got cable here. Breakfast is at seven. After eight you're out of luck."

And that was the extent of their conversation with Conrad. After dinner they took a digestive stroll around the cove. The air was pine-scented and crisp. The only sound was the gentle lapping of the lake against the shore. Randy could hear his heart beat. They walked, holding hands, not saying a word to break the exquisite silence.

When they got back to the cabin, it was chilly inside. D.J., a former Eagle Scout, made a flawless fire, and they got undressed and tumbled into the big, lumpy bed and watched the shadow of the flames dance on the knotty pine walls.

For the first time in his twenty-seven-year career as a sportswriter Milt Zola blew a deadline. He phoned the paper at ten-twenty the night of the second game in Cincinnati and told them to put together a main story off the AP wire and run a sidebar filler, he was writing a major piece that wouldn't be ready until the morning.

When Gus Mercer saw the Monday-morning edition without Zola's story from Cincinnati he immediately tried calling his head baseball writer, but Milt Zola was unreachable, flying back to L.A. with the Vikings for Game Three. He had stayed up most of the night writing his piece and would submit it personally and stand over it through production to make sure they didn't fuck with so much as a comma.

Sleepless but buoyed with manic energy, Zola entered the *Valley Tribune* building and went directly to Gus Mercer's office. Before the editor could begin to vent his anger over the missed deadline, Zola put the article on his desk and said, "Read this."

"What is it?"

"It's a feature piece. I want you to run it on the first page of tomorrow's sports section."

Mercer riffled through the dozen typewritten pages, looked back up at Zola, and said, "It's three thousand words. I can't run three thousand words on the sports page."

"Just read it, for chrissakes, will you?"

Mercer put his glasses on and started to read the article. He got halfway down the first page and stopped. "What are you, out of your fucking mind?"

"Just read the whole thing."

"This isn't an article. This is a diatribe."

"Just read it, will you?"

Mercer started to read it aloud: " 'I accuse the commissioner of baseball, Francis Esterhazy III, of conduct detrimental to the best interests of baseball. I accuse him of malfeasance in office, of moral cowardice, of collusion, of violations of the rights and dignity of baseball players, American citizens, and human beings . . .

" 'I accuse Messrs. John D. F. White, Junior and Senior, of breach of contract and discrimination, of cupidity and hypocrisy, of failing to field the best team to compete for the World Championship, of refusing to accord to their employees the basic rights and privileges guaranteed them by their contracts and by their membership in the human race . . .' "

Mercer stopped and looked at Zola. "What the hell do you think this is—the French Revolution?"

"It's a travesty of justice. It's a blot on this country's character and honor. It's a violation of the Constitution, the Rights of Man, the whole ball game."

Quoting now from his own article, Zola went on, in a loud voice, " 'We hold these truths to be self-evident: that all men are created equal; that they are entitled to life, liberty and the pursuit of happiness. Et cetera, et cetera, et cetera. That they are permitted to play ball, whatever their sexual persuasions are . . .' "

"Jesus . . ."

"Gus, somebody's got to take a goddamn stand here. The whole country's bending over because Emmett Zion, Pointer Smith, Vincente Parza, John D. F. White, and a couple of filthy-rich old bigots and homophobes are afraid that if two guys who are in love with each other play baseball the game's going to fall apart. That's complete bullshit and you know it."

"We're sportswriters, not political activists."

"You're a journalist, for chrissakes. What happened to your commitment to telling the truth? Have you sold out too, Gus? Are you an employee of John D. F. White?"

Gus Mercer sat for a moment digesting this outburst. Then he took a deep breath, put his glasses back on, and finished reading the entire ten pages. He read the last paragraph twice, caught up in its wild eloquence: "I accuse America, the country of Thomas Jefferson, the country that spilled its own blood rather than permit enslavement, that held its beacon shining bright in welcome to the oppressed masses of the world . . . I accuse you, America, of turning your back on liberty and justice, of making a mockery of freedom, of permitting the persecution of two of its citizens, whose only crime was falling in love. America, I accuse you of forgetting who you are. America, I accuse you of taking a called third strike . . ."

When Mercer was done, he put the article down on his desk, got up, and walked over to the glass partition that separated his office from the city room. Out there several hundred people were busily at work putting Tuesday's paper together, editing the horoscope, the comics, the TV listings, composing ad copy for patio furniture. None of this had anything to do with the Rights of Man. He was the sports editor of a family newspaper. His job was to report who won the game and by what score. He was three years from retirement with a decent pension package. At this point in his life did he really need to storm the Bastille?

Zola went in for the kill. "If you have any integrity as a journalist left, you'll run the piece."

"I've got to run it by the guys upstairs."

"If you run it by the guys upstairs, they'll kill it. You can't pass the buck on this one, Gus. It's three-and-two, bases loaded, two out. It's your game to win or lose. What do you say?"

As soon as Milt Zola had walked the story through copy editing and layout, he drove home in the Honda with the bad master cylinder, took the phone off the hook, and went to bed. He slept all that day and night. He slept the sleep of the condemned, oblivious to the commotion that would explode around him as soon as the paper came out in the morning.

All over Los Angeles Tuesday morning people innocently padded out to their driveways to get their papers and wander back inside, rubbing sleep dust out of their eyes, unaware that they were holding a live grenade in their hands. John D. F. White, Sr., had been about to crack the shell of his three-minute egg when the paper was brought to him by his houseman. The owner of the Vikings turned immediately to the sports page, saw the headline, read the first two paragraphs, and hit his egg so hard that he knocked it off the table and into the pool. Then he shouted for a phone.

Frank Anatolia, the publisher of *The Valley Tribune*, was awoken at his home by an irate John D. F. White, Sr. "How the hell can you print this garbage, Frank?" he bellowed into the phone. Not having read the piece, Anatolia was somewhat at a disadvantage, but not for long. John D. F. White, Sr., read him the piece in its entirety. When he finished he said, "Do you know what defamation of character is, Frank?" And he hung up.

Anatolia then phoned Gus Mercer at his home, and demanded an explanation for why the Milt Zola manifesto was published on the sports page of his paper.

"Everyone's got the right to an opinion," Gus Mercer said.

"He's got the right to an opinion, all right," said Anatolia. "He's got the right to *my* opinion."

The publisher ordered Gus Mercer to be in his office at nine sharp with his head sportswriter in tow. Mercer tried rousing Zola, whose phone was still off the hook, and wound up having to drive to Silver Lake to pound on his door.

"Get dressed," Mercer growled, "we've got a meeting with Anatolia in an hour."

"He didn't like the piece?"

"He loved it. He's going to submit you for a fucking Pulitzer. Just get dressed, will you?"

When they reached Anatolia's office a few minutes before nine, they found the paper's legal staff already assembled, along with the editor in chief and the managing editor.

Mercer and Zola were not even offered coffee. They were ushered to the far end of the enormous leather couch and informed that the paper was going to print a retraction of the piece and that it had to be ready by five that afternoon.

"What are we supposed to be retracting?" said Zola.

"Milt, you've defamed the commissioner of baseball, the owners of the Vikings and several other teams, the players, the sportswriters, the fans . . . the entire goddamn country. You didn't miss anyone. The only person you didn't defame was Thomas Jefferson."

"Yeah, but it's true."

"True?"

"Look, don't I have the right to my opinion?"

"Milt," one of the lawyers said, "we're not talking about opinions here. Breach of contract, collusion, malfeasance—these are specific allegations of serious wrongdoing. You can't make uncorroborated charges that these people engaged in this behavior."

"The Whites breached Dreyfus's and Pickett's contracts by barring them from the team plane. They colluded with Emmett Zion,

Pointer Smith, and Fritz Esterhazy, among others, to deny them their rights. Esterhazy committed malfeasance by misusing the powers of his office."

"Article Nineteen . . ." said one of the lawyers.

"Article Nineteen is unconstitutional. Denial of due process." Zola retorted.

"I didn't know you went to law school, Milt," Anatolia said dryly.

"Jesus Christ! Don't you see what's happening here? We're sitting on an enormous story. It's not just the suspension. It's the whole thing in Dallas. The cover-up. The substance-abuse bullshit. This is bigger than the Black Sox scandal. It's baseball's Watergate . . ."

The executives and the lawyers all looked at one another gravely, as if to confirm that they were dealing with a man who had skidded off the rails. Overwork, stress, pressure. It had been a long season.

"Listen, Milt," said Anatolia, "you're overtired. All this deadline pressure and traveling. We'll write the retraction and run it over your signature. You take a couple of weeks, relax, cover a little golf if you want, some high school football—"

"No one runs anything over my signature that I didn't write. Try it and I'll haul your ass into court for plagiarism."

Milt Zola sat there, his hemorrhoids killing him, threatening a staff of highly paid lawyers and his boss with a plagiarism suit for crediting him for something he didn't write. But at this point it made little difference. He had already gone too far to retreat. He was crouching in a foxhole with machine-gun bullets whizzing over his head.

There was a long moment of silence, the lawyers checking the creases in their trousers. Zola looked over to Gus Mercer.

Et tu, Gus?

The sports editor cleared his throat, coughed a few times, then said, "I'm sorry, Frank, but we're not running a retraction. If you want to get a new sports editor and senior baseball writer in the middle of the World Series, that's your prerogative. Otherwise, can we end this meeting because we've got work to do."

Zola welcomed him into the foxhole.

It was only the beginning. In a matter of hours a groundswell movement would begin in the country that would demand the reinstatement of Randy Dreyfus and D. J. Pickett to their rightful positions as shortstop and second baseman of the American League Champion Los Angeles Valley Vikings. But at that moment it was merely two men against the publisher of a major Los Angeles newspaper and his entourage of legal muscle.

Soon they would be joined by a burgeoning and disparate coalition of reawakened Americans, who some time ago had put their commitment to life, liberty, and the pursuit of happiness in their back pocket and sat on it. They would rise up and phone in their collective indignation to reinstate Dreyfus and Pickett. But not before a short, violent civil war of rhetoric and *sturm und drang* the likes of which the country had not seen since the days of Sacco and Vanzetti.

XXIV

Milt Zola's war cry was picked up by the wire services in a matter of hours, and by noon that day it was a national story. Every newspaper and TV and radio station in the country printed excerpts and quoted substantial portions of the three-thousand-word litany of accusations. Schoolteachers used it as a springboard for discussion in civics classes; congressmen quoted from it on the floor of the House; members of the clergy based their sermons around it; the Human Rights Committee of the United Nations passed a resolution condemning discrimination on the basis of sexual preference; The Ad-Hoc Majority for American Community Values compared it to *The Communist Manifesto*. . . .

The article completely overshadowed the World Series that was to resume that night. Milt Zola became both the rallying point for the reinstatement movement and the target of vilification for the anti–Dreyfus-Pickett faction.

There were small towns in the Deep South that were trying to find out what he looked like so they could burn him in effigy. There were rumors that he was homosexual, Jewish, communist, Iraqi, epileptic, psychotic, a child molester, an abortionist, a vegetarian . . . The paper had to hire extra security guards to keep people out who wanted to beat the shit out of Milt Zola. Two men were arrested outside the *Valley Tribune* building carrying a bomb with his name on it.

Families were split in violent disagreement over the matter. Husbands and wives stopped talking to each other. College students demanded that their universities pass resolutions in support of the two ousted ballplayers, while a number of American Legion posts issued statements commending Esterhazy and the suspension. Fistfights erupted in bars and subways. A group of gays went on a hunger strike on a baseball diamond in Golden Gate Park. The commissioner's office on Park Avenue was the target of around-the-clock demonstrations. Viking Stadium was picketed, and the pickets were attacked by youth gangs from Boyle Heights. Police riot squads had to be called in to preserve order. There was discussion of postponing Game Three of the World Series or moving it to another venue to prevent violence.

As for the main characters in this drama—Milt Zola, Randy Dreyfus, and D. J. Pickett—they were unaware of this maelstrom that had sprung up around them. Milt Zola was home in his house in Silver Lake still trying to catch up with his jet lag. And Randy and D.J. were sitting in their rowboat in the middle of Lake Pinoski learning how to fish.

Conrad had provided them with fishing rods and a can of worms. They had put the worms on the hooks, dropped the lines into the water, and sat there waiting for something to happen. After an hour or so, Randy said, "Boy, this is a pretty relaxing sport, isn't it?"

"You have to be patient."

"Hey, it's okay with me. I ain't going anywhere. It's nice and quiet here. No TV, no radio, no papers. No batting practice. I could get used to this. . . . So who do you think Charlie's gonna start in Game Three?"

"I don't know, probably Gambetta."

"He throws gopher balls, that guy."

"Tell me about it."

"Well, it's not our problem anymore."

"Nope."

"Maybe Conrad'll let us watch the game on his TV tonight."

"His TV doesn't work."

"Right . . ."

At this point Randy felt a tug on his rod. "Jesus, I think I got something." He reeled in the line and pulled a small fish out of the dark waters of Lake Pinoski.

"Hey, I caught a fish. I caught a goddamn fish."

He threw it into the pail and beamed like a little kid.

"You know something, D.J.?"

"What's that?"

"It doesn't get any better than this."

That afternoon, *Geraldo*, *Oprah*, and *Donahue* each managed to dredge up ex-ballplayers who were willing to come out of the closet on national television and talk about what it was like to be gay in the major leagues. One of them, Marcel Sprout, a journeyman relief pitcher with various teams in the seventies, said that being gay in major league baseball was like being a kid in a candy store without a nickel. The tune-in was substantial.

Time magazine pulled its cover and replaced it with a picture of Dreyfus and Pickett with the words I ACCUSE written across the top in bright red letters. A dozen publishers commissioned quickie books by gay athletes. A number of movie scripts were put in development, with noted directors and stars already attached.

Telephone and street interview polls were launched, and public opinion was running about fifty-fifty between reinstatement and continued suspension, with a small but not insignificant minority for crucifixion.

Fritz Esterhazy sat in his suite at the Beverly Wilshire studying the results of the polls with a mounting sense of anxiety. As a man of considerable political savvy, he could recognize the slow but ineluctable shift of public opinion and was aware of the limits within which you could operate when it turned against you. He had taken his position for what he considered the best interests of baseball. It was beginning to look now as if he may have miscalculated.

The phone rang. Esterhazy picked up. It was Emmett Zion.

"Let me tell you something, Fritz. What's going on in this country disgusts me profoundly."

"Well, we don't know yet—"

"Have you been watching television? They have homos on the goddamn Oprah Winfrey show talking about having committed sodomy while they wore major league uniforms. Now you have the right as commissioner to punish desecrating of the uniform, don't you?"

"Not exactly . . ."

"What do you mean, not exactly?"

"We can refuse to license the use of major league insignias and paraphernalia, but I don't know what we can do about ex-ballplayers who go on television and talk about their past sex life—"

"Well, you *can* bring charges against that writer for conduct detrimental to the best interests of baseball."

"I can't do that, Emmett."

"Why the hell not? He's a baseball writer, isn't he?"

"He's out of my jurisdiction."

"Well, he's not out of *my* jurisdiction. I'm suing his ass. So is Pointer. We'll send him up for thirty, forty years for libel, defamation, and inciting to riot."

Esterhazy hung up and took a call from *The New York Times* asking if he was considering reinstatement. "Not at the present time," he replied. He gave the same answer when asked if he was considering postponing Game Three, which was scheduled to start in a few hours.

By noon that day, crowds had already started gathering around Viking Stadium. People without tickets had gone out to the mammoth facility off Sepulveda to demonstrate and express their opinions. Traffic became hopelessly ensnarled. Both teams had to be helicoptered in for early batting practice.

But in spite of the turmoil going on outside of Viking Stadium and throughout the country, Game Three was going to proceed as scheduled. Without Randy Dreyfus, D. J. Pickett, or Milt Zola, all of whom had been relieved of their duties. As Fritz Esterhazy was fond of saying, the game always went on. It was bigger than any of them. Eighteen alleged heterosexuals would go out on the field and compete for money, a ring, and the right to call themselves champions of the world.

• • •

Cleon Gambetta sat in the trainer's room getting his right arm iced down. Willie St. James climbed into a whirlpool and sat there with the financial section of the paper. He could give a shit about the reinstatement or suspension of Dreyfus and Pickett. His soybeans were in the toilet.

"Fuck this," he said out loud.

"What was that?" asked Gambetta.

"You in soybeans?"

"Huh?"

"Get out."

Bernie Lazarre entered and said that there was going to be a team meeting in the locker room, called by Axel Most. St. James cursed and climbed out of the whirlpool soaking wet. He hated team meetings. The same old bullshit about running out ground balls and hitting the cut-off man.

This was a players-only meeting. Charlie Gonse, Al De Mun, and the other coaches were excluded. The players gathered around Axel Most's locker, in various stages of undress, tape wrapped around knees and ankles.

"Okay," said Axel Most. "This is what I been thinking. I been thinking it's about time this team took a position on this whole thing. I don't care what you think personally about Randy and D.J., but they've been fucked over. Royally."

"That's for sure," said Harry Glugg with a smirk.

"Shut up, Harry," Most snapped. "This is serious. It's not just Randy and D.J. It's all of us. If we let the owners get away with this, then they can get away with anything. I mean, they can decide that playing golf is detrimental to the best interests of baseball. Or eating pizza. Or going to the goddamn movies."

"What are you saying we should do?" said Rennie Pannizardi.

"I'm saying we should sign a petition for reinstatement and send it to Esterhazy."

"And what if he doesn't do anything about it?"

"Then I think we should go on strike."

"What are you, crazy?"

"No. I think we have to take a stand here."

"Fuck that," said Willie St. James. "You want to give up a World Series share because of those two fruitcakes?"

"It's not just for them. It's for us. They have no right to throw a guy out for what he does off the field that doesn't have any connection with the game."

"The fuck it doesn't," said Rennie Pannizardi. "They put on that uniform, they become a reflection of the Los Angeles Valley Vikings. And I don't want *my* kids coming out to the ballpark and seeing those guys in Viking uniforms. What kind of an example is that?"

"Would you rather lose the Series?" Bernie Lazarre said, then turned quickly to Howie Jarvis and Bo Caliper and added, "No offense."

"Where do you draw the line?" said Rennie Pannizardi.

"What do you mean—draw the line?"

"They get into major league baseball, pretty soon you're going to have them running General Motors. . . ."

Axel Most's resolution was passed fourteen to seven with four abstentions. He faxed the petition to the commissioner before going out and watching Cleon Gambetta get hit all over the ballpark.

Fritz Esterhazy had watched the Reds rout the Vikings 11–2 earlier that evening. They had pounded Gambetta and a procession of Viking mop-up relievers for seventeen hits. By nine-thirty he was back in his suite at the Beverly Wilshire having a room-service dinner. Axel Most's fax was lying on the desk beside the bottle of Chivas.

He had a goddamn labor dispute on his hands. His authority as commander in chief of baseball was being questioned. If the Vikings walked, he'd have to make a difficult decision. He could simply call off the World Series. Invoke force majeure and let the networks come after him for lost advertising revenues. He could disqualify the Vikings and start the Series over with the runner-up Yankees. They were from a major media market. The networks might buy that. Or . . . he could reinstate.

He didn't like any of the three alternatives. The idea of canceling the Series violated the principle he valued most—the continuity of the game, the orderly succession of World Series contests that had been going on for almost a century. Playing the Series with the Yankees was equally repellent. They weren't the American League Champions. There would be an asterisk next to this Series in the record books, and Fritz Esterhazy would be responsible for that asterisk. And reinstatement? Capitulation. Erosion of his rights as commissioner and the primacy of Article 19.

All day long the situation had been getting more serious, as the polls continued to show a trend toward reinstatement. It was that goddamn article by Milt Zola. It had stirred up all the turgid liberal bullshit that periodically turned the country into an ungovernable mess. As soon as you started taking Thomas Jefferson literally you were in trouble.

What would Kenesaw Mountain Landis have done with this predicament? What would FDR have done? He would have sent in troops to force the striking workers back into the coal mines. For a moment, Fritz Esterhazy imagined the sight at Viking Stadium of federal marshals standing in the dugout and sending the players out on the field at gunpoint.

As these unpleasant thoughts went through his beleaguered brain, the phone rang. He instinctively knew who it was. He considered not picking it up. What the hell was *he* going to suggest?

"Hello?" Esterhazy said into the phone, and heard the same inflectionless voice ask if he would hold for the president. Esterhazy drained his Chivas in one big swallow and held.

"Fritz, how are you?" The voice sounded cheerful, almost demented.

"Fine, Mr. President."

There was a short silence as if the man were trying to remember whom he had called and why.

"Fritz, let me tell you why I called. I'm concerned."

Jesus. Here we go again.

"Fritz, I'm concerned about basic American values. I'm concerned about this country's commitment to liberty across the board."

"I understand, sir."

"Fritz, I received a delegation from both houses of Congress this evening. A bipartisan delegation. They came to tell me of their deep concern about the situation out there in Los Angeles. They tell me that the American people are troubled that this World Series is not being played by the best available players. They're troubled, deeply troubled. Even though they don't for a minute think that inversion has the slightest iota of relevance to the American Way of Life or to baseball—in fact they'd just as soon institute treatment programs as early as the third grade to lick this problem—and I think with the right allocation of resources we can lick this problem—in fact, I intend to introduce legislation on this in January so we can tackle this problem and get the upper hand on it. In any event, uh . . . what was I saying?"

"About the World Series."

"Yes . . . Fritz, I think we're going to have to go with strength up the middle, inverted or not. Do you see my point?"

"I believe I do, sir."

"Great nations can conquer great obstacles, Fritz. We've pretty much gotten rid of cholera and polio in this country. And we knocked the dickens out of Saddam. So I don't see why we can't all get together and lick this baby too."

"We'll do our best, Mr. President."

"Thank you, Fritz. God bless you. My best to Marilyn . . ."

The commissioner of baseball announced the following morning that he was lifting the life suspension of Randy Dreyfus and D. J. Pickett. John D. F. White, Sr., was awakened by a phone call from Ken Teffner, who had been up watching the *Today* show on his Exercycle.

"He did fucking *what?*" John D. F. White, Sr., yelled into the phone on his bedside table.

"He reinstated them. Effective immediately."

"Why the hell did he do that?"

"The players threatened to strike if he didn't."

There was a deep moment of silence, punctuated only by the sound of the old man's phlegmy morning cigar cough. Then, even louder, "Anybody on my team strikes, they're through. Send them down to Class C. And not even on a plane. Get them goddamn bus tickets. One way . . ."

"Well, they're not striking anymore."

"How's that?"

"Because of the reinstatement."

"Listen, Teffner, I don't want those two queers in Viking uni-forms."

"I'm afraid that if you don't go along with the reinstatement, the players aren't going to play."

"We'll see about that. You call Gonse and tell him not to start those two fruits tonight."

"Well, as it turns out, you may not even have to do that."

"How's that?"

"Nobody knows where they are."

"What do you mean, nobody knows where they are?"

"They seem to have disappeared. Nobody has seen or heard from them in nearly a week."

"Well, for chrissakes, don't find them. . . ."

Since Randy and D.J. had slipped out of town at 4 A.M. the morn-ing after the suspension, there had been no news of them. Susie had been besieged by the press once again. They refused to believe her repeated claim that she didn't know where her husband was. Nor did Barry Fuchsia know where Randy Dreyfus was, nor did Randy's mother, who, when reached in Lakeland, said that she didn't know where he was but if *she* were looking for him, the first place she'd check out had four letters and began with *H*.

Pete Zabriskie had a few notions, but nobody asked him. He was off the clock. So was Mendes Fuad, who had been following the developments with academic interest while continuing to treat Su-sie Dreyfus for depression and insufficient ego strength. Susie had told him that Randy had said that he was going to go to Maine with . . . his lover. She still choked over the word.

"A honeymoon," said Fuad.

"I suppose so," murmured Susie.

Fuad had stared off at his fish for a moment and then said with uncharacteristic loquacity, "Frankly, it's dreadfully painful, this honeymoon business, suddenly being face-to-face with the dailiness of the fantasy object, confronted with the toothbrushing and toilet-flushing aspect of the human experience . . ."

As soon as news of the reinstatement broke, there were attempts to contact the two ballplayers and to get them into uniform for Game Four that night. Esterhazy issued an appeal for the two ballplayers to come forward so that they could play the World Series at full strength.

As the hours passed, there were reported sightings of Randy Dreyfus and D. J. Pickett in all fifty states, Canada, Costa Rica, and Romania. Hospitals and morgues were checked and rechecked for John Does. State police and the National Guard were put on alert.

The only person who knew the exact whereabouts of the two reinstated baseball players was the proprietor of the Devil's Island Cabins in northeastern Maine. But his TV had been on the blink for months now, and he went into Caribou only once a week for groceries. And since he had given up baseball thirty-one years ago, he didn't know who the hell Randy Dreyfus and D. J. Pickett were, anyway. As far as he was concerned, they were quiet people and the worst fishermen he had even seen. They couldn't have caught a flounder in a bathtub with a harpoon.

Game Four went off on schedule Wednesday night at Viking Stadium in spite of the continued absence of the two reinstatees. Axel Most had called another pregame meeting and said that since they had successfully gotten the commissioner to back down, they could play ball again with a clear conscience. He suggested, however, that they wear arm bands to express their solidarity with their missing teammates.

"How about pink ones?" said Rennie Pannizardi.

The third baseman refused to wear one of the dark blue arm bands with the initials RMD and DJP on them. So did Willie St. James, who claimed he didn't get involved in politics.

An enthusiastic crowd turned out to support the beleaguered team. There were signs all over the stands that said things like COME HOME, RANDY AND D.J. and WE LOVE YOU—ALL IS FORGIVEN. The Nazis and the gay bashers were now in the minority.

Axel Most, pitching with three days' rest, held the Reds to four hits through seven and two thirds, with Hube Henry finishing up by getting the last four hitters. Howie Jarvis and Bo Caliper turned three double plays and didn't make an error. Jarvis even got a hit, a wind-blown fly ball down the left-field line that went for a double, and he came around on Glen Ephard's smash to the gap in right-center with what turned out to be the winning run.

And so the Vikings, without their star shortstop and second baseman, had managed to even up the Series at two games apiece. But the mystery of the missing players overshadowed the game. The entire country wanted to know where they were. Milt Zola had made them into heroes or, in the worst-case scenario, martyrs.

As for Zola, he had been woken up that morning by a phone call from Gus Mercer telling him that he was now a national hero. I AC-CUSE had mobilized the country, and the groundswell had been so massive and immediate that Esterhazy had had to act. Now everyone wanted to interview Milt Zola. Book publishers were after him. He was a star.

Zola stood there in his underwear, scratching his two-day growth of beard, and nodded silently.

"No shit," he mumbled.

"We're talking a Pulitzer here," Mercer said.

"A Pulitzer?"

"You're a lock."

Zola hung up and stood in the middle of his cluttered living room, reflecting on the irony of it all. He had written a suicide note, which had turned out to be a big hit. They didn't want to accept his sword. They wanted to decorate him. Go figure.

He trundled into the kitchen, put a pot of water on the stove, spooned some instant coffee into a reasonably clean cup, and tried to figure out what to do now. Since he was apparently no longer banned from baseball, he should be covering the Series. But the Series wasn't the story anymore. The Series was only a sidebar. The story was the missing shortstop and second baseman. Where the hell were they?

There were appeals in newspapers and on TV stations all over the country. Either something terrible had happened to Randy Dreyfus and D. J. Pickett or they weren't interested in being found. If he could find them . . . Shit, not only would he live up to his Pulitzer, but he could put the World Series back on the level it should be on, the best baseball in the world.

There was one person who might know where they were. It was

worth a try. He dressed hurriedly, not even bothering to shave, got into the Honda, and headed out to Valley View Estates.

Susie had gotten the security patrol to keep the reporters at some distance from the house. But they wouldn't go home. There was still a rumor that Randy Dreyfus was hiding out in the home of his estranged wife. Up in Thousand Oaks, reporters had already bribed the condo manager to check D.J.'s unit, but Susie wasn't letting anybody in. She had taken calls from John D. F. White, Jr., Ken Teffner, and Fritz Esterhazy and told each of them that she did not know where her husband was.

When an unshaven Milt Zola showed up in front of the house on Caravaggio Place, he was intercepted by the security police and told that he had to keep at least fifty feet away from the property. Zola then took out his press card, identified himself, and caused a commotion as the other reporters gathered around to interview him. One of the cops went up to the door, rang the bell, and told Susie that Milt Zola was there and wanted to talk to her.

"Who?"

"Milt Zola. The guy who wrote the article."

She agreed to see him in back of the house, on the patio. The cops escorted Zola around through the fence no longer patrolled by Calvin to the patio, where Susie was waiting.

She put her hand out and said, "It's a pleasure to meet you, Mr. Zola."

"Likewise," said the reporter.

"Please, have a seat." She beckoned to a couple of chairs in the patio conversation nook, and they sat down facing each other.

"Excuse my appearance, but I rushed over here as soon as I heard. I think time is of the essence."

"I beg your pardon?"

"We have to find Randy and D.J. Before it's too late."

"Too late for what?"

"The Series. There's only three games left—at the most."

Susie looked at him, searching for a sense of sincerity behind a face creased with what seemed to be both fatigue and intelligence. He had written I ACCUSE. It was a beautiful, eloquent appeal to the basic instinct for justice and fair play in America. It had gotten Randy reinstated, with a chance to play ball again and reclaim his rightful position as the best shortstop in baseball. Reading it, tears had come to her eyes.

Still, she hesitated, wondering if she was violating a trust.

"If you know where he is, you could avoid a great tragedy by telling me. Do you realize that there are a couple of guys playing shortstop and second base that don't even belong in the major leagues, let alone in the World Series? It demeans the game. And it's irrevocable. Once it goes down in the record books, there's nothing you can do about it. Besides, most of the country, with the exception of the lunatic fringe, wants them to play. So what do you say? Do you know where they are?"

What the hell. He hadn't said not to tell anyone. Susie sighed and nodded slowly. "I think so."

"Where?"

"Well, I don't know *exactly* where they are but I think they're in Maine."

"In Maine? What are they doing there?"

"Fishing."

"Mrs. Dreyfus," said Zola, already on his feet, "can I use your phone?"

It took a while, but Zola's call was eventually routed through to Camp David, where the president was vacationing. He had been in the recreation lodge relaxing with his model trains when one of the Secret Service men told him that Milt Zola was on the phone.

"Who's that?"

"The reporter who wrote the piece in Los Angeles about the two homosexual ballplayers."

"Well, I'll be damned."

The president shunted the locomotive onto a siding, turned off the transformer, and picked up the mobile phone.

"Milt, how are you?"

"Very well, Mr. President."

"Hell of a piece you wrote there."

"Thank you, sir."

"In fact, I think we ought to put it over there in the National Archives. What would you say to that?"

"I would be honored . . ."

"And I'd like to have you down here for a little softball on the south lawn. Fritz Esterhazy, a couple of senators, some of the guys from State. Slow pitch, seven innings . . . losers buy the beer . . ."

"Mr. President, I believe I know where Randy Dreyfus and D. J. Pickett are."

"You do? Hell, the FBI can't even find them."

"I think they're in Maine."

"In Maine? What in the dickens are they doing there?"

"Fishing, sir."

"Well, I'll be damned."

"The problem is we don't know where exactly in Maine they are."

"It's a pretty big state."

"Not as big as Iraq, sir."

"Beg your pardon?"

"Mr. President, if we could find SCUD missile sites in the desert, we could probably find a couple of guys fishing in a rowboat."

"Lot of guys fishing in rowboats in Maine, Milt."

"They got a Dalmatian with them."

The president hung up with Milt Zola and dialed the Secretary of Defense, beeping him off the golf course.

"Norm, how you doing?"

"Not so good, Mr. President. I just bogeyed the fourth hole."

"Sorry to hear it. Norm, how many of those AWACS surveillance planes we got in the Northeast?"

"Where in the Northeast?"

"Within striking range of Maine."

It took the former general only a few seconds to calculate the precise number. "Twenty-eight. There a problem up there, sir?"

"We got a couple of lost ballplayers."

"Ballplayers, Mr. President?"

"Affirmative, Norm. They're in a rowboat with a Dalmatian. Find 'em."

XXV

$\mathbf{I}$t took Calvin a while to learn to lay off the catfish. Not that there were so many of them to lay off of. Though they had made a great deal of improvement since first dipping their rods into Lake Pinoski several days before, Randy Dreyfus and D. J. Pickett weren't breaking any records in the angling department. Most of the time they just sat out there in the pleasant Indian-summer sun watching the colors turn and fade on the thinning trees along the perimeter of the lake, munching on liverwurst sandwiches that Conrad provided, and drinking iced tea from a thermos. Calvin sat between them, sharing the liverwurst sandwiches and staring at the catfish that swam listlessly in a pail of water.

It was a life of simple pleasures. Fishing in the morning, a nap after lunch, a long walk through the mulch of dead leaves in the woods around the lake. Early dinner, early to bed.

As Mendes Fuad had pointed out to Susie, it was a honeymoon. And very different from the honeymoon Randy had taken with Susie ten years before in Maui, where they had enjoyed a week of nonstop luaus, discos, and rum-and-Cokes. There weren't any luaus at the Devil's Island Cabins. Nor any rum-and-Cokes. And the nearest disco was quite a ways downstate. It was fishing and iced tea on Lake Pinoski.

On the Thursday morning of Game Five of the World Series, with twenty-eight high-tech AWACS surveillance planes crisscrossing the state of Maine in search of them, Randy, D.J., and Calvin were out on the lake after breakfast, as usual, waiting for a bite. Randy cast his line out into the water and got himself comfortable, his hat down over his eyes like an outfielder in a sun field with a high blue sky.

In the distance they could vaguely hear the bells tolling at Devil's Island Baptist Church. It put Randy in a religious frame of mind.

"You believe in God?" he asked.

"Not really," D.J. replied, carefully slicing a worm and impaling it on his hook.

"Not even a little bit?"

"Well, maybe a little bit."

"I'll tell you what I think," said Randy. "I think you got to have somebody in charge. It may not be like the guy with the white beard and the angels and that shit. But unless there's somebody running the show it all doesn't add up to a whole lot. You know what I mean?"

D.J. nodded.

"I get this feeling sometimes," Randy continued, "that it's all worked out in advance. Whatever's going to happen is going to happen whatever you do about it. And we're like working on a tape-delay type thing. Sometimes you get a quick advance glimpse, sort of a preview of coming attractions, like at the movies. Sometimes I'm standing out there at short and get this feeling that the guy's going to hit the ball to me, maybe to my left. So I cheat over a step and sure enough, the guy hits it to my left. But it doesn't happen all the time."

"If it happened all the time, you'd be in pretty good shape."

"Remember the squeeze play against Oakland?"

"The squeeze play?"

"You know, when you were on third and I bunted you across, the last game of the season . . ."

"Oh yeah, I remember that."

"How'd you know I was going to bunt? There was no sign. Charlie nearly shit a brick."

"I didn't know you were going to bunt."

"You *didn't*?"

"Uh-uh."

"I thought you knew. I was sending you, like, telepathic signals."

"Well, I didn't pick them up."

"So how come you broke for the plate?"

"I picked up a hitch in the guy's motion every time he threw a change. So I figured if I got the jump and the change, I had a shot at stealing home."

"No shit."

"Actually, I was kind of pissed off when you bunted. I had the base stolen."

"Son of a bitch."

"I mean, maybe there was telepathy that I wasn't aware of. Unconscious telepathy."

"Maybe . . ." Randy leaned back against the oar lock.

"Hey, come on, don't pout," D.J. said.

"I'm not pouting."

"Yes you are. I know that look."

D.J. wedged his fishing rod securely under one of the seats and, moving over beside Randy, put his arm around him. Randy fought it for a moment and then let himself sink into the embrace.

"Maybe it *was* telepathy," D.J. said. "I mean, the idea of stealing home could have come from you . . ."

"Maybe . . ."

They kissed. Then they kissed some more. Calvin realized what was happening and barked. He had started to bark every time they made love. The only thing that quieted him down was letting him up on the bed with them.

The dog came over and joined in. They had already gotten fairly involved by the time they heard the motor. It had started low in the distance and gotten progressively louder, like a droning insect. When they realized it was heading for them, they had to scramble around slipping their shorts back on and rezipping.

The seaplane came in low over the lake, landed with a splash, and taxied over to the rowboat, its wash causing water to overflow the gunnels. Calvin was apoplectic, barking his head off.

The door to the seaplane opened and a guy in a gray suit with sunglasses looked out at them and called, "Mr. Dreyfus? Mr. Pickett?"

"Who wants to know?"

"The United States Secret Service. Jim McGinty. How're they biting?"

Randy and D.J. mumbled something vague.

Jim McGinty checked his watch, then, "If we hurry we can just about make it."

"We can just about make it where?"

"To L.A. for the game. *Air Force Two's* waiting in Bangor."

Because of a stiff headwind, they didn't make it into Burbank Airport until twenty minutes before game time. There were crowds at the airport to greet them, TV cameras, news crews. They hurried to a helicopter that was waiting to take them to Viking Stadium.

Most of the 125,000 people cheered wildly as the chopper appeared from behind the left-field stands and angled in, alighting perfectly on the artificial turf between the pitcher's mound and home plate. Randy and D.J. stepped out, still wearing their Maine fishing outfits, into the roar of the hometown fans.

They waved to the crowd and then trotted toward the Viking dugout, where they were greeted with high fives by their teammates. Then they went down into the clubhouse to get into uniform for the start of the game. There were stacks of letters and telegrams piled up near their lockers but no time to read them. A national TV audience was waiting for Randy Dreyfus and D. J. Pickett to take their positions in the Los Angeles Valley Viking infield.

Randy and D.J. had a brief moment alone before going through the tunnel to the dugout.

"Can you believe this?" Randy said.

"Crazy."

"Couple of hours ago we were fishing in Maine. Now we're back in the World Series."

"There's still a lot of crazies out there aren't very happy about this."

"Fuck 'em."

"Be careful," D.J. said.

"What do you mean, be careful?"

"I don't know—just be careful."

Randy looked at him, wondering what he meant, then he shrugged, grabbed his glove, and trotted up the tunnel.

When they were introduced, there was wild cheering again, sprinkled with some booing. And some dead silence. The consensus that had pushed the president to push Fritz Esterhazy to reinstate them was fragmented and fragile. There were still people out there who didn't buy Milt Zola's thesis that baseball had nothing to do with where one put one's penis.

The game began badly, with the Reds scoring three runs in the first inning. Back in the dugout Charlie Gonse was already throwing up his hands in despair. Neither D.J. nor Randy had swung a bat in a week. They were rusty, jet-lagged, and mellowed by their honeymoon on Lake Pinoski.

In the first, D.J. popped to short. Randy stood there, swinging the bat in the on deck circle, trying to get ready. The cry started up again, the cry he hated so much. "Ran-DEE, Ran-DEE . . ." Here he was again, in the coliseum with the lion.

He stepped into the batter's box and glared out at the Reds' pitcher—a veteran right-hander with a nasty split-fingered fastball. The bat felt funny in his hands. Like a weapon he had forgotten how to use.

He barely saw the first two pitches. The third one missed his head by a sixteenth of an inch. He could almost feel the stitches of the baseball graze his ear. *Be careful.* That's what D.J. had said. There were people out there that wanted to kill him.

Randy struck out looking on a low outside fastball. It was a lousy call. He didn't even bother giving the umpire the satisfaction of a nasty look.

He went back out and played shortstop, fielding his position, making the plays. That was always the easy part for him, playing the field. His body moved naturally with the sound of the bat. It was like dancing to easy-listening music.

The game crept along, still 3–0 Reds. The Vikings mounted a couple of rallies that died on the basepaths. D.J. got a single in the sixth but was caught stealing. Randy walked in the third and flew deep to center leading off the seventh. He was finally beginning to feel the bat in his hands the way it had to feel before he started to hit.

The crowd was quiet, restless, morose. The game was slipping away. The Vikings were dying a slow death. It would be over soon. A game without drama or greatness. Just twenty-seven routine outs with a couple of cheap hits thrown in.

Randy sat by himself at the end of the bench in the dugout, watching the game drain away, wondering whether they should have even bothered showing up. They had been happy fishing in Maine. Nobody was throwing baseballs ninety-five miles an hour at their heads.

By the bottom of the ninth, with the score still 3–0, half the crowd had already left. They wanted to beat the traffic. It was that type of town. A goddamn World Series and people left early to beat the traffic.

Rennie Pannizardi got a broken-bat bloop single to lead off. The organist hit a crescendo of notes. CHARGE flashed on the message board. The sixty thousand people left in the stands yelled back, "Charge!" on cue. The Reds manager went out to the mound and changed pitchers. A kid with a howitzer arm came out of the bull-pen. The guy had an E.R.A. of 1.25. Randy had never gotten a hit off him.

He struck the next two guys out on six pitches. More people headed for the parking lot. Then the kid hit Spic Mendoza in the left shoe, which was lucky. Because anyplace else he hit him would've killed him. D.J. came up. First and second, two out. Randy sat there mesmerized, as if he were watching a movie, until Charlie Gonse yelled at him to go out on deck, where he was supposed to be.

Randy grabbed a bat and walked slowly out to the on-deck circle. He stood there and watched the man he loved trying to hang in and keep the game alive. He had never loved D. J. Pickett as much as he did at that moment. There he was, exhausted, overmatched, trying to figure out how to get on against a kid with a ninety-eight-mile-an-hour fastball.

Randy didn't give a shit about the game. Or the Series. All he cared about was D.J. He didn't want him to make the last out, to become the object of even more hate than he already was. He just wanted this to be over so that they could go fishing someplace and forget about trying to hit a round ball with a round bat.

It was just a copper plaque on a wall in upstate New York. Right?

D.J. managed to work the kid to three-and-two, fouling pitches off, just managing to get enough wood on them to stay alive. Randy closed his eyes and prayed that the guy wouldn't strike D.J. out.

He heard the cheers, opened his eyes, and saw D.J. throw the bat away and trot down to first with a walk.

The crowd got to its feet. Randy was coming up, representing the winning run. He took a few extra practice swings, milking it. He didn't care anymore. D.J. was safe from the wrath of the crowd. Nothing bad could happen now.

Randy walked up to the plate like it was the stairway to heaven. All he could see was a blur of lights and shirts and the blue-black sky. He didn't see the pitcher, or any of the infielders, or the three runners on base. And he didn't see the thin man with the trim mustache up in Section 19-A behind first base reaching into his 7-Eleven cooler bag.

Randy saw nothing. He stood in the batter's box, smiling, waiting for it to be over. It was all on tape delay anyway. It was settled beforehand. It was just a matter of playing it out. So what the fuck. Take a shot.

Randy guessed fastball. Low and inside. He adjusted instinctively, inching the front foot forward, and then swung as soon as he got that nanosecond glimpse of the white bullet heading toward him. He guessed right. The ball hit the sweet part of the bat and was in the parking lot in left field before the cheers could even go up. He had never hit a ball that hard in his life.

Son of a bitch. He stood and watched it, shaking his head. And then he laughed. What else could he do? He had no idea how the hell he'd hit the ball.

As Randy trotted to first base, the thin man with the trim mustache in Section 19-A behind first base removed the high-powered pistol from the 7-Eleven cooler bag. As if to make his point, he waited for Randy to circle the bases. Then, just as Randy Dreyfus touched home plate and lifted his arms up high in triumph, the thin man with the trim mustache in Section 19-A squeezed the trigger.

XXVI

The E.R. nurses kept asking him if he was next of kin. D.J. kept replying that he was his second baseman, which was about as next-of-kin as you got in baseball. He sat in the small waiting area, among the victims of domestic violence, animal bites, and automobile accidents, waiting for news about Randy.

They had driven an ambulance right onto the field, through the gate in the left-field bullpen and over to where Randy had fallen. They had loaded him onto a stretcher amid the deafening dead silence of Viking Stadium and driven him away.

D.J. had ridden in the ambulance holding Randy's hand and talking to him in a quiet, reassuring voice. At the hospital, he watched helplessly as they took Randy away through the swinging doors. Now there was nothing to do but wait.

He sat there listening to the sounds of muffled sobbing, coughing, whispered conversations, as the nurses and doctors came and went. Outside in the corridor the TV crews were already gathering.

D.J. heard loud noises as the door to the emergency room opened and Susie Dreyfus entered. In the split second that the door was opened, flashbulbs popped, shutters clicked, minicams whirred. Susie looked appropriately sober in a demure gray dress, flats, and a cardigan thrown over her shoulders. Her eyes searched the room, found D.J.

She came over and sat down beside him.

"How is he?" she asked.

"They're working on him now."

"What are they doing?"

"A procedure. That's all they're saying."

"I heard on the radio that it's not life-threatening. The bullet hit below his waist."

D.J. nodded, then shook his head and mumbled, "I knew it . . ."

"What do you mean?"

"I knew something was going to happen. Something had to happen."

"I don't understand."

"You can't do what we did."

Susie looked at him quizzically, still not sure what he meant.

"We stepped over the line," D.J. said, shaking his head again. He didn't say anything more. They sat there in silence, side by side, waiting together.

Eventually a doctor came out of the emergency-surgery area and said, "Dreyfus?"

D.J. and Susie got up simultaneously.

"Mrs. Dreyfus?" the doctor asked, coming over. Susie nodded. The doctor looked quickly at D.J. and nodded, acknowledging that he knew who he was.

"We're in good shape here," the doctor said. "Nothing very serious."

D.J. exhaled very slowly. Susie contracted her abdominal muscles in a yoga technique for suppressing outcries of pain or grief.

"The bullet entered the left clunis and lodged itself in the fatty tissue in the sublateral femus muscle. We were able to remove it cleanly. There's a small amount of phyectopia and some edema near the coccyx, but there was no significant blood loss and no organ damage. We were nowhere near the kidneys, liver, or spleen . . ."

"Doc, where the hell was he shot?" D.J. said.

"He was shot in the buttocks."

"He was shot in the *ass*?"

The doctor nodded.

"No shit . . ." murmured D.J.

"Tell you something," the doctor said, "if you have to be shot, that's exactly where you want to get it."

"Where is he now?"

"We're transferring him upstairs. We'll keep him twenty-four hours, forty-eight tops, just as a precaution to make sure there's no secondary infection."

"Thank you, doctor," said Susie, always polite.

"It's okay." Then he turned to D.J. "How about an autograph?"

D.J. signed a copy of *Health Today* magazine that was lying on a table, and the doctor disappeared.

For a moment D.J. and Susie stood there, not knowing what to say. Finally Susie said, "Why don't you go see him first."

Randy was lying propped up on his good side in bed, watching the end of the eleven o'clock news. D.J. stood in the doorway for a moment, caught his breath, then entered the room.

"Hey, how're you doing?"

Randy turned his head and flashed one of his boyish smiles. "Okay."

"You had me worried there for a moment."

"Son of a bitch shot me right in the ass."

"Good thing too."

"Yeah, that's what the doc says. Anyplace else and it could've been hairy. . . . Looks like I'm not going to be sliding for a while."

"You hit 'em that far you don't have to slide."

"I really hit the shit out of that sucker, didn't I?"

"You sure did. It got out of there fast."

D.J. sat down on the chair beside the bed. Randy lowered the volume on the TV. "You see the news?"

"No . . ."

"It was the lead story. They showed the home run, the ambulance, the whole thing. . . . The guy was some sort of whacko, just lost a promotion in the Department of Motor Vehicles to a faggot . . ."

D.J. winced.

"Sorry . . . A gay guy."

"Right."

"I still got a lot to learn."

"Yeah . . ."

They sat in silence for a moment before Randy said, "So you going to Cincinnati, huh?"

"I guess so."

"You don't seem so excited."

"It's just a baseball game."

"It's the World Series."

"I'll tell you something—after what's gone down the last few months, it doesn't seem so important, you know what I mean?"

"Yeah. You hit the ball, you run around the bases. Big deal, right?"

"Right."

"It's just a plaque on a wall in upstate New York."

"Right."

"But it sure as hell beats working for a living." D.J. smiled. Randy smiled back.

"I bet you get MVP," D.J. said.

"Nah."

"You led the league in hitting, fielding percentage, consecutive errorless games . . ."

"Yeah, but they don't give MVP's to lefties."

"To who?"

"Guys like us. You know something? I bet you there were a lot of lefties that nobody knew were lefties that did some great things in baseball."

"Probably."

"I mean, what about Wally Pipp?"

"Wally Pipp?"

"Yeah, I mean with a name like that . . . What about Pie Traynor and Snuffy Stirnweiss? What about Billy Cox? You see Billy Cox giving it to Pia Zadora?"

They both started to laugh, so uproariously that the nurse had to come and ask them to keep it down. They sat there watching TV together.

On the screen there was a commercial with a bunch of guys sitting around drinking beer and saying how it didn't get any better than that. Bullshit. What the fuck did *they* know? It could get a hell of a lot better.

Randy looked back at D.J. and asked him a question he didn't want to ask him.

"So what are you going to do after the Series?"

D.J. shrugged. They sat there, the TV going softly in the background, avoiding eye contact. The question lay unanswered between them, like a ground ball up the middle. Somebody had to go for it. Finally, Randy said in a very quiet voice, "So what do you say, you want to go fishing?"

It seemed to take an eternity for D.J. to reply. He looked at Randy, his eyes creased with a mixture of tears and laughter, reached over, and gently brushed away a strand of hair that had fallen across Randy's face. Then he nodded slowly and said, "Why the hell not . . ."

XXVII

The morning of October 21, two days after the Reds won the Series by sweeping the last two games at Riverfront Stadium, was cold and foggy. A fine mist fell on the San Fernando Valley. You could even have called it rain, with just a small stretch of the imagination. The gauges picked up .03 of an inch at the Civic Center.

A flatbed truck got off the northbound 405 at Sherman Way and turned left into Van Nuys Boulevard. The driver had to switch his wipers on coming through the Sepulveda Pass. By the time he reached Van Nuys the mist had nearly evaporated into the metallic Valley air. An illegal Salvadoran with a straw hat sat beside the driver, his eyes half closed, dozing. The guy didn't speak a word of English. But at twenty-five bucks for the day, that's what you got.

The driver continued north into the far reaches of Van Nuys until the shopping center appeared. It looked forlorn in the wet early-morning light. This was the third time the driver had done this job in the last few months. But it was a job, billed by the hour. He'd put in for a full day again, take it easy, pay the illegal out of his pocket, and make out with a nice piece of change.

He sent the guy up in the crane to start taking down the old letters. By eleven-thirty they had the old sign down. The driver went over to the Pizza Hut by himself and had a medium meatball-and-anchovy pizza and a large Pepsi while the Salvadoran ate something from a paper bag.

After lunch they put the new sign up. A couple of people stopped to watch on their way into the Alpha Beta. The drunk who lived behind the garbage Dumpsters saw the new sign, blinked rapidly a few times, wondering if more of his life had passed him by than he'd imagined. He'd seen that sign somewhere before.

The job was done by two-thirty, the old letters stored back in the truck, the crane lowered, the illegal slouched into the shotgun seat, two tens and a five in his pocket.

By three o'clock the sun had burned through the mist. The driver started the engine and turned the truck out of the shopping center and back toward the freeway. He'd drop the guy on Ventura, hit the topless lounge on Lankershim, and pull back into the yard at five.

In his rearview mirror he saw the bright letters of THE RANDY DREFYUS SHOPPING CENTER. They had misspelled the name. Fuck it. They'd leave it there. See how long it took people to notice. Then he'd come back out and fix it again.

About the Author

PETER LEFCOURT lives in Los Angeles most of the time and is no relation to Alfred Dreyfus.